KALEIDOSCOPE

KALEIDOSCOPE

A JOANNE KILBOURN MYSTERY

GAIL
BOWEN

McCLELLAND & STEWART

Library and Archives Canada Cataloguing in Publication

Bowen, Gail, 1942–
   Kaleidoscope : a Joanne Kilbourn mystery / Gail Bowen.

ISBN 978-0-7710-1689-9

   I. Title.

PS8553.08995K35 2012   C813.'54   C2011-906531-2

We acknowledge the financial support of the Government of Canada through the Canada Book Fund and that of the Government of Ontario through the Ontario Media Development Corporation's Ontario Book Initiative. We further acknowledge the support of the Canada Council for the Arts and the Ontario Arts Council for our publishing program.

Published simultaneously in the United States of America by McClelland & Stewart Ltd., P.O. Box 1030, Plattsburgh, New York 12901

Library of Congress Control Number: 2011938747

Cover art: bullet hole: © Alptraum | Dreamstime.com;
splatter: © Domen Colja S.P. | Dreamstime.com;
background © Aliaksey Hintau | Dreamstime.com

Typeset in Trump Mediaeval by M&S, Toronto
Printed and bound in the United States of America

This book was produced using paper that is 20% recycled.

McClelland & Stewart Ltd.
75 Sherbourne Street
Toronto, Ontario
M5A 2P9
www.mcclelland.com

1 2 3 4 5   16 15 14 13 12

For my friend, Marjorie Gerwing,
With thanks for over two decades of great conversation

CHAPTER

1

On the afternoon I retired from our university's political science department I dreamed of my first husband. It was a strange dream; in fact, it was strange that I dreamed of Ian at all. He had been dead for fifteen years. My time of wrestling with grief was long over. I had remarried, and I was deeply in love with my new husband. I was leaving the university with few regrets, memories that were mostly good, and a buoyant sense of possibilities.

Spring that year had been warm and rainy – tropical weather for a prairie province. Trees were in full leaf, lawns were lush and green, bushes and plants were flowering. The air was heavy with the scent of lilacs and wet earth. A Mediterranean languor, enervating but soothing, had settled on our city. It was a good day to retire.

I arrived home at a little after two-thirty. My husband, Zack, a trial lawyer, was in court. Our fourteen-year-old daughter, Taylor, the last of my children who still lived at home, had surprised me by appearing at my retirement lunch and was now back at school, studying for end-of-year exams. Our dogs, Willie and Pantera, were waiting at the front door. I bent to give them head pats. "Just me," I said. "Get used to it because the three of us are going to be spending a lot of time together from now on."

I checked the mail, poured myself a glass of iced tea, and went out to the yard. A half-dozen Halos, my favourite Martha Washington geraniums, were waiting to be planted in a spot by the fence that Zack and I decided could use a splash of colour. Dark red and rimmed with silver, the Halos would be just the touch we needed from the summer palette, but I had larger plans. I positioned one of the lounges so that it would catch the sun, lay down, closed my eyes, and drifted off. And then, on that June afternoon, green with promise, I dreamed of Ian.

My dream was not elegiac. I was in the kitchen of a church basement, pulling steaming roasting pans of cabbage rolls out of an oven. No matter how many pans I pulled out, there was always another one. I was running out of space on the counters. I was hot and I was angry. Over an ancient PA system I could hear Ian talking about building a better world. I was only half listening because I'd written the speech, and I'd heard him deliver it a dozen times, but when he stumbled, I gave the disembodied voice my full attention. I waited as he searched for words. When they continued to elude him, I slapped down the pan I was holding. "Damn it, Ian, you know I finish every speech with the same sentence: 'Security for any one of us lies in greater abundance for all of us.'" Ian's disembodied voice repeated the words, and I woke up.

When I opened my eyes, my husband, Zack, was beside me in his wheelchair. As always when he came straight from work, he looked like an ad in *GQ* – a lightweight taupe linen suit, a matching shirt, and a lime-and-pink-striped silk tie that I particularly liked. He smoothed my hair. "You're hot," he said.

"You're hotter," I said. "You are such a good-looking guy. How long have you been sitting there?"

"Long enough to worry that you might be getting too much sun, but you were smiling, so I didn't want to interrupt your dream."

"My dream wasn't that great," I said. "Just one of those frustration things. I was smiling because I realized that all those cabbage rolls I was supposed to find a place for were a little joke from my unconscious."

Zack raised an eyebrow. "You're going to have to explain the cabbage rolls."

I sat up and sipped my iced tea. "I was dreaming about Ian," I said. "I hardly ever think of him any more, but I guess he was on my mind because today was my last day at the university."

"Another goodbye?" Zack said.

"Something like that. Anyway, even in my dream, Ian was just a voice making political promises at a rally while I was in the kitchen of some church basement doing a slow burn."

"Carl Jung says that a dream is a message," Zack said. "You have to treat it the way you'd treat an unfamiliar object – turn it over and over until you understand its purpose."

I took another sip of my sun-warm iced tea and looked hard at my husband. "You know the most surprising things."

"I'm a trial lawyer. Knowing things is my business. So what do you think your dream meant?"

I shrugged. "Beats me. Probably that whatever I choose to do next shouldn't involve cabbage rolls."

Zack's voice was warm and intimate. "You must have known that thirty years ago. You've always been smart enough to be the one making the speeches."

"Maybe, but Ian was the one who was running for office. I was home with the kids, writing speeches, organizing coffee parties, and being a good political wife."

"You sound as if you're still doing that slow burn."

"I'm not. When I think about that time, the only feeling I have is remorse. That's probably why I don't talk about Ian very much. He was thirty-seven when he died – too young, and he and I had a lot of unfinished business. Your pal Carl Jung says that dreams lead us to deep inner truths. But I always knew the truth about Ian and me. We loved each other, but we had problems – at least I did."

"And Ian didn't."

"To be fair, he was just too busy to notice. Everything happened so fast: the move to Saskatchewan, Mieka's birth, the election win, and then suddenly our party was running the province."

Zack chuckled. "I remember seeing the new premier on the news just after he was sworn in, asking a reporter where the men's room was."

I smiled at the memory. "The new premier was livid that they ran that tape. Anyway, after Ian became Attorney General, he was never home."

"And you were."

I nodded. "When Ian and I were married, we promised each other we were going to be like D.H. Lawrence's twin stars, 'revolving in never coinciding orbits.' But after that first election night, there was only room for one shooting star. Ian was it, so I became the stargazer." My voice caught. I took a breath and finished. "And that's the way it was until he died."

Zack leaned towards me and took my hand. "Let's go inside and have a drink and a smooch," he said.

"You always know exactly what I need."

"Maybe that's because it's always exactly what I need."

I pulled a stool up to the counter so I could watch Zack make our drinks. As he did with everything, he brought total concentration to the process of mixing Bombay Sapphire and Martini & Rossi. Zack is a handsome man – balding, heavy-browed with an actor's large features, a vertical fold in his right cheek, a full-lipped, sensuous mouth, and extraordinary eyes, green flecked with brown. He lined up his mixing glasses, jiggers, and the gin and vermouth and began. When the drinks were ready, he removed our martini glasses from the freezer, filled them, dropped in a curl of lemon, and handed me my glass.

"This seems like an occasion for a toast," he said. "What would you like to drink to, Ms. Shreve?"

"How about dreams – past, present, and future?" I said.

Zack grinned. "Very Jungian."

We touched glasses. "You never tell me about your dreams," I said.

"You don't want to know," he said. "They're mostly triple X."

"That explains all that midnight groping."

"Any port in a storm," he said cheerfully. His face grew pensive. "You know something weird, Jo? In my dreams, I'm not in the wheelchair. You and I are walking or doing dishes or dancing and my wheelchair is nowhere to be seen. I haven't walked in forty-four years, but in my dreams I have a fully functioning body." His eyes met mine. "Then I wake up, and there's the chair."

"Does it bother you?'

"No. That wheelchair is just part of my life, and I have a great life. We're lucky people."

"And we're smart enough to know we're lucky," I said. "A double gift – and now I have all the time in the world to be grateful."

"No second thoughts about leaving the university?"

"Not a one."

"So how was your retirement lunch?"

"Exactly the same as every other retirement lunch at the Faculty Club. Good food. Bad speeches. Everyone checking their watches to see how much longer they had to stay. Hey, one nice thing – the kids were all represented. Mieka read a funny e-mail Angus sent from Calgary. Peter brought Taylor and they both said a few words. Then our grand-daughters sang 'Frère Jacques' in a round until Mieka gave them the hook."

Zack frowned. "I should have been there."

"You had to be in court. How'd that go, by the way?"

"The judge kicked my ass six ways till sundown, but I took it manfully, so I think the jury's on my side."

"Are you going to win?"

Zack took off his jacket and loosened his tie. "Fifty-fifty. Find out tomorrow."

"If I'd had a choice I would have been in court with you. Watching you get your ass kicked six ways till sundown would have been more fun than listening to people trying to remember me being incisive or funny."

"But you are incisive and funny."

"Apparently I leave it in the locker room. My colleagues were really grasping for memorable moments today."

"They don't know you the way I know you. Their loss."

"Well, they did give me a great present. Follow me. It's in the bedroom."

The dogs loped down the hall after us. My gift was original and thoughtful – a glass kaleidoscope that the accompanying card described as "fused, kiln-textured, stained, and formed." Whatever process had gone into its creation, the kaleido-scope was exquisite. I'd placed it on a low table by the window, where it caught the sun. Zack wheeled his chair close and picked it up. In the warm late-afternoon light the saturated colours of the glass seemed to undulate, flowing into one another with the fluidity of ocean water – now blue, then green, gold, white, black. In gold cursive script, the artist, Linda Sutherland, had written *Security for any one of us lies in greater abundance for all of us.*

Zack read the sentence aloud.

"That line was in my dream," I said. "I've used it a hundred times to finish political speeches. I guess we can take Dr. Jung off the case." Zack held the kaleidoscope to his eye, pointed it towards the light, and turned the tube. "This actually works," he said.

"No surprise there," I said. "Ed Mariani chose the gift, and he knew I'd get a kick out of a kaleidoscope that I could play with."

Zack's eyes widened. "How did Ed get to be the gift-buyer? He's at the School of Journalism."

"True, but he's had a couple of cross-appointments with our department, so he knows us. Ed figured if my colleagues in political science were left to their own devices, I'd end up with a La-Z-Boy, so he volunteered to choose a gift."

Zack placed the kaleidoscope in its stand on the table. The rays of sun pouring in the window seemed to penetrate, swirl, and become part of the glass. Zack's eyes were still fixed on the kaleidoscope. "There's nothing wrong with La-Z-Boys," he said, "but I'm glad Ed and his impeccable taste stepped in. This really is amazing."

I put my hands on Zack's shoulders and rested my chin on the top of his head. "Do you ever think about how lucky we are to have beauty like this in our lives?"

"Probably not often enough, but yes, I do." Zack covered my hands with his own. "Where did that question come from?"

"Just a conversation Ed and I had after lunch."

"Let me guess. It was about his wedding."

"No," I said. "It was about the anger that builds in people who never have beauty or much of anything else good in their lives. Last semester Ed's senior class in investigative journalism interviewed gang members in North Central about what had led them to join gangs."

"I imagine those students had tales to tell," Zack said dryly.

"They did," I said. "But they also heard some provocative rumours."

I straightened and Zack turned his chair around to face me. "Such as," he said.

"Apparently, the students turned up credible sources that a young agitator named Riel Delorme had convinced The Warriors and The Brigade they should join forces with him to stop the Village Project."

"Delorme – the name sounds familiar . . ." Zack said.

"He was one of my students. It was a while back – at least five years ago. We met a few times, talked about directions he might take for a master's thesis. I remember he was very interested in Che Guevara. He seemed keen. Then he didn't show up for a meeting we'd scheduled. I e-mailed him a couple of times suggesting he get in touch, but he never did. I asked around, and one of the other grad students told me Riel had dropped out."

"Well, unless he's a miracle worker, there's no way he could get The Warriors and The Brigade to enter into any sort of alliance. I've defended some of their members. Those guys couldn't agree on how to make a trip to the shit house."

"Ed thinks there's some truth in the story," I said. "He's not exactly a novice. He took up where his students left off and he's been working on it for months now."

"Then he's lucky he's still walking around," Zack said. "North Central is the worst neighbourhood in the country, according to the media. Gangs like The Warriors and The Brigade are high rollers. There's big money in drugs, prostitution, and old-fashioned robbery."

"Ed said many of them are clearly victims of fetal alcohol syndrome," I said. "Problems with impulse control and impaired judgment are almost guaranteed."

The line of Zack's mouth was grim. "Could be that. Could be they just get off on sticking knives into people. But whatever their thought processes, they are dangerous. Jo, I know how fond you are of Ed. I like him too, but he's a gay man who's effeminate, affluent, and not exactly in fighting trim. Easy pickings. Tell him to stay out of North Central and leave the undercover work to the cops."

"I did tell him that. He won't listen. Any more than you listen when I ask you to cut down on your workload."

Zack raised his hand, palm out, in a halt sign. "Let's park that one for the moment. What's Ed hearing on the street?"

"The big story seems to be that the project manager who was killed on the site of the old fur factory that was being demolished was not the victim of workplace negligence."

"So how did Danny Racette die?" Zack said.

"According to Ed, some members of The Brigade and The Warriors think Riel Delorme's opposition to the Village Project is ineffective. They've defected and joined a gang called Red Rage. Ed's sources tell him that Red Rage is really hard core. They decided that the on-site death of one of Leland Hunter's workers was the only way to make their point."

Zack's body tensed. He was Leland Hunter's lawyer. A problem for Leland was a problem for him. "So the explosives were set to go off when Racette was still sweeping the building to make sure nobody was inside? Shit. Now I really do need a shower."

My husband's life was high stakes and high stress – not a good combination for anybody, but particularly not for a paraplegic who'd had a health crisis just months earlier. I stroked his shoulder. "Want some company?"

"Always," he said. "But won't Taylor be home soon?"

"No. She and Declan are playing Ultimate Frisbee after school and then going out for pizza."

Zack grinned. "In that case, let's lather up."

After we made love, Zack stretched lazily. "That never gets old, does it?"

"Every time's an adventure," I said.

Zack groaned. "I wish we were staying home tonight."

"That's my line," I said. "You're the party boy."

"Tonight the party boy would like to hang up his tap shoes and stay here beside you and watch the sun go down."

"We have a whole summer to do that. And we both like Margot."

Zack raised an eyebrow. "And it really is time you met Leland."

"Leland's a busy man. Peyben's an international company. He's always travelling, and when he's here, he has Margot, his son, and his redevelopment project."

Zack sighed. "And you're still pissed off because Leland's project put the kibosh on the plans you and Mieka had to open UpSlideDown2 in the Warehouse District."

"Not much point in opening a community play centre when the community it was supposed to serve is being demolished," I said.

Zack kissed my hair. "Hey, we just had some great sex. Let's not ruin the moment. Besides, we've been through this a dozen times. As far as Leland's concerned, The Village isn't going to demolish a community. It's going to replace a bunch of rattrap houses, abandoned warehouses, and empty factories with a model neighbourhood. You've seen the ads. The Village is going to be a renaissance for the downtown area."

"A renaissance that will leave the people who live in North Central now without housing," I said. "Zack, you know as well as I do that they won't be able to afford to live in the shining city."

"Be fair, Jo," Zack said wearily. "Overall, this will be a good thing. I've seen where those people live. You know that one of my current clients is a slum landlord. Cronus probably owns a third of the houses in North Central. They're a disgrace, but Cronus takes great pride in how lucrative his hellholes are. He was trying to get me to invest in some houses on Winnipeg Street. He says the secret to turning a rental house into a moneymaker is simple – minimal repairs and maximum use of space. He showed me how he creates an extra source of income by stapling cheap insulation over what was once a living room window, then wiring in a microwave and a bar fridge and renting the room out as a suite."

"I've noticed that insulation in front windows in the Core," I said. "I didn't realize what it was for. How does a man like Cronus sleep nights?"

"Like a baby," Zack said. "But Leland isn't Cronus. He really is trying to make The Village work for everybody. Peyben has made a serious attempt to recruit people from the community to do the work."

"And six months into the project, the worker who's shadowing the project manager is killed on the job," I said.

Zack's voice was even. "If Ed's information is right, it had nothing to do with workplace negligence. The police are still investigating, but my guess is they'll discover that Leland Hunter is not the bad guy in this."

"You really like him, don't you?"

"It's hard not to," Zack said. "He's a straight shooter, and he's a nice guy who loves my law partner the way I love you."

"Truly, madly, and deeply," I said. "Okay, I'm still not sold, but if Leland makes Margot happy, I'll reserve judgment."

————

The building where Margot and Leland lived had a history. The year before, a call girl named Cristal Avilia had been murdered in one of the two condos on the top floor. Cristal's list of clients was gold-edged, and before we met, Zack had been one of them.

Cristal was only one of many women in Zack's life. There had been other risky behaviours: high-stakes poker games that lasted three days, fast cars, speedboats, and heavy drinking. A friend told me Zack had lived like an eighteen-year-old with a death wish. The truth was more complex. As a paraplegic who knew his days might be numbered, Zack believed in seizing the moment.

When we met, Zack's perspective changed. He wanted to be part of the future that included our family and me, and he was willing to do what it took to be with us for as long as possible. He cut back on his drinking, put limits on his gambling, drove within hailing distance of the speed limit, and committed himself enthusiastically to monogamy. He was a changed man, but the past always leaves debris, and there were still enough shards of Zack's former life around to wound us both.

Cristal Avilia's real estate dealings were complex and their legacy had endured. Not only had she owned the condo in which she lived and conducted her business, she had heeded the wise counsel of realtor clients who saw the shape the Warehouse District was assuming and advised her to purchase the renovated warehouse on Halifax Street in which it was situated. When Cristal died, her sister, Mandy, inherited the property.

Mandy worked at a beauty shop called Cut 'n' Curl and was content with her immaculate bungalow on a corner lot in Wadena, the small town where the Avilias had grown up. She had no interest in relocating and she had no idea how to unload a high-end property with an unsavoury history.

Luckily for Mandy, Margot Wright was a Wadena girl too, and she believed in community.

A month after Cristal's death, Margot paid Mandy a fair price for the condo. In midsummer, the renovations on Margot's new home were complete, and she threw a party to celebrate. Leland Hunter came with a group of friends. When the party was over, the friends left, but Leland stayed. The next morning Margot took him on a tour of the building. The owner of the only other condo on Margot's floor had put his property up for sale the morning after Cristal's murder. Leland had just moved back to Regina and was looking for a place to live. For both Leland and Margot, it seemed like kismet.

As a developer, Leland knew the importance of timing. He saw the potential in the area around the building on Halifax Street. There had been a civic push to reclaim the Warehouse District, and already the areas to the north and west of Leland's building were a pleasant mix of high-end condos, trendy bars and restaurants, and specialty shops, but the areas south and east of the building were still classified as "unimproved." Leland's first step was to buy the building on Halifax Street. As plans for the Village Project took shape in his mind, Leland began buying the properties that stood in the project's way.

The quickest route between our house and Leland and Margot's place was along College to Broad down 7th, but that night I took a longer path, through the narrow downtown streets with numbers for names and big-city problems. The weather had changed. The sky had darkened and the wind had picked up, whipping debris into the air. Half-naked kids, dirty and laughing, darted out from between parked cars while the adults who might have cared for them sat smoking on front stoops, laughing as the dogs they had tethered to metal spikes by short leashes snarled and lunged impotently towards passersby.

In front of a building where teenaged members of the community association had painted a mural that featured a dove bearing an olive branch, hookers, both male and female, many of them younger than our daughter Taylor, stood on corners, their pelvises thrust forward provocatively, their eyes dead.

Zack's face was bleak as we moved through the Core. "God, this is depressing," he said.

"Tell me something I don't know," I said. "I come down here all the time. I keep hoping I'll find another site that might work for the new play centre."

The idea of opening a place in North Central where children could play and their parents could sip coffee and visit was my daughter Mieka's. By training, Mieka was a caterer, but caterer's hours aren't good for a single mum with two young daughters. UpSlideDown, Mieka's first café/play centre, was an invention of necessity, and from the moment it opened in an area of our city with boutique shopping, heavy foot traffic, and plenty of young families, it was a hit. When Mieka noticed that parents were getting more out of visits to the new play centre than happy kids and the chance to kick back with a good cup of joe, she took note. While they sipped their coffee and watched their kids play, the parents who came to UpSlideDown were sharing questions about child-rearing and picking up parenting skills from one another.

Parents in North Central were often very young with troubled histories, and Mieka and her friend Lisa Wallace, a community development worker in North Central, realized that opening a place where young parents could learn parenting skills while they watched their kids play might serve a real purpose. They found an old school-supply warehouse that was ideally situated and solidly built. I was enthusiastic, and after he had engineers check out the building, Zack bought it for me as a pre-retirement gift. We were in business, and then Leland's Village Project came along. Our perfect dream stood in Leland's way. I received a substantial cheque from Peyben for the building, and within a week it had been demolished.

"Finding another piece of property for the play centre shouldn't be a problem," Zack said. "You made a tidy profit on that deal with Leland. Money always opens up options."

"I'm reminding myself of that," I said. "I also remember that the property was a gift from you."

"And probably paid for by Leland's money," Zack said. "And so the dance goes on."

"I guess the question is who gets to dance and who gets to watch," I said.

Zack chuckled. "Careful, Ms. Shreve. Your socialist roots are showing."

A fifteen-foot chain-link fence topped with razor wire surrounded the manicured lawn and the shimmering swimming pool set like a jewel in the Japanese courtyard behind the condo where Margot and Leland lived. Still visible on the brick face of the four-storey building were the words COLD STORAGE. When I tapped in Margot's security code, a gate in the fence slid open. We followed the driveway to the garage, where we again tapped in the security code. The door opened and we drove inside. There were perhaps a dozen other cars there – all new, all expensive.

Zack opened his door, reached into the back seat, pulled out his wheelchair, and unfolded it. When I didn't move, he turned to face me. "Are you feeling weird about going to Cristal Avilia's old condo?"

"A little," I said.

"Well, don't," he said. "This is Margot's place now, and
there's been nobody else for me since the day I met you. You
fill me to the brim."

A walking path wound through the grass of the courtyard to
the back entrance to the condo. Wrought-iron chairs with
yellow-and-white-striped cushions were arranged in conversational groupings between clusters of flowering bushes.
The scent of barbecue hung in the air, but there wasn't a
soul in sight. After tapping in the security code for the third
time, we entered the building and stepped into a freight elevator that moved us smoothly to the top floor.

The foyer of Margot's condominium was spectacular: an
open-concept plan with a vaulted ceiling and skylights. Two
storeys of light, hardwood, granite, and glass. The furniture
was all simple and elegant: soft pale leather couches and
chairs, bronze lamps that cast a gentle glow, huge ornamental jars filled with dried grasses. It was a stunning setting for
a woman who was pretty stunning herself.

Margot was a natural blonde with creamy skin, delicately
arched brows, full lips, and dagger nails that were always
painted a shade of red that hinted at danger. On more than
one occasion I'd seen her in court, and even in her barrister's
robes, Margot was a man magnet. We met frequently at social
events. She never showed up with the same date twice,
although the glitter in the eyes of her escorts suggested they
would welcome a return engagement.

But that night, as she and Leland Hunter greeted us, Margot
was radiant with the knowledge that she had found the lover
with whom she wanted to spend the rest of her life. At first
glance, Leland Hunter did not appear to be a man who would
make a woman's loins twitch. The contours of his shaved
head were not pleasing. His face was long and angular, his
eyes were hooded, and his nose was large and appeared to

have healed imperfectly from a break. His body was taut, sinewy, seemingly without an extra ounce of flesh. He looked like a fighter, not a lover.

Zack, Margot, and I were dressed casually, but Leland was wearing a grey summer-weight suit, a white shirt, and a brilliant aubergine and grey silk tie with matching pocket handkerchief. A power suit, but Leland didn't need expensive tailoring to announce his power. Before he uttered a word, we all knew the room was firmly in Leland's command. "I hope you know how pleased I am to finally meet you, Joanne," he said, extending his hand. "Our children are close, you and Margot are close, and Zack and I are close. It feels as if tonight, the final piece is sliding into place."

Leland's handshake was firm and he didn't release the pressure until I'd responded. Even his movements were efficient. "I agree," I said. "It's time we met."

"Would you like a tour of the place before we have our drinks?" His voice was gravelly, throaty.

Zack shot me a quick look and waited for my response.

"That would be fun," I said.

"Fun for us, too," Leland said. "Margot and I don't entertain often."

Margot laughed and slipped her arm through his. "Try never," she said.

"Okay, never," Leland said. "All the more reason why we welcome the chance to show off." Hand in hand, they led us through the condo, pointing out the skylights in the twenty-four-foot ceiling, the original exposed brick wall, the hickory kitchen cabinets, the polished granite counter, the sleek fixtures, the two-sided gas fireplace, the skyline views from the terrace.

"It's gorgeous," I said.

"It needed work," Margot said tightly. "It looked like a place where men could live out their fantasies, which, of

course, is exactly what it was." She had no knowledge of
Zack's connection with Cristal, but she was clearly still
baffled and angry at the turn Cristal's life had taken.
"Anyway, I'm pleased with it."

"You should be," I said. "It's beautiful."

"Leland's is the only other condo on this floor – same plan
as this one, but it's spiffier. He cheated, though. He hired
a decorator."

"You'll notice where I choose to spend my nights,"
Leland said.

"Oh, I notice," Margot purred.

The sexual heat between them was palpable. Zack and I
exchanged a glance, then his gaze moved towards his law
partner. "The faster you feed us, the faster we'll be out of
here," he said.

Margot had one of the all-time great dirty laughs. "In that
case," she said, "let's get dinner on the table." She gestured
towards the balcony. "I was hoping we could eat outside,
but that wind is wicked and it looks like rain. Leland pulled
the table over so we could still have the view."

"Not much to see now," Leland said. "By next year, we'll
have something very nice to show you."

Margot shot a look of distaste at her perfect kitchen.
"Meanwhile, all we can offer you is the sad spectacle of me
making dinner."

"Can I help?" I asked.

"God, yes," she said. "All the food came from Evolution,
and Aimee has given me written instructions for every dish."

Margot passed the list to me, and I read through it.
"Absolutely straightforward," I said. "Let's crank up the
oven to 375 and as soon as it's ready, we'll put in the beef
tenderloin and the potatoes. The meat will take about
forty-five minutes for rare. Aimee has everything else
timed. The roasted red pepper soup needs a crème fraiche

drizzle at the end. I can show you how to do that in about a second and a half."

"I'm ready," Margot said. "Send me in, coach." When she clapped her hands together, I got a good look at her engagement ring, a pear-shaped solitaire.

"Wow, that's a gorgeous ring."

"It is, isn't it?" she said. "Leland had it specially made, and it took a while to find exactly the right stone."

"It was worth waiting for," I said.

"Just like Leland," she said. "By the time I met him, I'd decided I was happy on my own. I liked my work. I earned a lot of money. I had a reliable vibrator, and there were plenty of men to take me to social functions where my vibrator wouldn't have been welcome. Then along came Prince Charming."

"And out went the vibrator," I said.

Margot's grin was wicked. "It was an old friend. I gave it an honourable send-off." She opened the refrigerator and took out a bottle of champagne. "Let's get rolling."

The food was excellent, the wine was splendid, and the talk was good. Not surprisingly, given the company, the first topic of conversation was marriage. But the wedding we spoke of was not Margot and Leland's, which was still more than three weeks away; it was Ed Mariani's marriage to Barry, his partner of twenty-seven years.

On Sunday, Barry and Ed would be married in the rooftop garden of the condo on Halifax Street. "I am over the moon about the garden," Margot said. "When I was a kid, I spent half my life in the Wadena Library. One afternoon I found a coffee-table book about roof gardens. God knows what a book like that was doing in a local library on the bald prairie, but I lugged it home, and every night I just stared at the pictures, dreaming. I kept renewing it until finally the librarian told me I might as well keep it, but if anybody else wanted to check it out, I'd have to lend it to them. And now here I am on Halifax Street with a roof garden of my own."

"We were lucky," Leland said. "The developer who did the initial renos on this property completed the structural work on the roof garden before she ran out of money, so we just had to do the finishing and choose the plants and the furniture."

"Actually, Ed had to choose the plants and the furniture," Margot said. "Leland was travelling, and I was working sixteen hours a day on the Zwarych trial. I didn't want to wait till next year, so Ed took over. He did a great job."

Leland's smile was slow in coming but worth waiting for. It softened his face, made him seem approachable. "Margot and I are so pleased that Ed and Barry chose to have their wedding here, and according to the forecast, Sunday will be a perfect June day."

"That's good news," I said. "Ed and Barry have waited a long time for this."

Leland turned to me. "Margot tells me you're the best man."

"I am," I said. "We struggled with the title. 'Matron of honour' sounded like I should be wearing a feathery hat and support hose, and Zack pointed out that 'chief witness' sounded as if I was testifying in court, so we stuck with 'best man.' I kind of like it."

"So do I," Zack said. He turned to Margot. "So, how come you aren't getting married in the roof garden of your girl-hood dreams?

"Because I had another girlhood dream. I wanted an old-fashioned, small-town Saskatchewan wedding," Margot said.

"At heart, Margot is just an old-fashioned, small-town Saskatchewan girl," Leland said.

Margot gave him a sidelong glance. "Hardly," she said. "But despite my big-city ways, I wanted a Wadena wedding – not the ones they have now, which are just the same as weddings anywhere – the kind people had when I was a kid. No floral arrangements – just everybody emptying out their gardens and bringing all the flowers to the United Church in jam jars. And everybody in town sitting in the pews whispering about how beautiful I look and checking my waistline to see if I'm pregnant."

Zack choked on his wine. "Are you?"

"Focus your laser gaze on me at the wedding and decide for yourself," she said. Margot leaned back in her chair and closed her eyes. "This is going to be a great wedding, and the reception's going to be so much fun. It'll be at the golf course and everybody in town's invited. Sis Gooding will do the food – she does the food for everything in Wadena. There'll be perogies and cabbage rolls and turkeys and hams and jellied salads that match my attendants' dresses and crepe paper and fairy lights looped through the tree branches and a country band that plays 'Careless Love' for the bride-and-groom dance, and people clinking glasses to make Leland and me kiss." In the candlelight, Margot's face glowed. Leland reached over and touched her cheek. Then he gave her his slow-blooming, transforming smile.

In addition to his wedding day, there was another significant event on Leland's agenda. The next morning our university was awarding him an honorary doctorate. It wasn't his first, but Leland didn't dwell on himself, he focused on me. "It must be a thrill to have an earned doctorate."

"At the time it was simply a relief," I said. "I was a widow with three children, and if I was going to get a job teaching, I had to finish my dissertation. Most academics just see the Ph.D. as a union card." I met Leland's eyes. "Of course, there are circumstances where a union card can be a powerful tool."

Zack picked up on the challenge in my words and cleared his throat. Margot watched with interest, but Leland was unruffled. "Because a union prevents people like me from shoving workers around," he said.

"If you understand that, why is the Village Project non-union?" I said.

"You know the answer to that, Joanne. A union project costs more. That means more investors – more people to answer to. There's a saying in the development business: 'Beg for forgiveness, not for permission.' I'm not going to waste time begging for permission. I'm going to do whatever's necessary to take this district back to what it once was."

"And tomorrow you get your reward," I said. "The scarlet hood with the gold silk lining,"

"And I can't wait to see you in it," Margot said.

Leland's voice was even. "You may get to see more than that." He turned to me again. "You're on campus, Joanne. You must have heard something about the protest that's apparently being planned for the ceremony."

"From what I've heard, it's not going to amount to much," I said. "Some of the graduands on stage are planning to turn their chairs so their backs are to you when you speak."

"I can handle that," Leland said. "Actually, I can handle most things." His voice was flat. He wasn't bragging, simply stating a fact.

As Margot and I were bringing in dessert and coffee, Zack's cell rang. He took the call, exchanged a few words with his caller, said, "Okay, thanks," and broke the connection.

"Peyben's off the hook, Leland," he said. "The police are now treating Danny Racette's death as a homicide."

Leland tented his fingers and stared at them silently for a few seconds. "That doesn't make Danny any less dead," he said at last. "So what makes the police suspect murder?"

"They discovered a treasure," Zack said. "Sifting through every square inch of that grid they drew over the detonation area finally paid off. The cops were looking for something that shouldn't be there, and this afternoon, they found fragments of what appeared to be a timing device."

"And our crews use electronic detonators," Leland said. "That blast was scheduled for 3:00 p.m. and it went off at 2:20 when Danny was checking the site so he could give the all clear." Leland sipped his coffee. "Do the police have any theories about who did it?"

"If they do, they're not sharing," Zack said. "Leland, this afternoon Joanne told me that Ed Mariani was looking into rumours that the group opposed to The Village has been recruiting gang members. Has he mentioned anything about this to you?"

"Ed and I haven't really had much chance to talk," Leland said. "But the gang connection is worth looking into. Danny Racette joined The Warriors when he was eleven. He was twenty-two when he decided there might be a better way to lead his life. He went back to school, got his ticket, and started working in construction."

"So Danny Racette's murder could have been some sort of Warrior retribution?" Margot said.

Zack shook his head. "I don't think so. There's a protocol for gang members who want to leave. It's called 'stomping out.' When a kid joins a gang, there's an initiation ritual called 'stomping in.' It involves selected gang members taking turns beating the shit out of the prospective member for a predetermined number of minutes. If he or she is tough enough to take the punishment, they've proven they've got 'heart.' They get their Warrior tattoos, and they're in. 'Stomping out' also involves a vicious group assault, but this time if the member is able to walk away, he or she gets to keep on walking." Zack turned to Margot. "Gangs have their own code, and part of the code is honouring the stomping out. If Racette got through his stomping out, The Warriors wouldn't touch him. Of course, The Brigade is another story."

I felt a chill. "From what Ed told me, a lot of gang members are just kids," I said. "It's hard to imagine children making a decision that will commit them to that kind of life."

"Or death," Zack said. "I have all this gang lore at my fingertips because I defended a fifteen-year-old who killed another kid during a stomping in."

"And all this fun and games takes place five minutes from where we live," Margot said.

Leland frowned. "I think we would all welcome a change of topic." He went to the door that opened onto the terrace. "Rain's stopped," he said. "Let's go up to the roof and check out the view."

We took the elevator to the roof garden. Even beaten by rain, the garden was beautiful. Pots of bougainvillea and hydrangea in deep purple, dusky pink, and purest white vied for pride of place with roses hitting June perfection. Leland led us past the flowering plants to the ornamental grasses Ed had used to create a barrier between the beauty of the roof garden and the ugliness of the construction sites below. The rain had flattened the grasses. Margot bent to straighten them. "Now that the rain has stopped, they'll dry quickly," she said. "When the wind blows, they rustle and make a kind of music. It's otherworldly."

Leland moved aside two of the planters to give Zack a clear view of the area surrounding their building.

"It all started with Margot, of course," Leland said. "She likes living here. It's close to her work, and there are good restaurants within walking distance that stay open late and have live music that's worth listening to."

"It sounds inviting," Zack said.

"It is, but it could be more. We shouldn't have to be living behind fifteen-foot security fences topped with razor wire. We shouldn't have to swipe our security passes four times to enter our own home. The logical move seemed to be to change the neighbourhood."

Leland's words resonated with me. Changing the neighbourhood was also the idea behind UpSlideDown2, but the approach Mieka, Lisa, and I were taking was different from Leland's. Our plan was to work slowly from the ground up. UpSlideDown2 would be a co-operative that would give people the will and the tools to transform their neighbourhood. Working from the inside out was slow, and the change might be generational. Leland's way was fast – top down, outside in.

As I gazed at the mud and the construction hoardings that had replaced the abandoned factories, crumbling houses, and condemned warehouses, it didn't seem as if, so far, Leland's plan had changed much for the better.

Leland had been watching my face and he saw that I was unconvinced. "Joanne, I know the landscape is bleak now," he said, "but there can be no phoenix without the ashes."

Leland may have viewed the world through the unsentimental eyes of capitalism, but as he spoke of recreating a Regina with the vibrancy it had in the early 1900s, he had a visionary's passion. His dream was an appealing one: a community not just of warehouses converted to high-end condominiums but also of small businesses, offices, mixed-income family homes, a public school, a high school, a branch library, and green space – small parks and backyard gardens, community gardens, even individual roof gardens.

When he finished speaking, he studied our faces, gauging our reactions. "Well, we've all seen the ad campaign," he said. "The intent of our slogan – Reclaiming Our Heritage – is to suggest the pleasures of moving back to a simpler time."

"Will the people who lived here before the redevelopment be able to afford that simpler time?" I asked.

"No," he said. "But the jobs we're bringing to the community will give them a way out of North Central. There are always casualties along the way, Joanne, but this is a journey worth taking." His eyes bored into me. "You don't agree?" he said.

"I don't know," I said. "I guess it depends on whether you're one of the casualties."

"Sometimes people choose to become casualties," Leland said. "With projects this size, we always try to recruit from the community. When we advertise in the United States or in Central America or Africa, we have to hire security to control the crowd of people desperate to work. Do you know how many applications we got from North Central? Ten. Five of the men responding to our ad never showed up for an interview. Two of them didn't make it through the first day on the job. Two are working out fine. And the fifth was Danny Racette. He was our success story."

"And now he's dead," I said. "All night long I've been trying to remember what Danny Racette looked like. When he died, there was a picture of him in the newspaper. I've been trying to remember his face, but I can't."

Leland's eyes held mine. "Count yourself lucky," he said. "I can't forget it."

CHAPTER

2

The evening ended soon after that. Margot offered us a nightcap, but when Zack and I declined, she didn't press the invitation. As we moved towards the elevator, Leland touched my arm. "I hope this is the first of many evenings we'll all have together," he said.

"We had a great time," Zack said. "Margot, you'll have to give me the recipe for that soup."

"No problem, big guy," she said. "Just call Evolution Catering and ask for Aimee."

As I eased our car through the gate onto the street, Zack stretched and yawned. "Well, it could have been worse."

"It was a very pleasant evening," I said carefully.

"That bad, eh?" Zack said.

"Not bad at all," I said. "I always enjoy being with Margot, I love you, and Leland's a very compelling man."

"You wanted to clean his clock, didn't you?"

"Was it that obvious?"

"Just to me, and only because I spend my life attuning myself to your nuances."

"How much wine did you have anyway?"

"Not enough to miss the way you bit your lip when Leland talked about how some people choose to be casualties."

"Bullshit is bullshit," I said. "Even when it's delivered by a gracious host."

"Well, thanks for holding back," Zack said. "Leland wants you to like him, Jo. Cut him a little slack."

"I will. One of my retirement goals is to stop being judgmental. I'll start with Leland."   .

"A perfect way to end the evening," Zack said contentedly. He reached over and turned up the volume on the radio. "And," he said, "the cherry on the cheesecake – we get to listen to Miles playing 'Springsville.'" There were two more cuts from *Miles Ahead* before the news came on. Zack turned off the radio. "Do you think Margot really is pregnant?" he said.

"She had a couple of sips of champagne and nothing else. She's forty-two years old and she and Leland want a child, so if she's not pregnant now, I think she and Leland are working on it."

Zack was mellow. "Another baby in the firm – that will be nice."

"Margot will be a great mother," I said.

"Do you think she'll want to take maternity leave?"

"Don't pamper her," I said. "Give her the day off, but deduct it from her billable hours."

"You're mocking me, Ms. Shreve."

"Got to get up pretty early in the morning to put one over on you," I said. "And here's another bulletin. Guess what? We're home."

When Zack and I went in to say goodnight, Taylor was in bed wearing her current favourite sleepwear: an orange tank top and white silk shorts. One of my old university poetry anthologies was propped up on her knees.

"How's the assignment going?" Zack asked.

Taylor's mouth curled. "What's the point of similes anyway?"

"Beats me," Zack said. "When it comes to poetry, I'm like a eunuch in a harem."

Taylor looked at him blankly, and then the penny dropped. "Wicked," she said. "Thanks, Dad."

"My pleasure," Zack said, kissing her goodnight and heading down the hall to our room.

"So did you have fun with Declan's dad and Margot tonight?" she asked.

"We did," I said.

"Do you think we could invite them up to the lake some time?"

"Of course."

Taylor placed the anthology face down on the bed. "I think Declan needs to do something normal for a change. His parents are piling stuff onto him. His dad wants to make up for all the time he was away when Declan was a kid. Declan likes Margot, but he has to be super-careful because his mum gets hysterical if he even mentions Margot's name."

"Remember what Mieka did when Lena was little and she had a tantrum?"

"Ignored her till Lena realized nobody was watching and stopped," Taylor said.

"That technique works with adults, too," I said.

"I'll tell Declan," Taylor said. Then she slumped. "It probably won't work with Louise, though. Nothing does."

It had been a long day. I had eaten well that night and drunk moderately, but as I listened to Zack's contented snore, sleep eluded me for a long time. The wind howled along the creek, rattling the glass patio doors.

I believed Leland was sincere when he stood in the roof garden envisioning the grey and desolate neighbourhood beneath us transformed into a place where dreams could take root. But his vision had already claimed its first casualty, and Zack's account of the gangs' stomping-in and stomping-out rituals had been chilling. People who invented and practised rituals like that wouldn't be likely to back down from a fight. I couldn't stop myself from wondering who might next be caught in the middle.

The next morning when I awakened, our mastiff, Pantera, was sprawled across the threshold to Zack's bathroom; the shower was on full blast and Zack was singing "Ring of Fire" in the leathery bass he favoured when he tackled Johnny Cash tunes. Willie and I checked the weather through the glass doors to the deck. The sky was pewter, and the wind along the levee was whipping the frail branches of the newly planted trees along the bike path. "That's one rotten day out there," I said. Undeterred, Willie ran for his leash and Pantera lumbered after him.

Our run was cold and miserable. The wind cut; the path on which we ran was littered with tree branches, and the night winds had been sufficiently powerful to uproot some of the saplings. The dogs and I circled the levee and came home – a good workout, but not a great one. By the time we got back, Zack had finished breakfast and was dressed for the day.

"Coffee's ready and porridge is in the pot," he said. "I've got a few things to check out before I go to court."

"Are you going downtown already?"

"Yep. I have to stop off and get you something for the lake."

"Is there something I need?"

"In my opinion, yes, but it's a surprise. What I do with it will bring you pleasure and it costs less than ten bucks. No more hints." With that, he wheeled off towards the front door.

When Taylor appeared in the kitchen, she was wearing a white eyelet blouse, black capris with cuffs, and her favourite black-and-lime rainproof flats. She looked as crisp as a new apple – a rare, lovely girl. She was carrying my poetry anthology.

I poured her juice. "So any luck with the poetry assignment?"

"I found a poem. It's called 'A Dream Deferred.' It's short, so the people in my group won't hate me, and it has a tonne of similes."

"Good news all around," I said.

Taylor looked in the porridge pot and wrinkled her nose. "Is this it?"

"We have the usual options, and I bought some crumpets to take to the lake. They're in the fridge."

"Excellent." Taylor pitched the anthology onto the table, where it landed with a thud. "I copied out my poem, so you can have the book back," she said. She popped two crumpets in the toaster and began melting butter in the microwave. As she had since she was little, she tucked a tea towel bib-style around her neck before eating. When she'd finished her crumpets, she poured herself another glass of juice.

"Ready for the day?" I asked

She nodded. "I hope it's better than yesterday."

"What was the matter with yesterday?"

She shrugged. "Well, the day was okay – actually it was great. I thought I'd hate Ultimate – I'm not exactly a jock, but it was fun pitching the Frisbee around and our team actually won. The other kids invited us to go for pizza with them, but Declan knew his mum would be alone, so we took a pizza over to their house."

"That was a nice thought," I said.

Taylor sighed. "I guess, but it didn't work out. Mrs. Hunter didn't eat anything. She just drank. Finally, she decided she wanted a bowl of cereal. There wasn't any milk in the house so Declan went out to get some, and as soon as he left, his mum brought out this journal she kept when she was fourteen. It was creepy. All about how she'd just met this boy, and she knew they were 'destined' to spend the rest of their lives together."

"And the boy was Leland Hunter."

Taylor cringed at the memory. "Mrs. Hunter wanted me to read her journal out loud. It was filled with all these intimate things about how she and Leland Hunter were fated to be together forever. Finally, I just couldn't do it. I gave the journal back to her. She was really drunk, and she started off for bed. Then she turned around and said, 'Don't ever let go of your destiny.'"

"Did she explain what she meant?"

"No. By that time, she was pretty close to passing out. Declan got home and we helped her up the stairs."

I felt my gorge rise, but I kept my voice even. "I remember having to do that with my mother. I hated it."

Taylor shrugged. "Those stairs are steep and they're slippery. Somebody has to help her."

I chose my words carefully. "You know how fond your dad and I are of Declan," I said. "He shouldn't have to be Louise's nursemaid." I touched her hand. "And, Taylor, neither should you. You're fourteen years old."

She leapt to her feet. I'd touched a nerve. "And that means that I should be" – her fingers flashed furious air quotes – "'seeing other boys.' We've talked about this a hundred times. You just don't understand."

I lowered my voice. "Then help me understand, Taylor. You just told me how disturbing you found Louise deciding at fourteen that Leland Hunter was her 'destiny.'"

Taylor took a deep breath. "Declan and I don't believe we are each other's destiny. We just know that right now, being together is the best thing for both of us."

"You've always enjoyed meeting new people."

"It's more complicated now. Jo, there are plenty of boys who want to be with me, but I don't want what they want."

"Sex."

She held my gaze. "You don't know what it's like now. Boys expect girls to do things to them that I just don't want to do. And if the girl doesn't do it, they tweet or text about her and they put things about her on Facebook. And if she *does* do it, it's even worse!"

"What kind of things?"

"Guess?" Taylor said. "Before Declan and I got together, I saw stuff about me on Facebook. Boys said I was frigid. They called me an icebox and other stuff that was way worse. I don't know if I'm frigid. I don't even care. I just know I don't want to be a skank like my mother."

"Taylor . . ."

She clapped her hands over her ears. "I know. I know. I shouldn't have called her a skank. She had a complicated life. But the articles I read about her say she slept with all these men and all these women. I don't hate her, Jo. I never knew her. All I know is her art, and it's incredible. But I'm not like her. I don't like it when boys paw at me. Declan keeps them away."

"By . . . ?"

"As long as boys think Declan and I are a couple, they don't bother me." Her smile was tentative. "Jo, most mothers would be relieved that their daughter weren't sexually active."

"I am relieved. Taylor, Zack and I are proud of the decisions you make."

Her smile grew broader. "Then get off my case about seeing other boys. And I'm not warping Declan. He sees other girls. Girls who are older than me."

"Girls who *are* sexually active."

Taylor jumped up from the table. "Can't you ever leave anything alone?" she said. "I don't care what Declan is doing as long as he's not doing it to me. I know exactly what you're going to say next and I don't want to hear it. I don't want to hear your lecture about sex and respect. Declan is respectful of those girls. He takes them out to eat and go to movies and hear bands, and unlike a lot of boys, Declan never tweets or goes on Facebook to talk about what he does with them afterwards. Those girls are happy and Declan's happy and I'm happy. Can't you please – for once – just leave my life alone?"

Taylor was the fourth child I'd seen through adolescence. Apparently I had learned nothing. "Okay," I said. "It's miserable out there. Want me to get your raincoat?"

She sighed. "I'm fourteen, remember? I know enough to come out of the rain."

After Taylor left, I went to our room to make the bed. I looked at the tangle of soft cotton sheets with longing. At my retirement luncheon there had been many hoary jokes about the lazy life of retirees. I'd been retired less than twenty-four hours and this would be my second nap. So be it. I took off my jeans and shirt, slipped on my pyjamas, and slid between the sheets.

Tired as I was, I couldn't help worrying about Taylor. She was handling herself with real maturity, but the presence of Louise Hunter in her life was troubling. My first meeting with Louise had come the previous December. She and Leland had been divorced for several years, and she had spent much of that time drinking heavily. After a bizarre incident in which Louise gave a stranger the keys to her Mercedes and asked him to drive her home to head off the possibility of yet another DUI charge, Declan called Zack for help. I went with Zack to Louise's and while he paid off Louise's volunteer driver, I readied her for bed and tucked her in. The sequence of tasks was painfully familiar to me, and it was not something I wanted Taylor to learn, not now or ever. Nor did I wish it for Declan.

Not long after that night, Louise stopped drinking, and for a few weeks it seemed as though she might be truly on the road to recovery. But on Valentine's night, Leland asked Margot to marry him and she accepted. In Regina, lovers don't need a photo on the social page to announce an engagement. Kind friends will carry the news. By noon the next day Louise had been told that Leland was remarrying, and by five she had washed down a handful of pills with vodka. Her suicide attempt was not successful, but Zack told me about the note she'd written. It ended with a poignant quote from Tennyson: *It is the little rift within the lute, / That by and by will make the music mute, / And ever widening, slowly silence all.*

I finally did doze off for a while, and when I awoke, it was time to begin getting ready for convocation. Ed Mariani and I had arranged to go together. As it had been since before I'd begun teaching at the university, convocation was held at the Conexus Arts Centre. The centre offered ample parking, but after a major event, getting out of the lot caused tempers to fray. Ed and Barry lived five blocks from Conexus, so I'd arranged to leave my car at their place and walk to convocation with Ed.

That afternoon, it was not a pleasant walk. The weather had moved from wretched to iffy, but the garment bags that protected our academic robes against the weather made them unwieldy. Ed was a heavy man, and by the time we arrived at the centre his breathing was laboured. I was relieved when the brightly lit lobby came into view, but there was one more hurdle to clear before we were inside.

A group of protestors had gathered. About half were Aboriginal, half were Caucasian. They were nearly all young men, mostly heavily tattooed and rough looking. The demonstration appeared to have been hastily organized. The signs were crude: hand-lettered on poster board and stapled to scrap lumber. The message was unequivocal: Leland Hunter wasn't a developer, he was a destroyer, and he should get out of their neighbourhood. Ed and I recognized the group's leader at the same moment he spotted us. Ed knew Riel Delorme only by reputation, but I remembered him from our academic meetings. We exchanged the awkward nods of those who find themselves in a situation that etiquette books don't cover, and then he surprised me by coming over.

Riel had changed. As a student, there had been something sweet and gentle about him, but in the five years since I had last seen him he had hardened. His face was deeply lined, his lips compressed, and his obsidian eyes had dark circles around them.

The changes in the man standing in front of me on that windy convocation day were not simply physical. With his shining blue-black hair centre-parted and flowing to his shoulders, powerfully muscled arms, tight blue jeans, and combat boots, Riel Delorme was an urban warrior.

"Good to see you, Professor Kilbourn," he said.

"Good to see you, too," I said. "This is my friend Ed Mariani from the School of Journalism. Ed, this is Riel Delorme."

"Professor Mariani knows who I am. He's been asking people in my neighbourhood about me."

Ed was genial. "We could cut out the middleman," he said. "You could talk to me face to face."

Riel was noncommittal. "Maybe someday." He cocked his head towards the protestors. "I'd better get back to work."

I held out my hand and touched his arm. "Do you ever think about coming back to university?"

"That was another world."

"It's still there, Riel," I said. "I don't know what shape your academic record's in, but if you are interested in coming back, give me a call. I'm in the book."

"I know." He lowered his eyes. "Every so often I look you up. There's something I should talk to you about . . ." He met my gaze. "This isn't the right time," he said and then walked away.

Ed's look was quizzical. "What was that all about?"

"I don't know," I said. I checked my watch. "But we'd better get inside."

The lobby was filled with families – happy, proud, wearing their Sunday best, cameras slung from their necks. It was a nice crowd. Ed and I tunnelled our way through and headed downstairs. He pulled me aside at the bottom of the stairwell. "Do you think Riel Delorme wanted to talk to you about Danny Racette's death?"

"It's possible. I might be the only person from Leland's world Riel feels he can really talk to," I said. "He might have heard something, but I don't believe he would have been involved. When Riel was my student, he was an admirer of Che Guevera. He believed Che was right about revolution – that someone had to make it happen – but he was definitely questioning the validity of violence."

"Riel didn't look like a pacifist today."

"No," I agreed. "He didn't."

———

There is more than a whiff of the medieval about convocation: the solemnity and unhurried pace of the rituals, the arcane symbolism of the ceremony that marks a scholar's rite of passage, the elaborate design of the faculty academic robes and hoods, the timeless optimism of the participants. Convocation ceremonies are not without their charms, but they are usually long, often hot, and, after the novelty of being part of the platform party wears off, always mind-numbingly boring.

Normally, after the graduating students and platform party have been piped in, the national anthem sung, the invocation offered, the chancellor's message delivered, and the candidate for the honorary degree presented, my colleagues and I furtively pull out BlackBerrys or smartphones and settle in for the duration. But this time I was entirely alert.

After the dean of the Faculty of Business Administration finished his introduction, Leland stepped forward for the conferring of the degree: a scarlet hood was slipped over his head onto his shoulders, he signed the register, and moved to the podium to deliver the convocation address. At that point, perhaps twenty students stood and turned their chairs so their backs would be to Leland when he spoke.

I had expected Leland to ignore the protestors, but he shifted his position so that he could face their backs. His voice was even. "Never turn your back on the enemy," he said. "It makes you vulnerable, and it undercuts your ability to react effectively. Sun Tzu's *The Art of War* says that strategy requires quick and appropriate responses to changing conditions. That's true in war; it's true in business; it's true in life. If your back is turned, you can't assess the situation and that means you can't take advantage of it. I'm about to start my prepared text, so now would be a good time to turn your chairs around and take the measure of your enemy."

Had this been a TV movie-of-the-week, one student and then another would have turned to face Leland. No one did.

In the silence, audience members began to stir uneasily in their seats. "Well, that's your decision," Leland said. He moved closer to the podium, adjusted the gold silk lining of his scarlet hood, and began his prepared speech. I heard more than one sigh of relief. My left-hand neighbour, who taught constitutional history and dreamed of Greece, pulled out his BlackBerry and began thumbing through images of Crete, Rhodes, Lesvos, and Kos. When Leland finished, the applause was polite but perfunctory.

We were back on track. A student pianist played a piece he had composed for the occasion. The university president delivered her message, and then the real business of the day – the awarding of degrees – began.

Beside me, my colleague found a website that allowed him to take a virtual tour of Athens. I watched the students trooping across the stage and thought about the next graduation in our family – our younger son Angus's from the College of Law. It was a year away, but Zack was already determined that his stepson would join the firm, and he had dangled the shiny bauble of a summer job in the new Calgary office to entice Angus to work at Falconer Shreve. The Calgary job was a sensible solution to a prickly problem. Working with the firm would be an impressive line on Angus's resumé, and except for Zack's partner, Kevin Hynd, nobody in the Calgary office knew or cared about Angus's relationship with Zack. I was thinking about how much fun Angus must be having in Calgary when my colleague said goodbye to Greece, flicked off his BlackBerry, tapped my arm to get my attention, and stood. The last graduate at the last convocation I would attend as a faculty member had received her degree. It was time to leave the stage.

The basement room where the members of the platform party removed their academic garb was hot and crowded. Leland was handing his robe to a woman from the registrar's office. His face brightened when he saw me. "I was hoping we'd connect," he said. "I'm meeting Margot and Declan in the lobby, and they were looking forward to seeing you and Ed."

I gazed around the room. "Ed's here somewhere," I said. "Let me find him, and we can go upstairs together. Incidentally, congratulations – not just on the honorary doctorate but on your speech. I liked what you said to the protestors."

Leland's expression was amused. "They didn't."

"Sometimes it takes a while." I spotted Ed coming towards us. "Here's our man. Let's find Margot and Declan."

Walking through the lobby with Leland was an odd experience. He had just received an honorary doctorate. I would have anticipated that someone would have reached out to shake his hand or called out congratulations. No one did. People weren't hostile. They simply stepped aside and gave us a wide berth. Leland moved quickly, eyes straight ahead towards his destination.

Margot and Declan were waiting a few feet from the glass entrance doors. Both were elegantly dressed for tea at the president's house, Margot in a cream jersey wraparound dress that hugged her curves and Declan, for the first time in my memory, in a suit and tie. His outfit was clearly new and very expensive, but his dark blond dreadlocks were, as always, tied back with a piece of hemp. He was, after all, sixteen years old, and he, too, had a statement to make.

As soon as we reached Margot and Declan, we exchanged a few words and started through the crush towards the exit.

The sequence of events that followed had the jumpy, unfocused quality of a video shot by an amateur. Leland and Margot were following Ed, Declan, and me through the doors when seemingly out of nowhere Louise Hunter appeared, grabbed her ex-husband's arm, and attempted to pull him back into the building. Two factors worked against her: the press of people seeking to get out of the hot and airless lobby was intense and Louise was drunk. Leland pried her fingers loose from the arm of his jacket, whispered something, and made his escape.

The car that would take Leland, Margot, and Declan to the president's tea was waiting. So were the protestors and the police. The scene was anything but tense. After three hours outside, the fire had gone out of the bellies of the protestors. The officers sent to keep order as Leland left the Conexus Centre were vigilant but relaxed.

When Leland reappeared outside, the demonstrators took notice and began chanting and raising their signs. It seemed they were simply going through the motions, and no one, including the police, looked alarmed. However, when a cameraman from a local TV station, who had been taking feel-good pictures of happy families, turned his camera on the confrontation, the stakes were raised. The protestors began jockeying for position, and in the confusion Riel Delorme was knocked towards Leland Hunter, and the handle of Riel's sign struck Leland's head before clattering to the ground.

Reflexively, Leland's hand went to the wound; it came away covered in blood. The police moved quickly to clear the area, herding the protestors away from Leland. One officer pulled on gloves and picked up the sign. There was an ugly jagged piece of metal where the wooden handle had been joined to the placard. The cop brandished the sign. "Who was holding this?" he asked.

Riel Delorme stepped out of the crowd. "I was," he said. He seemed both resigned and defiant. Two officers moved into position beside him.

Margot opened her bag and took out a pocket pack of tissues. She ripped it open and carefully removed all the tissues so they formed a pad. She placed it against Leland's wound. It was soaked immediately, but even when fresh blood ran down her arm, Margot maintained the pressure on the wound.

Declan was staring at Margot's arm; he seemed frozen. "Dad, this is bad," he said.

"Head wounds always bleed," Leland said. "Get me to emergency, and they'll stitch me up."

One of the police officers flanking Riel Delorme took in the situation. "There's an ambulance on its way. Did anybody see what happened?"

No one said anything. Finally, I spoke. "People were jostling one another. The man holding the sign was pushed towards Leland Hunter and the handle hit him. It was an accident."

The EMT team arrived, imposing order on our chaos. They began checking out Leland. The bleeding had slowed, but he was pale, and despite his impatience to get to the hospital where he could be stitched up and sent on his way, the EMT people were thorough: maintaining the pressure on his wound and monitoring his heart and blood pressure. Margot, blood-spattered but composed, sat on the concrete beside Leland, holding his hand and whispering things that made him smile.

Louise Hunter had broken down, weeping and straining to get close to Leland. Declan and a woman with fiery red hair who appeared to be a friend of Louise's were keeping Louise firmly in hand, well away from her ex-husband.

My statement that Leland Hunter's injury had been inflicted accidentally brought me attention from a young uniformed officer with a badge identifying him as Kevin Toews. I didn't have much more to offer him: the account of what I'd seen, the nature of my connection with Riel Delorme, and my contact information. Riel's eyes never left my face. When Constable Toews walked away, I gave Riel what I hoped was an encouraging smile; he nodded acknowledgement and walked over to the ambulance. It was a gutsy move. The EMT people had just picked up the gurney on which Leland was lying. Riel leaned towards Leland. "I'm very sorry," he said. "I didn't mean to hit you."

Leland met Riel's eyes. "Never ruin an apology with an excuse," he said and then he turned away.

The EMT people loaded the gurney into the ambulance. Margot and I watched together until Leland was inside and the doors were shut.

"I'll take a cab and meet you at the hospital," I said.

Margot shook her head. "There's no need. Declan's meeting us there. And Leland is right. Head wounds always bleed a lot. I have five brothers. I know Leland will be fine." She held out her hands. They were trembling. Margot tried a smile. "Apparently my body didn't get the memo that I'm taking this in stride."

"That's always a problem when you're in love," I said.

"A lesson I'm just now learning," Margot said ruefully. When she turned to open the door to the passenger's side of the driver's compartment, Louise Hunter appeared. The red-haired woman was with her. The woman seemed to have a firm grasp on Louise's arm, but Louise managed to shake her off. When Louise attempted to shove Margot out of the way, Margot put her hands on Louise's thin shoulders and gazed down at her as if she were disciplining a child. "I'm the one who's going with Leland," she said.

Louise's intake of breath was sharp. "I'm his wife," she said.

"Not any more," the red-haired woman said, and her voice was firm. "Louise, don't do this to Declan and don't do this to yourself. Let me take you home."

Margot shot the woman a grateful look. "Thanks, Sage," she said. "I'll make sure you get an update on Leland's condition." Then she climbed into the passenger's seat and shut the door.

A knot of protestors had been watching the scene unfold. They appeared to be delighting in Leland and Margot's pain. As the ambulance sped off, a boy who didn't appear to be much more than sixteen raised his arm in a power salute and yelled, "I hope you die, you rich fucker."

The ambulance had disappeared, but the young boy kept cursing Leland and uttering obscenities about what he'd like to do to Margot if he ever got her alone.

"Let's get out of here." Ed's hand was on my arm. He looked at anxiously. "You seem shaken," he said. "Do you want me to call a cab?"

"No, the wind's died down. I could use some fresh air."

Ed and I had never felt the need to chat when we were together, so we walked home in companionable, if thought-ful, silence. When we reached his house, I kissed his cheek. "See you on Sunday," I said and started towards my car.

"Jo, can we talk for a minute. I'd like your opinion on something."

"You're not having second thoughts, are you?"

"Not a one. This is a gift Barry and I never dreamed would come our way. What I wanted to talk to you about are the orchids I've been growing for the wedding."

"Cascading white phalaenopsis and dendrobium – exactly what you gave me to carry when Zack and I were married. They were so spectacular no one noticed my dress."

"Zack did," Ed said. "When you joined him at the altar he couldn't stop beaming."

I smiled at the memory. "It was a nice moment."

"I want that moment, too," Ed said quietly. "Joanne, I know I'm not Adonis. I see myself in the mirror every day. I'm middle-aged, I'm fat, and my hair is thinning, but I want Barry to look at me the way Zack looked at you." Ed's voice was husky with emotion. He cleared his throat. "So what do you think? Would I look foolish if I carried the orchids when I walked up the aisle to join Barry?"

"Raise high the roof beam, carpenter," I said. *"Like Ares comes the bridegroom, taller far than a tall man."*

"Meaning?"

"Meaning, it's your wedding day, Ed. Carry the orchids. You and Barry have earned that moment."

CHAPTER

3

I was staring at my academic robes, pondering their fate now that I'd retired, when Margot called, sounding tired but relieved. "Good news," she said. "The doctor in emergency stitched Leland up, said that he should take it easy for the rest of the day but that he's fine."

"That is good news," I said. "So you're home safe."

"We are, and we may never leave again. That was a real adventure in crazy town this afternoon. Thank God Sage Mackenzie was there to hustle Louise away."

"Is she Louise's companion?"

"No. She's the lawyer Leland pays to keep Louise out of legal trouble. Sage doesn't come cheap, but as you saw today, she earns every penny. I promised I'd give her a call, so I should move along, but I knew you'd be worried."

"I *was* worried. Tell Leland to let you pamper him for a while. Actually, after the afternoon you had, you could probably use a little pampering yourself."

Margot chortled. "Leland and I will take turns playing nurse. Have a good weekend, Jo."

"You, too."

After I hung up, I decided that the fate of my robes could be determined another day. I zipped them back in their garment bag and took them down to the closet in the mudroom where we kept everything we didn't know what to do with. The weekend could not begin too soon for me.

Taylor, too, was ready to rock and roll. She loped through the door, threw her backpack on the kitchen table, and did a full body stretch. "It's only Thursday, but it's the weekend," she said.

"That's right – you have study days on Fridays till exams start."

Taylor's lips curved in a smile. "Just because it's a study day doesn't mean I have to study every single second. And Declan's coming to the lake Saturday night and Ed and Barry are getting married on Sunday, so it's going to be great."

It was just a little after five when Zack came in. He had his trial bag on his lap, and he looked   i d.

"I got shellacked," he said.

"You didn't win your case."

"Nope. You overestimated my charms, Ms. Shreve."

I bent down and kissed him. "No, I didn't."

The creases that bracketed Zack's mouth like parentheses were deep. He rubbed his hand over his eyes – a sure sign that he was tired. "Well, win or lose, the lawyer always gets to come home. But the good news is that I haven't got anything urgent on for tomorrow, and now that Taylor's prepping for finals, and you, Ms. Shreve, are a retired lady of leisure, we can head for the lake tonight."

"That sounds so good," I said, "but are you sure you're not too tired?" I stood behind his wheelchair and massaged his shoulders. "We could stay here tonight and drive to the lake in the morning."

Zack covered my hands with his. "No. You like waking up at the lake, and I like waking up with you. We can pick up steaks and whatever else we need for dinner at that store on the point."

"Sold," I said. "Want me to make you a drink before we go? I'll drive."

"This weekend is looking better and better," Zack said.

He followed me into the kitchen and watched as I took the gin and vermouth from the refrigerator. "Big one or little one?" I said.

"Do you really have to ask?"

I made him a generous martini, and I poured a short vermouth for me. Zack took a sip, sighed contentedly, and closed his eyes. "Better already," he said. "So how did convocation go?"

"You didn't hear?"

"I've been busy: went to court, had lunch with my client, went back to court, got squashed like a cockroach, and crawled back home to you. So what happened?"

"Well, convocation itself was fine. About a dozen students turned their chairs when Leland began to speak, but he handled it well – addressed them directly and when they didn't respond, he carried on. The problem came afterwards. There were demonstrators outside the Conexus Centre, and when a TV cameraman showed up, the protestors broke through the police line. One of them got jostled, and the handle of his sign hit Leland. There was a piece of metal in the wood. Leland's all right, but he got a scalp wound that needed stitches."

"I take it the signholder is under arrest," Zack said.

"It was an accident," I said. "I was beside Leland when it happened. Riel Delorme was the person holding the sign."

Zack's eyes were questioning. "You were the only witness?"

"I don't know," I said. "I guess you'd have to ask the police."

"I should call Leland."

"I talked to Margot, and she said all was well, but I'm sure Leland would like to hear from you. Let me know when you're ready, and we'll hit the road."

Before we were out of the city, Zack closed his eyes and began to snore. The dogs were bagged out in the back of the station wagon, Taylor was listening to her iPod, her cats had settled into their cages on the floor. The drive to Lawyers' Bay was less than an hour. Till then, I was alone with my thoughts.

When I turned off the main highway onto the road that led to the lake and smelled the sharp scent of evergreens and the faint tang of skunk, I felt the weight lift from my shoulders. On the day we bought our house in the city, Zack had given me a charm bracelet with two charms: one was of the Bessborough Hotel in Saskatoon, the place where we'd been staying the night we decided to get married. The other was a key that Zack said was to everything – the house, the car, his heart, the place at the lake, the boat, the whole shebang.

The whole shebang turned out to be substantial. Before we married, I had considered many factors. The one dynamic that never entered the equation was the fact that Zack was a very rich man.

As a single parent with four children, I had always been careful about money. My first husband's death had been unexpected, and at thirty-seven, he hadn't had much time to build an investment portfolio. I was not without resources. There was insurance, and I had a tenure track position at the university. I owned our home, but my kids had always had to have paper routes and babysitting jobs to pay for non-essentials. It hadn't done them any harm.

Old habits die hard. I was still careful with money, but the station wagon I was driving was a new Volvo and our summer house was in a gated community. The only other people who lived on our bay were Zack's law partners and their families. For my birthday the year after we married, Zack had given me a second home on the property for my grown children to use when they visited. Our lives were privileged and I knew it.

When I drove through the gates, Zack reached over and squeezed my knee. "Better?"

"Yes. That business with Leland after the ceremony shook me. And not just because he was hurt. The men demonstrating against Leland's honorary degree were frightening. They were obviously trying to look tough, wife-beater shirts and arms covered in tattoos, but I've had students who went for that look. What scared me today was the hatred. Those people hated Leland because he was rich, and they hated Margot because she was beautiful and she was with Leland."

"And Leland's honorary degree gave them a convenient excuse to vent their rage."

"It did. Zack, I always liked Riel Delorme, and I hate to see him making rotten choices. In his address today, Leland talked about the importance of facing those who oppose you. He made a lot of sense. I just wish that Riel had been inside listening."

"Instead of outside protesting."

"No flies on you," I said.

We had been at the lake the weekend before, but Willie and Pantera raced around sniffing with the fervour of creatures discovering a new world. Taylor's exit was more leisurely. She picked up the cat cages from the seat beside her and sauntered towards the house. "I'm going to text Gracie and Isobel, let them know we're here," she said. "Then I'll come back and help you unload. Okay?"

I smiled at her. "Great," I said.

Restored by his nap, Zack reached for his wheelchair. "Okay," he said. "I'm ready to boogie. I'll fire up the barbecue and pour us a glass of wine."

We ate outside, cleaned up, and Taylor headed for her room. I looked at Zack. "Want to stay out here and watch the sunset?"

"We've seen sunsets. Let's go to our room. I have a surprise for you. You'd probably better take off your clothes," he said. "I lack experience in this area."

"So all those women who claim to have enjoyed your favours are just indulging in wishful thinking?"

"No. I spread my favours around, but you're the first woman I've ever done this for. Follow me." When we got to our room, Zack handed me a small bag. Inside was a bottle of nail polish. "Ms. Shreve, I'm about to paint your toenails."

I examined the bottle. "Mochaccino Mama," I said. "Nice shade."

Zack ran his fingers along my arch. "Nice feet."

Zack and I and my Mochaccino Mama toenails were in bed before the sun set.

I was sleeping soundly when Zack's cell rang. I opened my eyes to the first light of early dawn. I wasn't alarmed. The clients of trial lawyers keep irregular hours. But I was awake, and although Zack kept his voice low, I could hear what he said.

"Was anybody hurt? Well, that's the main thing."

My heart began to pound. I sat up and moved closer to Zack so I could hear everything.

"Do you need us to come back to the city this morning?" he said. "Good. Any ideas about who did it? Yeah, I know. We'll meet you at the house at nine. And, Deb, thanks for the call. I know how busy you must be."

We only knew one "Deb" – Inspector Debbie Haczkewicz – and she was an inspector with the Major Crimes Unit of the Regina Police Force. My stomach clenched.

Zack hung up and turned to face me. "You did hear me say that no one was hurt?"

"What happened?

He held out his arms. "Come here."

Suddenly, I was very cold, but Zack's arms were warm. "There's no way to break this to you gently, Jo. About an hour ago, some kind of explosive was detonated in our garage. My car was in there, and I'd filled the tank on my way to court yesterday, so the fire department's still trying to deal with the fire."

"Oh my God. How bad is it?"

He shook his head. "I guess we'll see how bad when we get back to the city."

"I'd better call Mieka and the boys – let them know we're here and safe."

When I hung up after delivering the message to each of our three grown children, I turned to Zack. "How did I sound?"

"Cool. Reassuring. Matter-of-fact." He held out his arms again. "Now, feel free to go crazy."

I'd started to shake. "We could have been in that house," I said. "If you hadn't suggested coming to the lake a day early, the three of us would have been asleep, and we would have died."

"But we weren't in that house," Zack said. He drew me close. "We're at the lake, and we're alive. So let's take it from there."

I burrowed in. "I just can't understand why . . ." I said.

Zack roughened his voice into that of a tough guy. "Why . . . of all the gin joints in the world someone decided to blow up ours?"

In spite of everything I laughed. "I didn't know you did a Bogart imitation," I said.

"Neither did I," Zack said. "Today just seemed as good a time as any to give it a whirl."

CHAPTER

4

It was clear that neither of us were going to get any more sleep that morning, so I went to the bathroom, splashed my face, brushed my teeth, and put on my running clothes. Routine had saved me many times, and I was hoping the familiar pattern of a run before breakfast would calm my nerves and clear my mind. When I went into the kitchen, Zack already had the coffee on; bacon was in a pan ready to be put in the oven; and the eggs, bowl, and whisk were on the counter. Zack's ability to compartmentalize always dazzled me. Clearly he'd decided that if we were going to have a lousy morning we should at least have a great breakfast. I kissed him and made an effort to match his sangfroid. "We have some chives growing in that sunny patch by the front door. Want me to snip some for the eggs when I come back from my run?"

"Chives will be nice," he said. "But I am adding an ingredient that will make this dish brilliant."

I picked up a package of boursin au poivre and checked the date. "You do realize that the 'best before date' on this cheese is tomorrow."

He cocked his head. "That's why we're using it today. I'm being thrifty. I lost big-time at poker Wednesday night." I didn't ask for elaboration. The day was already off to a sketchy start.

When the dogs and I got back from our run, everything was ready. Breakfast was Zack's specialty: the bacon was crisp, the boursin gave the eggs a savoury bite, the rye toast was buttery, and the coffee strong and good. As we sat at the ancient partners' table that we used for all our meals at the lake, it seemed that God was in Her heaven and all would eventually be right with the world.

Our dining room had floor-to-ceiling windows on three sides. To the north we looked out on a copse of lilac bushes, to the west on the broad sunlit lawn that sloped to the lake, to the south on the blooming perennial beds that the land-scaper had put in fifteen years ago when Zack bought the property. Beauty everywhere.

We didn't talk about Debbie's phone call until after we'd finished eating. Then Zack moved his wheelchair back from the table, balanced his plate and cutlery on his lap, and wheeled to the sink. "Time to face the music," he said. "So do we take Taylor with us?"

"No," I said. "We'll tell her what happened, but there's no need for her to see the house today."

"Agreed," Zack said. "The Wainbergs are here. Taylor can stay with them while we're in the city. From what Deb said, the damage is extensive, and there'll be police and media everywhere. Taylor doesn't need that."

"She's already known enough loss," I agreed. "It's taken her years to feel safe in the world."

Zack tented his fingers. "And now fresh evidence that we're never safe."

I winced. "Let's not put it that way to Taylor," I said.

———

Our daughter has always been a deep sleeper, and that morning we had to rap on her door vigorously before she called out to us to come in. Her bedroom was the prettiest room in the cottage. She had just turned twelve when Zack and I were married. He told us to make whatever changes we wanted to in the house at the lake. I'd changed nothing, but Taylor had transformed a tastefully generic guestroom into a place that, even in the dead of winter, spoke of summer: white walls, sheer white curtains, a wicker reading chair with pale blue linen pillows, a small glass table that held her collection of shells, a white dresser and nightstand, a brass four-poster bed with a crisp white cotton bedspread, and over the bed a piece of art Taylor's birth mother, Sally Love, had made for the child of a friend. Zack had been vague about how much he'd paid for the lustrous acrylic of a black cat sunning itself in a bed of violets, but that morning as I looked at Taylor curled up with her own cats, her face rosy with sleep, her dark hair tousled, I realized once again that whatever Zack had paid had been money well spent.

When she saw us, Taylor yawned and frowned. "What's up? I thought this was a sleep-in morning."

"Change of plans," I said. I sat on the bed and glanced back at Zack.

He moved in close. "Something's happened," he said. "Everyone's fine, but there was an incident at our house last night."

Taylor sat up, her dark eyes wide. "What kind of incident?"

"There was an explosion in our garage. Your mother and I have to go into town and talk to the police about it."

Taylor clutched her knees to her chest. "Why do you have to talk to the police?"

"Because the explosion wasn't an accident," Zack said. "Inspector Haczkewicz was the officer who called us. She thinks what happened was deliberate."

"Is the house still there?" Our daughter's voice was small and frightened. "Are my paintings gone?"

"I don't know," Zack said. He took her hand. "We'll have a better idea after we see the situation for ourselves. The Wainbergs thought you might like to spend some time with them while we're in the city."

Taylor's eyes travelled between Zack and me. "Do the police think that the people who killed the man working on the Village Project did this to our house?"

Zack shrugged. "Nobody knows. Both cases involved explosives, so it seems logical. Taylor, your mum and I aren't holding anything back. We really don't know anything more than what we've already told you."

I put my arm around her shoulders. "The important thing is that no one was hurt," I said.

"Not yet," Taylor said. She was trembling.

Her hair smelled of rosemary and mint. I closed my eyes and held her closer.

"No one's going to be hurt," Zack said. "The police will see to that."

I thought of Mieka and her girls, and of our sons. From the tension in Taylor's body, it was obvious that she, too, realized, we had entered a new and complex world.

"I'm scared," Taylor said, "and not just for me."

"I won't lie to you," Zack said. "This is not a great situation. Until whoever did this is caught, we'll take precautions we never thought of, and we'll live our lives differently. But we'll be safe. I promise you that. Lawyers' Bay is a gated community. Nobody gets in here but us, and we'll make arrangements for a secure place in the city."

"We're fine," I said. "And we're going to continue to be fine." My voice was calm and assured. When I gave Taylor a final hug, I hoped she couldn't feel the pounding of my heart.

I like driving, and usually Zack asks if I want to take the

wheel. That morning he didn't. He got into the driver's seat, folded his wheelchair, snapped on his seatbelt, and shut the door. "Ready?" he said.

"As I'll ever be," I said.

The landscape pulsed with the extravagant beauty of late spring, but our talk was grim.

Zack waded right in. "Have you ever seen a house where there's been an explosion?"

"No."

"I have. It was years ago. A client of mine – an estranged husband – blew up his wife's house with a concoction he improvised from fertilizer and diesel fuel."

"Isn't that what was used in the Oklahoma City bombing?"

"It's a popular choice," Zack said. "It's cheap, easy to get, and it does the job. Farmers use it to clear land or dig ditches." Zack fell silent as he concentrated on passing a semi.

"Did the wife survive?" I asked finally.

"No. She was blown to kingdom come – along with most of the house. The Crown had an explosives expert testify. A lot of these guys are so in love with the sound of their own voices that they bore the tits off the jury with jargon, but this guy was good. I was watching the jury when he testified, and after he explained what happens during an explosion I knew he'd nailed my client."

"What did the expert say?"

"He said that an explosion is just a very rapid expansion of a gas – it was as if a really powerful balloon had been placed inside the house of my client's ex-wife and it had been suddenly inflated. Where there was nothing strong enough to stop it, the balloon just pushed through."

"And your client's ex-wife wasn't strong enough to stop it."

Zack's nod was distracted. "She weighed 104 pounds. She never had a chance."

"Oh God," I said.

"There's more," Zack said. "But if you've heard enough . . ."

"I'm going to see the house in a few minutes," I said. "I might as well be prepared."

"Okay. Well, Debbie says they're still having trouble getting the fire in the garage area under control – probably because of that full tank of gas in my car."

"Shit," I said.

Zack gave me a quick grin. "That's the spirit. And you know, Jo, unlike Humpty Dumpty, houses can be put back together again. We still have the number of the contractor who did the retrofitting. And he was good."

"He was," I agreed. "So were you. I've never seen anyone as committed to anything as you were to finding that house and getting it ready for us to move into the day we were married."

"Never underestimate the power of love and fear," he said.

I turned to him. "What were you afraid of?"

"Losing you."

"There was never any danger of that," I said.

"I thought there was. When we flew to Saskatoon for that retirement dinner, I knew you were wavering. People were falling all over themselves telling you what a prick I was, and then that night one of my exes got a snootful and asked you if I was still into threesomes."

"I remember," I said. "I also remember that was the night I told you that I couldn't imagine my life without you."

"I needed to nail it down, Jo. I thought that if I found a good solid family house, you'd know that I was willing to do whatever it took to make us a family."

"And now we are," I said.

"You bet we are," Zack's voice was strong and comforting. "We're going to be okay, Ms. Shreve."

Our street was blocked with police cars and media trucks. There was no way we could fight our way through, so we

parked on Leopold Crescent. As we walked down the alley
that joined Leopold to our street it became increasingly
difficult to breathe. It was unbearably hot, and the air was
heavy with the acrid stench of burning fuel, rubber, and who
knows what else. The house we left when we went to the
lake had been pleasingly designed and nicely landscaped –
unexceptional except for its accessibility ramps. Now the
place where Zack, Taylor, and I had lived with our dogs and
cats looked like a dollhouse that a wilful child had kicked
hard in a fit of temper. The force of the explosion had blown
out the windows and doors and ripped off a section of the
roof that we had reshingled the spring after we moved in.
The new roof had been guaranteed to last twenty-five years.

A young woman, whom I recognized from our local six
o'clock news, was doing a stand-up on the sidewalk in front
of our house. As she pointed to the police barricades surrounding our property, she noted that the police had established a security perimeter to protect the public and the
evidence. One glance suggested it had been a wise precaution.
The explosion had strafed the property: our lawn was covered
in chunks of concrete, wood bristling with nails, and shards
of glass blown from windows. It was chaos, but the forensic
investigators moved through the chaos purposefully with
measuring equipment and grid markers.

When I saw the charred, ragged remains of our family
room, the enormity of what we had lost hit me like a slap.
The room had been the heart of our house and now it was
destroyed. I gazed at what was left of the walls. Zack and
Taylor and I had pored over a lot of paint chips before we
found a colour we could all live with. We had settled
on hibiscus.

Zack followed the angle of my vision. "Don't," he said
gruffly. "We'll have a Christmas tree in the family room
again, and we'll watch movies together, and the dogs will

steal our popcorn and throw up on the rug. It's just going to be a while. Now, come on. Let's find Debbie."

Friendships between police officers and trial lawyers are few and far between, but Debbie and Zack were tight. When Debbie's son crashed his motorcycle and awoke to discover he was a paraplegic, he attempted suicide. At Debbie's request, Zack spent hours with Leo, convincing him that life in a wheelchair could still be sweet. It had taken a while, but Leo was now teaching English in Japan. He had married a Japanese woman and they were expecting a child. It was a happy ending, and Debbie credited Zack with helping to write it. When she approached us that morning, her first concern was personal, not professional. "I know how much you loved your home. This must be devastating."

"We're still alive to complain about our lousy luck and that's a definite plus," Zack said.

Tall and forceful, Debbie was all cop when she was on the job, but her smile was warm and her insights were solid. "So I don't have to waste my energy feeling sorry for you."

"Nope," Zack said. "In the next few days we'll probably do a pretty good job of that ourselves, so you might as well concentrate on finding the bad guy."

"Why don't we sit in one of the squad cars?" Debbie suggested. "We'll be out of the sun and our friends in the media won't be able to hear the conversation."

"You're the boss," Zack said. We followed Debbie to a car that was parked in the shade. Zack and I slid into the back seat. Debbie reached towards the dash, started the motor, and flipped on the air conditioning. "It'll kick in soon," she said. She turned back to face us. "Okay, I already know the answers to the first two questions, but protocol must be followed, and my colleagues will be covering these topics with your neighbours."

I took Zack's hand. "The Van Velzers will be in their glory."

Debbie stiffened. "Your neighbours don't like you?"

"No, they like us, and we like them. The Van Velzers just enjoy being involved."

"They watch and they listen," Debbie said. "Worth their weight in gold – at least to me."

"So what are you going to be asking Mr. and Mrs. VV?" Zack said.

"First, we'll ask them if the relationship between you and Joanne is solid."

"As a rock," Zack said. "Next question."

Debbie tapped her pen on her notebook. "I hate interviewing lawyers. Next question. Are the Shreves having financial problems?"

"Nope, we're raking it in. If you need to talk to our accountant, I'll give you her number."

"That won't be necessary – at least not yet. So, do the Shreves have any enemies?"

Zack laughed. "C'mon, Deb. I'm a trial lawyer. I've got nothing but enemies." Zack turned to look again at the wreckage of our home, and his smile faded. "Obviously, there's at least one person in town who doesn't wish us well," he said more quietly.

Debbie changed position so she could focus on me. "Joanne, is there someone who might have a grudge against you?"

Debbie's question surprised me, although it shouldn't have. Zack and I both lived in the house, but from the moment Zack told me about the explosion, the connection with the Village Project was so glaring I never even considered that the target might have been me.

Now I was forced to consider. "Once in a while, a student is angry about a grade or a comment I made in class," I said. "But they limit their retribution to firing off an angry e-mail to my department head or the dean. A student wouldn't have done this."

"You sound very sure," Deb said.

"I am," I said. "Students these days have a high degree of self-interest. They wouldn't risk their future to get even with a professor."

"Does either of you have any theories about what happened?"

"It's hard not to believe there's a connection between Danny Racette's murder and this," Zack said. "But they didn't use dynamite here?"

Debbie shook her head. "No. Fertilizer mixed with diesel fuel."

"So – homemade," Zack said.

"Out of ingredients that are easily obtainable in an agricultural province," Debbie said. "They'd need a detonating device, but they could easily have found one by breaking into a construction shed. Where there's a will, there's a way."

Zack rubbed his head. "Anybody trying to scare Leland into stopping work on The Village is wasting his time. There's serious money involved. People are expendable. Investment isn't. You know how long they stopped work after Danny Racette died? Two minutes. If I'd been blown sky high, Leland would have had another lawyer by lunchtime. I'm small potatoes, Deb."

"You're also one of Leland's groomsmen."

"Only because there's nobody else around," Zack said.

Debbie tapped her pencil on her notebook. "So no insights about why your house was targeted?"

Zack shook his head. "Nothing you haven't considered," he said.

Debbie turned her eyes back to me. "I understand you witnessed the incident between Riel Delorme and Leland Hunter yesterday after the university's convocation."

"I did, and as I'm sure you know from your officer's report, I said it was an accident."

"And you were certain of that."

"Yes."

"You're aware of who Riel Delorme is."

"He was a student of mine. It was at least five years ago, but he's the kind of student I remember. Riel and I talked about his plans for doing a master's and then he dropped out."

"What was his thesis topic?"

"He seemed to have trouble settling on one, but he finally decided on Che Guevera and the politics of revolution."

Debbie raised an eyebrow. "'The revolution is not an apple that falls when it is ripe. You have to make it fall.'"

"You've been studying Che Guevera?" I said.

"Just Googling," she said. "Outside the Conexus Centre yesterday, the protestors were shouting, 'Make them fall.' The chant seemed familiar. One of my colleagues suggested I Google Che Guevera. And there was our quote."

"There's no incitement to violence there," I said.

"How about, 'I don't care if I fall as long as someone else picks up my gun and keeps on shooting?'"

"Those were Che's words, not Riel's," I said. "Debbie, when Riel was deciding on a thesis topic, he was looking for a model that would be effective in battling what he saw as systemic racism and poverty."

"And he decided that violence was the answer."

"History is filled with people who believe they're justified in destroying a society that degrades them," I said.

"And most of them believe the end justifies the means," Debbie said.

"Riel didn't believe that. At least not when I knew him," I said. "In those days, he believed that people who were marginalized could change the system by working together."

"And now he's working with gangs," Debbie said.

"So, guilt by association?" I said.

Debbie made no attempt to hide her annoyance. "No one who associates with The Warriors and The Brigade is an innocent. Gang members are mad dogs, and if Riel Delorme was smart enough to get into graduate school, he's smart enough to figure that out. He should also be smart enough to realize that by brokering an alliance between The Warriors and The Brigade he's given them twice the power they had before."

Zack leaned forward. "You mean Delorme actually pulled off a coalition?"

"He did," Debbie said. "Of course, it hasn't worked out quite the way Delorme anticipated. The Warriors and The Brigade did come together to fight the Village Project, but the love affair didn't last. Gang members are gang members. It didn't take long for some of them to get bored listening to Delorme's rhetoric about empowering disenfranchised youth and joining forces with sympathizers outside North Central to change the system. So they defected and joined Red Rage—"

"The destination of choice for the maddest of the mad dogs," Zack said. "The guys who've been threatening a full-on war over the land that Leland and Peyben have targeted for redevelopment. Did they blow up our house?"

Debbie's shrug was weary. "Your guess is as good as mine."

"Yesterday outside convocation, Riel said there was something he should talk to me about, but the time wasn't right," I said.

Debbie's eyes were piercing. "And you think that what Riel wanted to talk about had something to do with your house being blown up?"

I shook my head. "No. If Riel was part of the plan, he wouldn't have sought me out. I guess it's possible that he knew about what was going to happen, but I can't believe that if Riel knew about the bombing, he wouldn't have warned me."

Zack turned to Debbie. "Have you interviewed Delorme?"

"As a matter of fact, I have. He was down at headquarters this morning, bright and early. He volunteered to do whatever he could to help with the investigation."

"That's a surprise," I said.

"It is," Zack agreed. "Did Delorme give you anything useful?"

"Nothing that hadn't occurred to us. He suggested that we look into Red Rage's recent activities."

"There's always mischief afoot with those boys," Zack said.

"True, but you'll notice they aren't under arrest," Debbie said. "We need evidence and we need a motive."

"The motive for killing Danny Racette is pretty straightforward," Zack said. "Somebody wanted to demonstrate that Peyben regarded the workers from the community as expendable. Blowing up Danny Racette was a sure way to keep the anger level against the Village Project high."

"I'll buy that," Debbie said. "So why would Red Rage blow up your house?"

"Obviously they wanted to kill us," Zack said. "But since that didn't work out, I guess they'll have to settle for the pleasure of watching us twist in the wind."

When I shuddered, Zack put his arm around me. "Let's not give them the satisfaction."

We exchanged a long, hard look. "Okay," I said finally. "Screw them. Let's get on with the rest of our lives."

Zack grinned. "You're a lot tougher than you look, aren't you?"

"I don't know," I said. "But I have a feeling we're about to find out."

CHAPTER

5

It was a shock to move from the cool interior of the car to the heat of the sidewalk. When Zack was back in his wheelchair, Debbie slipped her coiled notebook into her jacket pocket. "I should get to work," she said. "I'll keep you posted."

"Is it possible for us to go inside the house?" Zack asked. "Taylor's anxious about her paintings. So are we."

Debbie was vehement. "No way," she said. "Zack, I'm not even crazy about having our own people in there. It's dangerous. There might still be explosives around, and there's no way of knowing if the structure is stable."

"Any idea about how long it'll be before we can move back?" Zack asked.

"I'm not an expert," Debbie said. "But you won't be able to start construction until the investigation is finished, and that's going to take time."

"So are we looking at weeks – months? Zack asked.

"Depending on the extent of damage and your luck at getting a contractor, I think you're looking at six months minimum, but that really is just a ballpark figure."

Zack grimaced. "Jeez, Deb, you could have sugar-coated the pill."

"You wouldn't have swallowed it," she said. "Now, I should get back. The faster we get our work down, the sooner your contractor can start." She squeezed Zack's shoulder and gave me a quick smile. "I'll be in touch."

After Debbie left, a truck from Rapid Rent-All pulled up. Zack and I watched as the driver and two workers took out a portable toilet and temporary metal fencing. They set the portable toilet on an area near the sidewalk that was clear of debris and began to fence off our property.

"We don't need to watch this," Zack said. "Let's go."

When we turned into the alley, we met Leland Hunter and Declan walking towards us. About four inches above Leland's right eyebrow was a neat line of stitches. He placed a hand on Zack's shoulder. "I'm so very sorry," he said.

"We are, too," I said.

"As soon as I heard the news, I called your place at the lake," he said. "Taylor told me you'd come into Regina to check out the damage. I was hoping we'd catch you – is there anything I can do?"

"At the moment I don't think there's much any of us can do," I said. "But in the next while, I imagine we'll need all the help we can get."

"I'm available," Declan said softly. "Is Taylor's studio all right?"

"I didn't think to ask," I said. "It's a fair distance from the garage, so there's a possibility . . ." My sentence trailed off. The enormity of what had happened seemed to come in waves. The memory of Taylor painting in her studio, bathed in the light that poured from the north window, was another blow.

"I'll call the officer in charge of the investigation," Zack said. He picked up his BlackBerry. His exchange with Debbie was brief but positive. "The studio's fine," he said. "Thanks for the reminder, Declan."

"No problem," Declan said. "I can't get my head around this. What if Taylor—" His voice broke and he swallowed hard. Leland put his arm around his son's shoulder, and Declan leaned into him.

It was a nice moment and a significant one. There was a time when Leland wouldn't have been there to meet his son's needs, and Declan would have turned to Zack, whose job it was to handle Leland's personal business. There was plenty to handle. Leland's family was small, but their problems were large. The alcoholic ex-wife of a very rich man is easy prey to the bottom feeders who insinuate themselves into the lives of the vulnerable. In Leland's absence, Zack spent hours protecting Louise from herself.

Leland and Louise's only child had his own share of crises. On Declan's sixteenth birthday, Zack had taken him to the Broken Rack to shoot a little pool and teach him exactly what the Youth Criminal Justice Act meant for the kind of young offender Declan seemed determined to become.

Zack was good with kids who were danger freaks, probably because he'd lived on the edge most of his life. He and Declan clicked, and the birthday game of pool was just the first of many. Between shots, Zack and Declan talked, and Zack heard enough to alarm him. He called Leland and told him that if he wanted to salvage his son, he should move back to Regina. Leland did. The sudden presence of his father in his life seemed to convince Declan that it was time to pull back from the precipice. He was a changed young man.

Leland's arm still rested on his son's shoulders as he turned to Zack and me. "Have you had a chance to think about living arrangements?"

"Not really," I said. "We have the place at the lake, but the Cronus trial starts Monday, and it's going to be demanding."

Leland raised an eyebrow. "A slumlord accused of killing his girlfriend who also happened to be a cop? I imagine it will be demanding."

"I'll be keeping crazy hours," Zack said. "And Taylor still has school and exams."

"It's only 145 klicks round trip from Regina to Lawyers' Bay," I said. "We can manage it, but we're going to be making a lot of round trips."

"Too many," Zack said flatly. "Living at the lake during the week isn't going to work, Jo. We're going to have to find something in Regina."

"My condo's available," Leland said. "I'm already living with Margot and we're going to be travelling with Declan in August, so there'll be nobody on the top floor. As you saw the other night, the condo is fully accessible, and God knows, that building is secure.

Zack looked up at me. "Do we want to talk about this?"

Life was moving too quickly. "It'll take weeks to find a fully accessible rental with a solid security system," I said. "And we don't have weeks. It's a generous offer, Leland, and we accept."

"It's settled then," Leland said. He handed me his key card. "Why don't you and Zack go by Halifax Street and take a look before you go back to the lake. My housekeeper's number is by the phone in the kitchen. Her name is Jasmina Tervic, and if you call her, she'll have the place ready so you can move in tomorrow. In the meantime, I'll get some of my guys over here to look at what it will take to rebuild."

I dropped the key card in my bag. "I don't know how to thank you, Leland."

"No thanks necessary. You and I both know that this is the least I can do." He looked at his son. "Ready to go, Declan?"

"Not quite," Declan said. "I need to talk to Zack and Joanne for a minute."

Leland shrugged. "Do you want me to go on ahead?"

Declan shook his head. "No. It's not a secret or anything. It's just – I got a text from Taylor. I was supposed to go out to the lake tomorrow night. Taylor said she still wants me to come. I told her I'd ask you." He shifted his focus to us. "Look, I really understand if you'd just like to be by your-selves for a while."

"If Taylor wants you at the lake, and you want to be at the lake, then that's where you should be," I said. "We could get the boat out and go to Magoo's for dinner. The sooner we get back to real life, the better,"

"Exactly what is Magoo's?" Leland asked.

"It's a diner across the lake from us," Zack said. "We usually take the boat over. They make their own burgers, and their French fries and onion rings are greasy enough to satisfy Joanne and Taylor. Magoo's also has a jukebox that doesn't play anything that was written after 1980 and a wooden dance floor that I dominate."

"You dance?" Leland asked.

"He's very good," I said. "He's also exhausting. As long as the Beach Boys have one more chorus about the advantages of quitting high school and getting married, Zack won't leave the floor."

"Litigator by day, Beach Boy by night," Leland said.

"That's pretty much it," I said. "But why don't you and Margot come out to the lake with Declan so you can see for yourself?"

"Another time," he said. "You don't want people around when you're dealing with a crisis."

It would have been easy to blow off Leland's concern with polite words about how he and his family were always welcome, but I seemed to have moved past easy answers. I touched his arm. "Actually, Leland, I don't know what we want," I said. "All I know is that Taylor has been rocked by this. Spending an evening with people she likes, doing what we've done dozens of times, might help her believe that the old safe world is still in place."

Leland's smile was ironic. "Thanks for considering me part of the old safe world. I'll check with Margot."

The call was brief. "She'd be delighted," Leland said. "When would you like us?"

"Early," Zack said. "Come around four. You can have a swim and we can all have a drink before dinner. Magoo's doesn't serve anything stronger than milkshakes."

When we were buckled into our seats, Zack turned to me. "We're alone. You can take off your game face."

"Was it that apparent?" I said.

"Only to me," he said. "You're making all the right moves, Ms. Shreve."

"Having Leland as a friend smoothes the rough edges," I said, and my voice was tight. "Our house blows up and twelve hours later we've already got a condo and the promise of a contractor. No wonder the people in North Central hate us."

Zack's eyes flashed. "Guilt isn't going to help here, Jo. We had some lousy luck and now we're having some good luck. Let's just play the hand we've been dealt."

"Easier to play the hand we're dealt when we get so many of the good cards," I said.

"Jesus, Jo. Could you let it go?"

I looked at my husband who hadn't walked in forty-four years. Who hadn't known a day without pain and who never complained. I unbuckled my seat belt and moved closer to him. "Do you know what we need?" I asked.

"A referee?"

"I was thinking more along the lines of forty-five minutes in the No-Tell Motel."

Zack's smile started slow and ended big. "Forty-five minutes? You flatter me."

I kissed him hard. "I was counting on a quick game of rummy first."

"You're on," Zack said. "But let's wait till we get back to the lake. I've got a thing about bedbugs."

"In that case," I said, "why don't we stop by Mieka's and see the girls? The kids could probably use some reassurance that we're all right."

"I could use a little reassurance myself," Zack said.

The front entrance was not accessible, so as we always did, Zack and I headed for the backyard. We heard the fluty voices of our granddaughters before we saw them. Mieka and the girls were throwing around a beachball, but as soon as we rounded the corner and the girls spied Zack, the beachball was forgotten and they sped towards him. After two and a half years, he was still their shiny, star-spangled top banana. Lena leapt on to his lap and Madeleine stood close to his chair. Mieka stayed where she was, holding the ball in front of her.

The week before I had taken the girls shopping for swim-suits, and they were wearing their purchases. Madeleine's navy suit was simply cut and functional; Lena's, a pink and purple homage to the Disney princesses, had a little skirt. Both girls were sporting summer haircuts. As the girls twirled to show off their new 'dos, Zack murmured appreciatively. "Très mignon," he said. "You obviously went to Paris."

Lena scrunched her face. "Granddad, you know that Chantelle at Head to Toe always cuts our hair, and Head to Toe is just up at River Heights."

"True," Zack said. "Still there's a certain je ne sais quoi about your hair. Perhaps Chantelle is from Paris."

"She's from Shaunavon," Madeleine said flatly, and there was something in her voice that suggested discussion of Paris was now fini. "Granddad, why don't you and Mimi come watch us swim. My dive is getting better, and Lena can swim almost the whole length of the pool underwater."

The pool was an albatross with an ancient and cranky circulation system and a whining need for constant and expensive repairs. But Madeleine and Lena, like their mother, her brothers, and Taylor, found magic in its waters, so year by year, the pool's life was extended. As with many aging beauties, a trick of the light could do wonders for the old pool, and that June day, the shafts of sunlight hit the water at exactly the right angle, restoring the pool to its former glory.

Mieka had put down the beachball and was walking toward the house. I took my granddaughters' hands. "Let's go over and say hi to your mum, then we can all come back and watch you."

Lena was impatient to get moving, so she let go of my hand and skipped ahead. "Mum has a new bathing suit," she called over her shoulder. "It's a bikini."

"Not really a bikini," Madeleine said. "Just a two-piece bathing suit," but Lena had already moved out of earshot.

My older daughter and I were unusually close. When Ian died, I had needed her help. When Mieka's marriage broke up and she moved back to Regina, she had needed our help; but it went beyond that. Mieka and I loved each other but we also liked each other, and after a rocky start, she had come to welcome Zack as a friend and as the primary male presence in the girls' lives.

"We heard about your new suit," I said. "It's a knockout."

"Thanks," she said absently, barely returning my embrace. Mieka was tall and very slender. She had a lovely body, but she had always chosen clothes that concealed rather than revealed it. The bathing suit she'd worn every summer since Lena was born was faded, shapeless, and, except when Mieka was swimming, covered with a sweatshirt. The new bikini

was black with a pattern of deep pink passionflowers. Mieka
had obviously been tanning. She looked radiant. She also
looked distracted. Her eyes kept travelling past me to the
house. "Just let me run inside for a minute, would you?"

Mieka's timing was off. Riel Delorme came out before she'd
even reached the deck. I was taken aback, but after an
awkward moment, Riel eased the situation. He extended his
hand to Zack. "I'm Riel Delorme."

Zack shook Riel's hand. "Zack Shreve." He looked questioningly at Mieka.

"Riel came by for a swim," she said.

Zack was sanguine. "Well, it's certainly a pleasant day
for that."

"The girls are anxious to get in the pool," Mieka said. "Why
don't we let them show us their stuff? We can talk later."

"Fine with me," Zack said and turned his chair towards
the pool. We all followed silently and watched as Madeleine
dove in. Her entrance was a little shaky, but she didn't belly
flop. "Well done, young grasshopper," Mieka said, and she
and I exchanged a smile. As it turned out, it would be the
last smile of the morning.

After Lena had been praised for her stellar underwater
performance, Mieka turned to Riel. "I just made some iced
tea. Could you and Zack keep an eye on the girls while
Mum and I bring it out?"

"A cool drink sounds good," I said. My voice was falsely
bright. I took a breath and tried again. "We just came back
from looking at the explosion. It was hot and there was a lot
of dust."

Mieka's face was pinched with concern. "How bad is it?"

"It's unbelievable," I said. "This time yesterday, we had
a home. Now it's a crime scene."

Mieka chewed her lip, her invariable gesture when she

was distressed. She took down four glasses, filled them with ice, poured in the chilled tea, and finished off each drink with a sprig of mint. She passed me my glass, then picked up two of the others and headed for the yard. "I'll be back in a second. I'm just going to take these to Zack and Riel."

Her relief at being given a reprieve from facing me broke my heart. Suddenly, it was all too much. The house. Leland. Riel. The gangs. I wanted to run, but there was no place to run to. I held the cold glass against my forehead and then my temples, took a sip of tea, and gazed around the kitchen that had been mine and was now Mieka's.

When Mieka's marriage ended, she moved back to Regina into the house where Ian and I had raised her and her brothers. Like me, my daughter was no fan of change. After Maddy and Lena decided to share the room in which their mother had grown up, Mieka moved into my old room, and everything else was pretty much as it had always been.

My daughter still handled special catering jobs, so the shining cookware and the knives hanging on a knife board were top of the line. The rest of the kitchen, right down to the red-and-white-checked cotton tablecloth, was as it had been when I'd lived there. I looked at the sampler I had brought from Ian's mother's house after she died.

I hadn't had much luck in the mother sweepstakes, but when it came to a mother-in-law, I had been blessed. Ian's mother, Hazel Kilbourn, had a generous heart and an endless enthusiasm for the pleasures of life. The sampler she'd made captured her spirit. "I'm Not Cluttered," the lettering said, "These Are My Treasures." And in a glorious needlepoint jumble Hazel had displayed those treasures: depression ware, hooked rugs, dolls, teddy bears, clocks, the collection of Santas that was still in a display case in Mieka's living room, Hazel's old cat, Dusty, and her dog, Major. Major had been a rescue dog. The name on his tag was Sparky, but my mother-in-law noticed that when Sparky walked, he raised his legs like a drum major, so she'd changed his name. I was smiling at the memory when Mieka returned.

"I was thinking about your nana's dog," I said. "Do you remember him?"

"Major, the marching dog?" Mieka said. "You bet." She picked up her tea. "But you didn't come here to talk about Major."

"No," I said. "Actually, we just dropped in so the girls would know we were all right, but now that we've seen Riel here – Mieka, what's going on?"

She traced a wavy line down the condensation on her glass. "Riel and I are friends. We met when Lisa Wallace and I were planning UpSlideDown2. Lisa and I wanted to involve the community. Riel had helped Lisa with projects at the rec centre, and she thought he'd be a good person to have on our side."

"And he was?"

"He was exactly what we needed – smart, knowledgeable, warm, kind, great with kids." Mieka's face flushed, but her grey-green eyes remained fixed on mine. "Actually, we're more than friends, Mum."

I shifted my chair so Zack was in my line of vision. He was at the edge of the pool. I could hear the girls' voices through the open window. Riel had drawn his chair close to Zack's and they were deep in conversation.

"When were you planning to tell us?" I asked.

Mieka raked her fingers through her hair. "I don't know. I guess I kept hoping that Leland Hunter and the Village Project were just going to go away."

"That's not going to happen," I said. "Both Leland and the project are here to stay, and the sooner you and Riel accept that, the better."

Mieka's voice was strained. "Better for Leland, you mean."

"Better for everyone," I said. "Mieka, I was sick about having to sell the property we were planning to use for UpSlideDown2, but when we had dinner with Leland and Margot the other night, he made a convincing case for creating a mixed neighbourhood. I still have reservations, but in theory The Village will be a place where all kinds of people can live together. The high-end properties will remain where they are, in the warehouses. But the houses will be for people with low to middle incomes. The landscape architect for the project specializes in small urban parks and public horticulture. There'll be community gardens where people can grow vegetables. At the moment, as you know, there's not a single store in North Central that sells fresh produce. The Village is designed for pedestrians, so people don't have to own cars. If Leland can pull it off, The Village will be exactly the kind of neighbourhood this city needs – human scale and accessible. It's a compelling vision."

Mieka's lips were compressed. "A vision that will put money in Leland Hunter's pocket."

"Leland already has money," I said. "This is about something else."

"He's obviously won you over."

"That's not true," I said. "I still have a lot of questions. For one, there doesn't seem to be a plan for helping those who have to leave the area find new homes. That's a serious omission, and I'm going to talk to Leland about it. He's very forthright, and he's fair. Leland could have used the incident with the sign to make trouble for Riel, but he didn't. He accepted Riel's explanation that what happened was an accident.

Mieka looked at me coldly. "Skull wounds heal," she said. "What Leland Hunter did to Riel's neighbourhood is irreparable."

I could feel my anger rising, but I kept my voice calm. "Why don't you and Riel get together with Leland and Zack and me? Look at the plans for the Village Project. Talk things through."

"You've got to be kidding."

"I couldn't be more serious. Mieka, I understand Riel's opposition, but this is already ugly, and it's getting uglier. We have to find middle ground before something else happens."

"Mum, something *has* to happen. Maybe you need to take another look at the inscription on that kaleidoscope they gave you at your retirement luncheon. Refresh your memory about what you and Dad were fighting for."

"My memory doesn't need refreshing," I said. "And I can't look at the kaleidoscope. It was in our house and our house was bombed."

Mieka flinched, but she didn't back down. "Riel wasn't responsible for what happened. Your house was bombed because Zack is Leland Hunter's lawyer."

"And the days and nights of pro bono work Zack does for people in North Central aren't part of the equation," I said. "Mieka, you might want to revisit that quotation on the kaleidoscope yourself. The emphasis is on creating abundance, not on destroying other people's security."

As we walked across the lawn towards the pool, I was quivering with anger, and Mieka was close to tears. Zack was quick to pick up on the fact that things had not gone well between us.

"Looks like it's time to go," he said softly. I nodded. Zack called to the girls and they came out of the pool and ran, dripping, towards us.

We're a demonstrative family, and we always part with an embrace or a touch. That morning, the girls gave us the usual soggy hugs. Even Zack and Riel shook hands, and but when it came time for Mieka to say goodbye to us, she said, "Take care" and moved towards the far end of the pool, picked up a rake, and began fishing out inflatable pool toys. Madeleine noticed. "Mum, you forgot to hug Granddad and Mimi."

Mieka gave her a fleeting smile, and then she went back to corralling a bright and silly plastic whale.

When we got to the car, I buried my face in my hands. Zack squeezed my leg. "Guess we should have chosen the No-Tell Motel. Do you want to talk about it?"

"No," I said.

"But things between you and Mieka are going to be all right."

"They will be," I said. "Right now, we're both hurt and angry, but Mieka knows I'd crawl over broken glass to stay close to her and the girls."

"She'd never make you do that," Zack said. He turned the keys in the ignition. "Do you want to skip checking out Leland's condo and just go straight to the lake?"

"No. Ed and Barry's wedding is tomorrow, and Monday Cronus's trial starts and Taylor's in school. This is the only chance we'll have to see what we need to bring with us."

"Your call," Zack said.

Absorbed by our own thoughts, we fell silent for a while. After Zack turned left and headed for the Warehouse District, I said, "What did you and Riel talk about?"

Zack shrugged. "Basically, I told him that if he was going to hang around with our daughter and our granddaughters, he should decide what kind of man he wanted to be."

"How did he take that?"

"He said he'd die before he'd let anyone harm Mieka or the girls. I told him if anyone even remotely connected with him laid a finger on any of them, he wouldn't have to make a decision about dying."

"I guess that tore it," I said.

Zack made a dismissive gesture. "Nah. My tone was kindly. After that, we just chatted and watched the girls swim."

"I think Mieka's in love with him," I said. "Really in love. I've never seen her this fierce about a man."

"Not with the girls' father? I've always assumed that things started out hot there and just cooled down."

"No. Mieka and Greg's relationship was never 'hot.' They kind of drifted into marriage, and then the girls came along, and they were both committed to being good parents, so they stuck it out."

"And then Mieka had her 'aha' moment. She told me about it."

"I'm surprised," I said. "She's careful not to talk about Greg."

"We didn't exactly talk about Greg. It was after dinner one night at the lake. I was noodling around with an old Peggy Lee song, and Mieka sat down to listen. When the song was finished, she said that for a while, she felt as if that piece of music had been written just for her."

"So what was the song?"

Zack sang the opening bars of "Is That All There Is?"

For the past twelve hours, the news had been unremittingly grim. Leland's condo was a glorious surprise. Its structure was the twin of Margot's, but the ambience here was Tuscan – simple, welcoming, informal. Most of the furniture was wood. The tables were carved and hand painted, the chairs and sofas were upholstered in durable fabrics in the warm colours of late afternoon: cream, terra cotta, honey-gold, burgundy, orange-red.

The appliances in the kitchen were the newest and best, but the tiles above the counters had the soft patina of age. The centre of the kitchen was a large wooden butcher-block table.

"Wow," Zack said. "This does not look like Leland."

"Leland said his decorator came highly recommended," I said.

"I can see why," Zack said. "Do you like it?"

"Very much," I said. "It's what I would do if I knew half as much as Leland's decorator does."

"You know all the things that matter," Zack said. "Now that we've oo'ed and ah'ed, let me see if I can get around this place in my chair."

Taylor would have the upstairs master suite to herself, and in addition to the oversized bedroom, she had two bathrooms, a large sitting room, and a second small bedroom. There were two more bedrooms and two bathrooms on the main floor. While Zack checked out the width of the doorways, the turning spaces, and the height of the counters in the kitchen and the bathrooms, I wandered over to the huge windows overlooking the street.

On the corner of the next block there was a wholesale party supplies store that looked similar to the building we'd planned to turn into UpSideDown2. The first time Mieka had shown me the Markesteyn property, her face had shone with excitement. As I remembered my daughter's joy on that cold winter morning, my eyes stung.

I didn't realize Zack had come back from inspecting the condo until I heard his voice beside me. "Well, it works for me," he said. "Nothing too high, too low, too sloping, or too steep."

"Good," I said, turning away from the view. "Zack, you spent some time with Riel Delorme today. What do you think of him?"

Zack was slow to answer. Finally, he said, "Well, he's no Wayne Gretzky."

"Where'd that come from?"

"Gretzky always knew instinctively where the game was going – not just where his teammates were but where they were going to move next. Riel's right in the middle of the action, but he can't seem to see what's going on, and he can't figure out where the game is headed. I don't get it."

"Maybe he just doesn't *want* to see what's really going on. Maybe, with all his good intentions, he's in over his head and doesn't want to face it. Maybe Riel is what Ian used to call 'terminally naive.'"

Zack nodded approvingly. "Nice turn of phrase."

"Most of the time the phrase was directed at me."

"You're not naive."

"Not any more," I said, "but once upon a time I was a lot like Riel."

CHAPTER

6

That day I really needed the calming effect of driving. Without comment, Zack took his place in the passenger seat. "Wouldn't take many mornings like this one to make a dozen, would it?" he said. •

My laugh was forced. "No, but we're headed for the lake now so soon all will be well."

"About that," Zack said. "Joanne, I have to call Debbie Haczkewicz and tell her about our new living arrangements."

"Every move we make, huh?" I said.

"Yep – and every breath we take – at least till all this is cleared up."

"I'm assuming that Mieka's relationship with Riel is now going to be on record at the police station."

Zack nodded. "Yes, if it isn't already. Jo, did you tell Mieka that we were moving into Leland's condo?"

"No. I didn't want to pour salt on the wound."

"Just as well," Zack said. "For the time being, the fewer people who know we're living on Halifax Street during the week, the better."

"Can I tell Peter and Angus?"

"It might be simpler not to, but that's your call."

"I don't like lying to them."

"You don't have to lie," Zack said. "Just don't say anything. They'll assume we're driving in from the lake every day."

"A sin of omission, not commission," I said.

Zack's smile was wry. "Get used to it," he said. "Now, I'd better call Debbie. It never pays to withhold information from the cops."

When we came through the gate, the dogs roared up to meet us. I scratched our bouvier's head. "Somehow I don't see these guys as condo dwellers," I said. "I hate the idea of not being with Willie and Pantera every day."

Pantera rested his huge jaw on the arm of Zack's chair. "Me, too," Zack said. "But I'm sure the condo has a no-pet rule, and a bouvier and a mastiff are not easy to sneak in."

"So what are we going to do?"

"Well, Noah Wainberg's up getting the cottages ready. I'm sure he wouldn't mind taking care of the dogs during the week, and as soon as the Cronus trial is over and Taylor's finished exams, we can move up here till September. Are you okay with that?"

"I guess I'm going to have to be," I said. "Let's find Taylor and fill her in. We might as well get it all over with at once."

We walked down to the lake into a scene from Norman Rockwell. Taylor and Isobel Wainberg were on the swings that Isobel's father, Noah, had suspended from a high branch of an elm years ago. They were pushing themselves slowly, deep in conversation, their toes dragging through the dirt on the paths worn through the grass. The girls were very different. Taylor was tall and loose-limbed with the quick smile of the extrovert; Isobel was small-boned, tightly wound, and hesitant about revealing her private self. Yet from the moment they met, Taylor and Isobel had been fast friends.

Not wanting to disturb the sweetness of the moment, neither Zack nor I moved, but the dogs loped ahead and the girls turned. Their young faces were anxious.

"How bad is the house?" Taylor asked.

"It's bad," I said.

"Were the paintings wrecked?"

"We don't know," I said. "The police wouldn't let us go inside. It wasn't safe."

Taylor lowered her eyes and began scuffing the dirt with her toe. Isobel was a girl quick to sense the moods of others. She jumped off the swing and touched Taylor's shoulder. "I think maybe you and your parents need to be alone to talk about this."

Zack smiled at her. "Thanks, Izzie. We'll see you later."

When Isobel left, Taylor looked at her father and me. There were tears in her eyes. "Will we ever be able to move back?" she asked.

"It'll be a while," Zack said. "But it will happen. Until the house is back to normal, we've got the lake and we've found a place to stay during the week. It's not far from your school."

"Where?" Taylor asked.

"Leland Hunter's condo on Halifax Street."

"But the bedroom is upstairs," Taylor said.

"You've seen it?" I said.

"Declan left his jacket there one weekend and we went to pick it up." Her face pinched with worry, she turned to Zack. "You're coming with us, aren't you?"

"To the ends of the earth," Zack said. "But in this case, just as far as the main floor. You'll have the big bedroom on the second floor. There are a couple of other bedrooms downstairs. Joanne and I will take one of those."

"I knew there were bedrooms downstairs, and I knew Jo and I would never move without you. What's the matter with me?"

"The same thing that's the matter with all of us," I said. "There's just too much to absorb. And, Taylor, there's something else. We're not going to tell anyone where we're living. Declan and his dad and Margot will know, of course, and the police have been told, but that's it."

Taylor's dark eyes widened. "Not even Gracie and Isobel?"

Zack's voice was even. "I've known those girls since the day they were born. I love and trust them, but we can't afford a slip. I honestly don't think we're going to hear anything more from those apes who blew up our house, but until the cops get them, we can't tell anybody where we're living."

Taylor got off the swing. "Okay," she said, and her voice was small. She started up the slope towards the house, and we followed. I could see Zack's weariness as he pushed uphill. My own legs felt like lead.

We had a sandwich and when I suggested a nap, Zack didn't fight me. Two hours later, I woke feeling if not reborn at least ready to face what lay ahead. I turned so I could look at my husband's face. The creases that bracketed his mouth were deep. His paraplegia affected every area of his life. Routine made it manageable, but in the next month, there would be no routine. We'd be adapting to a new house, a new schedule, and Zack would be carrying the burden of convincing a jury that his client, a slumlord with unsavoury connections, hadn't murdered his girlfriend. I went into the bathroom, picked up my nail polish, and came back to bed. When Zack awakened, he stretched lazily. "So any new crises while we slept?"

"Nothing major," I said. "But I seem to have smudged the polish on my baby toe." I handed him the bottle of

Mochaccino Mama. "How about a quick repair job before we go to Magoo's?"

When Margot, Leland, and Declan arrived, Margot, a dog lover without a dog, dropped to her knees and began crooning endearments to Willie and Pantera. Leland's stitches still looked angry, but he wasn't the only member of his family among the walking wounded. Declan had a line of stitches along his cheekbone, and the area around his right eye was an ugly rainbow of purplish-blue and yellow.

"What happened to you?" Zack said.

Declan looked away. "I walked into a door."

Zack cocked his head. "Just an educated guess, but I'd say the door was about five-foot-ten, hundred and eighty pounds."

A small smile quivered across Declan's lips. "Closer to six feet, two hundred pounds."

"We're lucky you're still with us," Zack said.

"So I've been told," Declan said. "Is Taylor around?"

"She's inside studying," I said. "She'll be glad to see you."

When the door shut behind him, Zack turned to Leland. "So what did happen?"

Leland sat on the corner of one of the lounges. "Declan was upset about what had been done to your house," Leland said. "He went into North Central to ask some questions."

"And people were reluctant to answer," I said.

Leland's voice was devoid of expression. "According to Declan, he gave as good as he got."

"Jesus," Zack said. "He's lucky he didn't come home in a body bag, but I'm sure you explained that."

Margot came up the porch steps. Her tone was dry. "Actually, being on the receiving end of a beating with a sawed-off baseball bat made the point for us."

Zack shuddered. "Who's for a drink?"

"Sparkling water for me," Margot said.

"I could use something stronger," Leland said. "Zack, I remember you saying that you make a fine martini."

"He makes a great martini," I said. "And I'll join you."

"Good," Leland said. "We'll drink to better days."

Part of the allure of Magoo's was the fact that we could get there by boat. As we nosed out into the lake, I turned to make certain that all the life jackets had been snapped on. They had. Margot and Leland were seated in the back; Taylor and Declan were directly behind us. Taylor had tipped her head back to catch the sun, and Declan was watching the play of light and shadow on her face with an intensity that made my heart ache for him. Taylor may have felt their relationship was a friendship of convenience, but clearly Declan's emotions ran deep.

From the May long weekend to Thanksgiving, Magoo's rocked. Most nights as we passed the midpoint in the lake, we could hear the music. Tonight, it was Buddy Holly singing "Oh Boy."

Zack and Margot joined Buddy at the second verse. Zack had a tuneful bass, and Margot sang with wild down-home abandon. As she and Zack hit the "Dum dee dum dum dums," even Taylor and Declan were laughing. It seemed an auspicious start for the evening.

Magoo's was a favourite with our family, and it was fun to see the restaurant through fresh eyes. When Margot spotted the distinctive rounded top and the glass front of the vintage Wurlitzer jukebox, she clapped her hands with delight. "This is the real thing, isn't it?" she said, bending to check the playlist. "There was a jukebox like this in Northey's ice-cream parlour in Wadena when I was a kid. I spent hours standing in front of it watching people put in money, and punch the buttons, hoping they'd choose a song I liked. They seldom did, but I still danced." Margot continued to pore over the playlist. "Leland, give me a loonie, would you? C-5 is the song I want for our bride-and-groom dance."

Leland smiled and handed over the loonie. Margot put it in the slot, hit C-5, and Slim Whitman began singing "I Remember You." "Slim has always been a favourite in Wadena," Margot said, then she held out her arms to Leland and they began to dance. Taylor and Declan followed suit.

Zack looked up at me. "Want to dance, Ms. Shreve, or shall we just find a quiet corner and smooch?"

"It's been a long day," I said. "Let's smooch."

We were in luck. There was one empty table left on the deck and it overlooked the lake. Zack moved a chair out of the way, wheeled in beside me, and took my hand. The sun was starting to fall in the sky, leaving a shaft of light across the water. A lone red canoe was heading for shore. "Let's just stay here, forever," I said. "Listening to Slim, watching the canoe, and canoodling."

"I'm not going anywhere," Zack said.

"Neither am I," I said, and then we shared a deep, lovely kiss that I wished could have lasted forever but, in the way of deep, lovely kisses, didn't. Margot and Leland and the kids joined us. Herb McFaull, who owned Magoo's, came out to say hello. The late, great Ritchie Valens began singing "La Bamba" and the sensory overload that was the true Magoo's experience began. Everything at Magoo's was superlative. The burgers were the sizzlingest, the shoestring fries the skinniest, the onion rings the greasiest, the coleslaw the most savoury, and the milkshakes in their old-fashioned metal containers the coldest and the thickest.

A meal at Magoo's demanded and deserved full attention, so none of us talked much while we were eating. That didn't mean there weren't some nice moments. Zack, as he always did, solemnly unloaded his onions onto Taylor's burger because she loved onions, and she never remembered to order extras. When he attempted to open his mouth wide enough to take a bite of his burger, Declan winced with pain and slid his burger back on his plate. Wordlessly, Margot reached over and cut his burger into bite-sized pieces. Declan gave her a grateful smile and Margot leaned close to him and whispered, "I have brothers."

After we'd eaten, Taylor and Declan gravitated towards the dance floor to put a little hip-hop into the sock hop, leaving the four of us to savour the pleasures of the gloaming. Only good friends can be comfortable sharing silence, and that evening I began to feel that Margot and Leland – in spite of the differences we might have – had entered that special category. When Leland's cell shrilled, the spell was broken.

As Margot watched her fiancé move to the edge of the deck so he could be out of earshot, she made no attempt to hide her annoyance. "That will be the ex–Mrs. Hunter," she said. "I wish someone could break Louise of her compulsion to drink and dial."

"Many have tried," Zack said.

"That's right," Margot said. "You were on Louise duty for a while, weren't you? Before Sage Mackenzie took over."

"Took over and took off to open her own law firm," Zack said.

"I thought most young lawyers would trade their first born for a chance to be an associate at Falconer Shreve," I said.

"Most would," Zack replied. "But Sage isn't a dewy-eyed young graduate. She was a cop before she was a lawyer."

Margot turned to me. "You saw her, Joanne. She was the redhead trying to control Louise after the convocation. Anyway, I never had much to do with her, so all I know is the gossip."

Zack gave her a sharp look. "So what's the gossip?"

"Just that Sage left very suddenly. People were surprised. You must know what happened, Zack."

"Part of it," he said. "Sage and I were working late one night and she came onto me."

"When was this?" I said.

Zack squeezed his eyes shut in concentration. "I don't know – late January, early February. We were working on the Lance Retzlaff case. We'd been talking to witnesses all day and were looking through the interview notes. Sage kept moving closer to me. I ignored it, then she reached down and started rubbing my penis."

"How come you didn't tell me?" I said.

"Because, as I explained to Sage, I was a happily married man and I wanted it to stay that way."

"And that was the end of it?" I said.

"No," Zack said. "Sage unzipped my fly and reached in. She was quick – I'll give her that."

Margot sputtered with laughter. "Sorry, Zack," she said. "It's just the image of you as the innocent maiden being ravished is pretty hard to swallow."

Zack scowled at her. "It wasn't funny at the time. If it hadn't been for the delivery man . . ."

"The delivery man?" I said. Now I was laughing, too. "Where did the delivery man come from?"

"God knows," Zack said. "He just wandered in, so I zipped up, told him he had the wrong office, put on my coat, and came home to you."

"And you never told me about your incredible adventure," I said.

"You were asleep, and Sage was gone the next week, so it was no longer relevant. Are you angry?"

"Of course not," I said. "But I am grateful to that delivery man."

Margot and I had both smeared our mascara laughing, so we excused ourselves to go to the ladies' room. Whatever your purpose, the women's bathroom at Magoo's is worth a visit. The mirrors are surrounded with lights like the makeup mirrors in old movies and the walls are covered with photographs of movie stars of the 1950s and 1960s posing with Mr. Magoo, the cranky, myopic, W.C. Fields–like cartoon character who gave the restaurant its name.

As Margot and I stood in front of adjacent mirrors repairing our makeup, I was struck by the new softness in her face. She was clearly a happy woman. Remembering her tenderness with Declan, I said, "You're going to be a good mother."

Margot flushed and ran her hand over her stomach. "Am I showing?"

"No. I just meant . . ." I turned towards her. "You *are* pregnant. Congratulations!"

"I'm over the moon. So is Leland." Margot's eyes were swimming. She dabbed at them and made a face of mock horror. "Hormones. What happens if I start blubbering in court?"

"The jury will melt," I said. I put my arms around her. "How far along are you?"

"Three months. It's going to be a Christmas baby!" She stood sideways and narrowed her eyes critically at her reflection. "I can't wait till I have a baby bump."

"Your breasts are already a little fuller, but you've always had nice breasts."

"I like your breasts, too," Margot said. She laughed her wonderful dirty laugh. "Be sure to tell Zack about this little womanly exchange. It'll keep him awake all night."

When Margot and I got back to our table, Leland was there and he seemed preoccupied.

Margot looked at him carefully. "Problems?" she asked.

Leland nodded. "One problem, and it's solved – at least I hope so. That was Sage Mackenzie."

"Ah, the woman of the hour," Margot said.

"I'm glad she was around tonight. Apparently, some goon showed up at Louise's. He told Louise she'd promised him 'a couple of grand' if he'd put a scare into somebody. The goon was there to get instructions and money. Louise had no idea what he was talking about. She must have made the arrangements when she was drunk and then lost it all in a blackout. Luckily Sage showed up and handled the situation."

"What did Sage do?" Zack asked.

"She gave the man some money for his trouble and he left. Sage says she's sure Louise won't remember any of this in the morning, but she thought I should know." Leland tried a smile. "And now I do. End of story."

Margot touched Leland's cheek with her hand. "Let's hope," she said.

After Leland, Margot, and Declan left to go back to the city, I took the dogs for a short walk on the beach and Zack returned some phone calls. Then we both went to Taylor's room to say goodnight. At fourteen, she was past the age for tucking in, but she continued to welcome a hug and a moment together at the end of the day, and so did we. That night, she was in bed with her cats, reading Pablo Neruda's *Odes to Common Things*, a collection celebrating tomatoes, chairs, cats, wine, bread, and other objects that bring beauty to our everyday lives that I'd given her for her birthday the previous November.

"I was just thinking about the sock paintings," Taylor said. "They were in the family room, so I guess they're gone."

The sock paintings were a Neruda-inspired sly response to a private joke between Taylor and me. Taylor believed that socks, like air, belonged to everyone, and she was an unrepentant and chronic borrower of mine. Her Christmas present to me the previous year had been two rectangular canvases: on one, she had copied out Neruda's "Ode to a Sock" in English; on the other, she had written out the poem in Spanish. The margins of both canvases were decorated with whimsical drawings of socks that she and I had jointly known. With a pang, I realized that the paintings had been in the family room and had almost certainly been destroyed by the explosion.

"We'll know more tomorrow," Zack said. "But, Taylor, you're here. You'll make new paintings."

"They won't be the same," Taylor said. "Because I'm not the same." There was no anger or self-pity in her voice. She spoke with the same cool detachment her mother exhibited when she confronted an unpalatable truth. "I've been thinking about this. When I painted those socks for the first time, I was so excited. I felt like the person who invented socks. But now I'll just be making art about socks that have already been painted. The newness won't be there any more." Her dark eyes moved slowly from Zack to me and back to Zack again. "Nothing stays the same," she said.

"That's not necessarily a bad thing," Zack said.

Taylor smiled her mother's smile, broad and generous but always tempered by a tiny flicker of mockery that played across her lips. "It's not necessarily good either," she said.

After Zack and I got into bed, like many busy couples, we checked our messages. News about the explosion had spread, so my e-mail was full of notes from friends expressing sympathy and offering whatever help we might need. I answered the notes, put down my BlackBerry, and plumped up my pillow. "Ready for lights out?" I said.

"Not quite." Zack took off his glasses and lay them on his bedside table. "Jo, when we were at Magoo's, I didn't tell the whole story about what happened with Sage."

My stomach clenched as I tried to summon Sage's image.

All that came to mind was a flash of red hair as untameable as wildfire. "Was there more between you two?" I said.

"God, no," Zack said. "One encounter was more than enough. But the week after that incident Sage attacked Norine, and we fired her."

"Attacked? You mean physically?" I said. "I can't imagine that. Norine's such a good person."

"Agreed, but apparently Norine did something Sage didn't like and Sage blew up. In addition to using some ugly language, Sage grabbed Norine's arm and twisted it."

"What had Norine done?"

"Nothing. You know how short of space Falconer Shreve is. The room Sage was using for an office had been a dumping ground for old Rolodexes, files, and agendas. Norine had it cleaned out. When Sage accused her of stealing, Norine asked her what was missing, but Sage wouldn't say. Anyway, that was that. We had a quick partners' meeting and decided that Sage had to go. We agreed to support her story that she wanted to open her own office, but we made certain she left the office immediately."

"How did Sage get connected with Louise Hunter?"

"That was my idea. Louise never quite understood that the retainer Leland paid me to take care of her legal affairs didn't include being on-call 24/7. As you well know, Louise was a lot of work, and to be honest, I felt sorry for Sage. I've lost my temper a few thousand times, but I've never been fired. I figured that Leland's money would give Sage a cushion until she got her practice going."

"You're a good guy," I said. We turned off the lights and I moved in close. "Hey, I forgot to tell you the big news. Margot's pregnant. The baby's due in December."

"That's nice," Zack said. "Really nice. And great timing. The office is usually quiet over the holidays, so Margot won't have to miss much work."

"I'm sure that was her first consideration," I said.

"You're mocking me," Zack said. "But I'm bulletproof. How come Margot told you first?"

"It was just a miscommunication. Anyway, that doesn't matter, but Margot did want me to tell you that when I said she had lovely breasts, she told me she'd always admired my breasts, too. And then we kissed."

"Seriously?"

"Think about it," I said.

"Oh, I will," Zack said. "I'll be awake all night thinking about it."

CHAPTER

7

If a couple spends twenty-seven years planning a wedding, it seems especially fitting that the event is perfect in every way. Ed and Barry's wedding was everything they had hoped it would be. The skies were blue, the sun was bright, the air was warm, and there was just enough breeze to make flower heads nod and ornamental grasses rustle.

Half an hour before the ceremony, Ed met me in the lobby. He was carrying two florist boxes and wearing a summer tuxedo the colour of latte froth, a white shirt, a cream vest, and a striped cream and white Windsor tie.

Until that day, I had never seen Ed in a suit. In his day-to-day life, he favoured shirts custom-made to hide his girth. He had dozens of them in different shades and materials.

"You look sensational," I said.

"So do you," he said. "Did Zack like the dress?"

"He loved it. From now on, you're in charge of my wardrobe."

Knowing that I would be a reluctant fashionista, Ed had scouted the Internet until he came up with a shimmering silvery-lilac silk sheath, closely fitted and sleeveless with a plunging neckline that revealed discrete but noticeable cleavage.

When I'd tried the dress on, I'd been dubious. It was flattering but expensive and very revealing. "I don't know about this," I said as we stood in front of the mirror.

But Ed's mirrored self was beaming. "Trust me," he said. "Gay men know these things."

Now, however, his brow furrowed with concern. "How are you doing, Jo?"

"Fine," I said. "Really. Seeing the house was grim, but it could have been worse. When Zack came home after court on Thursday, he suggested we go to the lake that night. He'd lost his case and he was tired, so I said we should just wait and go in the morning. Zack knows how much I love being at the lake, and he insisted."

Ed shuddered. "Coincidences like that make you believe in fate."

"They do," I said. "But the only fate we should be thinking about today is yours and Barry's. You were born to be together. This is going to be a beautiful day. Now let me have a look at the bouquets."

Ed handed me the smaller of the boxes. "Yours, madam." The bouquet inside was simple and elegant – a duplicate of the one I'd carried when Zack and I were married: a mix of pale green and cream cymbidium, their stems braided with ribbons into a handle. "Acceptable?" Ed asked.

"Perfect," I said.

"Good. Now here is mine." Ed removed the lid of the larger box. The bouquet inside was exquisite: cymbidium, gardenias, peonies, and roses – all white – their stems braided with white ribbon. Ed took it in his hands. "You're sure about this?"

"I'm sure," I said. "You look exactly the way a man in love should look."

"In that case," Ed said. "Let's find Barry."

The ceremony was conducted by a judge named Penney Murphy, an attractive woman with spiky red hair and an affable manner. Judge Murphy spoke of how Ed and Barry gave themselves freely and generously and of how we as a community of friends and family were present to celebrate and support the married couple. She was plainspoken, but her words were heartfelt. When I saw Barry's eyes as he gazed at Ed holding his spectacular bouquet, I felt a catch in my throat and hoped that the mascara I'd paid far too much for truly was waterproof.

Taylor, who had always held a special place in Ed and Barry's lives, read a passage from the Song of Solomon. Barry's nephew read Paul's meditation on love from 1 Corinthians. As their vows, Barry and Ed together recited Sir Philip Sidney's sixteenth-century poem "The Bargain."

My true love hath my heart, and I have his,
By just exchange one for another given;
I hold his dear, and mine he cannot miss,
There never was a better bargain driven.
My true love hath my heart, and I have his.
His heart in me keeps him and me in one,
My heart in him his thoughts and sense guides;
He loves my heart for once it was his own,
I cherish his because in me it bides;
My true love hath my heart, and I have his.

After Ed and Barry exchanged rings, Judge Murphy said that she was honoured to join together two men whose commitment to each other had never wavered in twenty-seven years. When she pronounced Ed and Barry legally married, an oriole – an infrequent visitor to our city – flew over the newlyweds. Ed and Barry noticed the bird simultaneously and smiled at the omen, and at each other. Then the string quartet began playing the old Broadway tune "Mr. Wonderful" and a new phase of Ed and Barry's life together began.

As the wedding party walked back down the path between the chairs of the guests, I was struck by the joy in the faces I saw. Leland and Margot were beaming – their turn was next. Our son Angus was a surprise guest. He'd caught a flight from Calgary and he was sitting with Peter. Mieka was sitting at the back with Zack and her daughters. Both my sons gave me the thumbs-up sign. So did Zack. The girls jumped up and hugged me, but Mieka's face was strained. I stepped closer to her and bent down to brush a strand of hair from her cheek.

"I love you, Mieka," I said.

"I love you, too, Mum," she said, "but you and I are going to have to talk."

After I posed for photos with the rest of the wedding party, I found Mieka and we sat down together at a café table tucked away in a corner that promised privacy. Our table was next to a raised bed of hydrangeas whose blooms were the same pale pink as Mieka's dress. She was tanned, there were new lowlights in her ash-blonde hair, and she had the glow of a woman who was well and truly loved. "Pink's a great colour for you," I said. "You look beautiful."

Mieka's gaze was steady. "That's what Riel said."

"Right to the topic at hand, eh?" I said.

But having zeroed in, Mieka changed course. A copy of the wedding program was on the table in front of her. She tapped the photograph on front with her forefinger. "I've always loved this painting," she said.

"So have I," I said. "'The Old Gardeners' is my favourite Sally Love. Every time we go to Ed and Barry's, Taylor wanders off just to spend time with it."

"I can understand why," Mieka said.

In the painting, two men are looking out at their summer garden. One of the men is wearing a battered gardening hat. We see only the backs of the couple's heads, but the line of their bodies as they lean towards each other, their shoulders almost touching, speaks volumes about the closeness of their relationship.

"Do you remember the quote Greg and I used on our wedding program?" Mieka asked softly.

I nodded. *"Love does not consist in gazing at each other, but in looking outward together in the same direction."*

"It was never true for Greg and me," Mieka said. "We were never looking outward in the same direction. Riel and I are. We see life the same way. We want the same things."

"Twin stars," I murmured.

"If that was an allusion, it flew right past me."

"It was what your father and I believed our lives would be when we decided to marry."

Mieka's eyes were thoughtful. "It didn't work for you, did it?"

"No, it didn't," I said. "But that doesn't mean it can't work for you and Riel."

A server came offering flutes of champagne. Mieka and I each took one and placed it, untouched, on the table. "You love him," I said.

"I do," Mieka said. "And he loves me."

"You're going to have to give me a little time to absorb this," I said. "Until yesterday I didn't realize that you and Riel had even met."

"I know it must seem strange," Mieka said, "but at first my relationship with Riel was no big deal. He was just someone I was working with. Lisa Wallace and I were determined that UpSlideDown2 wouldn't be one of those projects outsiders imposed on the people of North Central. We wanted the community's support. Lisa knew Riel, and just before Christmas she asked him to organize a meeting."

I was incredulous. "You've known Riel since Christmas and you never mentioned him?"

"There was nothing to mention. We were just two people interested in creating a play centre, and then, well, the timing was never right. By the time Riel and I knew we were serious about each other, Leland Hunter had started demolishing the neighbourhood to clear the way for The Village, and Riel was scrambling to organize a resistance." Mieka ran her hand through her hair. "Mum, we were happy and we were in love. I guess I just didn't want to risk what we had."

Across from us, Zack, Madeleine, and Lena were still happily munching appetizers and watching koi in the stone pool at the corner of the garden. "Where are the girls in all this?" I said.

"Where they've always been," Mieka said. "They're my first priority and they're Riel's first priority, too. We've been careful not to confuse them about our relationship. The girls saw Riel at UpSlidedown, but he didn't start coming to the house until we were sure the relationship was serious."

"But now he does come to the house."

"Yes and when he comes, he stays overnight."

"And the girls are all right with this?"

"They think he's terrific. He's great with them. He's great with me. Can't you just be happy for us?"

"It's more complicated than that, Mieka. This is shaping up to be a very ugly battle, and Riel and our family have wound up on opposite sides."

"Not the *whole* family, Mum. And Riel is still grateful to you for encouraging him to pursue a master's, and Zack has a good reputation in North Central. He's taken on a lot of very unpopular cases for not much money. It's not you two personally. It's just . . ."

"Political?"

Mieka shook her head vehemently. "It's beyond that," she said. "Riel's world is different from yours."

"And it's different from the world you know, Mieka. Have you considered that?"

Mieka chewed her lip. "Yes, I've considered that, and Riel and I are dealing with it."

Across the garden, Leland and Margot had joined the girls and Zack by the pond. They were all laughing, and the wedding photographer was catching the moment. The girls were wearing matching green sundresses and Lena had attached the fake ponytail from the dollar store that she favoured for parties. It would be a nice picture.

"We can't lose you and the girls, Mieka."

"We don't want to lose you either, Mum, but you're going to have accept Riel. He's part of my family now."

I couldn't think of anything more to say so I picked up my champagne flute. "We better drink this while it still has some fizz."

Mieka's smile was shadowed, but she raised her glass. "To all of us."

We sipped our champagne, and for a moment it seemed that all was right with the world again, but suddenly Mieka's face tensed. I glanced over my shoulder and saw that Leland Hunter was about to join us. Mieka half stood, but Leland was too fast for her. "It was a beautiful wedding, wasn't it?" he said. "Margot and I were marvelling at how smoothly everything went and, of course, hoping that ours will be just as flawless."

"It will," I said. "Leland, this is my daughter, Mieka Kilbourn. Mieka, this is Leland Hunter."

Leland's craggy face had regained the ruddy glow of a man who spends time working outdoors, but my daughter's eyes were fixed on the stitches that ran from his forehead to his skull. They still looked painful. "I heard about what happened," she said. "I'm sorry you were hurt."

"It looks worse than it feels," Leland said. "It did earn me some points with your daughters. They were fascinated by the stitches."

Mieka frowned. "Did you tell them how it happened?"

"They didn't ask. And Lena's hair was far more intriguing. When I admired her ponytail, she took it off and handed it to me."

Mieka's voice softened. "I'll have to talk to Lena about how to receive a compliment."

"I thought it was a charming gesture," Leland said.

Mieka didn't respond. She glanced across at Zack and the girls. "I should get my ladies and give Zack a chance to mingle."

"It was good to finally meet you," Leland said and extended his hand.

Mieka hesitated a beat before she took it. Then she smiled and walked away.

Leland indicated the chair my daughter had just vacated. "May I join you?"

"Of course." A server arrived at our table with napkins, small plates, and a tray of hot hors d'oeuvres. "Perfect timing," Leland said. We both chose panko-crusted scallops with wasabi and some grilled shrimp.

I took a bite of my scallop. "Food for the gods," I said. "I could live on appetizers."

"I'll remember that the next time you come to dinner," Leland said. "Joanne, there was a distinct chill when you introduced me to your daughter. Is she still upset about Peyben buying the Markestyn property?"

"No," I said. "It *was* a setback, but the price you paid was more than fair, and Lisa Wallace and Mieka and I have all been scouting other properties."

"But something *is* wrong," he said.

"Not necessarily wrong but certainly complicated."

Leland leaned forward, waiting for me to explain. I didn't want to explain. I wanted to crawl into bed and pull the covers over my head. I was running on empty, but escape was not an option. "Mieka and Riel Delorme are in a relationship," I said.

"So she's confident that he didn't have anything to do with Danny Racette's death or the bombing at your house," Leland said.

"Apparently."

Leland speared a shrimp. "But you're not."

"I'm confident that Riel wasn't directly involved. Beyond that, I'm not sure of anything. You know we're not telling Mieka that we're living at your place."

"Zack mentioned that."

"I hate this," I said. "Mieka and I have always been open with each other—" A server who didn't look much older than Taylor appeared magically at my elbow. "That champagne will be warm," the boy said. "I'll get you a fresh glass."

"What I'd really like is some water," I said.

"With ice?"

"Please."

The boy looked at Leland. "Sir?"

"I'll have a little water, too, but no ice and two fingers of Scotch."

"That's probably not the worst idea you had all day," I said.

"Care to change your order?"

"No, the best man has to set an example," I said. "Don't beat yourself up about the tension between Mieka and me. There was no way you could have foreseen any of this."

"But there were things I could have foreseen," he said. "There were signs, but I ignored them because I wanted to get this development underway. I've been involved in a dozen projects bigger than this one. Every one of them has presented problems, but I've never broken ground until I understood what those problems were and found a way through them. This time I rushed, and everyone's paying, including you."

"Why was there such a push?" I asked. "I'm not being critical, just curious. We bought the Markesteyn building in December. You bought it in January and it was pretty well gone by the end of the month. What was the rush?"

"In a word – Margot." He looked across the garden to where Margot, Zack, and Angus were sitting by a glorious hibiscus, deep in conversation. Leland's smile was rueful. "I wanted to give Margot a perfect neighbourhood. I should have had meetings with the community – explained what we were doing, reached a consensus, but I didn't, and now we have a situation."

The young server set our drinks in front of us.

"Situations can be dealt with," I said. "You have a good track record, Leland. This can be salvaged."

"Thank you for that," he said. He sipped his Scotch. "So is the condo going to work for you?"

"Zack went through it yesterday – we don't have to change a thing, and that is a huge relief. Until we retrofitted our house, I had no idea the number of accommodations paraplegia demands, but your condo meets all Zack's requirements."

"I wish I could take credit for that," Leland said. "But Shelley Gregg, the developer who converted the warehouse, insisted on universal design throughout the building. She was also the one who roughed in this gorgeous garden. All I did was buy the property."

"Because Shelley Gregg went bankrupt," I said.

"Doesn't seem fair, does it?" Leland said. "To do perfect, sensitive work and get kicked in the slats."

"It may not be fair," I said, "but it's almost inevitable."

Leland gave me a quick, assessing look. "True, but your husband had a thought today that might redress the balance. He suggested adding a multipurpose community complex to the plans for The Village. He and I just kicked around the idea, but we agreed that the complex should be a centre for real community-building: a gymnasium certainly, but also a performance space, meeting rooms, an indoor pool, maybe a media space where kids could make videos and recordings."

"And you want Shelley Gregg to design the facility?"

"She's the logical choice. I've seen her work first-hand here on Halifax Street, and while Zack and I were talking I Googled her. She's designing public buildings now, mostly for municipalities."

"This facility would be just for people who lived in The Village?"

"No, it would be open to everybody. Fees would be adjusted to income. People in North Central would have the same access as people in The Village, they just wouldn't have to pay as much."

"That's a brave idea," I said. "I guess I don't have to point out that the sooner the people of North Central are involved in the development phase, the better."

"No. I learn my lessons," Leland said. "Jo, do you think Riel Delorme would talk to me?"

I remembered Mieka's toast "to all of us." Making Riel part of the planning process would be a step towards healing the breach that had developed between us.

"I'll ask him," I said. "Leland, you're not the only one who's learning lessons from this. Riel is smart enough to realize that he's fighting a losing battle. The Village is going to be built. That's a fact. The people in North Central need a place that will foster community development, and that's been a fact for a long time. The kind of centre you're talking about could be the place where the two neighbourhoods can really come together."

"So you'll talk to Riel?"

"I will."

"Good." Leland sipped his Scotch. "Jo, what would you and Mieka think about making UpSlideDown2 part of the facility?"

"It's worth considering," I said. "But you're talking about a long-term project, and we'd like to open our doors this fall."

"Well, keep the possibility in mind," Leland said. He drained his glass. "Now Zack tells me you like to run in the morning. Would you be interested in running with me?"

"I hear you're into Iron Man training, Leland. You're out of my league."

"I'm adaptable. It's a new neighbourhood for you. I thought you might like company."

"I would. What time do you usually run?"

"Five, but if that's too early, I can make it five-thirty."

"Five is fine," I said. "I'll meet you by the elevator. Now I guess we should join the others."

Over the years, I'd come to know many of Ed and Barry's friends, so after Angus and I had caught up on each other's news, I just drifted and visited. Judge Penney Murphy and I talked fashion, a subject on which we were in accord. When Judge Murphy admired my dress, I told her I'd trade her the dress and my stilettos for the comfortable black slacks, elegant silk shirt, and sensible flats she was wearing.

Ed was as happy as I'd ever seen him. When we found a

few minutes to be alone together, I said, "I don't need to ask if today was everything you'd dreamed it would be."

"It was better. Thank you for everything."

"All I did was show up."

"That's all you had to do. You're very dear to me, Jo. I hate seeing your life turned upside down."

"It'll be right side up again," I said. "Meanwhile, there's a lot to take care of, and Zack's got the Cronus case starting tomorrow. I'm just relieved I'm free to handle things during the day and meet Zack at the door wearing Saran Wrap and holding a martini."

Ed's round face creased in a smile. "Glad your sense of humour is intact."

"I'm fine," I said. "After the first shock, the only option is to adjust."

"Have you been through your house yet?"

"No. The police say it's too dangerous."

"You shouldn't have to go through it alone," Ed said. "When the police say the time is right, I'll come with you."

"You and Barry have just been married. You'll want to have time together."

"We've been together for twenty-seven years, Jo. Our honeymoon will be in September when we go to Europe. We'll be gone two months, so of course Barry thinks he has to get two months of work into his business before we leave. Till September, I'm going to have plenty of time on my hands."

"You're a good friend."

"I hope so, but my offer isn't wholly altruistic. I'm not a greenhorn, Jo. I understand that there are compelling reasons to oppose the Village Project, but the people who killed Danny Racette and blew up your house have to be stopped. This is a big story and I want to be inside it. I'm going to keep working North Central."

I felt my heart clutch. "Ed, did you get a good look at Declan Hunter's face today?"

"I couldn't help but notice, but I didn't want to embarrass him by asking about it. What happened?"

"After he saw our house yesterday, he went to North Central to ask questions. He approached a boy he thought of as a friend. The friend came at him with a sawed-off baseball bat."

Ed winced. "Declan's lucky to be walking around."

"I think Declan's figured that one out. Ed, the activities of the gangs may be a great story, but those guys play for keeps. I'll be more than glad to have you come with me when I look at the house, but don't get involved in the fight about the Village Project. You and Barry have waited a long time for this marriage. You deserve a chance to live happily ever after."

Dinner was a relaxed affair. There was no head table, but our family sat with Ed and Barry and Barry's best man and the nephew who had read from Corinthians. It was a happy, happy meal. After we'd eaten, Ed's best man and I both proposed toasts that were affectionate and unmemorable. Ed and Barry cut the cake and thanked us all for coming, then following the old tradition, they announced that they were leaving early to start their new life together.

I was beside Angus when the moment came for Ed to toss his spectacular bouquet. Mieka and the girls were standing by the koi pool. When Ed raised his arm to throw the flowers, Angus yelled, "Go deep, Mieka," then pulled out his smartphone. A lifetime of playing touch football with her brothers paid off. Mieka went deep and when she caught the flowers she raised them above her head in triumph, and Angus got his picture. When Mieka bent to give each of her daughters an orchid, Angus kept snapping.

Madeleine took her orchid solemnly. Lena reattached her fake ponytail, shoved in the orchid, and swanned off. Angus held up his phone to show me the photos.

"Amazing," I said. I put my arm around his shoulder. "It is so good to have you around. You are missed."

"I'll be back for the long weekend."

"I know. I also know that you're having a great summer in Calgary, and I shouldn't be greedy."

"You're not greedy. You're a mother." Angus's resemblance to Ian was remarkable: the same dark good looks and grace, the same quicksilver mood changes. He had been beaming, but suddenly his face darkened. "Is there someplace we can talk for a few minutes, Mum? I mean privately."

"Sure. We can go downstairs to Leland's condo. He's letting us use it when we're in town. Angus, is something wrong?"

"No. Everything's great. There's just something I need to show you."

Angus went over to the table where he'd been sitting and picked up his briefcase. When he came back, he looked into my face and frowned. "I'm making too big a deal of this. Really, everything's fine, Mum. Let's go downstairs and I'll explain."

When Angus walked into Leland's, he gazed around and whistled. "Wow. Imagine living in a place like this." He pointed to the butcher-block table. "Okay if we sit here?"

"Of course."

Angus opened his briefcase and removed a bulging paper file folder. There were elastic bands around the file to keep the contents secure.

Angus handed the folder to me. "Patrick Hawley, one of the other summer students, dropped this on my desk this morning. He thought it must belong to me."

"Why?" I said.

"Take a look."

The file was filled with newspaper clippings. The one on top was a photo of me, blank-faced at Ian's funeral holding my children's hands. I turned to the next clipping. It was another picture of Ian's funeral. Angus was crying and the premier, our friend Howard Dowhanuik, had dropped to his knees to console him. There were more stories about the funeral and a half-dozen obituaries. And then, in chilling reverse chronology, the focus shifted to stories about Ian's death at the side of a snowy highway in what had seemed, for years, to be a random act of violence. Then the focus shifted again. This time to Ian triumphantly alive: being sworn in as Attorney General and deputy premier, making speeches, giving press conferences, answering questions in the legislature. And then a front-page photo of Ian and me, impossibly young, on that first election night when we won and were faced with the job of forming government. And then the prelude: stories of the campaign leading up to that amazing victory, and before that pictures of Ian winning the nomination for Regina Lakeview, and then finally to pictures and articles about the time when it all began when Ian, as a Crown prosecutor, began to dream big dreams.

I closed the file folder. "I don't get it," I said.

Angus shook his head. "Neither do I."

"How did this end up with Patrick?"

"Through a screw-up," Angus said. "When Falconer Shreve decided to expand, Norine MacDonald hired a guy to cull the paper files – keep what was relevant and send the rest off to storage. When the boxes kept arriving, the guy had a total breakdown. I guess he had no idea what a mountain of paper a firm like Falconer Shreve could build up in thirty years. Anyway, he spun right out. He sent half the boxes to the new Calgary office, squirrelled away everything else wherever he could find space, moved to Winnipeg, and got a job as a server at a Chinese restaurant called Hu's on First."

"Talk about a cautionary tale." I laughed.

Angus grinned. "I guess. Anyway, he made some work for Pat and me and the other summer students. We're doing what he was supposed to have done."

"Going through the files to decide what to keep," I said. I placed my hand on the folder. "And the most recent material in here is fifteen years old. Angus, do you know what this looks like? Material from a newspaper morgue."

Angus's look was questioning.

"An archive database," I said. "Although that term is probably outdated, too. Anyway, newspapers used to keep files like this for people who'd been in the news so they could write an obituary when the person died."

"Do you think you should talk to the police?" Angus said. "Given everything else that's happened, I'm not crazy about the idea of some nutbar out there keeping a file about you."

"This file isn't about me," I said. "It's about your dad. I was just incidental."

"It's still creepy."

"I agree," I said. I closed the file. "And I will talk to the police, but, Angus, don't tell Zack about this. He's got enough on his mind. I'll call Norine tomorrow and see if she has any idea about where the file came from, but my guess is that at some point in the past fifteen years somebody was doing research on your father's career and simply lost interest in the project."

"You're probably right," Angus said, but he didn't sound convinced. "Keep me in the loop, Mum. I hope this didn't wreck the wedding for you."

"It didn't," I said. I picked up the folder. "I'll stick this out of the way and pick it up later. It's time we got you and your smartphone back to the reception."

———

Angus had to leave early to catch his flight back to Calgary. Pete and his girlfriend drove him to the airport, so Zack and Taylor and I were able to take the elevator to the condo without subterfuge.

After Taylor went upstairs to check out her new digs on the second floor, I turned to Zack. "I'm going to take off the killer dress and the killing shoes. Do you want to watch?"

"You bet." As he wheeled into the bedroom after me, Zack's smile was wolfish.

He undid the back zipper slowly and kissed the middle of my back. "Are you busy for the next half-hour?"

I slid the dress off. "Nope. Nothing to do but bring you pleasure."

"Let's get at it," he said.

I went to the door and called up to Taylor. "Your dad and I are going to have a nap. If anybody calls, just tell them we'll call them back."

Zack grinned at me. "Do you hear the sound of our daughter's eye-rolling at that mention of a 'nap'?"

"It's good for her to know we love each other. But we are going to have to be a little quieter. This condo is all open space, and sound carries."

"No more yodelling when I come?"

I bent down to kiss him. "You can still yodel. Just dial it back a little."

We were showered, dressed, and Zack was making tea when there was a buzz from downstairs. Zack wheeled towards the intercom. "I'm expecting this," he said. "I have to work on my opening statement and Norine sent this stuff over so I wouldn't have to leave you and go over to the office," Zack said.

"It's Sunday, Zack. Whatever you pay Norine isn't enough," I said.

"Norine reminds me of that frequently."

———

I carried a cup of tea up to Taylor. She was studying at an old trestle table. "Leland must have used this room to work in," I said.

"He did," Taylor said. "He told me he liked this room because he could see so much of the city from up here. He brought the table up because it gave him plenty of room to lay out plans." She gestured at the contents of her backpack spilled across the table. "Works for me, too," she said.

I pulled the drapes, closing off her spectacular cityscape. Taylor made a face. "The lights look so pretty from up here."

"I know. Zack just thinks it might be smart to stay private for a few days."

Taylor's dark eyes widened. "Because we're not safe?"

"Because we're not sure yet what's out there." I sat on the corner of her bed and Taylor swivelled her chair so she could face me.

"Taylor, the people who bombed our house are going to get caught. The police are watching out for us. Closing the curtains is just a precautionary measure."

"So we just do what we always do?" Taylor said.

"That's all we can do. You have exams and the All-College to get ready for. Your dad's got the Cronus trial starting tomorrow and that's going to be a long, hard slog for him. I have to deal with the house and" – I paused – "whatever else comes up."

Taylor was studying my face. "Mieka told you about Riel, didn't she? I saw you two talking at the wedding and you were both so serious I thought she must finally be telling you."

"You knew about Riel?"

"I met him a few times when I went over to Mieka's after school. He's really nice, Jo. That thing that happened with Declan's dad was terrible, but it was an accident – you said that yourself. I know Riel's fighting the project Declan's dad's working on down here, but Riel never talks about any of that with me."

"What does he talk about?"

"My art. Riel says there are a lot of kids in North Central who could be helped by learning to make art. He thinks I'd be a good teacher."

"You would," I said.

Taylor cocked her head. "So you'd be all right with the idea of me volunteering at the Willy Hodgson Centre."

I was taken aback. "Taylor, where's this coming from? You've never mentioned teaching art till this moment."

"But I've been thinking about it for a while." She leaned towards me. "It's something I want to do, Jo."

There was hope in her voice; there was also determination. I touched her hand. "Then do it," I said.

It had been a long day, and when we turned out the lights, Zack fell asleep immediately. I didn't. It seemed suddenly as if the axis of our lives had shifted. The house. Mieka and Riel. And now Taylor wanted to work in North Central. It was exactly the kind of commitment I hoped she'd make some day, but not now. Working at Willy Hodgson would put Taylor right in the middle of a neighbourhood at war, and I knew that, as our daughter, Taylor would be seen as the enemy. My mind raced, but my thoughts were not productive. I slid out of bed, went out on the terrace, and pulled my chair into a corner where I could look down into the shimmering depths of the swimming pool in the courtyard. Lit from below, the pool was jewel-like – a brilliant gem in the velvety emerald grass.

When Leland and Margot appeared, I didn't move. They were wearing white terrycloth robes that they shed casually at the pool's edge. They dove in and, side by side, began doing effortless lengths. When they were through, they pushed out of the water, shrugged into their robes, and walked hand in hand back to their condo. Healthy, intelligent, successful, and in love, they were, in E.A. Robinson's memorable phrase, "everything to make us wish that we were in their place."

After Leland and Margot left, my eyes drifted to the razor wire that topped the security fence. Once long ago, a friend had related the words of the priest who had prepared her for confirmation. "God says take what you want," the old priest said. "Take what you want and pay for it." As I stepped back inside our condo, I wondered about the price we would pay for what we had taken.

CHAPTER

8

At five o'clock the next morning, Leland met me at the elevator in a faded blue T-shirt, running shorts, and a brand of performance training shoes that I knew were light and well balanced because I wore them myself.

Leland pressed the elevator button and we stepped inside. "Do you like to talk when you run?" he asked.

"Usually I run with our dogs," I said. "We only talk if there's something worth talking about."

"Good precedent," Leland said. "Let's follow it." The elevator doors opened and we were on our way.

My usual route was along the bike path that followed the gentle curve of Wascana Creek. The sounds of my morning run were pastoral: the rustle of branches in the wind, the plash of water as a duck or a beaver broke the surface of the creek, and the lyric urgency of birdsong.

Leland and I ran on cracked concrete past giant machines mired in the mud of construction sites and hoardings covered with the graffiti tags of gangs. No birds sang here. Feral cats yowled over territory and tethered dogs snarled behind welded steel mesh security fences that were indestructible and unscaleable. I slowed when we came to a pair of angry Rottweilers behind a security fence.

"That bothers you," Leland said.

"I hate seeing dogs chained," I said. "And I don't understand why dogs are being used to guard a construction site. Nobody's going to steal those machines."

"No, but somebody could screw around with them," Leland said. "Every development project teaches you something. Sometimes the lesson costs money, sometimes it causes pain, sometimes both."

"So what have you learned from the Village Project?"

Leland shrugged. "Too much to go into now, but the dogs are necessary, Joanne. These cretins need snarling dogs to remind them that their actions have consequences."

"They must know that," I said.

"Look at this," Leland said, pointing to a hoarding covered with graffiti. Gang members had painted over one another's marks indicating ownership. "Riel Delorme thought he could unite this bunch for a greater good. These guys can't even let one another's graffiti alone – and what are they claiming ownership of? A piece of scrap lumber. Property that belongs to a multinational corporation. So instead of getting a job and a paycheque, they waste their lives hating me and spraying meaningless symbols on cheap wood."

"Are you ever afraid?"

"Being afraid doesn't change your fate," Leland said. "When it happens, it happens." With that, we picked up speed and ran wordlessly home.

Usually my morning run centred me, made me optimistic about my ability to handle the day ahead, but my run with Leland had unsettled me. The world of tethered dogs and unseen threats was new to me, but it was my world now, and I wasn't at all certain I could find my way. When I opened the door to our condo, my nerves were raw, but everything seemed reassuringly normal.

Zack was at the kitchen table, thumbing his BlackBerry, dressed for the day in the suit he'd worn to Ed's wedding. He grinned when he saw me. "I won't ask if you found Iron Man training up to your standards. You look as if you just stepped out of a sauna."

"How would you like a long, sweaty kiss?"

Zack held open his arms. "Bring it on," he said. "Nothing like a whiff of pheromones to get the day off to a great start."

"You do remember that the suit you're wearing might well be the only suit you now own?"

"True enough," he said. We shared a careful kiss, and I poured myself a glass of water.

"What do you want me to do about clothes for you?" I said.

"Nothing. Norine will take care of it. She's been ordering clothes for me for years. She just calls Harry Rosen in Calgary. They know my sizes and what I need. It's summer. I've got a sports jacket and slacks at the lake. When I'm in court, I wear my barrister's robe, so nobody knows what I'm wearing. If I've got a heavy-duty meeting, I can wear what I've got on. You worry too much."

I felt my gorge rise. "What do you mean 'I worry too much?' I'm not like you, Zack. I can't just shrug all this off and go merrily on my way. Our lives have been turned upside down. All I do is worry."

Zack touched my arm. "Is it helping?"

"Don't patronize me."

"I wasn't patronizing you. Crazy as it sounds, I was trying to get you to smile." Zack's voice was soft and reasonable – it was the voice he used in court when he was dealing with someone who was rocketing out of control. "We need to talk about this," he said.

"Not now," I said. "You have to be in court. Taylor has to get moving. And frankly, I'm pretty close to the edge already. Good luck with your case."

"Jo, please." Zack held out his arms to me, but I turned away. Then I did the unforgivable. I ran upstairs where he couldn't follow me.

After I'd rapped on Taylor's door, I splashed my face with cold water and took some deep breaths. Then I waited in the upstairs hall until I heard the front door close and I knew Zack had left.

As I went downstairs, I felt sick to my stomach. I had never loved a man as completely as I loved Zack. Our marriage was everything I could have hoped for, and I was jeopardizing it because my life was disintegrating, and I didn't know how to stop the erosion. I picked up my Black-Berry to text him, but the red light indicating an incoming message was already flashing.

Zack's message was to the point: "We love each other too much to let this happen, Ms. Shreve."

I texted back. My message was an overly emotional, school-girlish declaration of love, but the moment I hit Send I felt relief wash over me.

By the time Taylor came down for breakfast, my pulse had slowed and my voice was steady. I poured us both juice. "We're going to have to go shopping for you after school," I said. "I'm going to need some things, too."

"And Dad."

"Norine buys your dad's clothes. She has for years – I wouldn't dream of trying to live up to her standards."

As she always did, Taylor was cutting her toast into the bite-sized triangles before she ate it. "How old is Norine?"

"I don't know. She must be close to fifty."

"When we talked about matriarchies at school, I thought about Norine," Taylor said, nibbling a triangle. "She's like a tribal queen."

"A tribal queen who wears nothing but Max Mara," I said.

"She does have great taste," Taylor said. "And she's so regal. I wonder why she never got married."

"Some people have everything they want without marriage," I said. "Norine loves her work and she knows who she is."

"And that's enough," Taylor said thoughtfully.

"It can be," I said.

Taylor picked up another triangle of toast. "That's something to think about," she said.

When Declan texted Taylor to say he was out front, I went down in the elevator with Taylor and walked her to the curb where Declan was waiting in his car. I leaned close to have a better look at his face. It was a relief map of contusions, swelling, and stitches.

"You sure you're okay for school?" I said.

He tried a smile but finished with a grimace. "It's going to hurt just as much at home as it will there."

"You sound like your dad," I said.

This time, he did manage a smile. "Thanks," he said. "I do my best."

My cell was ringing when I came back into the condo. My friend, Jill Oziowy, head of news at NationTV, was calling from Toronto.

"What the hell is going on?" she said. "I was in New York for the weekend, and I come back, start checking my 682 messages, and discover one from Ed Mariani telling me that somebody blew up your house. What happened?"

"The police are still trying to figure that out," I said.

"You sound remarkably cool," Jill said. "Especially since,

according to Ed, the explosion at your house was probably the work of the same people who killed Danny Racette."

"I'm glad I seem cool, Jill, because I don't feel that way. But we're all trying to keep some perspective."

Jill snorted. "No sane person has perspective about having their house blown up. Industrial espionage is big stuff, Jo, and not just for Regina. Leland Hunter has projects all over the world. If there's some sort of international terrorist agenda . . ."

"There's no international terrorist agenda," I said. "This is purely local." I gave Jill a précis of what I knew about the hostility towards the Village Project and then, because we'd been friends for more than thirty years, I told her about Mieka's involvement with Riel Delorme.

When she heard about Mieka and Riel, Jill groaned. "That certainly complicates the situation," she said.

"It does. A few years ago, Riel Delorme was a graduate student at the university. He was interested in doing a master's thesis on movements that battled systemic racism and poverty. I liked him, he was smart and idealistic, and I was disappointed when he dropped out. Until last week, I hadn't seen or heard of Riel in years. He's changed, Jill. I could feel the anger coming from him, even though it wasn't directed at me. I could also feel the strength. I can understand Mieka responding to him. In that much overused word, Riel Delorme is charismatic."

"The Che syndrome," Jill said dryly. "Those guys are so sexy. It probably has something to do with the rifles. I'll bet if you asked Mieka, she could tell you what has happened in Delorme's life since he dropped out of university."

"I'm sure she could, but I'm not about to ask her," I said. "At the moment, my relationship with my daughter is a powder keg."

"Bad image," Jill said.

"Bad but accurate," I said. "Just about anything can set us off. Jill, I really would appreciate hearing anything you can find out about Riel's activities in the past five years."

"I'll do what I can. Whoops. Time to go," she said. "Somebody who thinks he's important just waltzed into my office. Don't take any chances, Jo."

My next caller was Debbie Haczkewicz, although at first I didn't recognize her voice. It was hoarse and strained. "Nothing real to report," she said. "But I promised to give you updates. We have officers going door to door in North Central asking questions. Nobody knows anything – no surprise there." A coughing fit interrupted her.

"Are you all right?" I asked.

"Summer cold," she said. "No big deal."

"Sounds nasty," I said.

Debbie hacked again. "I've had worse. Anyway, since we're not getting much help from the community, we're trying to trace the supplies used in the bombing. Talk about a needle in the haystack. Any halfwit with access to the Internet could have done the job."

"So you're nowhere?"

"We'll get there," Debbie said, and despite her hoarseness, her voice was steely. "Whoever did this is not going to walk away."

I had to ask the question that I had been trying to put out of my mind for days now.

"Debbie, was Riel Delorme involved?"

"We don't know," Debbie said. She hesitated. "Joanne, we do know that Riel is in a relationship with your daughter Mieka."

"How long have you known?"

"Since January."

"Why didn't you tell us?"

Debbie made no attempt to soften the asperity in her voice. "Because Mieka is a grown woman. She hasn't done anything illegal. She is spending time with a man who is of interest to the department but who has not been charged with anything."

"I understand. Debbie, I'm sorry if I pushed. I appreciate the call. I know how busy you are."

"There's something else," she said. "I don't know whether it could be classified as 'good news,' but it is news. You can go through the house today. You'll be supervised – just for safety's sake – but I know you're anxious to know the extent of the damage."

"Should we arrange a time?"

Her voice had almost disappeared. "No need," she said huskily. "We have people there 24/7."

"Okay, thanks again. Take care of that cold."

"It will take more than a summer cold to finish me, but I appreciate the thought. And, Joanne, if you really want to know how involved Riel Delorme is with all this, you might be wise to talk to your daughter."

After I hung up, I stared at the phone. Mieka and I had never had trouble communicating. Now, in the course of a half-hour, two people had advised me to talk to her. But the stakes were high. Neither of us could afford a misstep. We were both proud, and I knew that neither Mieka nor I would walk away or give in.

I was still staring at my cell when it rang. I hoped it was Mieka offering me an opening, but it was Ed.

"I thought I'd check in and see how my best man was doing the day after."

"I'm okay," I said.

"Just okay?"

"Reality is starting to set in," I said. "Jill called."

"I was sure she would. Jo, I hope you're not angry that I told her about what happened to your house. I thought she should know."

"And you were right. You saved me from having to go through the story one more time."

"Do you want me to come out to the lake? You sound a little down."

I looked around Leland's condo. More sins of omission. More coals heaped upon my head. "Ed, can I take you up on your offer to go through the house with me? I was just talking to the police, and they say it's safe."

"Choose a time, and I'll meet you there."

"Taylor gets out of school at three-thirty. Could I meet you at the house at two?"

"I'll be there."

Ready or not, life was moving along. I picked up my cell and pressed Mieka's number.

"How's everything in your kingdom this morning?" I said.

"Tranquil," she said. "I just walked the girls to school. Lena insisted on wearing the orchid from the wedding in her fake ponytail, and Madeleine took her orchid to Madame Turmel because we have a bouquet of orchids and Madame has none."

"The showgirl and the socialist," I said.

"Genes will tell," Mieka said.

"I don't remember any showgirl genes," I said. "But who knows? Mieka, you mentioned the other day that Riel had found a couple of possible sites for UpSlideDown2. I have some free time today. Do you think I could call him and get the addresses?"

"More than one way to skin a cat, huh?" Mieka said and there was an edge in her voice. "Did you talk to Zack about Riel and me?"

"I did. You know Zack. He wants this problem between

you and me fixed. And he wants it fixed fast. Calling Riel seemed like a good first step, but if I'm wrong . . ."

"You're not wrong," she said. "This is just so hard. I've been staring at the phone trying to decide whether the story about the ladies with their orchids was a good enough excuse to call you."

"Since when did we need an excuse to call each other?"

"Since you found out about Riel, I guess. I don't want to do the wrong thing either."

"We're all determined to make it through this. Just remember that we're on your side."

"And Riel's."

"And Riel's," I said, and I hoped I was convincing. "Mieka, Leland and Zack have been talking about adding a multipurpose complex to the Village Project – recreation centre, art gallery, and so on. It would be a shared facility with North Central. Leland wants to talk to Riel about it."

"Does Leland really want to talk to Riel or is he just doing it as a favour to you?"

"Does it matter? This isn't high school, Mieka. A man died. We've lost our home – at least for the foreseeable future. Someone has to *do* something."

"I'll call Riel," she said. "He'll be at work, but he can phone you. Are you at the lake?"

"Doing errands," I said quickly. "Just have him call my cell number. And, Mieka, I know Zack would appreciate a photo of the girls with the orchids."

"Check your BlackBerry. I already sent you both one."

I hung up and found the picture of the girls. They were both wearing crayon-bright T-shirts and shorts. Lena had half turned to give the camera the best possible shot of her ponytail; Madeleine was holding her orchid in both hands and gazing straight at the camera. I sent Zack a text telling him to check his BlackBerry and that I was going to try to connect with Riel. I knew Zack was in court, but it wasn't long before his answer arrived. It was to the point. "Do whatever it takes."

When I went into the living room to shut the terrace doors before I headed out to do errands, I noticed the file Angus had brought where I'd left it on the bookshelf. I took it down, carried it to the coffee table, and started to go through the clippings. I didn't get far. The picture of me holding my children's hands at Ian's funeral took me to a place I wasn't anxious to revisit.

In the months after Ian's death, friends and acquaintances praised the way I was handling the tragedy and getting on with our family's life. Their perception couldn't have been farther off the mark. I went through the necessary motions, but I had shut down. The only memory I have of that time is one I'd like to forget.

Every morning for what must have been weeks, I awoke to find Mieka at my bedside, her eyes anxious, asking me to get up and help her give the boys breakfast so they could all go to school. When the children left, I started my day. I did laundry, grocery shopped, answered phone calls, cleaned the house, stared at my unfinished dissertation, made supper, and counted the hours until I could tuck the kids in, take a sleeping pill, and be oblivious until morning. I survived, but those weeks left me with the knowledge that I lived on the edge of a crumbling cliff, and that I had to be very careful not to lose my foothold.

I flipped through the clippings till I came to a page recording an election victory. I stared at the pictures of that triumphant night and tried to remember what it was like to be young and unafraid.

I took a cab to the Volvo dealership where I filled out the forms for leasing a station wagon that was the twin of my car, which Zack would have to drive until a new car could be fitted with hand controls.

Zack had always driven a Jaguar, so my next stop was the Jaguar dealership for some brochures. I was sitting in a deep, swank leather chair, thumbing through photos of cars that cost more than many families earned in a year when Riel called. The irony was not lost on me.

Riel and I greeted each other with careful politeness.

"If you're serious about looking at a couple of possibilities for UpSlidedown2, we're in luck." Riel said. "I work for Northern Tree, and our chipper just broke. It's going to take a couple of hours to fix, so if you'd like company, I'm available."

"Then we're on," I said. "Where shall we meet?"

"I caught a ride to work with a buddy. We could save time if you picked me up. We're out trimming poplars at the old cemetery. Corner of 4th and Broad."

"I'll be there in twenty minutes."

Riel was wearing work clothes, and they were soiled. He didn't get into the car right away. "Have you a got a towel or something I can sit on?" he asked.

"Don't worry about it," I said. "This is the same car I have. We chose it because the leather can be wiped off. Hop in."

Riel's body was tense as he entered the car, and when he spoke, he stared ahead, not looking at me. "There were two places I thought we might look at, a deconsecrated church that's become a drop-in centre and a deconsecrated synagogue that's become a dance studio."

"Signs of the times," I said.

The church was depressing, but even from the curb, the old synagogue was appealing. I opened the door, but Riel made no move to get out.

"Aren't you coming?" I asked.

"The building's open. I called ahead. There's a class going on. I'll stay with the car. You don't want to come back and find it keyed."

"The last time our car got keyed, it was parked in front of our house," I said. "Riel, I'd like us to look at the building together."

The main floor of the old stone synagogue was open and spacious, with shining wooden floors and a mirrored wall for the dancers. There was indeed a class going on – a dozen little boys in the four-year-old range were jumping, rolling, leaping, waddling, and having what appeared to be a grand time. Their teacher, a whip-thin brunette, waved us in and moved back to her charges.

Riel and I stood for a moment at the edge of the dance space, watching the action, and then we moved along the edge of the space towards the kitchen, bathrooms, and office at back. Everything was bright and solid, but the old syna-gogue was about half the size of the building that we had sold to make way for the Village Project.

"I like this one," I said. "What do you and Mieka think about the size?"

"No question – we'd have to expand it. You think it's worth looking into?"

"Sure. Who owns the building?"

"A nice young hippie couple with a baby. They had a dream, but it betrayed them by making them rich."

"What was their dream?"

"To introduce SYLVANI to Saskatchewan." Riel smiled "And don't ask me what SYLVANI is. All I know is that it's some kind of dance and that Prairie and Rhyse can't keep up with the demand for classes, and they need a bigger space."

I walked across the room to check out the kitchen and bathrooms in the back. "This place definitely has possibilities," I said, "but expansion costs money. How much do the nice young hippies want for this building?"

I whistled at the sum Riel named. "I guess the big bad world of capitalism taught Prairie and Rhyse a thing or two about real estate. Anything else we should look at?"

Riel shook his head. "These were the only two sites that I thought might work. I know the idea behind UpSlide-Down2 is outreach, but unless we're prepared to have a crack house or a shooting gallery next door, our location options are limited."

"What's a shooting gallery?"

Riel raised his left arm and mimed the action of injecting himself. "You don't want kids playing next door to a shooting gallery," he said. "There are needles all over the ground."

"And this neighbourhood is safe?"

Riel's mouth twitched. "Everything's relative, but yes. I talked to Prairie and Rhyse. They have classes all day and well into the evening and they say they've never had a serious problem."

When we walked back, I stopped for a moment to watch the little boys. They were dancing a freestyle hip-hop on the shining floor and admiring their moves in the mirrored wall. "This place has a really good feel," I said.

"It does," Riel agreed. "So the synagogue is top of the list?"

I smiled at him. "It's a short list, but yes. This building feels right to me."

Nobody had keyed the Volvo. I ran my finger along the doors on the passenger side. "Look at that," I said. "Not a mark."

"That's a relief," Riel said. "So do you want me to arrange a meeting with Prairie and Rhyse?"

"Let's sleep on it," I said. "The building has potential, but we should find out if the buildings on either side are for sale, and if they are, whether they're in our price range."

Riel's laugh was short and bitter. "I still don't think things through, do I?" he said. "That's what you wrote on one of my papers: 'Dig more deeply here. Think things through.' I wish I'd listened."

"Riel, I've written those words on dozens of student papers. They weren't a comment on your life."

"It would have been a valid comment."

I met his eyes. "Were you involved in what happened to our house?"

He pounded his fist into his palm. "Jesus, if I were involved in the explosion at your house, do you think I would have come along on this little shopping expedition of yours? Do you think I would have gone to the cops the morning after your house blew up? Give me a little credit, Professor Kilbourn, and while you're at it, *you* dig a little more deeply. *You* think things through. Ask yourself who was responsible for creating an atmosphere where destroying someone else's home was seen as an acceptable option."

"You believe we brought the explosion on ourselves because of our association with Leland Hunter?" I said.

Riel's eyes were cold. "I think it might be time for you to take a look in the mirror."

I was close to telling Riel to find another way back to work, then I remembered Zack's message when Mieka sent the pictures of the girls with their orchids. "Do what it takes," he'd texted. So I tried again.

"I think we're all aware that mistakes have been made," I said, "but that doesn't mean they can't be rectified. Did Mieka tell you about Leland's plan to make a shared multipurpose complex part of the Village Project?"

Riel's jaw was set. "I'll believe it when I see it."

"Would you at least talk to Leland?" I said. "Find out what he has to say."

"Leland Hunter wouldn't talk to me."

"He's already agreed to," I said.

Riel's eyes flashed with anger. "So if I refuse to meet with him, I'm the guy who would rather lead his people over the cliff than take the enemy's hand."

"If your ego trumps the interests of the people you represent, I guess so," I said.

He gave me a sharp look. "That's how you see it?"

"That's the truth, isn't it?"

Riel spit out an expletive. When he started walking towards the bus stop, I didn't protest. I just sat and watched.

I was only a few blocks from Peter's clinic on Winnipeg Street so I called him and invited myself for coffee. I once described my sons by saying that Angus was the one who gave me an aerobic workout, but Peter was my yoga. From the beginning, there was a natural peace about Peter that seemed to move into me by osmosis when I was with him. That morning I was in serious need of an infusion of serenity.

In deciding to open a walk-in vet clinic in the Core, Peter had pretty well abandoned any hope of ever retiring. Except for a loyal group who had been Peter's friends since they were in pre-school together, most of Pete's clients paid him little or nothing. When income didn't match outlay, Zack and I helped out and we were happy to do it. We were a family of animal lovers and we understood the bond that exists between a pet and its owner.

In its previous life, Pete's clinic had been a pawnshop and because there were drugs on the premises, Pete had been forced to leave the bars on the windows. That detail aside, the walk-in clinic was a cheerful place. The walls were bright with posters giving advice about pet care and crayoned thank-you notes from satisfied clients. Even on school days, there were always kids with pets in Pete's waiting room. School attendance was regarded as optional in this neighbourhood, but whatever else was going on in their lives, the boys and girls of the area always found time to bring in pets with problems.

When Pete's new assistant, Ruth, ushered me into his examining room, Pete was explaining spaying to a young girl with a litter of new kittens. Ruth, a lithe and serious young woman from Botswana, took over the explanation without skipping a beat, and Peter and I went back to the staff room, where he poured us each a mug of coffee.

I took a sip. "Hey, this is a definite improvement," I said.

"You mean from the floor sweepings we usually have," Pete said. "Well, thank Ruth. She doesn't even drink coffee, but she said no one should be forced to drink swill."

"So Ruth's working out," I said.

"She's great," Pete said. "It's only been two weeks, but it's as if she's been at the clinic forever. She seems to know instinctively what needs to be done and she does it."

"Good. And how's Dacia?"

"After Ed and Barry's wedding, we had a long talk and decided to go our separate ways."

"Peter, I'm sorry. We really liked Dacia."

"I liked her, too, but it never seemed to get beyond that."

"Is there somebody else?"

He smiled. "Not yet. I'm not Angus, Mum. I usually wait till the ex is out the door before I bring in the replacement."

I laughed. "Angus is bringing Leah's replacement to the lake for Canada Day. The new woman is a lawyer and a lacrosse player, and her name is Maisie."

"And she's a knockout," Pete said.

"You've seen her."

"Nope. I'm just going by past history."

I took another sip of coffee. "Have you met your sister's new man?"

"Riel Delorme? Sure, we live in the same neighbourhood."

"And . . . ?"

Pete shrugged. "I'll say what you always say, 'as long as he makes her happy . . . '"

"But you don't like him."

"I like him. I just can't see him with Mieka. I never thought of her as political and Riel's a real firebrand."

"He is that," I said. I went to the sink and rinsed my mug. "You're really okay about the breakup with Dacia."

"More than okay. It wasn't going anywhere. We're both relieved it's over."

I hugged him. "Be sure and thank Ruth for the new and improved brand of coffee."

Pete chuckled. "You are so not subtle," he said.

"Comes with the territory," I said.

After I left Peter's I drove to 13th Avenue to buy the ingredients for paella – a dish that Zack and I liked but Taylor adored. As I stood in Pacific Fish watching Cassie, the owner, wrap the prawns, mussels, and clams, I felt as if once again I was on familiar turf. I picked up baguette at the bakery and crossed to the supermarket. As I strode up and down the aisles filling my cart, my confidence flowed back, as bracing as good health after an illness. This was my world – large, safe, and predictable.

When I got back to Halifax Street, I put away the groceries and went to our room to change into my jeans. I'd just put on a fresh T-shirt when I heard a crash upstairs. Under normal circumstances, I would have simply gone up to investigate. But circumstances were no longer normal. My heart was racing; my mind leaped to the conclusion that whoever had blown up our house had found us here, and I panicked. I looked frantically around the room for my phone, then remembered it was in my purse in the kitchen. I ran in sock feet across the condo, skirting the open living room, terrified that whoever was upstairs would see me. I held my breath and, hands shaking, fumbled through my bag for my BlackBerry. I was just about to hit 911 when I heard a cry from upstairs. The voice was female and my first thought was that it was a trick to get me to the second floor where I'd be more vulnerable. The woman called again. "Help. Leland? It's Louise. I need help!"

I dropped my BlackBerry back in my purse and ran upstairs. "Louise, where are you?" I said.

There was no response.

I called her name again. This time she answered. "Go to hell, Margot. Just leave me alone."

Louise's voice was coming from the master suite. She was in the bathroom. A highball glass had shattered on the porcelain floor. Louise was standing in the middle of the room, swaying slightly, staring at the melting ice and broken crystal.

"What's the matter?" I said. There was a triple mirror in the bathroom, and my reflection was a shock. I looked terrified.

"I dropped my glass," she said.

Suddenly I was furious. "So you cried for help." I turned away. "Clean up your mess, Louise. Clean up your mess and get out."

She stepped back and steadied herself against the bathroom counter. "What are you doing here, Joanne?"

"I could ask you the same question," I said.

Her laugh was forced. "Well, this is Leland's condominium, and he *is* my husband."

"Louise . . ."

She raised her hand to cut me off before I said more. "I know. Leland is my ex-husband, but that doesn't mean we've stopped loving each other. He's making a terrible mistake. He and I have been together since we were in high school. We swore we'd stay together forever . . ." She touched the platinum cuff bracelet that she was never without. "Leland gave this to me when Peyben opened its first international office. He said the world was ours."

"Louise, people change."

Her eyes, as blue as the eyes of a china doll, glittered unseeing. Though she was swaying, Louise was still sober, but her fantasy left no room for reality. "I called Leland's office. They said he was working at home. He and I need to talk." She took a step towards me. "He's not committed to Margot Wright. I knew that, but now I have evidence. He still has groceries here. I checked the cupboards and the refrigerator downstairs. Leland's particular about food. Everything has to be fresh, and everything here is fresh. He's not living with her."

She walked over and touched my hand. "Don't you understand, Joanne? He still has doubts."

I remembered how perfectly attuned Margot and Leland had been the night before, lovers swimming in unison, their powerful bodies illuminated by the lights embedded in the pool's aquamarine walls. They had found everything they wanted in each other.

"Let's go downstairs, Louise," I said. "We'll be more comfortable there."

I poured us glasses of cool water from the refrigerator. Louise drained hers, then opened one of the lower cabinet doors. She quickly found what she was looking for. When she splashed the Grey Goose vodka into her glass, her fingers were trembling. "I'll just have a small one – Dutch courage. Isn't that what they call it? Of course, this vodka is made in France." Her brilliantly blue eyes sought out mine. "I don't suppose you'd care to join me."

"I'm fine, but thanks."

Louise took her drink into the living room and perched on the end of one of the reading chairs. I followed her with my water. Neither of us spoke. When there was a knock at the door, Louise and I both started. I'd had no idea that Louise had the security code to our condo. Suddenly it seemed that somebody else did.

I opened the door cautiously. When I saw that the person in the hall was Sage Mackenzie, I relaxed.

She looked past me into the entrance hall. "I've come for Louise," she said.

"Follow me," I said. When we reached the living room, Sage and I stood side by side for a beat, waiting for Louise to make the next move.

It was sadly predictable. She drained her drink. As she placed her empty glass on the table beside her, Louise's frail shoulders slumped with defeat. Her shining plan for a surprise visit with Leland was in shreds and time was running out. My heart went out to her, and then I remembered the phone call Leland received the night we were at Magoo's. Louise was a sad figure, but apparently she was also a dangerous one. Sage Mackenzie was not my favourite person, but she stood between Louise and her worst impulses and for that I was grateful.

Sage also seemed to be making an effort. The file of clippings was still open on the coffee table. Sage glanced at it and raised an eyebrow. "Retired but still working on politicians," she said. Her eyes travelled around the room. "I'm assuming Leland Hunter is letting you use his condo until your own house is repaired."

"No," I said. "We're living at the lake. I just come here for a break if I have to stay in town to pick up Zack or our daughter." The lie had formed itself easily, and both Sage and Louise seemed to accept it.

Sage moved towards the window. "Well, you certainly have a great view while you're killing time," she said.

Up close, Sage was older than I'd thought on convocation day. Her eyes, pale-lashed and amber, were riveting, but there were already faint lines at their corners and at the corners of her small and determined mouth. Her fiery hair was smoothed back into a chignon and she was wearing the uniform of many successful female lawyers: a well-cut black business suit, hem slightly above the knee, expensive white blouse, minimal but good jewellery.

She placed her hand on Louise's arm. "Louise, let's get you home. I'll drive. I can take a cab back and pick up my car."

"I only had one drink," Louise said.

Sage's voice softened. "Let's not take any chances."

The misery drained from Louise's face. "You're a good friend," she said.

Sage smiled at her. "I do my best."

When the door closed after the two women, I made a note to ask Leland about the security in the building. The next person who managed to make it to our door might be someone more menacing than Louise's "good friend." I walked back into the living room, picked up the file, took it to the linen closet, and tucked it under a stack of pillow-cases. I didn't need reminders of the past; the present was troubling enough.

CHAPTER

9

Ten minutes after Ed Mariani and I began our inspection of what was left of our house on the creek, I knew that bringing him with me was a mistake. From the moment we arrived, Ed tried to keep my spirits up. When the police gave us hard hats to wear, Ed plunked his on, gave me a cherubic smile, and said, "Is this where I break into a chorus of 'YMCA'"? He was courtly as he presented me with a small paper notebook and a pen to record items that would need replacing, and he insisted on walking ahead of me in case there was danger.

I had seen the house the day after the explosion, so I had an idea of the extent of the devastation. Ed wasn't prepared, and as we looked at what remained of our double garage and the indoor pool that was essential for Zack's physical well-being, Ed was visibly shaken. I tried to keep it light. In my notebook, I printed a heading: NEED TO REPLACE. Beneath the heading I wrote: one garage and contents – car included. When I showed my list to Ed, his smile was strained.

I had known Ed for more than two decades. He was a man who savoured life's pleasures: a garden that bloomed from April through October, large airy rooms with furnishings that welcomed, convivial meals, chilled wine, the touch of a friend's hand. To him, the chaotic rubble that had been the kitchen and family room where we had been happy together was a rebuke. He shuddered as he took in the damage, but he couldn't seem to tear himself away. Finally, I touched his arm. "Time to move along," I said. He led the way, but his step, usually so light for a big man, was heavy and his face sagged. It was as if the destruction around us had penetrated his body as it had penetrated mine.

The farther we walked from the explosion site, the less acute the damage. The windows were blown out of our living room and the office Zack and I shared, but the bedrooms appeared to be intact. The two paintings that hung on the wall that faced our bed were unscathed. One of them was Taylor's first abstract; the other by colourist Scott Plear was a favourite of Ed's, but when I pointed out that both pieces were fine, Ed didn't comment.

When he moved towards the doors that opened from Zack's and my bedroom into the garden, Ed was pale. Our garden was Ed's pride. He had helped us plan it so that there would always be something in bloom, and many of the plants had come from his own greenhouse. I put my arm through his. "Come on," I said. "We've seen enough. We'll look at the garden another day."

For the first time in our relationship, Ed shook me off. "No," he said. Ed had a pleasantly musical speaking voice, but that day his voice was harsh and broken. "We have to know exactly what we're dealing with. We can't let those animals win."

Our backyard looked like a staging for a bizarre before-and-after photo shoot. The east side of the yard, the part that included Taylor's studio, still had the sweet greenness of June. The west side was a warzone. The explosion had strafed the copse of Japanese lilacs by the garage. A jagged black hole

was all that remained of our once thriving tomato patch. Fire
had scorched the lawn and dried the leaves of the forsythia
bushes, making them as brown and fragile as cured tobacco.

"Why would anyone do this?" Ed asked, and his voice
was both troubled and baffled.

"I don't know," I said. "When we were walking through
the house, I kept thinking of this client of Zack's. He was a
young offender, so of course I never knew his name. But he
had a record of serious vandalism. He'd break into homes
like ours and just wreck them. He didn't seem to care if he
got caught."

"Was they're some connection between him and the
homeowners?"

"None, and as it turned out that was the heart of the
matter. Zack was the boy's lawyer, so of course he tried to
talk with the parents. He made appointments with them to
come to the office, but they never showed up, so Zack went
to their house. It was on Winnipeg Street. Zack pounded on
the door, and when there was no response, he went in. His
client was sitting on the floor watching TV, fighting off a
cat for his plate of Rice-A-Roni. The mother was passed out
on the couch. The boy's sister was in the bedroom with a
paying client. The whole place was beyond filthy. Guess
what the boy was watching?"

"Cartoons?"

"A home improvement show. He told Zack that was all
he watched."

Ed winced. "Jesus."

"I guess at a certain point the rage just boils over," I said.

When Ed and I returned to the front of the house, two men
with clipboards were standing on the lawn, seemingly
assessing our property. Both were lanky with snub noses,
sandy blond hair, and the permanent sunburn of fair-skinned

people who work outdoors. I assumed they were father and son. I also assumed they worked for Leland. I was right on both counts.

The older of the two men approached me. "You must be Joanne Shreve," he said. "The police said that you and your friend were going through the house. I'm Andy O'Neill, and this is my son, Drew. We're project managers for Peyben. Mr. Hunter asked us to stop by."

"So what's the verdict?" I said.

"I can't say anything definitive until we've had a chance to look inside, but it's a solid house. The contractor did good work."

"Do you think the damage can be repaired?"

The son frowned. "It's too soon to make a decision. When a property sustains a blow like that, there can be weaknesses you can't detect at first. If the weaknesses are there, sooner or later, they can undermine the whole building."

"Life's full of metaphors," I said.

Andy's laugh was short. "You're a cool one, Ms. Shreve."

"Not really, "I said. "But I am working on it."

As it turned out, my coolness was put to an immediate test. When Ed and I arrived, I'd noticed a scattering of rubber-neckers gasping and gaping at the devastation that was once our home. Ed had muttered something about schadenfreude, and we'd moved along. But as we turned to go to our cars, I saw that the number of rubberneckers had been increased by two. Louise Hunter and Sage Mackenzie were on the sidewalk looking intently at the debris.

"Pretty awful, isn't it?" I said.

Louise turned, the flush of embarrassment at being caught gawking already spreading from her neck to her face. "It's terrible to think that you could have been here," she said. "Declan told me that if you hadn't gone to the lake a day early you would have been asleep and God knows what might have happened then."

Sage was surveying the scene coolly. "Remarkably, the explosion barely touched the bedrooms," she said. Her amber eyes shifted to me. "You must have been born under a lucky star, Joanne."

"I guess I was," I said.

On our way back from Taylor's school, she and I stopped off at the mall to pick up underwear and other essentials for the next few days. Clearly my definition of *essentials* differed from our daughter's, but it was fun to check out the frillies at La Senza, and Taylor got a dynamite deal on some Santa bras. When we got back to the condo, Taylor ran upstairs to her second-floor retreat and I headed for the kitchen.

I'm an orderly cook. I assemble all the ingredients before I begin. I make certain everything I need is at hand, and then I begin. It's important for me to know that if I plan carefully and follow the steps outlined in a recipe, I'll end up with the result I'm going for.

That afternoon, as the sun streamed in the condo windows, I checked my purchases against the list of ingredients in my paella recipe and felt the pleasure of being in control. Then unbidden and unwelcome, the memory of my old kitchen in the house on the creek filled my mind. I could have made a dish like paella blindfolded there.

But I wasn't there. I was here on Halifax Street in a kitchen that was as perfect and soulless as a magazine ad. As I waited for the olive oil to heat, I seasoned the chicken breasts and dusted them with flour. When the oil was sizzling, I sautéed the chorizo, then removed it and browned the chicken. As I chopped the onions, garlic, and parsley for the sofrito, the familiar aromas filled the air, and I knew how Alice felt when she stepped through the looking-glass and found herself in a world that was recognizable in many ways yet was not her own.

I was peeling and deveining the shrimp when Zack called.

"This is a nice surprise," I said. "How come you're not in court?"

"Ten-minute recess – just long enough for me to take a leak and check in with Norine. Guess what? Good news – the cops gave her the okay to have the art that survived delivered to Halifax Street and our clothing sent to a dry-cleaner who specializes in smoke damage. So what are you up to?"

"At the moment, I'm making paella."

"To make Taylor feel at home?"

"To make us all feel at home."

"Good call. Gotta go. Love you, Jo."

"I love you, too," I said. But I was talking to empty air. Zack had already hung up.

It was an afternoon where I had nothing but time, and setting the table on the terrace was a pleasant task. Like everything else in the condo, the linens and dishes evoked the lush beauty of Tuscany. The tablecloth I chose was a swirl of orange and red – the perfect complement for dinner-ware the colour of a ripe pear. As I moved, the sunshine and the moist heavy air pressed down on me. Finally, I sat in one of the chairs, tilted my head to the sun, and, eyes closed, listened to the rustling of ornamental grasses in the terra cotta pot beside the patio door. The Italians were right: *dolce far niente.* It can be very sweet to do nothing.

Zack was home at six. He had his trial bag slung over the back of his wheelchair and as frequently happened when I saw him, I felt a spark of lust. I leaned in and kissed him. He ran his hands over my hips and growled. "Is there more where this is coming from?"

"You have no idea," I said, "but Taylor's upstairs and if the paella burns, we're out $37.00 worth of seafood."

"There's always KFC," Zack said. He smacked his lips. "Paella, sex, and fried chicken. This could be a memorable evening. Do we have time for a drink?"

"We'll make time," I said. I followed Zack into the kitchen and watched as he mixed the martinis. When he handed me mine, I took a sip. "This is one of my favourite times of the day – the time when we have a drink and just talk."

"You might not love it so much today. Cronus passed along some troubling news about Riel Delorme. It turns out Riel's been a busy guy the past few years."

I felt a prickle of fear. "So what's he been doing?"

"Not to put too fine a point on it, screwing up and attempting to deal with the consequences. Anyway, as you know, Cronus built his empire renting out houses in North Central, so when Riel started talking to the tenants about their rights and showing them how to contact inspectors from public health and the fire department, Cronus hired somebody to do some digging. It turns out that when Riel dropped out of university, he was a full-fledged Marxist and revolutionary. Apparently, his apartment was filled with everything that had ever been written by or about Che Guevara."

"That's not surprising," I said. "Riel was considering Che as the subject of his master's thesis."

"Well, according to Cronus's information, Riel was doing some writing of his own that wasn't scholarly. It was incendiary, and the message was always the same: the only way for oppressed people to make progress was to unite and fight together."

"That's no different from anything Tommy Douglas or Gandhi or Martin Luther King advocated."

"Maybe, but none of them advocated violence. Riel told

his people that the oppressed had to match the oppressors weapon for weapon."

The image of Lena giggling as Riel swung her through the air flashed through my mind. "I can't believe Riel would incite violence," I said, but as I spoke the words, I remembered Riel's furious assertion that by associating with the man who had razed blocks of houses for the Village Project, Zack and I had invited the destruction of our own home. "Does Cronus have any evidence?" I asked.

"He says he had tapes of speeches where Riel called for an armed insurrection."

I was incredulous. "And the police didn't know?"

"They knew. Cronus isn't stupid." Zack's frustration was palpable. "Riel was turning out to be a major pain in the ass for him, so he took all the information he'd gathered and dropped it at the cop shop. Just being a good citizen, of course."

"Zack, if the police had all that evidence against Riel, why didn't they arrest him?"

"That's the question that Cronus raised with his previous lawyer. God, I wish I'd got this case sooner. Not to speak ill of the dead, but the late Guy LaRose must have been a real soup can. He was dying, but he knew that he had obligations to his client. If he couldn't do the job, he should have told Cronus to get another lawyer."

"And he didn't," I said.

"No. Guy forced Cronus to hang with him till death did them part, and at the end Guy made a real hash of his case. When Cronus told him that Delorme might have had a reason to set him up for Arden Raeburn's murder, La Rose told him that raising questions about Delorme was just a distraction."

"And Cronus accepted that?"

"Yes, because not long after Cronus dumped his information at the cop shop, Riel did a 180. Cronus thinks Riel finally figured out what any seven-year-old kid in North

Central knew – that the gangs are dangerous and they are uncontrollable. Anyway, that's when Riel stepped away from the secret meetings and militancy and began working out of the Willy Hodgson Centre and co-operating with the police."

"That doesn't explain why the police didn't follow through on the information Cronus brought them," I said. "Riel might have decided to back away, but he *had* attempted to recruit a group of armed militants to his cause."

"Agreed. Something stinks here, but right now I just don't have the time to go into it. I'm struggling for time, Jo. All I can do is try to dig up evidence that despite his un-savoury past, Cronus did not kill Arden Raeburn."

"Cronus's history isn't admissible, is it?" I said.

Zack sighed. "Not unless he testifies, which he will do over my dead body."

I winced. "Can't you just tell Cronus he can't testify?"

"Nope, all I can do is tell him that I strongly recommend against him taking the stand, and I've done that. If Cronus testifies, the Crown prosecutor can cross-examine him on everything questionable in his past, and believe me there's plenty: fights with tenants that ended up in front of the Rentalsman; perpetual litigation in small claims court, and behaviour towards women that, to put it charitably, has been less than chivalrous. Cronus is no Boy Scout, but I'd bet the farm that he was set up for this murder. The problem is I don't have a clue by whom or why."

I linked my fingers with Zack's. "You know what I think?" I said.

"I think we should have had a second martini."

"It's never too late," Zack said.

"It is for me," I said. "If I have another martini, I'll do a face plant in the paella."

"Rough day?"

"I've had better," I said. "But tell me about how things went in court."

"Let's see. I huffed and I puffed and I blew a few holes in the Crown's argument, and then Linda huffed and puffed and blew a few holes in my argument, so I'd say it was a draw."

"How did Cronus do?"

"He ignored my suggestion to dress down – he showed up in a $2,000 suit, a really great tie, and Ferragamo shoes."

"That's the way you dress."

"True, but the jury doesn't need to bond with me."

"So you're going to have to win on the facts?"

"Looks like."

Taylor and I carried the food out to the terrace, Zack opened a chilled bottle of pinot grigio, and we dug in.

I watched as Taylor took her first bite. "Mmm," she said. "This is good."

"As good as Barry's?"

She took another forkful and considered. "Close," she said.

"I'm going to count that as four stars out of a possible five," I said.

Zack turned to her. "So how did the kids at school react to the explosion at our house?"

She shrugged. "Fine. When I got there, everyone made a big deal of being sympathetic, and by second period they were all back to obsessing about what they were wearing to the All-College."

Zack stopped, fork in midair. "One of life's great lessons," he said. "Everybody's got their own shit. They don't really give a shit about your shit."

Taylor lowered her eyes, concentrating on her food, but her lips were twitching. She glanced at me, waiting to see if I was going to issue a language warning. I didn't. "Your dad's right," I said. "People have their own lives. And our family has more than enough to deal with. Ed and I went through the house today."

The news I was about to deliver was harsh, and Taylor and Zack both knew it. Zack reached across the table and took our daughter's hand.

"So how bad is it?" he asked.

"It's bad," I said. "Everything in the east half of the house is pretty well gone. The bedrooms are all right. The police wouldn't let us look at the basement, but I think it's safe to assume there'll be structural damage there."

"So what's left?" Taylor asked, her voice small.

"Your mother's paintings are still on loan to that retrospective, so they're safe. And the Scott Plear and your abstract were in our bedroom, so they're fine. Nothing in your bedroom was touched."

"But the room where the pool was is gone?" she asked.
I nodded.

"So the fresco I painted on the walls is gone?"
"Yes."

"And the self-portrait I gave Dad for Christmas?"
"It was in the family room."

"And the family room is gone?" Taylor's eyes brimmed with tears, but she set her mouth in a determined line and turned to Zack. "I'll paint another one."

"Thanks," Zack said. "Because that portrait was the last thing I looked at every morning before I went to work. If I was taking a beating in court, I'd remind myself that the girl in that painting was my daughter. That always put things into perspective."

"As soon as I get my supplies, I'll start," Taylor said. She hesitated. "Where am I going to paint?"

"Upstairs," I said. "We caught a break with your studio. It's well away from the house so your art supplies are fine. Norine called a company that will deliver everything tomorrow."

"Where are we going to put all that stuff?"

"That's up to you," I said. "You've got a huge space on the second floor. That master bedroom is three times the size of your bedroom at home, and the guest bedroom and the office are both large. I thought you might want to use the master bedroom as a studio and have the smaller rooms for your bedroom and whatever else you need."

Taylor's brow crinkled. "Are we going to be here that long?"

"It looks like we are. I didn't want to tell you before dinner, Zack, but Ed and I met some of Leland's men outside the house. They think we may have to start over with the house."

"You mean, tear it down?"

"I think that's a possibility."

Zack wheeled back from the table and looked around the condo. "This isn't all that bad," he said.

Taylor shrugged. "It's beautiful, but we're going to have to make it feel as if we really live here."

"I've seen what you can do to a room," Zack said. "I don't think that's going to be a problem."

For the first time since we started talking about the old house, Taylor smiled. "I do kind of unfurl, don't I?" she said. She had her mother's broad mouth and her smile was open and infectious. "Do you know what I think we need right now?"

"What?" Zack said.

"A swim. We're all tired and crazy. That pool in the court-yard looks really nice."

"I brought our suits from the lake," I said. "And Taylor's right, Zack. I think we all need to un-knot."

Zack scowled. "I don't feel like a swim."

Taylor went over and kissed his head. "Because you don't like strangers looking at your legs." Her voice dropped into the growl Zack used when he was uttering one of his saltier pronouncements. "You know, Dad, everybody's got their own shit. And they don't really give a shit about your shit."

Zack held out his hands, palms up, in a gesture of surrender. "Fair enough," he said. "Time for me to man up and hit the pool."

In Regina in mid-June the sun sets at around 9:15 p.m., which meant that after a half-hour of vigorous swimming with Taylor, Zack and I were still in bed in time to watch the fading of the last light of day.

For a while we were silent, then Zack said, "The swim was a good idea. We should do it every night."

"I'll hold you to that," I said, "but tomorrow night we'll be swimming late. It's Linda Fritz's dinner for Margot."

"I don't have it on my calendar."

"That's because you're not invited. It's for women only."

"Ah, Margot's stagette."

"Can you imagine Linda Fritz giving a party with girly drinks and male strippers?"

Zack's laugh was low. "No, I can't. Linda's fun, but she's not that kind of fun. So – just an all-female dinner."

"With a twist," I said. "Since Margot's so proud of being a Wadena girl, the menu is all Saskatchewan. The invitation said, 'Go locovores!' What are Leland's friends doing for him?"

"A bunch of us are going to the Broken Rack. I'm guessing we'll shoot a few games of pool, drink a few brewskis, and tell a few jokes."

"To each his own," I said.

Zack's only response was a snort that graduated into a satisfied snore.

CHAPTER

10

The next morning at five, when Leland and I stepped out of our building, he was quick to get to the point.

"Mind if we talk a little while we run today?"

"Not at all."

"The situation with the Village Project is not good," Leland said. "The police don't know for certain if Danny Racette's death and the explosion at your house are directly tied to the redevelopment, but that's the public perception, and it's hurting us. The media are no longer painting our mayor as the golden boy who's cleaning up the slums. Now he's the political bumbler who committed the city to an ill-advised project that's caused a man's death and a bombing in an upper-middle-class neighbourhood. People who have no stake whatsoever in the project are starting to take sides, and they're not taking our side. Joanne, I was sick about what happened to your house, but there was a small part of me that thought the bombing might have been providential."

"How could that possibly have been 'providential'?" I said.

"Because it exposed the thugs opposing the Village Project for what they are," Leland said. "Criminals whose only interest is destroying what other people work for. But nobody's giving our side the benefit of the doubt. The police have completely cleared us of fault, but people still believe Danny Racette died because of workplace negligence. "

"What's the public perception of what happened to our house?" I said.

Leland shrugged. "Some of our fellow citizens aren't crazy about people who are successful."

"Zack is the millionaire lawyer who takes on question-able clients and deserves what he gets?" I said.

Leland's smile was faint. "Something along that line."

"And I'm the wife of the millionaire lawyer who doesn't care if blood money pays for my nice life."

"Sticks and stones. It's the price of doing business, Joanne. But I have an idea about how to turn perceptions around. You and I talked about the possibility of Peyben building a shared multipurpose facility as part of the Village Project. Obviously, there are a number of issues that have to be hammered out between us and people like Delorme, who are opposed to the project. What do you think about us approaching Delorme and asking him to make the conver-sation between him and me public?"

"You mean a public forum?"

"No. The facts are on my side. I could win a debate against Delorme without breaking a sweat. But that would mean winning a battle and losing the war. Delorme and I need each other. He needs to show that he can do things for North Central."

"And you need to show that The Village isn't just a devel-opment, it's a way of changing the face of our city."

"Right," Leland said. "And that means getting as much publicity as possible. I think Delorme and I can stage some-thing that will work for both of us, and this is where you come in. I saw two of those shows you wrote for NationTV giving people an inside view of the institutions that govern their lives. Do you think your producer would be interested in showing a conciliation process from the inside?"

"Peyben sitting down with the group who opposes The Village?"

"More personal than that – me sitting down with Riel Delorme."

"Working out the agreement for the shared facility while the cameras roll? You and Riel would both have a lot on the line, Leland."

"We already do," he said. "Delorme doesn't trust me, and I'm not sure I trust him. If we make our deliberations public, there's more pressure on both of us to come through. If I commit myself publicly, he'll know I can't back out. And if Delorme can get this for the community, he'll show that he's a leader to be reckoned with."

"And Red Rage is just going to slink off into the sunset?"

"No. But they won't be able to take credit. They're criminals, Joanne, and criminals don't welcome the spotlight."

"I'm not sure about this, Leland. In theory the plan is great, but I don't think Riel will go along with it. Yesterday, I said you were interested in talking to him about the shared multipurpose centre. He was furious. He thought the invitation was a trap."

"Because if I made the offer public, and Delorme didn't accept, he'd look bad in his community."

"Riel's words were more dramatic. He said if he turned you down he'd be seen as the guy who would rather lead his people over the cliff than take the enemy's hand."

"That's a little self-dramatizing, isn't it?"

"He's young and idealistic," I said.

"Then it's time for him to grow up," Leland said. "He can't afford to lose this one. Neither can I. Neither can you. Neither can North Central. You're going to have to try again, Jo. Mention the TV angle. Delorme sounds like a guy with a big ego. I'll bet he'll go for it."

Okay," I said. "I'll talk to Riel again. And I'll call the producer I worked with at NationTV. Jill Oziowy's smart, she's fair, and she's principled. She can also be very convincing. I'll see if I can get her to talk to Riel."

"That's all I'm asking," Leland said. He gave me one of his slow-blooming transforming smiles. "I'm in favour of anything that will speed the day when we take down that security fence around the condo and Margot and I become part of the neighbourhood."

We spent the last half of our run talking about what would need to be done to the master suite in the condo to transform it into a studio, and Leland promised to get some of his men on the job that day.

Leland wasn't joking: Zack and Taylor had barely left when the crew from Peyben arrived. There were three men: all were muscular, all were young, and all were unnervingly deferential. I led to them to the second floor and explained what we needed.

When I expressed concern about the floors in the room that would be Taylor's studio, a freckled redhead who had introduced himself as Colton was reassuring. "We're installing temporary protective covering. We know our job, Ms. Shreve. You don't have to worry about a thing."

So I left them to it and went downstairs to read the morning paper and decide what to do with my day. As was often the case, the day presented its own agenda. I wasn't eager to talk to Riel, but I knew that I'd be fretting until I made the call. I didn't have Riel's number, so I had to phone Mieka. By now, Riel would have undoubtedly told her about our ugly exchange outside the old synagogue, so I was dreading the call, but Mieka was clearly relieved to hear from me.

"I was just going to phone you, Mum," she said. "Riel waited until this morning to tell me about the fight you two had yesterday."

"And . . . ?"

"And I told him I thought he should apologize. I also told him that the shared facility could be a great thing for North Central, and he should at least talk to Leland Hunter about it."

I was taken aback. "Wow. Thanks. Mieka, do you think I should call Riel?"

"No," she said. "He's proud – too proud sometimes – he has to learn that there are situations when he has to make the first move."

Shortly before nine, a courier arrived with the clothing Norine had ordered for Zack. After I'd put the new clothes in place, I stood back to make sure Zack could reach what he needed. Everything was accessible, and as always, everything was exquisite. Zack's closet always made me think of the scene in *The Great Gatsby* where Daisy Buchanan weeps over the beauty of Gatsby's shirts. Because of his paraplegia, it was vital that Zack care for his skin – the slightest irritation could turn into a pressure ulcer that could become infected, and even fatal – so his shirts were the softest cotton; his underwear was silk; and winter and summer, his socks were cashmere.

Satisfied that all was in order, I picked up the current issue of *The New Yorker*, told the workers upstairs that if they needed me I'd be in the roof garden, and headed for the pleasures of a soft June day. When I stepped off the elevator, I found myself face to face with Ed Mariani, who was carrying a tray of empty bedding-plant pots. Like characters in an old cartoon, we both jumped back. "What are you doing here?" Ed said.

Once again, my grandmother's maxim that *a lie will always find you out* had been proven true. "Putting in time," I said. "Leland offered us the use of his place when we were in town and at loose ends." Not the truth, but not a lie, and Ed seemed satisfied.

He held out his tray. "If you're at loose ends, you can help me do some planting. I found some healthy strays at the greenhouse, half price, and I thought I'd plant a little vegetable garden up here for Leland and Margot. I've just put in three kinds of basil, and I have tomato plants, thyme, rosemary, and seeds for romaine and lettuce in my car. By August, Leland and Margot will have fresh produce. Next year, I'll plan something more ambitious, but I thought this would be fun for them."

"It will," I said. "And I'd love to help. I need to get my hands in some potting soil."

For the next hour, Ed and I revelled in the smell of warming soil and new plants. "I get to put the tomatoes in," I said. "Nothing says summer like the smell of tomato plants."

"And basil," Ed said.

"And basil," I agreed.

I was so absorbed in gardening with Ed that I forgot about the workers from Peyben. When Colton's feet appeared beside me, I was startled. "Looks like you're having fun," he said.

I looked up at him. "I guess we're never too old to play in the dirt," I said.

He smiled. "I guess not. Anyway, Ms. Shreve, we're finished. At least to our satisfaction, but our satisfaction isn't what matters. Do you have time to check the rooms?"

I stood up. "Of course."

Ed looked at me questioningly.

I met his gaze. "I'm not just putting in time here," I confessed. "During the week Zack and Taylor and I are living in Leland's condo. We're going to be here for a while. This is Colton; he works for Peyben. He and his crew came this morning to rearrange the upstairs so Taylor has room for a studio."

Ed nodded, but his eyes were hurt. "I'm sorry," I said. "It's complicated. Would you come downstairs with Colton and me? I could use an inspired eye."

Ed pushed himself to his feet and the three of us walked to the elevator.

Colton had pulled out his BlackBerry to make notes as Ed and I inspected the rooms. The master bedroom was huge, and with a skylight and a wall of windows, including a northern exposure, it was an ideal space for an artist. The crew had covered the shining hardwood with an industrial protective covering that had been cut to fit snugly over the floor beneath. I turned to Colton. "This is perfect, thanks."

"Come see what you think of the rest of the job," he said. "We took out all the furniture in the guestroom so your daughter could have the suite from the master in there, but if she wants the guestroom bed back, just say the word. We think the office is nice for a schoolgirl. And there's a couch in there if your daughter wants to have a friend for a sleepover."

Ed and I followed Colton through the other rooms. In the smaller space of the guestroom, the bed from the master bedroom seemed enormous. "Taylor could sleep her six closest friends in that," I said.

"Somebody's idea of what a single man like Mr. Hunter needed," Colton said.

"Somebody who still reads *Playboy*," I said. "But the bed is fine in here. We appreciate your help."

Colton handed me his card. "My cell number is on there. If you have any problems, we'll be here within the hour."

After they left, I turned to Ed. "So now that the jig is up, can I offer you a cup of coffee?"

"Sure."

As he followed me down the stairs, Ed's step was ponderous. When we were together, Ed and I were seldom silent, but as I made the coffee, there was so much unsaid between us that we said nothing. I placed napkins and mugs on a small tray and filled the mugs. "I'm not sure what we have in the line of cookies," I said, "but there'll be something. Leland's housekeeper stocked the pantry, and she seems to have anticipated our every wish."

"No cookies, thanks." Ed cast a lugubrious gaze at the bar stools placed along the edge of the butcher block. "If you don't mind, I'd rather not perch on one of those," he said.

"I don't like them either," I said. "Too much like a diner. Why don't we go into the living room where we can actually look at each other while we talk."

As we settled into reading chairs, Ed said, "We've never had secrets from each other, Jo." He tried a smile. "You were my best man."

"Even my kids don't know," I said.

Ed's eyes widened. "I can't believe you haven't told your children."

"There was a good reason for that. Mieka's in a relationship with Riel Delorme. Apparently Riel has tried to sever his ties with the gangs, but that's easier said than done."

"God, Jo, you must be heartsick."

"Heartsick and scared," I said. "I'm trying to focus on externals, keeping our little ship afloat – making sure everyone's settled in and has what they need, but every so often the chasm opens and I see all the terrible possibilities."

"And I added to your worries by behaving like a petulant schoolboy. I'm sorry."

"Don't be. I'm glad not to have to lie to you any more. And I'm glad you're here." I leaned toward him. "Ed, you *have* pulled back on investigating the gang activity in North Central, haven't you?"

"I haven't stopped digging, but I'm keeping my distance. When I saw Declan Hunter's face the day of the wedding, I realized I wasn't the stuff of heroes."

"Thank heaven for small mercies," I said.

Ed patted my hand. "And for small discoveries," he said. "I've come up with something that isn't exactly earth-shattering, but it is another piece in the puzzle. Apparently, Riel Delorme has a sister – more accurately, a half-sister. She's an ex-cop who is now a lawyer. Her name is Sage Mackenzie."

"That's bizarre," I said. "I know Sage, and you've seen her, Ed – that day at the Conexus Centre – Sage Mackenzie was the redhead who pulled Louise Hunter away from Leland."

"She deserves a gold star for that," Ed said.

"Agreed," I said. "That whole scene was a nightmare, and Louise's antics made everything worse."

"And another plus for Sage. Apparently, Riel's conversion from militant to pacifist came about because she took him by the scruff of the neck and forced him to face some home truths about the people with whom he was associating. Given what you just told me about Mieka's relationship with Riel Delorme, you must be relieved to learn that there's a law-abiding member of the family keeping an eye on the rebel."

"My feelings about Sage are mixed," I said. "She's Louise's lawyer, and as you saw, Louise is a troubled soul. Sage seems to know just how to help her."

"So why are your feelings about her mixed?"

"Sage used to be at Falconer Shreve. One night when she and Zack were working late, Sage came on to him. Zack said that even after he made it clear he wasn't interested, Sage kept up her efforts. She unzipped his pants and put her hand in. At that point some delivery guy came into the office. Zack zipped up and that was that."

"That's a disturbing story," Ed said.

"It is," I agreed. "When Zack told me about the delivery man the first time, I thought it was funny, but since then I've wondered whether there was something more sinister going on."

"Such as?"

"Zack said Sage was pretty determined to get his penis out. I'm wondering if that delivery man was supposed to shoot some pictures."

"You think Sage was trying to solidify her position at Falconer Shreve with a little blackmail?"

"I don't know. The next week Sage was fired for assaulting Zack's executive assistant."

Ed's moon face was troubled. "I guess you never know about people," he said.

"No," I said. "I guess you never do."

Not long after Ed left, Riel called. His apology was terse, but it seemed genuine. Most importantly, he agreed to talk to Leland. When I put forward Leland's proposal about giving NationTV's audience an inside look at the mediation process, Riel said he would consider it. Our conversation was stilted, but we were at least talking and I was grateful for that.

Jill Oziowy could barely contain her excitement when I called to tell her that if Riel could be persuaded to agree, Leland Hunter was prepared to let NationTV's cameras record their meetings.

"Leland Hunter never – and I mean *never* – talks to the media," she said. "And to let cameras be there as the mediator brokers an agreement between Leland and the man who wanted to destroy his project – this is going to be amazing!"

Her exhilaration was infectious. "I agree," I said. "There'll be footage of the protest last week when Leland received his honorary doctorate from the university. All the chants and the signs: *Bring Them Down. What about our Heritage? Reclaim Our Neighbourhoods.* And I know the NationTV cameraman was there when Riel was jostled and his sign caught Leland Hunter's skull. It was an ugly cut – a lot of blood. Seeing two former enemies sit down and hammer out an agreement to share a multipurpose development will be a hallmark moment, and it'll be all yours."

"So," Jill said, "where's the worm in this shiny apple?"

"There isn't one," I said. "Everybody wins. Leland believes, and I agree, that the publicity focus will force both sides to reconcile their differences, and he's also hopeful that all the attention will drive the violent protestors – who may have bombed our house – into the shadows."

"Into the shadows but not out of business."

"No, but the reason buildings have security lighting is to keep the bad guys away. Leland's hoping the media glare will work the same way."

"And Riel – what does he get out of this?" Jill asked.

"If he co-operates, Riel will be front and centre again. Apparently he was hot stuff when he was the neighbourhood Che, but his pacifism has made him seem ineffectual. If Riel plays his cards right, the NationTV program will put him back in the spotlight, and when he brings North Central a multi-million-dollar facility, he'll be a force to be reckoned with."

Jill was thoughtful. "So everybody wins but the thugs," she said. "Why do I have a feeling they're not going to take this lying down?"

Zack and Taylor were going to Bushwakker's for dinner, but we had time for a cup of tea together before we headed our separate ways. When I relayed the news of the day to Zack, his ears pricked up at Jill's final comment. "She's right, you know. This program Leland is proposing is a real 'in your face' gesture, and haters don't react well to taunting."

"You think the television program is a mistake?"

"I don't know. I guess we'll find out."

I glanced at my watch. "I'm supposed to be at Linda's by six. People have to work tomorrow, so it'll be an early evening."

Zack gave me a lazy grin. "Good. I'll have the bed warm when you get home."

"What are you going to order at Bushwakker's?"

"Let's see. Maybe the wild boar burger with roasted hot peppers and a side order of those double-fried fries."

"Bushwakker's makes a very nice Greek salad."

Zack scoffed. "No man ever satisfied his woman by eating Greek salad."

"You'd satisfy me," I said. "I want you to live forever."

Linda Fritz lived in a small and carefully restored home on a double lot in the Crescents, not far from our house on the creek. As she greeted me at the door, I thought she looked remarkably fresh for someone who'd spent the day in combat with Zack.

Linda is an attractive woman: a tall, slim, self-possessed redhead with lightly lined pale skin, intelligent grey eyes, and a low but commanding voice. Zack had tried for years to lure Linda from the Crown Prosecutor's Office to Falconer Shreve. He admired her attention to detail, and her ability to read a situation and react effectively. He'd offered her money, a corner office, and a partnership, but she said that one of her great joys as a lawyer was going head to head with him in court so she was going to stay put.

"We're going to have dinner out back," she said. "But before we join the others I wanted to say how sorry I am about your house – especially your garden. I remember that when we were there for Zack's birthday last month, you said you finally had the garden you wanted and you were both looking forward to kicking back and enjoying it."

"Lucky we don't know what's ahead," I said.

Linda shuddered. "Isn't that the truth?" As she looked at me, her eyes were assessing. "You seem to be handling it."

"No choice," I said. "But tonight's for celebrating, not mourning. Let's go to the party."

As we walked through the kitchen, Linda handed me a platter. "Would you mind carrying this?"

"Do you trust me not to eat it before we join the others? It looks great."

"Thanks, it should be nice. Paté from the Hutterite colony at Kyle and high cranberry compote that I made from berries I picked myself near La Ronge."

"So you're serious about the locovore commitment," I said.

Linda sighed. "For tonight I am. Some nights I'm so tired when I get home, I could chow down on an endangered species."

She held the door open for me and picked up her own tray. "As you can see, the yard is low maintenance," Linda said.

The lot was deep and all grass except for a huge old cottonwood tree in the centre. "I imagine that cottonwood isn't low maintenance in the fall," I said.

"You're right, but it's so beautiful in the other three seasons, I accept those mounds of leaves as the price I must pay."

Linda had set a plank table under the tree and her other guests were already seated around it drinking wine. The light poured through the leaves of the cottonwood, making lacy patterns on the women below. "It's a gorgeous setting for a summer dinner," I said.

"We all have such busy lives," Linda said. "I thought we'd enjoy the peace."

There were only ten of us. I recognized most of the women there, but Margot and Linda were the only ones I knew well. All, except me, were lawyers. The invitation had stated casual, but I had learned that for Margot's crowd, "casual" was upscale, and I'd worn a pale grey silk shirt with matching pants, strappy sandals that Taylor had talked me into buying, and a filmy fuchsia scarf that added a splash of colour.

Margot took the platter of appetizers from me and placed it on the table. "You know everyone, don't you, Joanne?"

"Not as well as I'd like to," I said. "But I'm counting on tonight to remedy that."

A small, deeply tanned woman with shoulder-length greying hair poured a glass of Sauterne and handed it to me. "You'll find this a very welcoming wine," she said. "I'm Sandra Mikalonis. We've met, but it was at a law dinner, and you looked as if you were longing to find the exit."

"Zack always says I'd never make a poker player, but it's good to see you again."

"In a more congenial setting," Sandra said. She turned to the other women. "Why don't we all introduce ourselves?"

After the introductions, everyone expressed concern about what had happened to our house, then we got round to the real business of the evening: eating, drinking, and talking.

Given the fact that we were celebrating a wedding, it seemed inevitable that someone would ask Margot about how she and Leland met.

"It's not a long story," Margot said. "Somebody brought Leland to my housewarming party when I moved into the condo on Halifax Street. One thing led to another. Leland bought the building where I lived and moved in next door. Not long after he gave me this." She held up her left hand. Her spectacular diamond was fiery in the dappled light. "And neither of us has ever been happier."

"Sounds as if you were both ready," Sandra said. "Whenever I ran into him after his divorce, he was with a different woman."

"Palate cleansers," Linda said tartly. "Pleasant, forgettable little nothings to cleanse the palate before the really substantial dish arrived."

Margot roared. "Leland will love that." She took a bite of her chanterelle appetizer. "This mushroom thing is fantastic," she said. "And so is the pate. What's next?"

"Pickerel and wild rice from La Ronge; more mushrooms from my secret patch; and sugar snap peas from the market."

It was a splendid meal. By the time we'd polished off the last of the goat cheese soufflé with fresh strawberries, the sun was dipping towards the horizon, the air was cooling, and the conversation was heating up.

Diane, an athletic blonde with a husky laugh and a wicked sense of humour, had just told a story about a law school classmate named Ana who was drop-dead gorgeous but had a very tiny mind.

Margot leaned forward. "I remember her. She didn't really understand anything, but she had an incredible ability to focus."

"And she managed to pass her bar exams?" I said.

Diane chuckled. "Well, she had special tutoring. The male professors were falling over one another offering their services."

"What's Ana doing now?" I asked.

"She's house counsel for a cosmetics company," Diane said, stroking one of Linda's cats. "The lawyer who does the real work is a mouse of a guy – he hands Ana the material. She focuses her tiny brain hard and then sashays into the boardroom with her gorgeous hair and her pouty mouth and her four-inch eyelashes and delivers the goods."

"What if somebody asks her a question?" Sandra said.

"She promises to get back to them, and then she goes to Mr. Mouse," Diane said and rolled her eyes. "Ana's annual salary, not counting stock options, is probably four times more than mine."

"You're happy in your work," Margot said sweetly. "And, really, isn't that all that matters?"

Diane shot her an incredulous look. "You are kidding, right?"

"Right," Margot said, and we all laughed.

"Margot, what's the story on Sage Mackenzie?" Sandra asked. "I was really shocked when I heard she left Falconer Shreve. That's a plum job. What happened?"

Margot and I exchanged a glance, then she shrugged. "Bad fit. Sage spent five years as a cop in North Central and she went to law school committed to the idea that the community should have a lawyer who knew their world."

"And now the community's legal needs are being underwritten by a retainer from your intended," Diane said. "Or is my information wrong?"

"No, you're right," Margot said. "Sage has struck pay dirt, although she certainly earns it dealing with Louise."

"Sage was a good cop," Linda said. Her ginger cat, Trout, came up and rubbed against her leg. She picked him up and stoked him absently. "Determined, fearless, observant, fair. Perfect except . . ."

I picked up on her hesitation. "Except what?" I asked.

Linda continued to stroke Trout. "Sage has what we euphemistically refer to as an anger management problem. You know those YouTube clips of out-of-control cops beating up perpetrators? Sage had two of those to her credit. She is one of the most disciplined people I've ever known, but twice she just snapped. The consensus was that she'd seen too much when she was growing up."

I remembered Alex Kequahtooway, an Aboriginal man who had been dear to me, saying that he couldn't remember a day when he didn't wake up angry. "So was Sage discharged from the force?" I said.

"No. She'd always planned to be a lawyer, and after her second anger management 'failure,' Sage decided the time was right. She jumped through all the hoops. She finished law school, articled, passed the bar exams, became a lawyer, and then three months later she went back to the police force."

"That's strange, isn't it?" I said.

"Very strange," Linda said. "And there was a lot of chatter about it at that time. Apparently, Sage said she just missed police work – the excitement and the camaraderie, the bull sessions over coffee, and going out to the shooting range with the guys, that kind of thing. But then Delia Wainberg tapped her to go to Falconer Shreve. Apparently, Delia heard that Sage had the goods, so she convinced her to give the law a real try."

"Sage didn't try very long," Margot said. "She left after a couple of months. It's an odd pattern."

"Anyway, she seems to have landed on her feet," Linda said. "She's a success professionally, and when she's not tied up with Louise, she works closely with some of the kids in the gangs – trying to convince them to get out while the getting's good, I guess."

"The very model of a lawyer committed to 'giving back,'" Margot said, and she gave me a sidelong glance and winked.

Linda stood up and rubbed her bare arms. "The weather seems to be changing on us. It's getting cold, and those clouds look threatening. Shall we go inside?"

Diane stretched. "Thanks, but it's time for me to call a cab to ferry me back to the real world. This really was a great evening, Linda."

Diane's farewell acted as a signal to the rest of us to carry in our dishes, say our thanks, and arrange for cabs.

I was back at Halifax Street by ten. Zack was in bed reading. I kissed him and then started to undress. "Everything okay here?" I asked.

"Yep. Taylor and I had a nice dinner, then we came home and we both tackled our homework."

"Very virtuous," I said.

"How were the male strippers?"

"Every last one was a Greek god, and mine was a five-star lap dancer."

"I didn't know those guys lap-danced."

"They do if you stuff enough twenty-dollar bills down their Speedos."

Zack peered at me over his horn rims. "So what did you really do?"

"Had a great meal, drank wine, played with Linda's cats, and gossiped."

"Did you learn anything you didn't know?"

"I heard about Ana of the luscious lips, the small brain, and the prodigious ability to focus."

Zack shook his head. "So Diane Quennell was there. She and Ana were in the same class. Ana's success really sticks in Diane's craw – not because she's earning big bucks, but because Ana just uses the law as a means to an end."

I buttoned my pyjama top. "Don't all of us use our profession as a means to an end?"

"Probably, but Diane has respect for the law, and Ana doesn't. That's the real source of the antipathy."

"Speaking of antipathy, I learned something interesting about Sage tonight," I said. "According to Linda, Sage's anger management problem is long standing."

"That surprises me," Zack said. "Sage wasn't at Falconer Shreve long, but she was always very controlled. She only seemed to crack in the week before she was fired."

"I've been thinking about what happened that night," I said.

Zack closed his book. "Now that *doesn't* surprise me."

I slid into bed next to him. "Had there been any friction between you and Sage – I mean, before that night."

"No. We were both absorbed by the Retzlaff case, and we had a good working relationship. I had no cause for complaint, and I don't think Sage did." Zack looked at me questioningly. "I'm not connecting the dots here, Jo. If a woman is pissed off at a guy, does she usually ask him for a quickie?"

"No, and if a women makes a pass at a guy and he says, 'No, thanks,' she doesn't usually unzip him and pull out his penis. When you told us about what happened that night at Magoo's, Margot and I thought it was pretty funny, but I was talking to Ed about it today and something about the whole scenario just doesn't add up."

Zack frowned. "You don't think I encouraged Sage, do you?"

I shook my head. "Of course not, but a delivery man wandering into a locked office in a secure building after hours doesn't make sense. Have you ever wondered if Sage was thinking of blackmail?"

"So she arranged with the delivery man to catch the two of us *in flagrante delicto* and snap a couple of compromising pictures so she could get something she wanted."

"You don't look convinced," I said.

"I'm not convinced," Zack said. "I didn't have anything she wanted. She wasn't into money, and obviously she didn't care about advancing her career at Falconer Shreve or she wouldn't have taken on Norine. Something must have gone wrong for Sage – wrong enough that she fell apart."

"A love affair?"

"I have no idea," Zack said. "I don't know anything about Sage that wasn't on her resumé."

"Jill told me something today that wouldn't have been on Sage's resumé. She's Riel's half-sister."

Zack whistled. "Whoa. That's interesting."

"It is," I said. "It's also unsettling."

"Look on the bright side," Zack said. "We're in for some kick-ass family dinners."

———

The threatening grey clouds and the chill in the air we felt at
the end of Linda's party presaged a night of violent weather.
Twice the wind shuddering against the windows awakened
me. When I went to look out, nothing was visible through the
driving rain except the distant lights of the city – pointillist
dabs of colour in the blackness.

Storms didn't trouble me. Usually, I reassured the dogs
and enjoyed the show, but that night as thunder boomed and
lightning split the sky I was anxious. Overall, it had been a
good day. But I had lived long enough to be wary of loose
ends, and this day had more than its share. Jill's warning
that the haters would exact a price for Riel's co-operation
with Leland Hunter rang true, but Ed's assurances that he'd
back off his investigation in North Central did not. Mieka's
support had been an unexpected gift, but Riel had been cool
when he agreed to consider involving NationTV in the
process of mediation with Peyben. Sage Mackenzie was a
baffling figure and one whom I couldn't dismiss – unless
Riel Delorme disappeared from our lives, and it didn't look
as though that was likely to happen.

Finally, chilled and exhausted, I slid into bed, pressed my
body against Zack's, and soothed by his warmth and the
rhythm of his breathing, I slept.

CHAPTER

11

By morning the drama of the storm was over. When I walked out on our terrace, I saw that the wind had calmed and the rain was now warm and steady. I dressed for my run. The only time I wore a cap with a visor was when there was rain or snow. When Zack saw me tying back my hair in a ponytail so the cap would fit snugly, he said, "You're not running on a shitty day like this, are you?"

"The worst is over," I said. "And I like running in the rain – not too many other runners around. Will you be here when I get back?"

"Not sure," he said. "Declan's picking up Taylor for school, so I might take off early so I can talk to my client. The jury's going to be in court today, and I would like Cronus to reach out a little. What's that old joke? 'If you can fake sincerity, you can fake pretty much anything'?"

I kissed him. "Good luck with that. Give me a shout if you have a moment. Otherwise I'll see you after work. Remember you're on your own again for dinner. Taylor and I will be at the All-College."

"Take pictures," Zack said.

"You are the most doting father," I said.

"Making up for lost time. Have a good run."

Leland was waiting at the elevator. "I was afraid you wouldn't want to run in this weather."

"You and Zack," I said. "I like running in the rain. Besides, I have to do penance for that extra glass of Riesling I had with dessert."

"Margot said it was a great party," Leland said.

"It was, and it was exactly right for Margot – no bad jokes or gag gifts, just friends having fun."

Leland and I stepped into fresh cool air and streets that were slick but washed clean by the rainfall.

"You know, I've never had a woman running partner before," Leland said.

"I'm surprised. Last night we talked – not always kindly – about the many women who lined up at your door after the divorce."

"There weren't that many women." Leland ran his hand over his head. The stitches on his forehead were healing, but they were still apparent. "I'm not exactly Prince Charming," he said.

"Don't underestimate yourself," I said. "You're smart; you're good company; and you're a great running partner."

"Thank you," he said. "I don't seem to get close to many people."

"It's their loss," I said. After that we silently continued our run along what had become our usual route.

When we turned onto Rose Street, a late-model black suv peeled past us. The vehicle slowed but didn't stop at the stop sign on the corner. The door on the passenger side opened and someone threw a large bundle onto the pavement, slammed the door closed again, and the SUV sped off. The incident was over in a matter of seconds.

Leland turned to me. "Why would anybody do that?" he said.

"Too lazy to find a dumpster," I said. As we came closer to the corner, we heard crying: what had appeared to be discarded clothing was a naked Aboriginal child, perhaps nine years old, wrapped in a blanket. She was clutching a ten-dollar bill, and her eyes were wide with terror. A grey-white viscous substance was dribbling from her mouth.

I dropped to my knees. "It's all right," I said to the child. "No one's going to hurt you." Leland was already on his cell a few steps away. "I'm going to hold your hand," I said to her. "Is that all right?"

She didn't react, so I took her hand in mine.

Leland was talking to the police.

"We're going to get someone to help us," I said to the girl. "No one will hurt you, I promise." Still she said nothing, but she kept her frightened eyes on mine.

I longed to wipe her mouth, but I knew about contaminating evidence and I didn't want whoever had done this to a child to have a single loophole. Her chest was heaving and her body was tight with fear. So was mine, but I managed to keep my voice low and calm. Then, out of nowhere, I remembered something I used to do with my kids when they were young and exploding with emotions they couldn't understand.

I leaned closer to the child and whispered, "Close your eyes and think of the colour blue," I said. She hesitated and then she closed her eyes. "Okay," I said. "Now think of blue skies . . . and bluebirds . . . and blue cloth . . . and blue flowers . . . and blue Popsicles . . . and blueberries." The child's chest stopped heaving, and her breathing became more regular. "Now let's try green," I said.

We had moved to pink when a red Trans-Am roared down the street towards us. When the driver hit the brakes in front of us, I thought it must be a Good Samaritan, but I was wrong. The driver pulled so close to the curb I could almost touch his car. The man in the passenger seat leaned towards his open window. "Hey, cunt, what are you doing to that kid?" he said. His voice was low and menacing. He extended his arm out the window and I could see the tattoo of an eagle on his bicep. Flanking the bird were the linked letter R's. "We're on this street a lot," he said. "I'd like to get you alone – show you what Red Rage does to people who fuck with our kids."

Leland came over and focused his gaze on the men in the red Trans-Am. "The police are on their way," he said. "Are you planning to stay around and help with their investigation?"

I turned back to the child, whose eyes were still closed, even more tightly now. "Pink bubblegum, pink ponies, pink slippers," I said, trying to recapture her attention even though I could hear my own voice quavering.

"I'll find you," one of the men in the Trans-Am said, then the driver gunned the engine.

The ambulance appeared shortly afterwards. The EMT team was gentle and efficient. A woman knelt beside me and started murmuring assurances and then she gestured that I should move and let her take my place. I did. The crew made their preliminary check of the child's body and took their readings, and the police arrived to take a sample of the substance on the child's lips. The female worker stayed right with her as they lifted her onto a gurney and into the ambulance.

When the ambulance doors slammed shut, my intake of breath was sharp and Leland took my arm. "I'm going to call Zack," he said.

"No. I'll do it. I'm all right." I took out the BlackBerry Zack always insisted I carry when I ran and hit speed-dial.

"Good timing," he said. "I just pulled into my parking

spot – on my way to meet Cronus at the office and give him some charm pointers. What's up?"

"Leland and I were running on Rose Street and a little girl was thrown out of an SUV. She'd been assaulted." My voice broke. "Zack, there was semen coming out of her mouth. And when I was trying to calm her two men from Red Rage pulled over and one of them threatened me."

"I'll be right there."

"No. I'm fine. But we still have to talk to the police."

"What block of Rose Street are you on?"

I scanned the nearest building for an address. "600 block," I said.

"I'll be there in ten minutes."

He was there in five. Leland and I had just started talking to a young constable when Zack pulled up. I watched as he snapped his wheelchair into place and came towards us. He held out his arms to me.

"Don't touch me," I said. I was wet and dirty, and Zack's suit was immaculate. My concern was only with keeping his suit clean, but emotion gave my words a larger and darker meaning, and from the alarm in Zack's eyes I knew that he'd picked up on that.

"We're not going that route, Ms. Shreve," he said, and his voice was commanding. He pushed his chair closer. I wanted to bend towards him, but my limbs were heavy. Zack reached out and embraced my bare legs. I leaned forward and buried my face in his hair, hoping the familiar smell of my husband would connect me with the world again. It didn't. "I'm afraid, Zack," I whispered.

Zack pushed his chair back and gave me an assessing look. "You and Leland finish talking to the cops, then I'll drive you both home."

Leland's statement was comprehensive. He'd been able to identify the make of the SUV and the fact that it carried a Saskatchewan plate with the last two numbers 08. It was only a matter of time before the men who'd violated the child would be arrested.

I was a less satisfactory witness. I was able to identify the man who'd leaned out of the red Trans-Am as a member of Red Rage, but my description of his features was vague, and because I'd been focused on the child when the car pulled out, I didn't have information about the licence. Remembering the scene made my stomach churn, and I was relieved when the police took our contact numbers and sent us on our way.

When we arrived at the condo, Zack pulled in front of the gate to the parking garage. He took my hand. "Promise you'll text if you need me. I can be home in fifteen minutes."

"I promise," I said.

Leland moved closer to me. "And I'm going to stick around for a bit."

"Thanks," Zack said. "I'll call when there's a break."

Leland and I walked into our building and buzzed for the elevator. We didn't speak until we stepped off at our floor. "I need a shower," Leland said. "Do you want to get together and have breakfast somewhere afterwards?"

"Come over to our place. I'm not ready to face the world yet."

"Twenty minutes?"

"Twenty minutes."

I turned the shower on high and hot. After ten minutes, I'd scrubbed away the sweat of my run and the dirt of Rose Street, but as I towelled off I was still seething. I uttered an expletive, dressed, and went into the kitchen. By the time Leland arrived the coffee was ready.

Like me, he appeared to be fine – freshly showered, dressed, ready to meet the day. But I wasn't fine, and neither was he. I poured us each a cup of coffee and we sat on facing stools at the butcher-block table.

"How are you doing?" he asked.

"Not great," I said. "I seem to be in the middle of an existential meltdown."

"That's understandable," he said. "The fear in that child's eyes and the way she was clutching that ten-dollar bill will stay with us both for a long time."

"As it should," I said. I was sick with anger. "Who decides, Leland? Who decides which of two children gets a life of love and privilege and which ends up on the streets giving blowjobs for drug money?"

"I don't know," he said. "But I've been asking myself that same question. Margot and I have so many plans for the baby we're expecting. More than anything, we want our child to have a good life."

"No one seems to care if that young girl has a good life," I said.

Leland shook his head. "At least you and Mieka are doing something. UpslideDown2 is a worthwhile project."

"Is it?" I said. "Or is it just a sop to our consciences. What's the point of opening a play centre in a neighbourhood where a child is forced to fellate men who use her, then throw her out on the curb like garbage? What's the point of talking about parenting to people who send their child out on the street? Nobody gives a damn, Leland. I thought the man in the Trans-Am was a Good Samaritan. All he did was show me his Red Rage tattoo and threaten me. Maybe it's time Mieka and Lisa and I faced the fact that North Central is beyond saving."

Leland's voice was level. "You don't know that, Joanne. Neither do I, but we both know that walking away won't help."

The first fingers of a headache were pressing the back of my skull. "Leland, forgive me, but I'm not up for an inspirational speech."

"And I'm in no position to give one," he said. "There was nothing altruistic about my decision to redevelop the Warehouse District and North Central. I wanted to make money and please Margot. But lately it's occurred to me that The Village might serve other purposes. When Zack proposed building that shared facility with North Central, I leapt at the idea. I needed to cut the legs out from under Delorme and his supporters, so I offered them a project that they could never in a million years bring about on their own."

"No liberal guilt there, huh?"

Leland shook his head. "Not an iota. But maybe motivation doesn't matter. No matter why that facility gets built, it will be good for North Central and it will be good for The Village. It's a step towards showing that we're all in this together."

"So everybody wins," I said. "Peyben achieves its intended outcome, but there are unforeseen benefits for the neighbourhood and the city."

"You're not convinced," Leland said. "But there's logic here. We all accept the fact that collateral damage is possible, why not collateral good? Speaking of which, Riel Delorme called me. You obviously got through to him. He and I have a meeting scheduled for ten-thirty. We're supposed to discuss the NationTV project, but I can postpone."

"Don't," I said. "Riel is prickly. He's taken the first step, and if you postpone, he'll perceive it as a slight."

"Land mines everywhere," Leland said.

I walked Leland to the door. "I'll call you if I find out how the little girl is doing."

Leland's sentry eyes seemed to bore into me. "You're paying a high price for your association with me."

"Maybe it's a price I had to pay."

Leland touched my hand. "Collateral good?"

I tried a smile. "That remains to be seen."

———

When I heard the shrill of my cell and saw Mieka's name on the caller ID, I was on the roof garden, checking to see if the bedding plants Ed and I put in had weathered the storm. They looked hardier than I felt, and I almost didn't answer. Under normal circumstances, I would have gone straight to Mieka to talk about the tragedy of the child on Rose Street, but explaining why I was on Rose Street with Leland at five-thirty in the morning was impossible, and so I stared at the phone.

Then, anxious about the girls, I picked up. Mieka was keyed up but cordial. "How's life at the lake?"

"Tranquil," I said.

"Would you be willing to give up a couple of hours of tranquillity to come into town and stay with the girls? They're off school because it's a teacher's professional development day, and Lisa and I have a meeting with someone who's expressed an interest in making a sizable contribution to UpSlideDown2."

"Anybody I know?"

"Vivian Heinrichs."

"That's promising," I said. "Mrs. Heinrichs has deep pockets and a social conscience. What time do you want me there?"

"Is eleven too soon?"

"Eleven's fine," I said.

"Are you all right?" Mieka asked. "You don't sound like yourself."

"I was at a dinner party last night, and I drank too much wine."

Mieka laughed. "I assume since I'm talking to you, you made it safely home."

"I took a cab."

"All the way to the lake? That must have cost a fortune," Mieka said. "Well, we've all had at least one regrettable morning after. A couple of hours outside with Maddy and Lena will bring you around."

"I'm counting on that," I said. "See you at eleven."

Mieka and the girls were sitting at the kitchen table poring over some plans Riel had drawn up for a summer project. He'd agreed to build a kid-sized version of Milky Way, the girls' favourite ice-cream stand that had been on Victoria Street, unchanged, since my kids were little. Sitting on the benches outside Milky Way eating ice cream and watching other people eating ice cream under a cloudless Saskatchewan sky was one of the joys of summer in Regina. And the girls were determined to bring that pleasure into their own backyard.

Mieka handed me the plans. They were surprisingly professional. "Looks like Riel knows what he's doing," I said.

"He took the carpentry certificate at NIAST," Mieka said. "But I told him not to put too much effort into the project. I don't imagine the fascination with the ice-cream stand will last past summer."

"About as long as most summer romances," I said.

Mieka laughed softly. "Luckily, my romance is now three seasons long." She looked down at her shorts and T-shirt. "I'd better put on some grown-up clothes for my meeting with Vivian Heinrichs."

"Go ahead." I turned to my granddaughters. "Too early for lunch? I thought after we ate we'd see if the pelicans are still up by the bridge."

"I can always eat," Lena said flatly.

"So can I," said Madeleine.

"In that case," I said. "Let's get a move on."

After we'd washed our lunch dishes, the girls and I went off in search of pelicans. Our creek was filled with wildlife, but pelicans were rare visitors. The theory was that our rainy spring had swollen the creek enough to make it appealing, and if the cormorants were to be trusted, the fishing on the weir near the bridge was good. Madeleine stayed beside me and Lena ran ahead.

Our walk was uneventful. Lena spotted a small tree that bore the unmistakable marks of a beaver's attention. A boy on the other side of the creek skipped a stone across the water and startled a trio of brown ducks that had been peacefully squatted on the water's surface. A redwing blackbird, his scarlet and yellow shoulder badges bright as epaulettes, perched on a clump of bullrushes, belting out his tumbling song.

As always, we met dogs and dog owners whom we knew: a pair of Rhodesian ridgebacks owned by a neighbour at our old house, a Bichon named Daisy with whom the girls were taken, a rescue dog named Luke who had a maverick charm that won my heart. We greeted them all – dog and owner alike. This was our neighbourhood. People knew us here, and we knew them.

The willows on the creekbank near the weir grew out of the water in heavy clusters. For years I had witnessed the transformation from budding branch to first leaf to the full green leafing out of June, but the process never ceased to thrill me. As I watched my granddaughters run towards the weir where the pelicans were fishing, I felt a flash of joy. Then, remembering my morning, the dull anger that had begun when I saw that girl's body flung to the street filled my throat.

"Mimi, come closer. You can't see how they fish from up there." Madeleine's chiming little girl's voice was excited.

"I'm coming," I said. I made my way down the creekbank in time to watch two pelicans, their throat pouches expanded, catching their lunch. I stared at them without interest.

Lena was watching my face. "Why aren't you having a good time?" she asked.

"I'm having a good time," I said. "And I'm going to take a picture, so Granddad can see how much fun we're having." I pulled out my BlackBerry and recorded the moment. Then

I sent the photo to Zack with a note: "I'm fine. Wish you were here."

When we tired of the pelicans, we went to the playground, where the girls demonstrated their prowess on the monkey bars. Then, after a quick stop at Mac's for Popsicles, we went back to Mieka's.

Riel was unlocking the front door. He was wearing pressed jeans and a very new-looking white shirt. "Perfect timing," he said. He greeted the girls and then me – a little sheepishly. "Leland and I finished twenty minutes ago," he said. "Mieka was still at her meeting, so I hopped the bus so you could get on with your life."

"This *is* my life," I said. "We had a good time."

"We went to see the pelicans," Lena said. "And then we went to the playground and then to Mac's for Popsicles."

"So now you're ready to get down to work," Riel said.

Madeleine's eyes were bright. "Are we going to get started on the ice-cream stand today?"

"No time like the present," Riel said. "But if you're going to be doing carpentry, you'd better put on long pants, long-sleeved shirts, and real shoes and socks."

The girls raced into the house. I followed Riel inside to the kitchen. "Can I get you anything?" he asked.

"Thanks," I said. "I had a Popsicle. So how did the meeting go?"

"Pretty well, I think. It was at your husband's office." Riel shook his head. "That place is intimidating."

"I believe that's the intent," I said.

Riel smiled. "Anyway, I scored some points, and so did Leland. We established the ground rules for NationTV's coverage of the mediation. Nothing major except Leland agreed that we should hold our meetings at a place where people from North Central who wanted to be part of the process would feel at ease."

"Did you come up with a location?"

"Yes. The Willy Hodgson Recreation Centre."

"Good choice – for NationTV, too – more atmospheric than a lawyer's office."

My cell rang. I glanced at the caller ID. It was Debbie Haczkewicz. "Riel, I have to take this call," I said. "I'll go out on the deck."

As always, Debbie went straight to the point. "Zack asked me to give you a call."

"I'm glad you did. I meant to phone to see how your cold was, but there's been so much going on."

"Understood," Debbie said. "I seem to be on the mend, thanks. Zack said you wanted an update on the girl. There's nothing new there. Physically, she's still 'doing as well as can be expected.'"

"Having been raped and forced to fellate those animals."

Debbie sighed. "I used to get angry, too, Joanne. It didn't change a thing, except my blood pressure."

"Can the little girl have visitors?"

"She has visitors. From the police department and from social services. They'll be working together to develop a plan to keep her safe and get her off the streets."

"I thought I might stop by the hospital to see her."

"Bad idea for both of you, Joanne."

I waited, but Debbie didn't elaborate. "All right," I said. "Could I leave a gift for her?"

"What did you have in mind?"

"I don't know – something to help her pass the time in the hospital."

"That would be fine. The girl's name, incidentally, is April Stonechild. She just turned eleven. This is not the first time she has come to our attention."

The churning in my stomach had started again. "Thanks for the call, Deb," I said.

But once again, I was talking to dead air. Inspector Haczkewicz had moved along.

When I came back inside, Riel was sitting at my grandmother's maple table with the plans for the ice-cream stand spread out in front of him. He looked up. "Everything okay?"

I was about to offer a polite lie, but the lines his life and his choices had carved into his face stopped me. "No," I said. "Nothing's okay."

I sat down and told him about the incident on Rose Street – I didn't care if he wondered what I'd been doing running in North Central at five in the morning. As I talked, Riel's body tensed and his mouth tightened. His eyes never left mine, but they were so filled with pain and anger, I found it difficult not to look away. When I was finished, he said, "So now you're getting an idea about what it's like to live in North Central."

"Yes."

"And you wish you weren't." His laugh was jagged.

I stood. "I'd better go up and say goodbye to the girls. I have some errands to run and I'd like to get April's gift to her."

"What are you planning to get her?" Riel asked.

"I was thinking of an iPod."

"Her family will sell it to get drug money."

"Maybe April will be lucky and she won't have to go back there."

"Oh, she'll go back," Riel said.

"But if the police and social services can work out an alternative, why would she?"

"Because that's the only home she has," Riel said. And then he pounded his fist against the table with such violence that for a moment I thought he had split it in two.

CHAPTER

12

All our children attended Luther College High School. When Mieka had asked to go to Luther, Ian was opposed. He said that as an elected member of the people's party, his children should be in public schools. I pointed out that Mieka had been at Lakeview Public School from kindergarten to Grade Eight and that the boys were still there. I also pointed out that school had never been Mieka's primary interest, but that she was passionate about basketball, that Luther had a good basketball program, and that Mieka's best friend, Lisa Wallace, was going to Luther. I didn't win the argument on points, but Ian had bigger fish to fry. He lost interest in the dispute, and all our kids ended up at Luther, where they had been as happy as anyone ever is in high school.

As I pulled into the Luther parking lot on the night of the All-College, I had another "through the looking glass" moment. The campus was the same as it had always been: lush and well tended. The old brick buildings were as solid and handsome as ever. Sparkling in her tangerine silk botanical-print dress, Taylor had the same brio I remembered brimming over in Mieka and her friends on the night of their first big dinner and dance. The event would be as it had always been: girls bright in their summer dresses, boys wearing too much hair product, overcooked roast beef, and watery, lumpy mashed potatoes. Everything was the same, but I wasn't the same, and like Alice in Wonderland, I was nagged by the question "If I'm not the same . . . who in the world am I?"

As soon as we entered the building, Taylor made a beeline for her two best friends, Gracie Falconer and Isobel Wainberg. Gracie took after her father, Blake, a tall, husky redhead with freckles, and at fifteen, she was already six-feet tall and a star of the Luther basketball team. She was not fashion's slave, and that night she wore comfortable summer slacks, a cheerful shirt, and sandals. Isobel, delicate boned and with pale, translucent skin, intelligent eyes, and black wiry curls, was wearing a simple and flattering sleeveless white dress appliquéd with a black floral design at the neckline. The girls exclaimed over one another's outfits as if they hadn't spent the last month texting and chatting about every detail of what they would wear that night. I told them that they were beautiful, snapped a couple of pictures that I sent to Zack, then headed for the kitchen.

Margot was already there. When she spotted me, she grinned and extended her leg. "Check out the footwear," she said.

Margot's five-inch stilettos were part of her signature look. I had seldom seen her without them, but tonight she was wearing turquoise sneakers with soles that looked as if they had traction.

"You said the floors can get slick here," she said, handing me an apron. "I wasn't about to risk my neck or the heel of one of my Manolos. Anyway, thanks for the heads-up. I'm counting on you for further wise counsel in the years ahead."

I tied my apron. "Actually, 'wear sensible shoes' pretty much covers everything I know."

Margot handed me a potato masher. "In that case, make yourself useful."

When I'd helped at Mieka's first All-College, the kitchen was filled with women. Now the gender balance was even. Blake Falconer and Noah Wainberg were side by side at the counter where the roasts of beef were being sliced, and a couple of other fathers, whom I knew only slightly, were tossing salad and talking baseball at another workstation. As the parents worked, the conversation drifted pleasantly from talk of children, to high school memories, to summer plans. The familiarity of it all was lulling, and my nerves began to unknot. After the last potato was mashed and the grey roast beef was sliced and put in the oven to keep warm, the students began to take their places. As they filed in and sat at the long banquet tables, the kitchen grew quiet. The All-College may have been anachronistic, but watching your child reach the milestone of another completed school year was still a sweet moment.

We finished serving dinner to the students and sat down to begin our own meal. Margot was outgoing, and she had been quick to establish an easy camaraderie with the other parents, many of whom who were from places very much like Wadena. The conversation was pleasantly inconsequential – mostly about life in a small town: marathon perogie-making sessions before a big event, the pleasures of beauty salons that still knew how to style really big hair, and the fact that for good or ill, when you lived in a small town, you were never alone.

Margot and I noticed Louise Hunter at the same time, swaying in the doorway of the gym. Scanning the room for Declan, Louise seemed oblivious to everything else. The students sat at long rows of tables organized by grade. Taylor and the other Grade Nines were seated at the least desirable tables – the ones closest to the parents. Declan, two years ahead of Taylor, was in the centre of the room. Louise spotted her son and began weaving towards his row of tables.

Margot and I both rose from our seats before Declan noticed his mother's arrival. But Taylor caught my eye, and her worried look made me all the more determined to make sure Louise didn't ruin her son's, and my daughter's, night. Within seconds, Margot and I were at Louise's side. Margot took Louise's arm and began to lead her very firmly back towards the entrance, but Louise suddenly came out of her daze and fought back. "Get your hands off me," she said. "I mean it, don't touch me, Margot."

"Why don't you get back to your dinner, Margot," I said. "Louise and I will go outside and get some fresh air." I turned to Louise. "Okay with you?" She hesitated, then nodded numbly.

The gym had been warm and it was good to be outside. I took a deep, calming breath. The air was still and fragrant with the clean, moist scent of damp grass. The late-afternoon light was soft, but even the gentlest light could not disguise Louise's agony. She looked unwell and utterly exhausted. Louise's behaviour tapped into a well of emotion about my own alcoholic mother that I had worked long and hard to keep sealed. I wasn't an idiot: I knew that my identification with Declan skewed my judgment of Louise. I wasn't fair to her, and most of the time, I didn't care, but sitting beside her on the bench in front of Luther with the sun dropping in the sky, it was impossible not to respond to her suffering. "Would you like me to drive you home?" I said.

Louise shook her head. "I'll call Sage." Louise took her cell from her bag and hit speed-dial.

When Sage answered, Louise was close to tears. "I know you were planning to spend the evening getting caught up on your work, but I need to be picked up. I'm at Luther. Could you hurry, please? I don't think Declan saw me, but I don't want him to. I've already humiliated myself enough. I'll be waiting at the front." She paused. "Sage, I don't know what I'd do without you."

For a while, we sat without speaking: me watching the automatic sprinklers spraying water on the already soaking grass, Louise staring off into some private distance of her own.

"It would be easier if Leland died," she said suddenly. "Then I wouldn't have to spend every hour of the day imagining him with her. If he had a heart attack, I would be devastated, but at least there would be an end to it. There's no end to this."

I found her vehemence unsettling, but I also knew that the addicted live on an emotional roller coaster.

"Louise, give yourself a chance."

She tilted her chin defiantly. "Stop drinking?"

"That's your decision," I said. "All I know is that you have everything you need for a good life. You're healthy. You're talented. You're attractive. You have a fine son. You have friends, and you have enough money to do whatever you want – travel, study, get involved with the arts or a charity – you have many, many options. You're a very lucky woman."

Louise's smile was faint. "Nice try," she said. "But I'm not buying."

When Sage Mackenzie's Lexus appeared, Louise and I both had solid reasons for being relieved. My day had caught up with me. I was running on empty, and Louise's hands were shaking. When I stood to walk her to Sage's car, Louise waved me off. "You did what you could," she said. Then she moved quickly towards the Lexus and deliverance.

The falling sun's light was soothing and I was in no hurry to go inside, but I'd just settled back on the bench when Margot joined me. "Taylor was worried," she said. "So was I. Leland told me about what happened this morning with the little girl. He said you were both heartsick. I shouldn't have forced you to handle Louise."

"You didn't force me," I said. "We both knew it would be easier for Louise to deal with me."

"How is she?"

"Not good," I said.

"I try to be sympathetic," Margot said. "But it's difficult when Louise phones at all hours making threats and telling me Leland's just confused – that he doesn't really love me. And of course it's hard on Leland. Everybody thinks he's such a hard-ass, but he's not. This situation with Louise tears him apart."

"She needs professional help," I said. "Sage Mackenzie is doing her best, but Louise needs full-time care."

Margot clasped her hands between her knees and slumped forward. "Louise has the money to do whatever she wants with her life, so she decides to destroy it. Makes a girl ponder, doesn't it?"

"It does," I said. "But I'll have to ponder tomorrow. I'm dead beat."

Margot straightened and levelled her gaze at me. "You didn't sign on to chaperone the dance, did you?"

"No, just to help with dinner."

"Then you've discharged your obligation. Go home. I'll drive the kids back."

"That's the best offer I've had all day," I said. "Thanks. I'll just go in and tell Taylor what's happening."

Margot put her arm around my shoulder. "You didn't get to eat your roast beef," she said.

I leaned against her. "Every cloud has its silver lining," I said.

Zack was sitting at the dining room table in his shirtsleeves with a pizza, a beer, and a stack of papers.

When he heard me come in, he turned, pushed his chair forward with one hand, and held on to his slice with the other. "Hey, this is a pleasant surprise," he said. "I thought you'd hang on till the bitter end."

"The bitter end came sooner than anticipated," I said. "Louise showed up."

Zack winced. "God, I hope it wasn't a repeat of last year."

"It wasn't. Margot headed her off and I sat outside with Louise till Sage picked her up."

"Have you had anything to eat?"

"No."

"The pizza's still warm and there's cold beer in the fridge."

I got myself a bottle of Great Western, picked up a slice of pizza, and took a bite. "This is Chimney pizza," I said. "I didn't realize they delivered downtown."

"They don't. Stavros brought it himself," Zack said. "He misses having us in the neighbourhood. He thought you and Taylor would be sharing it with me, so he put extra anchovies on your portions."

The Chimney was the only pizza place in town that knew our preferences. My throat tightened. "Zack, I want our old life back," I said.

Zack's face was deeply furrowed and his eyes were weary. "So do I," he said. "But for a while, you're going to have to settle for extra anchovies."

After we'd finished eating, I pushed my chair back. "Time for this day to be over?" I said.

"Boy, is it ever." Zack tilted his head and winced.

"Muscles tight?" I said.

Zack rubbed the back of his neck. "I think they've turned to stone."

"How about a massage?"

"Let's make it a twosome – it's been a while."

Not long after Zack and I were married we hit upon the idea of nightly massages. We were deeply in love, but the simple intimacies of normal domestic life weren't simple for us. Nightly massages gave us both pleasure, relaxed us, and gave me a chance to check Zack's skin for warning signs of pressure ulcers.

That night as I squeezed the massage oil into my hand and began kneading the knotted muscles of Zack's shoulders, he groaned with pleasure. "Remind me. Why did we stop doing this?"

"Because somebody blew up our house."

"That's a pretty lame excuse."

"It was a trick question. So how was your day?"

Zack sighed. "Shitty. I'm losing my case and I shouldn't be."

"You can't win 'em all," I said.

"Yeah, but you should be able to win the ones where your guy is innocent."

I began working the area at the top of Zack's spine. "You really do believe Cronus is innocent, don't you?"

"I *know* he's innocent," Zack said. "And I'm doing all the right things to prove it, but none of them is working. I can read juries. I can usually spot at least one person who's soft on conviction. Not this time."

"But if Cronus is innocent and you're doing all the right things . . . ?"

"It's the human factor," Zack said. "The jury just doesn't like him. You know how it is. If you're favourably disposed towards someone, you cut them a little slack. And no one on that jury is favourably disposed towards Cronus. To be honest, I'm not too surprised. There's something reptilian about him, Joanne – that bullety head and those squinty eyes. I keep waiting for a little forked tongue to dart out at me. Linda shudders every time she looks at him."

I poured more oil into my hand and began to rub the base of Zack's spine. Pushing his weight in a wheelchair sixteen hours a day built muscle, and Zack's upper body was powerful, but his lower spine was incredibly vulnerable. The sight of the patchwork of scars that marked successive failed attempts to restore his ability to walk always made my heart ache. I was gentle when I smoothed oil on his scars, but because Zack had no feeling there, he never knew.

"Except for the fact that he's reptilian and he knows how to make a living room into an apartment with some insulation and a microwave, you've never told me much about Cronus," I said. "Is Cronus his surname or his given name?"

Zack chortled. "Neither. You'll like this because it shows that my client is capable of poetry. His birth name is Ronald Mewhort, Junior. The foundations of Cronus's empire were laid by his father, Ronald Mewhort, Senior. Anyway, Ron Junior went into the family business, but somewhere along the line, he and Ron Senior had a falling out, so Ron Junior screwed dear old dad out of his share of the business and had his name legally changed. He chose the name Cronus after the Titan who came to power by castrating his father."

I laughed. "Be sure to tell that story in court. It will win the jurors' hearts."

Zack sighed. "I'm going to need something. The worst part is I can understand the jurors' antipathy. Cronus is really a piece of work. He's a slumlord, but he walks into that courtroom as if he were king of the world. He's disdainful of the judge, the Crown, the jurors, and the witnesses. When someone makes a statement with which he takes issue, he turns his beady eyes towards the defence table and smirks. Of course, the suggestion that he and his defence team are buddies doesn't make the jury fond of us."

"It can't help that the girlfriend Cronus killed was a police officer," I said.

"Correction," Zack said. "The girlfriend Cronus is *alleged* to have killed. He didn't do it, Joanne. I've been through the depositions. I've interviewed Cronus a dozen times. And yes, the facts look bad. He was in a relationship with Arden Raeburn. He was in her apartment the night she was shot. The blood and skin under her fingernails were his, the bite marks on her body were made by his teeth, and his semen was in her vagina. But Cronus was scratched up too. The blood and skin under his fingernails belonged to Arden Raeburn and the bite marks on him came from her."

I began to move my fingers back up Zack's spine. "What am I missing here?" I said. "It sounds as if there's plenty of evidence to suggest that Cronus assaulted Arden Raeburn."

"He did assault her, and she assaulted him the way they'd been assaulting each other at least once a week for more than three years. Arden and Cronus were into rough sex: hair pulling, spanking, biting, handcuffs, whipping – the whole nine yards."

"And this hasn't come out in court?"

"Just obliquely. When the pathologist was on the stand, I asked him if Arden's injuries might be consistent with injuries suffered during rough sex. The good doctor agreed that they were, and then he delivered his punch line: 'All of them except for the bullet through her throat.' That guy's a laugh riot."

"Did the police find the weapon?"

"Yeah, it was in the apartment. It belonged to Arden – a Glock pistol – standard police issue. So Cronus is not going to be saved by the mystery weapon showing up in the real killer's dumpster. Jo, all we have is the fact that Arden liked it rough, and there's only one witness to that: Cronus. We've interviewed her colleagues, and they agree that Arden often had scratches or bruises, but she was a cop – scratches and bruises happen in the line of duty. And everyone says Arden was a very private person – we couldn't find anyone with whom she might have discussed her sex life."

"So you can't introduce the one fact that might explain everything."

"I can, but that would mean having Cronus take the stand. He's just chomping at the bit to get up there and announce that he and Arden liked their sex rough and that on the night she died they'd never been happier."

"Does Linda know any of this?"

"Linda knows all of it. She was thrilled when I told her Cronus was pressing me about taking the stand. It was as if she'd been touched by an angel."

"So what are you going to do?"

"We break our own logjams. I'll think of something. Now come on, Ms. Shreve. Off with that pyjama top. It's your turn."

Zack wasn't the only one whose muscles had turned to stone. I hadn't realized how tense I was till Zack finished unknotting me. I was rebuttoning my pyjama top when my BlackBerry began thumping on the nightstand. There was a text from Margot, and the message was simple: "Check your e-mail for photos."

The first photo was of Margot's feet. She was wearing her turquoise sneakers. I showed it to Zack. "That's your law partner," I said. "She wanted you to know she wasn't born wearing five-inch heels."

Zack grinned. The second photo was of Taylor and Declan on the dance floor. They were a handsome couple, but it was impossible not to notice that while Declan's eyes were on her, Taylor's were focused somewhere past his shoulder on her own private dream.

Zack was pensive as he looked at the picture. "What do you think is going to happen there?" he said.

I shrugged. "I don't know. I've given up thinking about what's going to happen next – it seems as though the universe just keeps pitching fastballs at us."

Zack's gaze was penetrating. "This is really getting to you, isn't it?"

."It is," I said. "The house was one thing, but that child this morning . . ."

"I hope you know that I feel like shit about all of this."

"Why, Zack? None of it is your fault."

"Do you honestly believe our house would have been blown up if I didn't work for Leland?"

"You're the one who always says the two most useless words in the language are 'what if.' We are where we are, Zack." I reached up and touched his lips. "And at this moment, where we are is fine with me."

CHAPTER

13

A restful weekend at the lake had me feeling almost like myself again by Monday morning. Leland and I had an uneventful run, and when I got home, Zack was showered and dressed for the day in one of the exquisite new suits Norine had chosen for him. "You look good enough to eat," I said.

Zack grinned. "'Had we but world enough and time . . .'"

I went over to the stove and stirred the porridge. "Where did you pick that up?"

"English 100 – the survey course – Beowulf to somebody else. *Had we but world enough and time* is one of the all-time great seduction lines. Every guy who was headed for law, medicine, engineering, or dentistry memorized it. It never failed."

"Do you remember the rest of the poem?"

"I never needed to. That first line always got me where I wanted to go." Zack wheeled in next to me and took my hand. "We're laughing again. So how do we keep the good vibe going?"

"Our doctor would say we should swim twice a day, give each other half an hour of deep massage every night, take plenty of long walks, avoid stress, sleep eight hours a night, and make love more."

Zack gave my hand a squeeze. "Henry's pretty realistic about our lives, Jo. I think he'd just tell us to do the best we can."

And that's what I resolved to do. After I had tidied up the breakfast things, the paintings from the old house were delivered, and I called Ed to come over and help me hang them. Scott Plear's *Firebrand* was instantly at home in the new space. It was a large painting, and its pulsing reds, golds, and yellows were a natural for a living room with a Tuscan feel and a two-storey wall of original warehouse brick. The cool indigos, greens, and blues of Taylor's first abstract gave an edge to Zack's and my large but generic bedroom on the main floor. When she was younger Taylor had been passionate about Miranda Jones's watercolours of geckos. She owned four, and after Ed hung them over her bed on the second floor, the room looked like Taylor's.

Finally, Ed and I sat with coffee in the living room. Ed looked around and his moon face creased with pleasure. "You know this isn't half bad," he said. I had to agree. We spent a pleasant hour chatting and unpacking our collection of Joe Fafard's miniature bronze horses and cows. Ed arranged them on fanciful glass-topped bronze table that seemed a perfect grazing place. For Zack's birthday in May, I'd given him a Fafard ceramic sculpture of an old boxer who'd gone one round too many. Zack had placed it on his dresser as a reminder, and after Ed and I said goodbye, I put the old boxer in our new bedroom. Then, because Zack was not the only one who needed to keep his focus, I placed the kaleidoscope that had been my retirement gift on my own dresser.

That evening we ate well, drank a little, and had a lei-surely family swim before climbing contentedly into bed.

For the first time in what seemed like ages, I was asleep almost as soon as I sank into Leland's cottony pillows.

On Tuesday, Margot's wedding dress arrived, and she took the morning off to indulge in some fizzy girl talk as she tried it on. The dress was exquisite, with a skirt fashioned of layers of draped silk organza petals that flowed with every step Margot took. She looked unbelievably lovely in it, but the bodice was tight and the new fullness in her breasts was evident.

Margot gazed at herself in her bedroom's full-length mirror. "So what do you think?" she said. "The seamstress said she can't let it out another quarter of an inch."

"You look sensational."

"And pregnant," Margot said.

"You look sensationally pregnant," I said.

"This will be a happy day for Wadena," Margot said. "Now for the love of God, undo that zipper. I need to breathe."

I spent the rest of the morning running errands and returned home in time to make a salad to go with the wonderfully crusty bread I had picked up at the Orange Boot Bakery. As I headed for the terrace with my lunch tray, I was still smiling at the prospect of Wadena's happy day. However, as I walked through the living room, I knew that, in Miss Clavel's immortal words, something was not "right." One of the drawers of the sideboard was partially open and the Fafard horses and cows had been rearranged on the glass tabletop. I put down my tray, trying to keep my hands steady, and counted the animals. One of the horses was missing.

"Louise!" I was furious that she had once again managed to disrupt my life with her self-pity. When there was no answer, I checked the rest of the apartment, calling her again. But it was clear there was no one else there. Louise wouldn't be interested in our sculptures – her obsession was

Leland. The image of the tattooed man in the red Trans-Am flashed through my brain. But how could Red Rage have managed to circumvent all the security codes?

The other mystery was that the intruder, or intruders, had done no damage and stolen only a small piece of sculpture.

I picked up one of the tiny horses. Each of the bronze animals cost $3,000, and we had owned twelve. A thief could have carried out the entire collection in a plastic grocery bag. Breaking into our home had been a huge risk for very little payoff. The intent clearly was to let us know that despite the fifteen-foot fence, the razor wire, and all the security swipes, we were vulnerable.

Out of nowhere, I remembered the Plains Indians custom of counting coup. If a warrior could walk into the enemy's camp and steal his weapons or his horse, he gained prestige. A member of Red Rage had walked into our home and stolen our horse – a clever urban twist on an old custom. If I hadn't been so terrified, I would have been impressed.

I put down the sculpture and called Debbie Haczkewicz, who sent over two constables. The male officer checked the security system, found nothing awry, then dusted the doorknobs and the surfaces of our furniture for fingerprints. The female officer took my statement, listened politely to my theory that in stealing our Fafard horse, Red Rage had replicated the act of counting coup, then got down on her hands and knees and found the missing bronze horse under the couch.

When I called Debbie to apologize for wasting her officers' time, she was understanding, but she cautioned me against letting my imagination run wild. I accepted her rebuke, but I knew what I had seen. The drawer to the sideboard *had* been open and the Fafard horses *had* been rearranged. I wasn't crazy, but it seemed someone was trying to push me in that direction. If that was the case, I had learned a lesson.

The next time I sensed that something was not "right," I would make certain I had hard evidence on my side before I passed along my suspicions to someone else.

By the time Zack got home, I had decided not to tell him about the incident with the Fafard horse. The trial was never far from his mind, and it was worry enough. Zack seldom second-guessed himself, but this time he knew he wouldn't be pulling any rabbits out of the hat. The physical evidence surrounding Arden's death was daunting, but if the jury could accept the explanation of consensual rough sex, Cronus would have a chance at acquittal. The only person who could offer that evidence under oath was Cronus himself, and understandably, he was determined to testify.

As his client's advocate and adviser, Zack was convinced that putting Cronus on the witness stand would be a mistake – he still couldn't see any of the jurors warming towards his client. But Zack was a gambler and a risk-taker, and he was running out of options. By Wednesday night, he was tipping towards going for broke and letting Cronus take the stand.

That night after we turned out the lights, Zack said, "So what do you think, Ms. Shreve? Should I let Cronus testify?"

"From what you say, your prospects can't get much worse," I said.

"Yes they can." Zack's laugh was a bark. "Cronus is the most alienating human being I've ever met. To know him is to loathe him."

"Well, Arden Raeburn didn't loathe him," I said. "And I don't know him."

Zack was pensive. "That can be remedied," he said finally. "Cronus and I always meet after the afternoon session in court. Why don't I ask him how he'd feel about having you join us tomorrow?"

———

The next day when I arrived at the courthouse, I was determined to keep an open mind about Zack's client. It wasn't
easy. Despite the immaculately tailored suit, the Countess
Mara tie, and the Italian leather shoes, Cronus was a snake.
When I shook his hand, it was unnervingly cold and smooth.
His head was shaven, and his eyes were hooded. His movements alternated between tense watchfulness and a quick
striking motion that I found alarming. His contempt for
women – or at least for me – was palpable.

He gave the witness room a scornful glance. "I know
you're not here for the ambience, Joanne. Zack tells me it
would be good for us to know how you react to what I want
to say on the stand."

Zack nodded. "It'll be useful to get a sense of how you
come across to an objective third party." Zack turned to me.
"We decided the best approach today is just to let Cronus
talk, and you or I can interrupt if anything leaps out at us."

The performance began with Cronus delivering a primer
on rough sex. Two minutes into his narrative, I knew he
needed coaching before he approached the witness stand.
Zack was playing an adversarial role, but even with a powerful and skilled opponent, Cronus was condescending. After
Cronus described the pleasures of hard and rhythmic spanking, Zack said, "Some might consider that sadistic." Cronus
looked at him pityingly. "It is *mildly* sadistic, it's also *mildly*
painful, but of course people who are into vanilla sex never
quite get the connection between pleasure and pain. Sexual
pleasure and a spanking both release endorphins. Rough sex
allows you to double your pleasure, double your fun."

Give him his due, Cronus was an enthusiast, but when he
moved from rhapsodizing about how women want a man
who shows them who's boss in the bedroom and began
explaining how a woman's *no* often means *yes*, Zack looked
as if he was about to spontaneously combust.

It only got worse when Cronus moved from lecture mode to personal history. When Zack asked Cronus to describe a typical evening he and Arden spent together, he said, "There's nothing to describe. We had sex."

"Surely you must have had dinner or gone to a movie or just taken a walk," Zack said.

Cronus was smug. "Arden might have done that with other men, but she knew what she wanted from me, and I knew what I wanted from her."

"And what was that?"

"Pleasure and pain."

"How did you meet Arden?"

"In the line of duty."

"Her duty or yours? Arden was a police officer and you are . . ."

"In real estate."

"You're a slum landlord."

"Sticks and stones." He smirked. "I provide a necessary service, and my ability to provide that service was being threatened, so I went to the police."

"Threatened in what way?" Zack asked.

"An agitator in North Central was distributing lists of telephone numbers to my tenants – community lawyers, tenants' associations, places where they could complain about my buildings. It's always wise to know the enemy, so I hired somebody to do some digging. Riel Delorme was bad news."

I was barely able to cover my gasp at hearing Riel's name from Cronus's mouth, but Zack, an experienced poker player, didn't miss a beat.

"Because he was making problems for you," Zack said.

"No, because he was disturbing the status quo – and the status quo worked for everybody. I didn't need a trouble-maker giving my tenants ideas. This Delorme guy was messing with them. Turns out his apartment was filled with

all kinds of crap about overthrowing the oppressors –
meaning guys like me – and books about people like Che
Guevera, whose biggest accomplishment was to get his
picture on a bunch of posters and T-shirts. There were even
tapes of Delorme telling his people that the oppressed had to
match the oppressors weapon for weapon. My tenants didn't
need to fight for their rights. They knew their rights. They
knew that in the houses I owned, they had the right to shoot
up, to entertain johns, to beat each other senseless, and to
drink till they passed out. They had the right to be left alone."

Zack was seldom at a loss for words, but the spectacle of
Cronus waving the flag for tenant freedom rendered him
speechless – at least temporarily. "So you took the results of
your 'investigation' to the police. And that's when you met
Arden?" he said finally.

Cronus pounced. "You got it wrong," he said. "Arden
wasn't the cop I gave the package to."

Zack was suddenly alert. "You told me you met Arden at
the cop shop when you went in to make a complaint –"

Cronus glared at Zack. "You're paid to ask the right questions," he said. "Yes, I met Arden because I was making a
complaint, but when I met her I was complaining about the
fact that the police hadn't done sweet tweet about the information that I'd brought them three weeks earlier. I'd have
thought those tapes would have got some pretty fast action."

"Shit," Zack said. "You're right. I made an assumption I
shouldn't have made. No excuses, but this file arrived on my
desk late. So you and Arden got together when she was following through on your initial complaint about Delorme."

"Right."

"And who was the first cop you dealt with?"

"A guy at the front desk who was obviously at the bottom
of the pecking order."

"But we could find out his name from the complaint you filed against Delorme."

Cronus's expression was almost pitying. "No, we couldn't because the report disappeared, along with the evidence. Hence my second complaint."

Zack tensed. "The file just disappeared?" This time he let his guard down enough to look over at me, brow furrowed.

"You seem surprised," Cronus said. "When people like me deal with the cops, there are all kinds of screw-ups."

"But you followed through."

"Of course I followed through, and so did Arden."

"And nothing was ever found."

Cronus shrugged. "Big surprise, eh? Anyway, it didn't matter because Delorme ceased to be a problem. He crawled back in his hole and left my tenants alone."

"Any idea why Delorme backed off?" Zack asked.

"Arden had a theory. Delorme's sister was a cop. Arden figured the sister lifted the report and the file and held them over Delorme's head as an incentive to straighten up and fly right."

"And Arden didn't report her suspicions to her superior?"

"No, and not because it didn't piss her off. Arden believed in the rules. But cops don't rat on other cops. Anyway, the situation remedied itself, like I said, and everybody was happy. Delorme had cleaned up his act, so his sister was happy; and he'd stopped being a major pain the ass for me, so I was happy. And the sister left the police force, so Arden was happy."

Cronus turned to me. "And that's the end of the story."

"It sounds as if your relationship with Arden went beyond just sex," I said. "You talked about the Delorme case."

"The Delorme case was a matter of mutual interest," Cronus said. "But talking wasn't our thing. Sex was our thing, and it was great." He leaned towards me. "And it was *always* consensual. We never did anything we hadn't agreed on. Neither of us made demands. We never fought. There was no reason for me to kill her."

His eyes shifted from Zack to me. "Do you have enough?"

I nodded.

"So do you think I should testify?"

"That's between you and Zack," I said.

"There are six women on the jury. How do think they'll react to me."

"I don't know." I forced myself to focus on the reason I was there. "I believed you when you said you had no reason to kill Arden. But you were patronizing when you explained the appeal of rough sex. You're not testifying to win converts. You're there to explain forensic evidence that otherwise is inexplicable. If I were in your position . . ."

Cronus raised an eyebrow. "And if you were into biting and handcuffs . . ."

Zack's voice was a growl. "Back off," he said.

I met my husband's eyes. "It's all right," I said. "Cronus, I understand that you have to make jurors understand what happens between a man and woman during rough sex. But keep it factual. The release of endomorphins is solid information. Focus on the fact that you and Arden both had high-stress professions and rough sex was a way of relieving stress. And don't challenge other people about their choices. You may be facing twelve jurors who are into vanilla sex."

"Sounds as if you think I should take the stand."

My eyes travelled around the cheerless witness room. "I think you and Zack should talk about it."

Zack walked me to the elevator. "Jo, I know this coincidence with Riel is weird, but we'll have to talk about it later. I'm under the gun, and Cronus and I have to focus on his defence."

"I agree," I said. "Do what you have to, but get Cronus off."

Zack looked at me closely. "You don't believe he killed Arden."

"No, I don't. But I can't imagine how you'll get a jury to believe that."

"Neither do I," Zack said. "In law school they told us that the trial lawyer's greatest fear is having an innocent client. With a guilty client, you give it your best shot, and if you lose, you know that justice has probably been served. If you have an innocent client, and you know you can't save him, you pretty much want to puke fifteen hours a day."

CHAPTER

14

Wadena is two hours northeast of Regina. The wedding was at two-thirty in the afternoon, so we were able to drive up and back the same day. Untried buildings were always a concern for Zack, but happily the church was fully accessible, and Margot had promised she'd personally throttle any able-bodied person who used the stall in the male bathroom reserved for people in wheelchairs.

On Saturday the sun was fiercely bright and the sky was clear. It was a perfect hot, still summer day. The drive through the gently rolling farmland was pleasant, and as he gazed out the window at the countryside, the tensions that had dogged Zack since the trial seemed to lift.

Swift and graceful, a hawk swooped out the sky; it picked up a gopher and sped away. "Did you see that?" Zack said.

"I did," I said. "Did you, Taylor?"

But our daughter, texting and listening to her iPod, was oblivious to the drama of Nature red in tooth and claw that had been played out seconds before.

"We should come out here more often," Zack said. "Just to catch the action."

Because Declan was under age, Zack was acting as the legal witness to Leland and Margot's marriage, so when we arrived at the church, Zack went straight to the rector's office to meet with the groom and his best man. Taylor and I went inside to stake out premium places near the front for us and for Barry and Ed. Margot's wish that her Wadena friends bring nothing except jam jars filled with flowers from their gardens had been honoured. No space was empty, and the mingled scents of the vibrant flowers of June hung heavy in the air.

Taylor was wearing the botanical print she'd worn to the All-College. She was growing her hair out. When she was making art, she either anchored her hair in a ponytail or knotted it casually atop her head. Her mother had done the same thing, but Taylor was always prickly about comparisons to her mother, so I never mentioned it. Today, Taylor's straight dark hair fell smooth and shining to her shoulders, and her eyes were bright. Exams were over – there were good times ahead.

"Have you thought any more about what you want to do next week?" I said. "We're going to stay at the lake tonight, but we have to go back to the city tomorrow. Your dad's going to be busy with the trial at least until Friday. You could stay with the Wainbergs or with Gracie and her dad."

"I'm coming back with you," Taylor said. "I talked to Lisa Wallace. She thinks I should spend the week teaching art at the Willy Hodgson Centre. It would give me a chance to see if I like the work, and give the staff and clients a chance to see if they like me. If it works out, I can volunteer in the fall."

I didn't reply immediately. Taylor read my expression and her forehead creased. "You said if I wanted to do it, I should do it."

"I still think that," I said. "But, Taylor, those kids have a lot of problems."

"That's why Lisa suggested a try-out. I don't want to make a big deal about volunteering and then drop out." Her eyes searched my face for a reaction. "Well . . . ?"

"I'm proud of you," I said. "Of course, I'm always proud of you."

"So it's okay?" Taylor said.

"Yes," I said. "But promise me that if you feel like you're in over your head, you'll let Lisa know."

"I will," Taylor said. She looked around the church. "Hey, this place is really filling up," she said.

"Margot predicted it would be SRO," I said.

When Ed and Barry came in, Barry looked around happily at the flowers and at the women in their filmy summer-bright dresses. "Good for Margot for going retro," he said. "This takes me back. When I was a kid I used to get so excited about the weddings in Stockholm."

Taylor's eyes widened. "I didn't know you lived in Stockholm."

"Stockholm, Saskatchewan," Barry said. "Population 323, so there weren't a lot of weddings, but I remember every single one of them."

The string quartet that had been playing softly as the guests arrived suddenly turned up the volume. Zack, Leland, and Declan came in from the rectory and faced the congregation. When Margot's seventeen-year-old nephew and the young man who was first trumpet in the Regina symphony walked up the aisle, the crowd hushed. The two men raised their instruments and blew the fresh, bursting opening chords of Jeremiah Clarke's "Trumpet Voluntary," and a chill ran up my spine.

Margot had five brothers and all were groomsmen. The five bridesmaids had all been at Linda Fritz's dinner party. Their dresses were of the same design as Margot's – layers of draped silk organza petals, but the bridesmaids' dresses were strewn with random splashes of colour. Margot's sister, Laurie, hugely pregnant, was the matron of honour.

Margot was an incredibly beautiful bride, but as she passed us, Taylor breathed the words that, as Margot predicted, would be on everyone's lips. "Is Margot pregnant?" Taylor whispered.

I leaned close to Taylor. "The baby's due in December," I said.

"So cool," Taylor said happily.

It *was* cool and the joy on the faces of the newly married couple was tonic.

When the ceremony was over and the last picture of the bridal party had been taken, we went to the golf club, where Sis Gooding and her assistants had prepared a prairie feast: turkeys, hams, perogies, cabbage rolls, jellied salads in colours that matched the splashes on the bridesmaids' dresses, homemade buns, vegetables from the garden. It was wickedly hot, but no one cared.

I was eyeing the spread. "No one will go hungry," I said to Sis Gooding.

"That's the idea," she said. "So what's your connection with the wedding."

"I'm married to Zack Shreve. He's one of the groomsmen," I said.

Sis looked at me with interest. "Zachary Shreve. I've read about your husband. I'll bet he keeps you hopping."

"He does," I said. "But he's worth it." I gazed at the table. "Did you and your assistants make all this yourselves?"

Sis laughed. "If I'd ignored the offers of help from people who wanted to contribute food to Margot's wedding, I would have been run out of town on a rail. No, what you're looking at is the best of Wadena. Everybody in town knows who does what well. My job was simply to co-ordinate."

"So what did you make?" I asked.

"The strawberry shortcakes," she said. "At the risk of sounding immodest, you'll never taste a finer dessert."

"I'll make sure to get in line," I said.

"Get some for your husband, too," she said. "He strikes me as a man who'd appreciate a fine strawberry shortcake."

I'd met Margot's sister, Laurie, when Margot and I paid a quick visit to Wadena the year before. I'd been impressed then by Laurie's common sense and humour, and when I lined up for a serving of Sis Gooding's dessert, I was pleased to see that Laurie was right behind me.

The sisters had chosen very different paths in life. Margot had wanted a successful career, and she got it. Laurie's life had always centred on Wadena, and the child she was expecting was her fifth. Physically, the sisters were much alike: the same cornflower blue eyes, the same wheat blonde hair, but they were alike in a more significant way: neither had time for bullshit, and that day in the dessert line, Laurie and I exchanged the usual pleasantries and got down to business.

Laurie's voice was low and musical. "I think people around here have always assumed I envied what Margot has – the recognition, the money, the great clothes – but I knew differently. Kids aren't for everyone, but Margot always wanted them, and I'm so glad she's not missing out."

"She and Leland have a great future ahead," I said.

"They really love each other, you know," Laurie said.

"You sound surprised," I said.

"I'm not," Laurie said. "It's just that mid-life marriages are often a matter of convenience." She laughed. "Maybe all marriages are a matter of convenience – at least to a degree. Their marriage won't be an easy one, but it will be worth the effort." After that gnomic remark, Laurie and I picked up our strawberry shortcake and shifted our discussion to the mysteries of adolescent behaviour.

———

By the third week in June, the sun sets late in Saskatchewan but most of the wedding guests were going back to Regina, so the dancing on the lawn began early. When Slim Whitman sang the first notes of "I Remember You," and Leland took Margot in his arms for the bride-and-groom dance, I thought I had never seen two happier people.

After Slim hit his last high note, Margot approached Zack and Leland held out his arms to Laurie. Laurie laughed and pointed to her stomach, so Leland turned to me. Not surprisingly, Leland danced with precision and grace. So did Zack. Taylor kicked off her shoes and she and Declan began dancing on the grass. Then people began joining us, but when Margot noticed that Ed and Barry were staying on the sidelines, she approached them. "You guys are newlyweds," Margot said. "How come you're not out there?"

"Community standards," Ed said.

Margot frowned. "Oh for God's sake." She held out her arms to me. "Joanne, may I have this dance?" I slid into her embrace, and we began a cheek-to-cheek number that by any criterion was a test of community standards. People smiled encouragingly at Margot and me, and when Barry and Ed joined us, there was nothing they could do but keep on smiling.

The reception was still in full swing when Zack, Taylor, and I left. We were anxious to get to Lawyers' Bay: it had been a full week, and Willie and Pantera were waiting. As so often after a hot day, there was a storm that night. Zack and I lay in the dark and watched as sheet lightning turned the entire sky to glowing white.

"You know, I'm glad the wedding's over," Zack said.

"So am I," I said. "There could have been a surprise visit from Louise or a mystery guest with explosives. But the day was perfect in every way."

"May the perfection continue," Zack said.

"Amen to that," I said.

Wednesday morning, Mieka called to ask if I was free to come to a press conference in the Warehouse District at noon. Concerned about the seepage of public support for The Village, Leland had decided to make an early announcement of Peyben's plans to build the shared multipurpose facility. Riel and Shelley Gregg, the developer who had done the renos on the Halifax Street building and who was designing the new building, would be joining Leland to answer questions. The press conference was to be held in the vacant lot where the facility would be built. The land bordered North Central and The Village, so the optics were good.

I arrived a little before noon and went over to stand by Mieka. She was on edge but happy. "I thought about bringing the girls, it's such a big moment for Riel and for the city, but I know how these announcements can drag on, so I decided not to."

"Good call," I said. "A couple of times when your dad was announcing some major initiative, I took you and your brothers to the press conference. You always got bored and started kicking each other."

For a hastily assembled press conference, the event went off smoothly. The mayor and the appropriate city councillors were there, as were local crews from each of the networks and a photographer and a reporter from our city's paper. Shelley, Leland, and Riel were all wearing jeans and T-shirts, and as they began the formal part of the announcement, they stood behind a worktable that held a mock-up of the latest multipurpose centre that Shelley had designed. In many respects that structure met the criteria for the proposed Village/North Central facility, so the model was a useful and appealing focus for their presentation.

Riel and Leland flanked Shelley at the table. That place-ment, too, was good optics. The men appeared cautious, cordial, and, most importantly, equal. Riel spoke first. He listed the benefits to the city of the proposed facility and, specifically, to North Central, whose community members would be part of the process from the beginning. Leland announced that he shared Riel's vision for the project and that while there were many details to work out, he and Riel would work them out publicly with the aid of a mediator. Peyben hoped to break ground at the beginning of September and open the doors a year later. Shelley Gregg gave a moving speech in which she said that a city grows from its heart. Her words were few, but the image was powerful and as the media people asked more questions and scrambled for more footage, I knew the press conference had been a success. Mieka and I hugged each other spontaneously for the first time since Riel had protested Leland's honorary doctorate.

"I'm glad you came, Mum," Mieka said. "I was nervous, but it went well, didn't it?"

"Very well," I said. "I liked Shelley's line about a city growing from its heart, and Riel and Leland said all the right things. It was a good start."

"There are so many reasons why this has to work," Mieka said.

I put my arm around her shoulders. "I know," I said. "And it will work."

Zack called when I was in the liquor store choosing a bottle of Reisling for dinner.

"What are you up to?" he said.

"Buying booze," I said.

"Get lots," he said. "I'm being drawn and quartered and the jury is trying not to look pleased."

"It can't be that bad," I said.

"It is," Zack said. "Get the biggest bottle of gin you can find and two straws."

I'd just turned north on Winnipeg Street on my way back to the condo when I noticed the red car behind me. My pulse quickened. At some level, I'd been waiting for the red Trans-Am to appear from the moment I'd knelt beside April Stonechild and the member of Red Rage flexed his bicep and pointed at his tattoo.

"We'll find you," he'd said, and now they had. My cell began to ring, I checked call display – "Number Withheld," it read. The ringing stopped. There was an underpass ahead. As I turned left onto 8th Avenue, the ringing began again. I could feel sweat breaking out along my hairline. I stopped for the light and looked in the rear-view mirror. The driver appeared to have his cell to his ear. The light changed and I gunned it.

I started up 8th and the Trans-Am fell behind, but I hit another red and he caught up with me. When my kids began driving, I'd passed along the tips I'd heard for dealing with a driver who seemed menacing. I couldn't remember any of them. Panic had made my brain porous. And then I saw Nicky's Restaurant, famous for its lentil soup and slow service, and I remembered: *pull into a space as close as possible to the door of a public building.*

Adrenalin pumping, I screeched into a space reserved for the handicapped. I opened my door, jumped out, and started for the restaurant. I heard a car door slam behind me.

"Wait," yelled a voice. "I've got your wallet."

I spun around. The man facing me was a reed-thin Aboriginal man with a brush-cut and a pleasant face. He was wearing a white T-shirt and blue jeans. No tattoos. The red car behind him was a Mustang, not a Trans-Am.

He held out my wallet on the palm of his hand. "You dropped this when you came out of the liquor store. I thought

I could catch you in the parking lot, but you took off, so I followed you." His eyes scanned my face. "Obviously it was a stupid move," he said. "I've frightened you."

Deeply ashamed, I took the wallet. "Thank you," I said. "I'm very sorry. I'm a little crazy right now."

"It's none of my business," he said. "But you should probably try to calm down before you drive again. You were speeding in a school zone back there."

I remembered my relief when the red car slowed on 8th. Unlike me, the driver was obeying the law. My knees were shaky. "I won't go anywhere till I know I'm ready to drive again," I said.

He nodded and walked away.

I sat in my car for five minutes cursing my hysteria and gulping air. Finally, when I'd had my fill of self-castigation and my breathing was even, I put the keys in the ignition.

At four o'clock, I picked Taylor up from the rec centre. She was wearing her painting clothes: a man's white shirt from Value Village, jeans, and sneakers. When she hopped into the car, she was paint-smeared and beaming.

"I don't need to ask you how your day went," I said.

Her words came in a torrent. "It was great. My first two days were terrible. I wasn't going to tell you that, but now that it's over I will. The kids in the program are pretty cynical, and when I tried to talk they made comments."

"What kind of comments?"

Taylor arched an eyebrow. "You don't want to know, but I didn't cry or explode or run away, so I guess that's something. Anyway, Lisa suggested that today we should begin with a group meeting. This time, when I started talking about how making art stretches you and allows you to really look at life and put what you see on canvas, a few kids began to listen.

"There was one boy who hasn't talked in weeks. The staff can't tell us specifics about people's histories, but this boy, Neil, is my age. Lisa said he'd been through something traumatic and he hadn't said a word since. For most of the morning, he just looked at the canvas, and then, finally he made this great bold red stroke. He stood there for about fifteen minutes staring at what he'd done. And then his brush began to fly. It was if the art he was making had been in him all along. Jo, it was so great." Taylor took a breath and gave me her self-mocking Sally smile. "And how was *your* day?"

"It was fine," I said.

"Good," she said. "Now I've been wondering whether art might give Neil a way to break through the things that are walling him in. I know it's not going to happen tomorrow or even soon, but if he keeps painting maybe one day he'll realize he's been talking through his art all along, and he'll start using words."

Taylor sighed with contentment, slipped out her iPod, slumped into her seat, and we drove the rest of the way without talking – two women absorbed in their own worlds.

When Zack came home, I met him at the door with his swim trunks. He scowled. "You were supposed to be holding a bottle of gin with two straws."

"The Bombay Sapphire's in the refrigerator and we have very nice Reisling to go with the pickerel we're having for dinner," I said. "All that's standing between you and pleasure is twenty minutes doing laps in the pool."

Zack was still grumbling when we stepped into the elevator, but later when he was towelling off in our bedroom and I handed him his martini, he was sanguine. "This was worth waiting for," he said.

"Let's hear it for delayed gratification," I said.

"You bet. So how was your day?"

"Fine. I lost my wallet and a Good Samaritan returned it." I was becoming expert at editing the truth.

"A story with a happy ending," Zack said.

"Yes, and we're going to have a pleasant evening," I said. "Taylor's third day as a volunteer was beyond wonderful. You'll get a contact high just by sitting next to her."

Zack was thoughtful. "I'm glad Taylor's volunteering at the rec centre. She has a lot to offer – not just her talent, but her sweetness. The kids she'll be working with can use a reminder that life isn't always brutal."

I kissed the top of his head. "You're a good guy," I said.

"Not always," Zack said. "But thanks. Hey, Leland tells me you were at the press conference to announce the new shared facility today."

"News travels fast."

"Leland and I arrived in the parking garage at the same time."

"Ah. Then he told you the conference went smoothly."

"He seemed pleased."

"He should be. It was a great first step."

"Let's hope it's just the first of many," Zack said. He pivoted his wheelchair towards the door. "Come on. Time to hear the latest news from Willy Hodgson."

That night, when I poured the massage oil onto my hands and began to knead Zack's shoulders, I felt as if my fingers had hit rock. "How can your muscles be this tight after a swim, a martini, and two glasses of Reisling?" I said.

Zack moaned. "In a word, Cronus."

"He's been on my mind, too," I said. "Zack, there has to be something you can do."

"I've been over the Crown's case a dozen times," Zack said. "And one thing keeps leaping out at me. Motive. As Cronus told you, he had no reason to kill Arden Raeburn.

If somehow I can just get the jury to see that, everything else falls away."

I began moving my hands down Zack's back. "The Crown must have suggested a motive."

"That's their Achilles heel. The first rule of litigation is to tell your story and make it stick. Linda hasn't told her story. She alluded exactly once to a possible scenario, and she hedged her bets by saying that there were only two people in the room that night, and since one of them was dead, all we had was conjecture. She sketched out a bare bones account of what might have happened. Cronus and Arden were in Arden's apartment engaged in their Saturday night activity of choice. Things got out of hand. Arden Raeburn's gun was in the room, and Cronus used it to kill her."

"Given Cronus's past and his demeanour, I can see why a jury might buy that."

"So can I," Zack said. "But they shouldn't because it isn't true. There's not a shred of evidence connecting Cronus to the gun that killed Arden. And Linda isn't sure of her theory either. She's meticulous, and she always builds her case very carefully. Every shred of evidence Linda presented in this case was calculated to make certain that Cronus was convicted. She doesn't leave loopholes because she doesn't want to lose on appeal. So I ask myself, Why hasn't she nailed down motive?"

"And the answer is . . . ?"

"And the answer is because she can't. Joanne, the forensic evidence is the lynchpin of the Crown's case. If we can establish Cronus and Arden agreed to rough sex, we remove the lynchpin."

"And Cronus is the only one who can remove the lynchpin," I said. "He'd have to testify and he'd have to make the jury believe he was telling the truth."

"He convinced you," Zack said. "Do you believe he could convince a jury?"

"I don't know," I said. "But I think you're out of options."

Zack pushed himself up to a sitting position, then used his arms to inch himself back so that the pillows piled against the headboard supported him. "Right," he said. "Hand over that massage oil, Ms. Shreve. Your turn now and you get to choose the conversational topic."

Given the tension I could still feel in Zack's body, I decided against what we both knew was Topic A and moved to something safe: our plans for the Canada Day long weekend at the lake.

The Canada Day weekend had always been special for the members of the Winners' Circle, the group that had gravitated towards one another in their first year of law school because they sensed they shared a destiny. There had been five of them: Blake Falconer, Zack, Chris Altieri (now dead), Delia Wainberg, and Kevin Hynd. At the end of their first year, the members of the Winners' Circle brought sleeping bags and tents to Lawyers' Bay and camped out on the beach. That weekend, they drank beer, ate hot dogs, and as they watched their campfires turn to embers, they dreamed dreams. It was a weekend none of them would ever forget, and they agreed that, in the years ahead, no matter where they were, the members of the Winners' Circle would always meet at the lake on July 1.

They formed their own law firm, and they kept their promise. No member of the Winners' Circle had ever missed July 1 at Lawyers' Bay. Once, Kevin Hynd had been exploring Mount Kailas in Tibet, but he managed to make his way to a phone, call in, and be marked present. As the partnership succeeded and the firm grew, the character of the Canada Day party changed. It was now very much a Falconer

Shreve event – the firm's chance to open the gates at Lawyers' Bay and give their associates, staff, clients, and rivals a day filled with the hottest, the finest, the freshest, the fastest, and the most succulent that money could buy. The Canada Day party was a hot ticket, but this year, due to the troubling events of the past month, the police had recommended rescheduling the party. This weekend's event would be family only, but deciding who was family turned out to be a knotty problem.

Big changes had come to Falconer Shreve. Counting Margot, there were seven new partners, and six were in the Calgary office. Zack, who was always in favour of including everybody, wanted to invite all the partners to the party. Delia Wainberg, who was still a true believer in the Winners' Circle, wanted this Canada Day gathering to be restricted to the original members. Kevin Hynd, who was in charge of the Calgary office, wanted to include his people. Blake Falconer, who like Delia had a reverence for the past, voted with her.

One evening, not long after we moved into Leland's condo, Zack broke the stalemate by asking Margot what she thought. She heard Zack out, then shook her head. "Did it occur to any of you that we new partners might have plans of our own for the long weekend? Leland and I are going to Chicago, and I somehow doubt that the new Calgary partners are panting at the thought of being invited to a lake forty-five kilometres east of Regina." Margot had looked approvingly at her very red dagger fingernails. "Here's a thought. Why don't you Winners' Circle guys have yourselves a big time that weekend. You can roast your weenies and sing 'Auld Lang Syne' all night long. The rest of us will do what we do and we'll show up for the command performance at Lawyers' Bay next year."

That night when I'd walked Margot to the door, she'd drawn me out into the hall. "Tell me honestly, Joanne.

Don't you ever find all that Winners' Circle stuff just a tad weird? Every single one of those partners is a millionaire now and they didn't get that way by being idealistic about the law or anything else."

"I know," I said. "But the one thing they can't buy back is the way they were. That's what they want to hold on to."

Margot had given me a long look. "So I should feel sorry for them."

"Not at all," I'd said. "Just learn the lesson."

Since the guest list was settled, Zack and I just conferred on the menu for the weekend. Usually, the affair was catered, but this year because our numbers would be smaller we were going to cook for ourselves. Zack had volunteered to bring the meat and we decided on boned prime rib and whole salmon – both of which Zack fancied himself an expert at barbecuing.

Despite the pleasure of massage and menu planning, Zack had trouble sleeping. After tossing and turning for two hours, he rolled over and mumbled, "I have to put Cronus on the stand."

"Good," I said. "The decision's made. Want me to come to court tomorrow?"

"Would you?"

"Of course. I'll drop Taylor off at Willy Hodgson, then I'll go straight over."

"We're in Courtroom B," Zack said.

"Got it. Now go to sleep."

And he did.

As I always did when I entered the courthouse, I spent a few seconds gazing at the mural of the God of Laws in the lobby. Over the years, I had been a parent-helper at many tours of the courthouse, and I knew that mural was a mosaic of 125,000 pieces of Florentine glass and that the female figures flanking the God of Laws were Truth and Justice. That morning, I gave Truth and Justice a few moments of extra attention. "Do your stuff, ladies," I whispered, then went inside.

The courtroom was crowded. The trial was winding down, so the media and members of the public were hoping for a last burst of fireworks. I found a seat where I had a clear view of the jury and settled in.

Cronus was already sitting in the prisoner's box, guarded by a provost who looked like she meant business. Zack and his associate, Chad Kichula, were already seated at the defence table, and Linda and her associates were at the table reserved for Crown counsel.

We rose as the clerk announced that Madam Justice Rebecca Cann was entering. Justice Cann lived across the creek from us and she owned a pair of Shih Tzus, so our paths crossed frequently. When we talked dogs, she had an easy smile and a bright enthusiasm. But today, the talk was not of Shih Tzus, and Justice Cann's expression was stony.

The day was hot, and as he walked from the prisoner's box to the witness stand, I saw that Cronus had dressed as any successful businessman might for an important meeting: a sleek white suit, a violet shirt, and a striped tie of violet and aubergine. As he raised his hand to be sworn in, I scanned the jury's faces. They were as representative as any twelve people I'd meet at Safeway on a Saturday afternoon. The majority were Caucasian, but one had the warm copper skin of the Caribbean and two were East Asian. Most were middle aged, but one woman appeared to be very old. I knew that the boy in the front row had to be nineteen to be called for jury duty, but he didn't appear to have been nineteen for long. The jurors were a disparate group, but as I watched them focus on Cronus, I knew that they were united in one signifi-cant way: they all heartily loathed the defendant. Zack was usually able to establish a good relationship with jurors, but as he steered his wheelchair towards the witness box so he could question his client, I saw that the jury's distaste for Cronus extended to my husband.

The realization that there was nothing Cronus could say or do that would sway that jury seemed to hit Zack and me at the same moment. We exchanged glances, then Zack shrugged and began trying to pump life into his still-born case.

Cronus acquitted himself well. Despite the jury's aversion to him, he attempted to establish eye contact. Without belittling their choice of sexual activity, he was clear in explaining what rough sex involved, and why he and Arden made the choices they had made. The defence needed to establish that the scratches and contusions found on both Arden and Cronus's bodies could have been the result of their normal sexual practices, so Zack guided Cronus through a description of rough sex that was graphic but not salacious. Cronus did well, but I could tell from the set of Zack's shoulders that he knew it wasn't enough.

When the court broke for lunch, both Zack and Cronus appeared drawn and tense. I went over. "That was a disaster," Cronus said.

"You only need to get through to one person," I said.

"You were watching the jury," Cronus said. "Did I get through to anybody?"

"Maybe that young man in the front row," I said. "He seemed to really be listening to what you said."

Zack gave me a quizzical look. "We'll focus on him after lunch," he said. "Ms. Shreve, would you mind very much having lunch on your own? There are some things Cronus and I should discuss."

"Not at all," I said. "I have some errands to run. I'll be back at two."

There was a linen sale at the Bay. Life at the lake was hard on towels, so I laid in a supply, had a chili dog and Orange Julius at the food court, and went back to the courthouse.

The snatches of conversation I overheard as I sat waiting for court to begin were not encouraging. I thought Pierre Trudeau had it right when he said that there was no place for the state in the bedrooms of the nation. Whatever consenting adults did once the bedroom door closed seemed to me to be no one's business but theirs. However, Cronus's account of the mechanics of rough sex appeared to have opened a rich and nasty judgmental vein in my fellow citizens. People were licking their chops as they rushed to condemn him.

As the jury filed back in, I hoped that at least one of them had heard the words "Judge not, that ye be not judged." It was impossible to tell what they were thinking, but when Cronus took the witness stand, they stared at him as if he were a specimen. His speaking voice was an oddly soothing monotone. As he described his relationship with Arden, the very old lady in the second row of the jury box drifted off to sleep.

Cronus's explanation that he had no motive for killing Arden Raeburn was persuasive, but by the time he offered it, the faces of the jury were closed.

The right to a trial by a jury of one's peers may be a cornerstone of our justice system, but seemingly, like the Queen in Alice in Wonderland, Cronus's peers had decided on "Sentence first – verdict afterwards."

Linda's job was easy. She sat back and watched through narrowed eyes as Cronus told his tale. When the very old lady in the second row of the jury box awoke with a start, Linda smiled at her forgivingly.

It had been another bad day for the defence, but Zack would have three days to lick his wounds. It was a long weekend, so we did what we had done a hundred times before. We picked up our daughter and headed for Lawyers' Bay.

My favourite piece of furniture at the lake was an old oak partners' table that Zack's decorator had found at a small town auction. It was large and ornate with twenty-four chairs upholstered in cracked maroon leather. Whether there were twenty of us or two of us, we ate there. That Friday night, eighteen of us sat down to dinner. In poker and in family life, Zack liked a full house. As he took in the faces at our table, he looked as content as I'd ever seen him – as always, I was amazed at how he could compartmentalize troubling thoughts and fully focus on enjoying the good times when they happened.

Everyone seemed to be getting along. When Angus came from the airport with his new girlfriend, Zack and I both swallowed hard. Maisie Crawford was six feet tall, with a body that rippled with health and power, an intelligent face, shoulder-length, curly brown hair, and a split lip.

"Lacrosse," she exclaimed with a grin that quickly turned to a grimace. "Shit," she said. "I just did it last night. It's still a little sensitive."

"Would a beer help?" Angus said.

"Probably not," she said amiably, "but it's still a good idea." She turned to me. "What can I do to help?"

"Thanks, but I think everything's under control. Get Angus to introduce you to the gang."

Zack and I watched as Maisie made the rounds. "Has Angus ever been without a spectacular girlfriend?" Zack said.

"Not to my knowledge," I said. "But even in the rarefied circle of Angus's girlfriends, Maisie's a standout. What kind of law does she practise?"

"She's a trial lawyer," Zack said. "And Falconer Shreve is lucky to have her. Calgary's still a ballsy town, and rumour has it that when Maisie walks into a courtroom, shaking the floor with every step, the manly parts of opposing counsels shrivel."

I laughed. "Tonight, I'm just grateful she's taking the heat off Riel. Mieka was worried he'd feel a little out of his element."

"I was looking forward to talking to him." Zack looked around. "Where is he?"

"He and Peter went to check on the roast. Man's work."

"I should be there," Zack said.

"No, you shouldn't," I said. "This is why we have kids. To leave you and me free to enjoy the party."

"In that case," Zack said, grinning, "allow me to get you some wine and lead you to a quiet corner."

It was a good weekend. There was no shortage of power-boats at Lawyers' Bay, so the big kids got in some serious waterskiing, and the little ones, including our granddaughters and Delia and Noah's year-old grandson, Jacob, had some spectacular boat rides. Zack and I swam, took the dogs for walks, came home, and ate ice cream.

Saturday night, when the sun smouldered against the horizon, the members of the Winners' Circle went down to sit by a campfire on the beach and the rest of us cracked open beers and caught the sun's last rays.

Maisie looked towards the beach. "Kevin has mentioned the Winners' Circle a couple of times. I thought it was a joke."

"Not to them," Noah Wainberg said. "And not to anybody who knew them then. I was in their year in law school – I was never in their league, but they were magic." He handed Jacob to me. "But one picture is worth a thousand words. I'll be back in a second." He loped off towards their cottage and came back with a large framed black-and-white photo. "That was the way they looked that first summer."

All the members of the Winners' Circle were there. Delia,

Kevin, Chris, Blake, and, in the middle, Zack. They were up to their waists in water – Zack too. He'd wheeled out so far that the lower part of his chair was submerged. Squinting into the sun, their faces suffused with joy, they were incredibly appealing. Maisie studied the photo and pointed to Chris Altieri. "Who's this? Isn't everybody supposed to show up?"

"Chris Altieri committed suicide three years ago," Noah said.

"What happened?"

Noah shrugged. "He couldn't forgive himself for being human."

After dinner, we regrouped, and I got some time to catch up with Angus.

Pantera had followed Zack down to the beach, but Willie, ever loyal, had stayed with me. Angus dropped to the grass and began rubbing Willie's stomach. "I don't want to dim your glow, Mum, but did you find out anything about that file Pat Hawley found?"

"No. You know, with everything that's been going on, I forgot all about it. But I showed it to Debbie Haczkewicz just after you brought it to me. She was polite, but after she found out that the file had just turned up randomly, she didn't seem particularly interested. It was pretty much the same story with Norine. She pointed out that the most recent clippings in that file were fifteen years old and that in fifteen years a lot of employees had come and gone at Falconer Shreve. The clippings could have belonged to any of them."

"So the file is weird but not significant," Angus said.

"That seems to be the consensus," I said. I gazed towards the point. "No sign of Peter and Maisie," I said with just a small question mark in my voice.

Angus shrugged. "Pete's probably still figuring out when to make his move."

"Really," I said. "And you're okay with that?"

"There's nothing between Maisie and me. She didn't have any plans for the long weekend, so I invited her to come to Lawyers' Bay."

"I'm glad you did," I said. "We all like Maisie."

Angus's grin was rakish. "But Peter likes her most of all."

On the night he died, Zack's partner Chris Altieri taught Taylor a riddle that she never tired of. *What three words make you sad when you're happy and happy when you're sad?* The answer was, *Nothing lasts forever.* As we drove back to the city Monday afternoon I remembered that riddle. The past three days had been free of care, now it was time to return to the real world. Zack was preoccupied, and as we approached the city, I could see the tension gathering in his body.

I tried to distract him. "Did you notice that there was some interesting chemistry between Peter and Maisie?"

"I did," Zack said. "Angus seemed cool with it." He shrugged. "It's a different world. When I was Angus's age I would have knee-capped the other guy, brother or no brother."

"Angus might have been into knee-capping mode if he and Maisie had been more than just buddies," I said.

"It's hard to imagine being 'just buddies' with a woman who has legs like Maisie's," Zack said. "But as long as everybody's happy . . ."

"They appear to be," I said. "Speaking of . . . how did your meeting on the beach with the Winners' Circle go?"

"Truthfully, it was a little sad," Zack said. "But it was also long overdue. We all agreed that everything is changing. Margot's reaction was a slap in the face, but she was right. We have to acknowledge that the Winners' Circle doesn't mean anything to the new people. Kevin says that, for the sake of the firm, it's time to stop worshipping those early years as if we were bugs stuck in amber."

"Last night Maisie asked about the Winners' Circle," I said. "Noah brought out that black-and-white photo of the five of you in the lake that first summer. You really did have something special. You still do. You're all at a good place in your life."

"Well, except Chris," Zack said.

"True. But you know, I've been thinking of that old riddle Chris told Taylor."

"Why's that?"

"Because the answer isn't true. Some things do last forever."

Zack reached over and squeezed my leg. "And thank God for that," he said.

CHAPTER

15

Tuesday morning when I came back from my run with Leland, Zack was making a hungry-man's breakfast for us both: scrambled eggs, sausages, and toast. I poured juice. "You must be planning to do some heavy lifting," I said.

Zack's lip curled. "I think it's more a case of 'the condemned man ate a hearty meal.'"

Mindful of my grandmother's adage "Never trouble trouble till trouble troubles you," we hadn't discussed the Cronus case at all over the long weekend. Nor had we brought up what we had recently learned about Riel's past. Zack and I were in desperate need of a problem-free weekend and we had taken it. Now the weekend was over. "Is it that bad?" I asked.

"It's bad," Zack said. "But I'll survive. Hey, the other day when you mentioned that juror number six in the front row might be open to persuasion, did you really pick up on something or were you just blowing smoke?"

"Cronus seemed pretty down. I was trying to be encouraging."

Zack sighed. "I was afraid of that. But just for the hell of it, I'm going to pretend juror number six is wavering."

Despite the fact that the courtroom was packed, I was able to get the seat with the unimpeded sightline to the jury that I'd had before the weekend. When the jurors entered, I noticed that the very old lady looked well rested, and for no reason whatsoever, I took that as a good sign.

Zack's closing statement was tight. He thanked the jury for their diligence. He also thanked them for their forbearance in remaining tolerant and restrained when they were confronted with graphic and unsettling testimony. He cited the same evidence the Crown had presented, but he said, as judges of the facts, the jurors were compelled to separate the facts from their reaction to the defendant and how he earned his living.

"I know how difficult that is," Zack said with a small smile. "I'm a lawyer. I've heard the jokes. Nobody even bothers to make jokes about slumlords. My client owns and rents houses in North Central. These are houses that, as he testified, serve the needs of a very specific population. You and I might not like Cronus's choice of occupation, and we may not share his choice of sexual practices. All of that is irrelevant. As judges of the facts, all you are being asked to do is decide whether the facts in this case are sufficient to declare my client guilty of murder.

"They are not. As the Crown counsel pointed out, this is a curious version of he said/she said. But this equation is more complex than the Crown would have you believe.

"You are asked to find this defendant guilty of murder. You have seen the autopsy photographs and you've heard the pathology reports. Arden Raeburn died from gunshot wounds. The bullets that killed her were fired from her own Glock pistol. There is not one iota of evidence connecting Cronus to that pistol. No fingerprints. No witnesses testifying that Cronus was in Arden Raeburn's apartment at the time the pistol was fired. Nothing. And none of Cronus's actions on the night of April 24, 2010, are those of a man guilty of murder.

"You heard his testimony. On that Saturday evening, he and Arden engaged in the same acts that they had indulged in for more than three years. At the ending of the evening, he and Arden had a drink together. Then, as he did every Saturday night, Cronus drove home, played with his cat, and went to bed. He made no attempt to dispose of the clothing he was wearing that night. As usual, he put what he'd been wearing in the laundry hamper where the cleaning lady who came every Tuesday would find it and wash it. He slept well, and when the police arrived to question him Sunday afternoon, he was sitting in his living room having a beer and watching a basketball game.

"These are not the actions of a guilty man, and I ask you to remember that when you determine Cronus's future."

As Linda Fritz rose to deliver her closing statement, every eye in the courtroom was on her. With her auburn hair smoothed into a French twist as carefully composed as she was, Linda was a commanding figure. She began by thanking the jury for their attention throughout the trial and commending them for the gravity with which they had accepted their responsibility as "judges of the facts." She then gave a careful précis of the evidence.

There was no dispute between the Crown and the defence about physical evidence. Both agreed that Arden Raeburn's regulation Glock pistol was the murder weapon and that it had been wiped clean of prints. There was no dispute about the ballistics reports that measured the distance and angle from which the shots were fired. The physical evidence on Arden's body and beneath her fingernails could have suggested either that she fought off her assailant or that she had been a willing partner in a session of rough sex. The blood, bodily fluids, and fibre remnants taken from Arden's body matched samples from Cronus, just as the blood, bodily fluids, and fibre remnants on Cronus matched samples taken from Arden. The defence had conceded that on Saturday nights, "date nights" for Arden and Cronus, the couple in the neighbouring apartment had often heard signs of struggle, but Zack had established that the couple had never approached Arden with an offer of assistance, nor had she requested help.

Only once did Linda falter. When she touched on what might have motivated Cronus to murder Arden Raeburn, Linda could only suggest that the only two people who knew what happened that night were Arden and Cronus, and Arden was dead. At that point I glanced over at Zack. He wrote something on his legal pad and drew his associate Chad Kichula's attention to the notation. Without seeing the legal pad I knew that Zack had written the number 3 on the page. For him, the fact that there had been three people in Arden's apartment the night of the murder had become an article of faith. One of the three was dead, one was unjustly accused, and the third, the real murderer, was still at large.

Madam Justice Rebecca Cann began her charge to the jury by giving the standard instructions about the credibility of witnesses, the weight of circumstantial evidence, and the concept of reasonable doubt. She delivered her charge on the law slowly and precisely. "As defined by the Criminal Code of Canada," she said, "murder is a culpable homicide with specific intentions. To be found guilty of murder, the person who causes the death of a human being either meant to cause that death, meant to cause the human being bodily harm that he knew was likely to cause death, or was reckless about whether death would ensue or not." Justice Cann gave further directions on first and second degree murder. She then instructed the jury that they could find the defendant guilty only if the Crown had established all the necessary elements, including intent.

Finally, the judge outlined the evidence presented during the trial, then without drama, the jury filed out to begin deliberations. After they left, there was the usual hubbub in the courtroom. A guard escorted Cronus down to the cell in the courthouse basement where he spent the periods of the day when court was not in session. The judge went back to her office. When the crowd thinned, I walked over to the table where Zack was sitting with his associate Chad Kichula.

It was the first time I'd met Chad, and as Zack introduced us, a smile played at the corner of his lips. Zack had told me Chad was a rock star, and his description was right on the money. Tall and lean, with dark blond hair, piercing blue eyes, and a dangerous smile, Chad was indisputably what Taylor and her friends called a stud muffin. The stud muffin and I shook hands and then he left the courtroom for the Barristers' Lounge.

One of Zack's favourite quotes was from a Regina prosecutor named Serge Kujawa. Kujawa said that speculating on what a jury was doing and why was a total waste of time, so he spent all his time speculating. As a rule, Zack wasn't a speculator. He had an uncanny ability to leave a case at the courthouse, but that day I knew that he would carry the burden of this case with him until the verdict came in, and I was worried.

"Chad's on duty," I said. "Any chance we could go home for a swim?"

"Sorry, Ms. Shreve. I have to be here. If the jury asks the judge questions, I have to know her answers. I may not agree with her interpretation of the law and that could be a problem down the line."

"If you don't get rid of some of that tension, there'll be another kind of problem down the line," I said.

"Then I'll have to deal with it. You know this is my job, Jo. During a trial everybody's on call: the judge, the staff, the jurors, the Crown, the defence, and the defendant. I don't want a mistrial because I was swimming when I should have been in the courtroom."

Zack looked grey and spent. I wasn't about to give up. "You trust Chad," I said. "I'll leave the phone by the pool. You can be back here in half an hour."

"Madam Justice Cann will be pissed."

"Maybe," I said. "But you'll be alive, and that's pretty much all I care about."

I won that small battle. Zack came home. We swam and he was back at the courthouse in a little over an hour, where he stayed until ten that night. I had a martini waiting for him. He thanked me for the thought, asked me to save the drink for the next day, and fell into bed.

The next morning we reached a compromise. Whenever Zack thought he could safely leave, he'd call me. There wasn't much down time, but we made the most of what we had. If there was a two-hour lunch recess, we'd eat on the terrace and take a nap or I'd swing by Mieka's and pick up the grand-daughters for some grandparent time in the roof garden.

By Friday morning, there was still no verdict in the Cronus case and we were both on edge. I blinked first. "It's been two full days," I said. "What do you think is going on?"

"Probably one of the jurors is holding out," Zack said. "I've been running through their faces in my mind, trying to figure which one of them seemed sympathetic."

"Does it matter?"

"Nope." Zack's smile was self-mocking. "I just get off on playing head games with myself."

I laughed. "What happens if the juror continues to hold out?"

"The foreperson will announce that the jury is unable to reach a verdict, and the Crown will have the option of running a new trial."

"And you'll be back to square one."

"Not really. The Crown will almost certainly decide to run a new trial, and there are things I'll do differently. Of course, there are things Linda will do differently, too."

"But for Cronus, anything is better than a guilty verdict."

"Yes, but we're not home free yet. Peer pressure is powerful. It's hard to withstand the arguments and the frustrations of people you've been working with closely – especially when there's so much at stake."

"So we just cross our fingers and hope for the best?"

"That's the usual legal advice," Zack said dryly.

That afternoon, we were coming home from a late lunch when Chad Kichula called. The verdict was in.

"Time to go back to work," Zack said.

"Do you want me to come to court with you?"

"I'd be glad to have you there. Cronus isn't going to have a lot of friends in that room."

"You think the jury will convict him?" I said.

"There are always surprises." Zack said, but he didn't sound as if he was expecting one.

When we got to the courthouse, it seemed that we weren't the only ones caught off guard. Linda Fritz's hair was damp. "I was at the gym," she said.

"I'll stay down wind," Zack said.

Linda's look would have curdled milk. "I showered," she said.

Zack opened his arms wide. "In that case . . ."

Linda turned to me. "How do you put up with him?" She didn't stick around for an answer. Zack shrugged, then wheeled down the corridor to get his barrister's robe and I headed for Courtroom B.

I was able to get a good seat again. I'd just pulled out my BlackBerry to check for messages when Cronus was brought in. He was dressed more casually than usual – in slacks, a crisp, casual-Friday cotton shirt, and loafers. He looked like the average guy, exactly the look Zack had been pressing for all along.

When Cronus strode to the prisoner's box, I saw that his face was drawn and dark circles of sweat were spreading under the armpits of his summer shirt. After the lawyers had taken their places, the jury filed in, and then finally Madam Justice Rebecca Cann entered. The courtroom was packed, and the tension was palpable, but the protocol that governed the delivery of the verdict was low-key.

The court clerk addressed the jury: "Ladies and gentlemen of the jury, have you agreed upon your verdict?"

The jury foreperson, a balding man who seemed to have grown smaller and more bent during the days of the trial, stood and announced that the jury had indeed agreed upon a verdict.

As Cronus stood to hear his fate, his hands were trembling. So were mine.

Then it was the court clerk's turn: "How say you? Do you find the accused guilty or not guilty on the charge of first degree murder?"

"Not guilty," the jury foreperson said.

"Do you find the accused guilty or not guilty on the charge of second degree murder?"

"Not guilty," the jury foreperson said.

Cronus closed his eyes and exhaled. Chad Kichula and two other associates from Falconer Shreve who had come to watch clapped Zack on the back. It was over. Except for one puzzling coda. As the jury filed out, the very old woman who had dozed during much of the testimony made sure she caught Zack's eye and then she winked. Zack's nod of acknowledgement was barely perceptible.

The associates formed a wedge in front of Zack and Cronus so they were able to get out of the courtroom. I joined them in the lobby. I offered Cronus my congratulations. "I really am innocent, Joanne," he said.

"I know you are," I said. "I'm glad the verdict went your way."

"So am I," Cronus said.

"Well. that's that," Zack said, shrugging off his robe. He turned to Chad and the other associates. "Keep the media away from Cronus till he gets to his car. After that go out and have a great dinner. Charge it to Falconer Shreve."

Zack looked up at me. "Show's over," he said. "Let's get out of here. Boy, I never figured the old lady would be our salvation."

I took his robe. "You always say, 'It only takes one.'"

"True enough," Zack said. "All that matters is that the puck goes into the net, and the red light goes on."

Having decided to wait till the next morning to drive to the lake, we were in bed and asleep by seven-thirty. We awoke to an acutely beautiful day – cloudless, bright, and warm. Zack and I turned towards each other and embraced wordlessly. Seemingly, the verdict had lifted the heaviness that had been weighing on us since the trial began.

As always, I met Leland at the elevator, and he, too, seemed light-hearted. "I almost stood you up this morning," he said. "I didn't want to leave Margot."

"The good thing about being married is that Margot will be waiting when you come back," I said.

Leland met my eyes. "I'm a lucky man, Joanne."

We exchanged a quick smile of camaraderie and stepped into the elevator. As we began our run, the sun was hot but there was breeze enough to keep us comfortable. Except for the sound of our footfalls hitting the sidewalk in unison, the world was silent. It was a perfect day for running.

Just as we turned onto Osler Street, Leland grabbed my arm. "Look out, Jo."

I glanced down and saw an ugly shard of glass from a broken liquor bottle on the pavement in front of me. A second later, I heard a percussive sound, then another, then a third – very close together. I knew immediately that it was gunfire. I turned towards Leland. "Did you hear that?" I said. But Leland wasn't there. I stopped and looked behind me. He'd fallen.

"Are you all right?" I asked, but I knew he wasn't. He was crumpled on the pavement and blood was pooling around his head. His brilliant blue eyes were still open, but his lean and powerful body was unnaturally still. I knelt on the sidewalk. It was a replay of the morning Leland and I had run to help April Stonechild, but this time, I knew I couldn't harm Leland by moving his body. I knelt, lifted his head on to my knees, and then hit Zack's number on speed-dial. He picked up almost immediately. "Leland's been shot," I said. I looked up at the building nearest me for the address. "We're at 630 Osler Street." Then I broke the connection and sat cradling Leland's head in my lap until the piercing bleat of the sirens grew louder and then, when the ambulance found us, fell silent.

With April Stonechild, the EMT technicians had been deliberate and thorough, but their treatment of Leland seemed almost casual. They checked his vital signs, and then finding no sign of life, one of the technicians gently closed Leland's eyelids and shut his jaw. When the EMT team lifted Leland's body onto a gurney, covered it, and stowed it in the ambulance, I didn't move. They turned their attention to me: checking my pulse and blood pressure and asking me questions that were designed to elicit information about how I was handling trauma. A female technician with a broad, kind face and a gentle voice took charge. "You've had a terrible experience. The police want to talk to you, but we think it would be best if they waited until we could get you stabilized at the hospital."

"I want to go home," I said. My voice was dead.

A young police constable stepped forward. He was firm but kind. "I'd like to ask you a few questions. Can you tell me your name?"

"Joanne Shreve."

"What happened, Joanne?"

"Someone shot him," I said. I looked past the officer's shoulder and saw the ambulance carrying Leland start its unhurried passage down Osler Street. There were no flashing lights. This was no longer an emergency. The young constable asked me again to tell him what happened, but I couldn't see the point of answering. The story was over.

I saw Zack coming down the sidewalk and pushed myself to my feet. "That's my husband," I said. "I'm going home now."

A female police officer stopped Zack a few metres away. "Stay where you are, sir," she said. "This is a crime scene."

"Fair enough," Zack said, stopping his chair. "But my wife wants to go home."

The officer took a step towards Zack. "You're Zack Shreve, the lawyer."

Zack nodded. "I am."

"Then you know it's essential that we talk to your wife. She was the last person to see Leland Hunter alive, and she's the only witness. There's the possibility a fragment of a bullet may have exited Mr. Hunter's body, so we need to check Ms. Shreve's clothing for residual evidence. I'd also like to run a GSR test."

Zack scowled. "Oh, come on."

I turned to him. "What's a GSR test?"

"It's a test to see if a person has fired a gun recently." Zack glared at the officer. "And in this case it's totally unnecessary." He turned to me. "Joanne, you're under no legal obligation to permit the officer to administer the test."

The young constable ignored Zack and addressed me. "It's a simple test. No more intrusive than having your hands wiped by a moist towelette. And, Joanne, by eliminating you, we can make sure we're looking for the killer as soon as possible."

I held out my hands. Another officer, this one older, came over to conduct the test. He started to explain what he was about to do, but I cut him off. "I don't care," I said, "just do it."

When the GSR test was over, I turned back to the young constable. "Leland and I were running together," I said. "He said, 'Look out' and grabbed my arm. I thought he was warning me about a broken bottle on the sidewalk. There were three shots. Leland fell. I went back to him, but he was dead. Can I go home now?"

As I walked towards my husband I felt as if I was encased in ice.

Zack took my hand and turned to the young constable who'd been interviewing me. "Here's what I propose," Zack said. "My wife has given you what she can, and she voluntarily submitted to the GSR test. I'm concerned about her. I'd like to take her to our family doctor." He took out his cell. "I'm going to call Inspector Haczkewicz in Major Crimes. I'll describe the situation and ask her if it's possible to interview Joanne more fully later. Then I'll hand the phone to you, and if you have concerns you can relay them to the inspector. Is that acceptable?"

When Zack put his cell back in his jacket pocket, the officer said, "We have to make certain your wife's clothing is handled in a way that will ensure continuity of the evidence. I'll send a female officer home with you to get your wife's clothing. Inspector Haczkewicz will make arrangements with you for the interview." I hadn't been paying attention to the call. One thought pushed everything else away.

"Zack, how are we going to tell Margot?"

Zack stroked my hand and looked at the officer. "I'm going to call Margot Hunter. I don't want her to hear about Leland from a stranger."

Zack's conversation with Margot was brief. I stood next to him, but it seemed as though he was speaking from a great distance. When he broke the connection, he turned to me. "She wants to go the hospital to see him."

I remembered Leland's unseeing blue eyes staring at the sky. "That's a mistake," I said.

"It's Margot's choice," Zack said. "We're going to have play this by ear, Joanne. Now let's get you home."

As soon as we crossed the threshold of our condo, I headed for the bedroom. Constable Lerat, who had followed us in a squad car, was close behind me. When I began to peel off my T-shirt, she slipped on a pair of surgical gloves and said, "I'll help you with that."

She dropped each item of my clothing into a separate clear plastic bag and marked the bag with an identifying notation. When I was naked, she said, "Well, that's it. Can I get you a robe?"

I looked at the smears of blood on my body, "I need to shower."

"I'll send your husband in to help you," Constable Lerat said.

When I stepped out of the shower, Zack was there with a towel and my favourite pair of flannelette pyjamas.

I put them on and got into bed. Zack moved close. "Could you stay with me till I fall asleep?" I asked.

Zack smiled. "Sure."

I don't know how long I slept, but when I awoke, Zack, who was always in motion – thumbing his BlackBerry, making phone calls, scribbling on legal briefs – was exactly where he'd been when I lay down. "Welcome back," he said.

Hearing Zack's voice, and seeing his silhouette in sharp relief against the sunny window, I felt the comfort of the familiar. Then the memories engulfed me. "Leland's dead, isn't he?" I said.

Zack nodded. "I heard one of the EMT guys tell a cop that it was over in an instant. Leland didn't suffer, Jo."

"We don't know that," I said, and I was surprised at the anger in my voice.

Zack rubbed my shoulder. "Can I get you anything? Some tea?"

"I can make tea," I said. I slid out of bed and walked towards the kitchen. One of my running shoes had left a faint track of blood on the floor. I soaked a towel, cleaned the blood off, then dropped the towel in the garbage.

Zack's eyes never left me. "Do you want me to call Henry Chan?" he said.

"Why?"

"He could give you something to help you get through the next few days. You're going to have to do a lot of things that you won't want to do. Debbie will be over later. Margot will want to know exactly what happened, and she's going to need us to be here for her. And we'll have to tell Taylor and do what we can to help Declan. I know you're strong, Jo, but everybody has a breaking point. There's no shame in getting a little help."

I shrugged. "If you think it's necessary, give Henry a call."

Zack called Henry's office. "He's sending a prescription for Ativan to the pharmacy on Broad Street. But he does want to see you. Gina says he can squeeze you in after lunch. Will you be okay here alone while I pick up the prescription?"

"Doesn't that pharmacy deliver?" I said.

"Not as fast as I do," Zack said.

After Zack left, I went back to our room and stared at myself in the full-length mirror. Running with Leland had been good for my body. "You can get through this," I said to the tanned, strong-looking woman in the mirror. And for about thirty seconds, I convinced myself that it was true.

CHAPTER

16

When there was a knock at the door, I opened it expecting Debbie Haczkewicz, but it was Margot. "What happened?" she said.

I put my arm through hers and led her into the living room. She listened without interruption as I told her about Leland's and my last run.

"He had death threats, you know," she said. "Including one from Louise the night before our wedding. He just shook them off." She exhaled. "Jo, all I want to do right now is crawl into a hole and never come out again."

"I know," I said.

"I have to tell Declan." Margot's eyes were miserable. "How do you tell a boy something like this."

I put my arm around her. "You'll find the words."

"I shouldn't be driving. I'll take a cab to the school and bring Declan back here. Would it be okay if I bring Taylor home too? Declan will want her around."

"I'll call the school and tell them you're coming."

Margot didn't answer. Her attention had drifted. "This morning when we woke up, Leland and I made love," she said. "Then I went back to sleep, and he went for his run with you." She swallowed hard. "I'm really glad we did that."

As soon as Zack came through the door, he handed me the bag with the pills. "Those things are supposed to kick in pretty quickly."

"Good," I said. "Margot was here. You just missed her. She's gone to Luther to get Declan."

"I could have done that for her," Zack said.

"I think Margot wanted to do it. She's bringing Taylor back, too."

"That's probably a good idea," Zack said. "The media will have the news about Leland soon, and the kids don't need to be dealing with a circus." He took my hand. "How's Margot doing?"

"I don't think it's real for her yet," I said.

Zack's laugh was short and bitter. "I don't think it's real for any of us."

"Before you came home, I looked in the bathroom mirror and told myself I just have to hang on until after the funeral, then I can fall apart."

"Let's hear it for short-term goals," Zack said. "But there's a lot to do between now and the funeral, and ready or not, you and I are going to have to step up to the plate."

"I'm not ready, Zack," I said. "I feel as if my skin's been ripped off. My default position is always fake it until I make it. But right now I'm not even up to faking it."

"Give yourself time," Zack said. "The big thing is getting Margot and Declan through this. Margot has significant decisions to make, and she has to make them fast. Peyben was Leland's company. He has a board and hundreds of people working for him, but it was a one-man show. Margot has to decide who's going to run the company now, and she has to make sure Peyben's board and its stakeholders know the company will continue to be strong."

"What's going to happen to the shared facility with North Central?"

Zack groaned. "If it turns out that someone associated with Riel Delorme killed Leland, it'll blow sky high, and that will mean more problems for The Village, for North Central, and for all of us."

"And there's the funeral to plan," I said.

"I've already asked Norine to help with that. If Margot gives Norine a general idea of what she wants, Norine will make it happen."

"Thank God for Norine," I said.

Zack raised an eyebrow. "Oh, I do. And if I forget, Norine reminds me."

When my cell rang and I saw that the caller was Mieka, I felt my nerves twang.

Mieka was agitated. "I just heard the news. Leland Hunter was shot this morning. He's dead, Mum."

"I know," I said. I took a breath. "Mieka, I was with Leland when he was shot."

She was clearly baffled. "But they said Leland was killed early this morning. You would have still been at the lake."

"No, we were in Regina. During the week, Zack and Taylor and I have been living in the building Leland owns on Halifax Street. Leland and I have been running together. And this morning someone shot him."

"I don't understand. Why didn't you tell me you were living there?"

"After the explosion at the house, the police thought that the fewer people who knew where we were, the better."

Mieka's voice was cold. "And of course I couldn't be trusted because of my relationship with Riel."

"I didn't tell your brothers, either."

"Because you knew I'd be hurt if I were singled out. Well, I am hurt. And I'm angry."

Suddenly the emotions I had walled in erupted. "I'm angry, too," I said. "Do you realize you haven't said one word about the tragedy of Leland's death or about Margot and Declan's loss. Not one question about how I'm reacting to watching a man I considered a friend die. Just schoolgirl pique about not being in on a secret. I love you, Mieka, but I can't deal with this right now." I broke the connection.

Zack looked at me questioningly. "That was Mieka," I said. "You heard my half of the conversation. I don't want to talk about it any more."

"Understood," Zack said. "I'll call Peter and Angus for you."

"Thanks," I said.

My cell rang again. It was Ed Mariani. His voice was choked. "Jo, I am so terribly, terribly sorry. I liked Leland, and I'm very fond of Margot. Please give her my condolences."

"I will. Ed, I was with Leland when it happened."

I could hear his intake of breath. "My God. Do you want me to come over? Are you okay?"

"No, but Zack's here. I will be. I think."

"It never ends, does it?"

"No," I said. "It never ends."

The afternoon passed in a surrealistic blur. Zack took me to our doctor's in the afternoon, and Henry pronounced me physically sound but said he was concerned about my emotional detachment so he had his wife and nurse, Gina, book an appointment for me the following week.

Then Debbie Haczkewicz came by. I'd answered her questions, but clearly I'd been an unsatisfactory witness. She was relentless as she pressed me for details. Had Leland's eyes been focused on the sidewalk or on one of the buildings when he shouted, "Look out"? I didn't know. When he pulled me back, had he used real force? I couldn't remember. Had he tried to shield me? I thought so, but maybe not. When did I notice that he'd fallen? Time didn't make much sense any more.

I was baffled by her persistence. Leland was dead, and I didn't remember much of what happened. It was that simple. When I walked her to the door, Debbie said, "I'll be in touch."

"There's no point," I said. "I have nothing to say."

Debbie looked at me oddly. "I know this has been a shock, Joanne, but I have to talk to you about the case."

"Which one?" I asked in my new detached voice. "The bombing of our house? The assault on April Stonechild? Leland's murder? I seem to have been involved in every major crime in Regina in the past three weeks. And I don't want to talk about any of them."

"You don't really have a choice."

"Yes, I do," I said, and then I closed the door on her.

Life went on around me. I listened and sat very still. Norine had agreed to deal with whatever came her way. She arranged for Peyben's media relations department to release a statement announcing Leland's death and reassuring corporate partners and investors that the company would continue to perform well. Media relations had sent a draft of the obituary they were releasing and Margot had okayed it.

Two issues remained unresolved. Leland's Peyben colleagues wanted his funeral to be a showing of the colours – a public affair with a broad spectrum of important guests celebrating Leland's professional accomplishments. Margot was opposed to a large public event. She and Zack had agreed to talk the problem through, but Zack assured Margot that she had the final word, and he'd support whatever she decided. The second matter was thornier. Declan wanted to live with

Margot and she wanted him with her. Declan was seventeen, so the choice was his, and his reasons were compelling: Louise's alcoholism was consuming her life and Declan had seen enough to begin to be afraid it would consume his. Leland's death and the news that Margot was expecting a child had opened an unexpected new place for Declan in Margot's life and he wanted to step into it.

The problem, as always, was Louise. Declan loved his mother, and he was afraid that without him, she would disappear into the bottle.

Saying that in his world food was the currency for love, Ed insisted on dropping off dinner for all of us. As I set the table, it occurred to me that this would be our first dinner party in our new home. Margot's sister, Laurie, had arrived from Wadena, so we would be six. At Margot and Leland's wedding, Laurie had been ripely pregnant. She was nearly at her due date, but this was her fifth child, so she felt she would know when to call her husband, Steve, to come into Regina.

Ed's spinach and ricotta cannelloni was an inspired choice, and although none of us believed we were hungry, we all cleaned our plates. Ed was right. No matter what, people have to eat. Even tragedy didn't keep Wadena girls from doing their duty as guests: Margot and Laurie insisted on helping us clear the table, then quietly returned to Margot's condo with Declan. Taylor gave him a long wordless hug as they were leaving.

When Taylor went upstairs to get ready for bed, Zack turned to me. "You're having a rough time, aren't you?"

"Was it that apparent?"

"Just to me. You were so quiet." Zack's eyes were worried. "Did you take another pill?"

"I didn't need one," I said. "I seem to have shut off all on my own."

"That's not good," Zack said.

"It's working for me," I said.

Zack took my hand. "Since you haven't had a pill since this morning, how about a shot of that Hennessey's xo cognac in the liquor cabinet before we hit the sack?"

"Why not?" I said. "I wonder if Leland bought the cognac for a special occasion?"

"Don't do that, Jo. You're just pouring salt in the wound. Anyway, I doubt if Leland bought the cognac at all. I imagine the housekeeper just kept the bar stocked."

We took the brandies into the bedroom. We got into our pyjamas, climbed into bed, then picked up our snifters. Zack held his glass out to me. "To Leland," he said.

I nodded and took a sip.

Zack smiled appreciatively. "Good stuff, huh?"

"Nothing but the best," I said.

Zack swirled his. "What do you think about Declan's decision to move in with Margot?"

"I think it will save his life," I said.

"So do I. I've already set the wheels in motion, so there'll be no turning back. When you were getting dinner on the table, I called Sage Mackenzie and told her that Declan was moving out of Louise's and that Margot and I knew we could count on Sage to smooth the transition."

"How did she respond to that?"

"With relief," Zack said. "Joanne, I know Sage isn't your favourite person – she's not mine either – but we may have underestimated the burden she's carrying. According to Sage, Louise has been in free fall since the wedding. She's drinking even more, and her behaviour has changed. Apparently Louise is normally a very angry drunk, but Sage says that today Louise has been 'chillingly calm.'"

"Maybe Louise was right," I said. "Maybe it's easier for her now that Leland is dead. But I can't believe Louise will accept the idea of Declan living with Margot, under any circumstances."

"Sage believes she will. So do I. I came to know Louise well during the time that I was paid to keep her and Declan out of trouble. Leland was Louise's life. Declan was not a priority. In fact, she told me many times that the only reason she had Declan was because Leland wanted a child."

"Then I'm glad he's getting away from her," I said. "Because if Louise told you that she never wanted a child, she's told Declan."

The next morning I woke up at 4:45, dressed for my run, took the elevator down to the basement, and ran for an hour on the treadmill. The exercise room in the building was windowless. There was a flat-screen TV on the treadmill. I turned it on and watched the last half of *Rosemary's Baby*. Mia Farrow was pregnant with the devil's child.

When I went back upstairs, Zack was in the kitchen, looking anxious. "Where were you?" he said.

"Running on the treadmill in the basement," I said. "And watching *Rosemary's Baby*."

His face relaxed. "That's a hell of a way to start the day. We can do better." He held out his arms and I leaned in. "Want me to make porridge?"

"That'd be good," I said. After I'd showered and dressed, I came back to the kitchen. The bread was in the toaster and the porridge was in the pot. Zack put the food before me, and I ate it dutifully.

Zack had pulled his wheelchair up to the table so he could face me. "So what are your plans for the day?" he said.

"I'm staying here," I said. "I'm not quite ready for the world."

"Are you afraid?"

I nodded. "Shouldn't I be?"

Zack's voice was low and comforting. "It's possible that now that Leland's dead, the attacks will stop. I know it's terrible to look at what's happened in that light, but there's a certain logic there. I was Leland's lawyer. The bombing of our house could have been a warning. With all the security it would have been much harder for Red Rage to bomb the condo or any of the Peyben offices than it was to get at us."

"Do you believe that Leland was the intended target all along?"

"I think it's possible."

"I'm still going to stay put," I said. "I only have two major tasks today and I can do them both from here."

"And those tasks would be . . . ?"

"Making peace with Mieka and being around for Margot."

When we cleared away the dishes, I noticed the time. "Taylor must have forgotten to set her alarm," I said. "I'll run up and give her a nudge." When I turned onto the landing halfway up, I saw that Zack had moved his chair to the bottom of the stairs and was watching me intently.

"I *am* going to be all right," I said.

"Can I take that to the bank?" Zack said.

I took a deep breath. "Yes, you can take that to the bank."

The kiss that Zack and I exchanged before he drove Taylor to her job at Willy Hodgson was a lingering one. It would be a long time before we took each other for granted.

Just after Taylor and Zack left, there was a knock at the door. My heart raced for a moment, until I heard Margot's voice calling my name. She was dressed in jeans and a turtleneck. Her hair, still wet from the shower, was hanging loose. Her eyes were pink from weeping, but she was still Margot – strong and resourceful. She didn't bother with preamble. "There are a couple of problems, and I need you and Zack and a small army to help me deal with them. Is Zack tied up this morning?"

"He's taking Taylor to her volunteer work. He'll be back in ten minutes."

"Good," she said. "There's something ugly brewing at Peyben. I can feel it. I've had a number of lugubrious voice-mails from members of Leland's board expressing sorrow at my loss and telling me they need to meet ASAP."

"What's up?"

"I'm not sure, but I'm guessing Leland's loyal associates are going to relieve my widow's burden by offering to buy me out – at fire sale prices."

"Bastards."

"They are bastards, aren't they?" Margot said thoughtfully. "Leland's only been dead a day, and they're already swooping in. Anyway, I'm going to need help. I've called Blake. Zack and I have learned a trick or two in court, but managing an international corporation is not part of our skill set. Blake understands that world, and he knows the right people. If I have to clear the decks at Peyben and start again, Blake will have suggestions. Anyway, he should be here soon."

"International finance is definitely not part of my skill set either," I said. "Is there anything else I can help with?"

Margot's smile was wan. "As a matter of fact, there is. I know you're still reeling, but Declan's moving out of Louise's after school, and he could use back up. Laurie turned the phone off last night so we could get some sleep, but Louise left a half-dozen hysterical messages saying that both she and I should be grateful that Leland was at peace now and he wouldn't be torn between us any more."

"That's delusional," I said.

"I know it is," Margot said. "And I can handle it, but I'm not sure about Declan. Louise doesn't seem to have thought about him in the least. He barely got his father back before losing him permanently. At this point we're all fragile, and I don't want Declan having to deal with Louise alone. I'd go myself, but I expect to be tied up with those buzzards from Peyben, and Declan trusts you."

"I'll go with him," I said. "Zack talked to Sage yesterday. She thinks that when Declan's gone, Louise might be ready to seek the kind of help she needs."

Margot exhaled wearily. "I hope to God she's right because Sage has given her notice. She says Louise is consuming so much of her time that her law practice is suffering. Sage has agreed to stay on until she gets Louise settled into some kind of rehab facility, but after that, it's *sayonara*."

"Maybe this is the push Louise needs to make some changes."

"You're just like my sister," Margot said. "Always able to find the pony in the pile of shit."

We exchanged wan smiles. "How are you feeling physically?" I said. The glow that pregnancy had brought Margot was gone. Her face was drawn and she was clearly exhausted.

"Fine. Aside from the obvious, I'm having a dream pregnancy." She laughed softly. "Of course, it's a little difficult to forget the obvious."

When Zack got back, I told him about Margot's concerns. "I'd better head over there," he said. Then he held out his arms. "Let's try to get back to normal tonight. Have a swim and do all the things that are supposed to guarantee that we'll be together forever."

After Zack left, I sank down on the couch in the bright living room and closed my eyes for a moment. But too much had happened, and my mind was racing. I collected my phone from the bedroom. There was a message from Norine. Margot wanted a small religious service. Did I have any ideas about a venue that might be suitable?

I called Norine and suggested a couple of possibilities. My own preference was for the Luther chapel at the university.

It was an intimate and attractive space and the Hunters had ties to Luther. Declan was a student at the high school, and Leland had been a generous donor to the Luther College building fund. Norine said it sounded promising and she'd check it out.

As soon as I hung up, I squared my shoulders and hit Mieka's number.

My daughter sounded as strained as I felt. "The girls and I were just talking about you. We wondered if you'd like to come for a visit this morning," she said.

It was an olive branch, and I was eager to seize it, but I wasn't ready yet to leave the safety of the building. "Could you come here?" I asked. "I don't think I'm up to driving."

"Sure." Mieka hesitated for a beat. "I never thought I'd be asking you this, Mum, but where do you live?"

"In the building on Halifax Street where Ed and Barry were married." I gave her the number she needed to buzz our condo. "It's a pretty day," I said. "We could have tea in the roof garden."

"The girls would like that," Mieka said. "Mum, are you okay? You sound pretty zoned out."

"I'm okay. There's just so much sadness here. It'll be good to see you and the girls."

"It'll be good to see you, too, Mum," Mieka's voice broke. "Everything's changed."

"We'll change it back again," I said, but even to my ears, the words sounded hollow.

Madeleine and Lena arrived with a greeting card. They took pride in making their own cards, but the situation was momentous, and they'd chosen a card from the drugstore. The girls watched my face carefully as I opened the envelope. The front of the card was a picture of a mournful basset standing in front of a carousel. Inside was the message "Without you, life is a sorry-go-round."

"Do you like the card?" Lena said.

"Very much."

"Do you understand the joke?" Madeleine asked. "The merry-go-round is a sorry-go-round because we miss you."

"But I'm right here," I said.

Lena frowned. "Not the way you usually are."

Madeleine nodded in agreement.

My eyes took in their small, worried faces. "You know what?" I said. "I could use a hug." The girls scrambled onto my lap. They smelled of chlorinated water and sunscreen. It was hard to let them go, but finally I said, "Why don't you help me put some cookies on the plate and then we'll go up to the roof."

While we had our tea, we talked about the roof garden. Madeleine wanted to know whether Ed had planted flowers that would attract butterflies, and if he had, whether butterflies would come up this high. As I always did when a student confronted me with a question for which I had no answer, I told Madeleine, I didn't know, but I'd find out. Lena was interested in how many people the roof garden could hold without crashing down. That question was easier. There had been 150 guests at Ed and Barry's wedding, and the roof was still intact, so in my opinion, the four of us were on safe ground.

After we had tea, Mieka handed the girls their backpacks and suggested they find a place to draw while we talked. The roof garden was filled with sunny nooks and shady hideaways where sisters could draw and whisper, and the girls ran off happily.

Left alone, Mieka and I were less ebullient.

"Where do we start?" Mieka said.

"With Riel," I said. "I'm sure the police questioned him."

Mieka's mouth tightened. "He was first on their list. Luckily for Riel, he was asleep in bed with me at the time. Even luckier, the new neighbours – you know, who moved into the Adams's house last year – keep careful watch on exactly when he comes and goes. They confirmed he didn't leave the house until he went to work at 6:45 yesterday morning."

"Your own little Neighbourhood Watch?" I said.

"Yes, and for once I'm grateful they're so nosy."

Mieka's eyes met mine. "I know the murder has been terrible for Leland's family and for you and Zack, but it's hard for us too. Riel is so committed to the future of North Central. He was over the moon when he and Leland had that press conference announcing the shared facility. Riel felt as if the new centre might really draw the people of The Village and North Central together."

"That's still possible," I said. "I don't know who will be managing Peyben, but whoever it is will be reporting to Margot and she's determined to carry out Leland's wishes."

"Even if the person who killed Leland was someone who'd been associated with Riel?" Mieka said.

I tensed. "Mieka, if you know something, you have to go to the police."

She lowered her eyes. "I don't know anything. It was just conjecture." She picked up a cookie, changed her mind, and put it back on the plate.

"Remember your grandmother's rule," I said. "'Thee took it; thee eat it.'"

Mieka smiled, picked up the cookie again, and took a bite. "Have they made the funeral arrangements yet?"

"No. Margot doesn't want a big production – just family and friends. Zack's assistant is checking into Luther Chapel at the university."

Mieka nodded. "That would be a good choice," she said. She levelled her eyes at me. "Riel would like to go to the funeral. He wants to honour Leland for his efforts to build the community, but we don't know if Riel would be welcome."

"Let me check with Margot," I said. "But I'm sure she'll want Riel there."

"I hope so, for all our sakes. Mum, if there's anything I can do to help Margot and Declan, let me know. I remember when Dad died. I thought it was the end of the world."

"So did I," I said. "But we got through it." I took her hand in mine. Mieka had her father's hands, long-fingered, graceful, and slender. Ian's hands had been the first thing I noticed about him. "I'm glad you came," I said. "Zack's at Margot's, but I'm going to text him and tell him to meet us in the hall. If he finds out the girls were here and he didn't see them, he won't be happy."

When we called the girls, they came running. Madeleine had made a bright spring pictures of flowers, trees, and birds. Lena had drawn a picture of Jesus on the cross. When we went downstairs, Zack was waiting, and they presented their pictures to him. He examined both pictures gravely: "The pleasures of the flesh and the prospect of redemption," he said. "These deserve a public exhibition."

We trailed Zack into our condo. I found magnets in a cupboard, and Zack fixed both drawings to the refrigerator door and wheeled back to admire his exhibit. "I think our new art collection is beginning to take shape," he said. "But we'll need more work before the grand opening. I'm prepared to pay a loonie a picture."

Lena's eyes sparkled. "We can do more work. We can cover this whole refrigerator in pictures."

"We can," Madeleine said. "But Madame Turmel is right, Lena. You're going to have to take time with your work. Your Jesus only has one foot."

Lena whipped out her marker and made a quick adjustment. "Not any more," she said.

When the elevator doors closed on them, I turned to Zack. "Are you, Blake, and Margot having another session this afternoon?"

"Looks like."

"Start an hour later. Give Margot a chance to have a nap."

Zack yawned. "You know I wouldn't mind a nap myself."

"I'll join you," I said. "After school, Declan and I are moving his gear out of Louise's, so I'll need to be in fighting trim."

The sense of rapprochement with Mieka, the time with our granddaughters, and the nap with Zack had strengthened me. Nevertheless, my pulse was racing as Declan and I approached Louise's massive house on the east side of the city. At the best of times, I hated confrontation, and this was not the best of times. But, as is turned out, I had feared the wrong thing. I had expected to be met by a heartbroken woman who would pull out all the stops to keep her son by her side. But the front door was locked. Declan had to use his key to open it. His suitcases, his guitar, and the usual paraphernalia of an adolescent boy were lined up neatly in the front hall. Louise was sitting in the front room with the curtains drawn. Declan called out to her, but she didn't move out of her chair. "I had Trudy pack your things and clean out your room," she said.

Declan went to her. "Mum, we've talked about this. You didn't have to take all my stuff out. I'm planning to come back to visit."

"Your old room is being turned into a guestroom," Louise said. "The painters are coming tomorrow."

When Declan bent to kiss Louise's cheek, she turned away.

It didn't take us long to carry Declan's things to his car. He was tall and slender, but he was strong, and he was able to pick up his suitcases, guitar, and backpack and easily carry them to the car in one trip. That left me with his laptop and a duffle bag that appeared to be full of sports equipment. I put the laptop on the passenger seat and went back to rearrange the helmets, boots, and runners in the duffle bag so that we could close the door to the trunk. When I finally got into the car, I saw that Declan was crying.

His face was still bruised and swollen from the beating he'd taken, and his misery tore my heart.

"You must think I'm a real wuss," he said.

I handed him a tissue. "You're not a wuss. You're a guy who has far too much to deal with, so let it out. We'll stay here till you're ready to go back to Halifax Street."

CHAPTER

17

We ate dinner at our place. Ed had offered to bring meals for the next few days and we accepted with alacrity. Tonight's choice was seafood chowder and sourdough bread. The food went down easily, but our conversation was less palatable. The Peyben directors were pressing for a full board meeting. Decency would have suggested they wait until after the funeral, but they were insistent. Seemingly, greed and the need to swoop when an opponent was vulnerable trumped compassion, but Margot was game. She said the sooner she established who was in charge, the better, and she had asked Blake to arrange the meeting.

Zack and Margot were careful to include Declan in the discussion of what was happening at Peyben, and he seemed keen to learn. As grave as our talk at the table was, there was a sense of shared purpose that united us.

Margot had decided that the funeral would be at Luther, and we talked about who should deliver the eulogy. Zack was the logical choice. He and Leland had become close, and he was much in demand to deliver eulogies for colleagues in the legal community because as Zack had pointed out to me on previous occasions, he was one of the few lawyers in town who realized that a eulogy was supposed to be about the guy in the box, not about him. But Margot finally made another choice. She wanted Declan and her to work together on the eulogy and to deliver it jointly. Laurie protested that Margot didn't need the added strain of speaking publicly, and I thought she had a good point, but it was Margot's decision.

As soon as we'd cleaned up after dinner, Margot and Laurie started moving towards the door. They were both exhausted and Margot wanted to be sharp for her meeting with Leland's business associates. When Declan started to follow them, Zack asked him to stay behind. They went out on the terrace and closed the doors behind them.

Taylor watched them and cocked her head. "What do you suppose they're talking about?"

"I don't know, but my guess is that Zack is asking Declan to sit in on that meeting with Leland's board tomorrow."

Taylor's eyes widened.

"If Declan decides that someday he wants to take over Peyben, he's going to have to learn how the company operates," I said.

Taylor was fervent. "Declan loved his dad, but that doesn't mean he wants to be like him."

"He doesn't have to be like Leland," I said. "I think he just has to be there for Margot."

"Declan will do it for Margot," Taylor said. "But I think it should be his choice. He's only seventeen. What if he doesn't want to work at Peyben?"

"Then he'll have the information he needs to make that decision," I said.

"Declan always resented his father's business."

"Because Leland was away so much?"

Taylor was thoughtful. "Yes, but it's funny. Sally's art took her away from me my whole life, but I never once thought that would stop me from making art. I've always known that's what I would do."

"You're lucky," I said. "There are people who go through their entire life without knowing what their work should be."

"Is that the way it is for you?" Taylor asked.

"I thought about that at my retirement party," I said. "I liked teaching university, but I never was passionate about it the way your dad is passionate about the law and you're passionate about making art."

"Maybe now you can find work that you really love," Taylor said.

"Maybe I can," I said.

Leland's apartment had a small assortment of books in the guest bedroom that Zack and I were using. The books were general interest – the kind an overnight visitor might enjoy curling up with before sleep. I chose a book of personal essays that began with Seneca and ended with Richard Rodriguez.

It was an intriguing collection, but I turned to an essay I'd read a half-dozen times before: E.B. White's "Once More to the Lake," a deceptively simple account of a man trying to recapture with his son the quiet joys of a lake cottage in August. It's a beautiful story about time and loss, and White's prose is as pellucid as the lake about which he writes. When Zack came in, I marked the page and handed him the book. "Some bedtime reading," I said.

Zack sighed. "As long as it's not a spreadsheet."

"So did you fill Declan in on what every young man needs to know?" I asked.

"Declan and I covered the boy-girl stuff when he was fifteen," Zack said. "It was humiliating. Declan knew more than I did. But tonight I was the smart guy. I told Declan what to look out for tomorrow, and I gave him a rough idea of the size and worth of Peyben."

"Was he impressed?"

"I think he was. You know there was no silver spoon for Leland. He did it all on his own."

"And you thought Declan should know that about his father?"

"Yes. There's no arguing the fact that Leland was an absentee father, but when he was away, Leland was building something impressive, and I wanted Declan to understand that." Just as Zack wheeled into his bathroom, there was a knock at the door. "I'll get that," I said.

It was Declan. "Could you give Zack a message for me?" he asked.

"Sure."

"It's about tomorrow. Could you tell him I have a suit, and I know how to tie a tie." He reached back and touched his dreadlocks. "But could you ask him if I should get my hair cut before the meeting?"

I reached out and squeezed his arm. "I'll ask him," I said.

"Who was that at the door?" Zack called from the bathroom.

"Declan. He wanted me to tell you he has a suit and he knows how to tie a tie."

"Good for him. I was thirty before I learned how to tie a tie."

"How did you manage?"

"Clip-ons," he said airily.

"Declan also asked if he should cut his hair for the meeting."

"That's a big move. I'll check with Margot, but in my opinion, Declan's his own man and the dreadlocks are his choice."

———

Zack and I both slept well that night. I awoke at my usual time and dressed for a run on the basement treadmill. I was tying my running shoes when I heard a soft knock at the door. It was Declan.

I smiled at him. "Change of heart about cutting your hair?"

Declan's face was grave. "No, it's Laurie." His face reddened and he lowered his voice. "Her water broke – I didn't even know . . . anyway, the baby's coming. Margot called Steve and he's on his way, but we're taking Laurie to Regina General. Margot thought you'd be worried if you checked our place and we weren't there."

"She's right. We would have been worried. Declan, there's nothing Margot can do, and she has to take care of herself. She should go back to bed. So should you. You have that meeting this afternoon. The baby could take hours. I'll go with Laurie and stay at least until Steve gets there."

Declan looked relieved. "I would have done it, but if things got out of hand, I wouldn't know what to do."

I smiled. "Delivering a baby and learning the inner workings of a multinational corporation would be a lot for one day."

He turned to go, then stopped. "Oh. Margot says I can do what I want to do about my dreadlocks."

"Good."

I went down the hall and stuck my head inside our bedroom door. My conversation with Declan had awakened Zack. "It's too early for a crisis. So what's going on?" he said.

"Laurie's water broke."

"Jesus, when did this turn into a soap opera?"

I kissed Zack's shoulder. "There are two pregnant women across the hall. That ups the odds. Anyway, I'm going to tell Margot to go back to bed. Babies are unpredictable. There's no point in her sitting around in a waiting room when she could be getting some sleep. She's having a good pregnancy, but her risk factors are high: she's forty-two, this is her first pregnancy, and she's under enormous stress. I'll take Laurie to the hospital and stay with her until her husband gets there."

"You ready to drive again?"

"Yes. I think I just needed a boot from the life force."

"Give me a call when you know what's happening."

"I will. Now go back to sleep."

Laurie was waiting for me in the hall wearing a flowery dress and sandals and holding an overnight bag. I took it from her. "I can carry that," she said.

"So can I," I said. "You only have a couple of hours left as a sacred vessel. Take advantage of it." I pressed the button for the elevator. "How are you doing?"

"Fine," she said. Then she grimaced. "Except for the contractions. They're close. I think we'd better gun it."

"The hospital's five minutes away. Another advantage of living in the Warehouse District."

Laurie's only response was a barely suppressed moan.

"If you want to holler, holler," I said. "The streets are deserted. I'm the only one who can hear you."

Laurie took me at my word.

I pulled up to the emergency entrance and ran inside to get a wheelchair. Laurie collapsed into it gratefully. The staff took over, and I settled in with an old copy of *Architectural Digest*. The design of Woody Allen's Upper East Side apartment was surprisingly conservative, and I had just learned that Woody typed all his scripts on his first typewriter when a nurse came out and told me that Laurie wanted company.

I followed her to Laurie's room in the second floor mother-baby unit. Laurie was propped up in bed with an electric fetal monitor strapped around her stomach. "This baby is on its way," she said. "If Margot wants to see the miracle of birth, she should get here pronto."

"I'll call her," I said. I went out to use the landline at the nurse's station. I called Margot's. Declan answered. He said he'd awaken Margot. "Tell her to hurry," I said. Then I went back and held Laurie's hand as the contractions intensified. Margot arrived just in time to see the baby's head crowning. The head came out quickly. The doctor tilted it down to release the highest shoulder and then the second shoulder. Finally the baby's body slid out. It was a girl and she had a lusty cry. The nurse cleaned her nose and mouth with a syringe and placed her on Laurie's stomach. The umbilical cord was clamped and cut, and Laurie introduced herself to her new daughter.

Margot's face was transfixed. "That's really something," she said.

"It really is something," I agreed. "Now, I'm going to go home so you two can have some time together." I leaned down and touched the baby's head. "Welcome to the world, baby," I said.

"Her name is Hunter," Laurie said.

Margot's breath caught. "Thank you."

"Steve and I couldn't decide on a name," Laurie said. "But I called him last night and we agreed that Hunter would be great for either a boy or a girl." As I left the room, Hunter's mother and aunt were exclaiming over her perfection.

It was a nice moment, and as I walked along the dimly lit hall, smelled morning coffee, and heard the kitten cry of a newborn, I felt at peace. When the elevator doors opened, an orderly pushed out a gurney. carrying a rail-thin blonde. Her hair was patchy as if she'd torn at it and her eyes were frantic. A nurse followed behind, holding a newborn. When she tried to hand the child to the mother, the girl closed her eyes and turned on her side.

"You'll have to take your daughter," the nurse said. "We're short-staffed. They need me downstairs." She tried again to give the child to her mother, but the girl hugged her own body tightly. "I don't want it," she said.

The nurse hesitated, then she nodded to the orderly. "Take Keeley to her room. I'll send someone up to help her settle in." She turned her attention to the girl. "Get some rest," she said. "They'll be bringing breakfast soon. After you've eaten, we'll bring your little girl up."

"Don't bother," the girl on the gurney said.

The nurse and I stepped into the elevator. I stood close enough to see the child. The nurse adjusted the blanket so I could see the baby's face. She was tiny but very pretty. When she began to cry, the nurse and I exchanged glances, but neither of us said a word.

Declan and Zack were in our living room poring over spreadsheets when I got back to Halifax Street. "It's a girl," I said. "She's healthy, blond, and beautiful, and her name is Hunter. Everyone is doing well."

Zack's smile was warm. "And you were there to see it."

"I was. More importantly, so was Margot. Thanks to Declan, Margot made it for the grand finale."

"I've never seen a new baby," Declan said.

"My guess is that Margot will want to go to the hospital again tonight, and I'll bet she'd like some company."

"Is that allowed?" Declan said.

"Family's allowed, and you're family," I said. "Incidentally, are you men just about through here?"

"We can be," Zack said. "What did you have in mind?"

"Why don't the three of us drive up to Crocus and Ivy and find the most elegant dress in the store for Hunter?"

"I'd like that," Declan said, and for the first time in a long time, he looked like a teenager.

———

The trip to Crocus and Ivy Kids was more diverting than any of us could have anticipated. The sight of a notorious and powerfully built trial lawyer in a wheelchair and a teen-aged boy with dreadlocks discussing the quality of pink sleepwear (o to 3 months) from a company called Mini Vanilla garnered more than a few stares and surreptitious smiles. After some spirited discussion, we chose a half-dozen soft and airy onesies, two sunhats, and a tiny summery dress that was appliquéd in apple blossoms.

When we got back to the condo, Zack and Declan headed off to change for the meeting, and I knocked on Margot's door to see if she was home from the hospital and up to checking out the baby clothes. Her face was wistful as she examined them. She held up the apple blossom dress. "I can't wait to see Hunter in that dress," she said.

"If you have a little girl, she'll be in line for hand-me-downs."

Margot smiled. "I hated hand-me-downs, but this one is definitely a keeper." She folded the dress and slipped it back into the box. "Hunter's early arrival was serendipitous. When I was holding her, everything else just melted away. Of course, then I have to come back to reality. Norine's been a godsend, but it's difficult to plan a funeral when you don't know when the police are going to release the body."

"Margot, I know you're dealing with a great deal right now, but Riel Delorme would like to come to the funeral. He wants to honour Leland and the work he was doing. It's your call. If you think Riel's presence would be a distraction, he'll understand."

"No, I want Riel there. I'm going to follow the path that Leland chose – Peyben will continue to work with North Central. That's what I'm going to tell the board today." Margot was pensive. "Leland was never a bullshitter. The

Village Project came into being because Leland wanted to make money, but the assault on that little girl shook him. Seeing a child suffer like that . . ." Margot's sentence drifted off and her eyes filled with tears. She brushed them away impatiently. "Anyway, Leland felt that he had an obligation to do something, and he also had the resources. This facility could end up being the most significant thing Leland will ever achieve," Margot said. This time when her eyes filled, she let the tears flow.

CHAPTER

18

The meeting with the Peyben board of directors was being held at Falconer Shreve. "Home turf advantage," Zack said.

He and Margot and Declan had just left when Debbie Haczkewicz called. Reasoning that Margot had enough to deal with, Zack had volunteered to be her liaison with the police, and Margot and Debbie had agreed to the arrangement. Obviously, Debbie had news. I could have told her that if she phoned Zack then, she could catch him before his meeting, but I didn't. Whatever information Debbie had would not lighten the burden of Leland's widow and his son.

The message Debbie asked me to deliver was to the point: Leland's body would be released on the weekend and the police had a lead about the identity of the shooter. Debbie didn't volunteer anything about the suspect, and I didn't ask. The truth was I didn't want to know.

There was a staff meeting at Willy Hodgson, so Taylor was just working a half-day. As always, she came out of the rec centre ebullient.

"So what do you want to do with the afternoon?" I said.

"Mieka texted me that Riel finished the ice-cream stand and put a base coat on. I thought I might go over there and see what Madeleine and Lena want me to do. And I wouldn't mind a swim in their pool."

"I've got an old suit over there, but we'll stop by the condo to get one of yours. Let me call Mieka and see if that works for her."

"I'll borrow one of Mieka's," Taylor said. "Since Riel came on the scene, she's buying some pretty cool stuff."

Mieka suggested we come straight to the backyard, where Riel and Lena were finishing off a game of croquet. As soon as the girls saw us, they raced over. "Mimi, I've only got two hoops to go," Lena called out. "Mummy and Madeleine are already finished."

Riel was leaning on his mallet, looking disconsolate. "And I'll never finish. Put me out of my misery, Lena."

Lena flashed him a smile and smoothly hit her ball through the final hoops and against the stake. "Game's over," she said. "Now everybody come see the ice-cream stand and the surprise Riel made."

Riel had done a good job – the stand looked sturdy – and the surprise was a child-sized picnic table where imaginary customers could enjoy their purchases.

"It's great," I said.

Taylor eyed it speculatively. "What did you girls have mind?"

"We thought we'd call the ice-cream stand 'CONES!'" Madeleine said. "Does that sound good?"

"It sounds perfect," Riel said.

"And easy," Lena said. "All we have to do is paint a bunch of ice-cream cones everywhere. And then we can have the party."

While Taylor and the girls had a final confab about design, Riel, Mieka, and I found a shady spot on the deck. Mieka brought out a pitcher of iced tea and poured us each a glass. "I know Taylor's morning was great," she said. "Lisa gives me daily reports. What have you been up to, Mum?"

"Something amazing," I said. "Margot's sister, Laurie, had her baby this morning. I drove her to the hospital, and I saw the baby being born."

Riel leaned forward. "And everything went well?"

"Everything went the way it should. The labour was short – which is how I ended up being there for the birth. My ob-gyn once told me that nobody can predict what happens during a pregnancy and delivery."

Mieka chuckled. "Doctors don't usually admit that."

"She was a friend," I said. "And we were at a dinner party where the wine was flowing. Anyway, I should have listened to her. When Laurie's water broke this morning, I told Margot that these things took hours, so she might as well catch some more sleep. Hunter was born less than an hour after we got to emergency."

"Margot must have been touched by the baby's name."

"She was, and holding a beautiful, healthy newborn did wonders for her. By now, Laurie's room at the hospital will be filled with pink flowers, pink onesies, and dresses that are so sweet they'll make your teeth ache."

Mieka shook her head. "All that pink," she said. "I remember that from when Madeleine and Lena were born."

"Two of the best days of my life," I said.

"Mine too," Mieka said. "We're lucky, aren't we?"

"Yes," I said. "We're lucky." I thought of the girl on the gurney turning her back on her newborn. "And so are Madeleine and Lena."

The three of us looked towards the girls. "Not many little girls have their own ice-cream stand," Mieka said. She reached out and touched Riel's hand. "It's nice to have a man around the house."

Riel lowered his eyes. "It's nice to be the man around the house."

Mieka's face grew serious. "Margot must feel as if the bottom has fallen out of her world," she said.

"It has," I said. "She and Leland were very much in love, and their life together had just begun. But Margot's handling everything she has to. Riel, I did tell Margot that you wanted to attend Leland's funeral, and she wants you there."

"Then I'm there," Riel said. "If there's anything I can do . . ."

"There may be something," I said. "Margot's determined that the Village Project, and especially the shared facility, goes ahead exactly as Leland had envisioned. This afternoon, Margot is meeting with Peyben's board of directors to tell them that there will be no change of direction. Zack and Blake Falconer are with her, but I know your public support would help make the point with the North Central community."

"Then she has it," Riel said. "I'll do whatever I can to help." His brow furrowed. "Joanne, I have a question. I didn't know Leland well, but I thought our 'accord' was pretty much a marriage of convenience. We were both pragmatists who got what we needed out of the arrangement. But it seems as if the connection with North Central meant more to Leland than I realized."

"Margot and I were talking about that this morning," I said. "Leland had a change of heart about the shared facility. At the beginning it was just something to silence Peyben's critics, but the assault on April Stonechild shook him. He began to realize that the only way to really affect the lives of the people in the area was to work with them directly."

"I wish I'd known him better," Riel said softly.

Mieka took Riel's hand. "So do I," she said. When their eyes met, the connection between them was electric. For a beat, they both seemed to forget I was there.

"I'd better see how Taylor and the girls are doing," Riel said finally.

"The girls are already planning the grand opening." Mieka turned to me. "Madeleine's written out the invitation list. It's very exclusive."

"Did Zack and I make the cut?"

Mieka grinned. "Barely." Her smile faded. "I don't think I ever told you that Riel has a sister. I really wanted to invite her, but when I suggested it, Riel was adamant. I'm going to keep trying though. She's the only family he has, and apparently they were close for many years."

"What happened?" I said.

"I don't know," Mieka said. "My guess is that it was Riel's activism. His sister sounds like she's establishment all the way. She was in the police force, then she went to law school. Actually, you might know her. She worked for Falconer Shreve for a while – Sage Mackenzie."

"We've met," I said. "Actually, Louise Hunter is one of Sage's clients."

"One more connection with the Hunters," Mieka said. "I wonder if Riel knows about it." She picked up the tea glasses and put them on the tray with the pitcher. "Well, if he doesn't, I'm not going to be the one to tell him. Whatever happened between Sage and Riel really wounded him. He's been hurt so often. I don't want him hurt any more."

When Mieka went into the house, I followed. "You and Riel seem to have a good thing going."

"Does that mean you approve?"

"I approve of whatever makes you happy."

Mieka put the glasses in the dishwasher. "Then maybe this news won't make you crazy. Riel has moved in with the girls and me."

"That's a big step," I said.

"It is." Mieka stood and faced me. "And it was unexpected. Riel and I talked about the possibility a couple of times, but we both agreed that until we were sure we were ready for a long-term commitment, living together might not be the best thing for Maddy and Lena. I thought the matter was settled. Then Leland was shot, and that day after Riel finished work, he moved in with us."

"No explanation?"

"No. He just said he wanted to be with us all the time. Of course, that was fine with me."

"Have you been worried about your family's safety?"

"I'm always worried about my family's safety," Mieka said. "But it's nice to have someone there to worry along with me."

After we had our swim, Taylor stayed behind to work on the ice-cream stand, and I grocery shopped, picked up wine for dinner, and drove back to Halifax Street. Ed was bringing our meal again, so my only task was to set the table. That left plenty of time to read and catch a few rays in the roof garden, but first I had to make a phone call.

Jill Oziowy was relieved when I told her that NationTV could continue tracking the changing relationship between Riel's group and Peyben. "I've been afraid to call you to ask," she said. "Leland Hunter's death was such a tragedy. And you were right there. Pressing you about a TV production seemed insensitive. But since we've crossed that bridge, let's deal with reality. The hook for this show was going to be Leland Hunter and Riel Delorme, up close and personal. Now we don't have a face for Peyben."

"Well, no guarantees," I said, "but I'm relatively certain that Margot Wright will do it."

Jill was incredulous. "You've got to be kidding. She's prepared to sit down with Riel and explain how his group reached an accord with Peyben? Margot's husband was killed two days ago. She must be made of steel."

"She's not, but Margot's convinced that this is what Leland wanted so she's going to see it through. There's so much drama here, Jill. Margot is fighting Peyben's board to make certain they don't change direction on the Village Project. If they don't go along with her, she's prepared to fire them."

"Holy shit. This will be amazing TV."

"I know, but it's amazing TV about real people. Both Margot and Riel will have a great deal on the line here."

"So I should back off?"

"No, just be fair. And in the interest of fairness, or at least full disclosure, I should tell you that Mieka and Riel Delorme are now living together."

Jill whistled. "And how do you feel about that?"

"I don't know," I said.

I took my book of essays up to the roof garden, pulled a chair close to an arbour of lemon-coloured roses, and read M.F.K. Fisher until my eyes grew heavy. The shrill of my cell awakened me. It was Zack. "How are you doing?"

"Fine," I said. "I'm in the roof garden, getting a sunburn, breathing in the scent of roses, and reading about food."

"Sounds better than my afternoon," he said.

"The meeting didn't go well?"

"Margot came out on top, but the members of the board didn't make it easy for her," Zack said. "This has been one hell of a day."

"The evening will be better," I said. "Ed's bringing lamb biryani."

Zack brightened. "Margot wanted to know if she could bring Laurie's husband, Steve, to dinner tonight?"

"Of course. Ed is a generous cook."

"I'll pass that along," Zack said.

"Good," I said. "Zack, do you have a second?"

"Sure. What's up?"

"Debbie Haczkewicz called just after you left for the meeting with the board. I didn't suggest she call you then. I figured whatever news she had would wait, and you and Margot and Declan had enough on your mind."

"True enough. So what was the news?"

"Leland's body will be released this weekend."

"Well, I guess that's good. Anything else?"

"Yes. Riel finished building the ice-cream stand. Taylor's over there now, putting on the finishing touches. And Riel and Mieka are now living together."

"Whoa! So a martini night."

"You bet," I said. "A night for doubles if ever there was one."

Zack, Margot, and Declan were back at Halifax Street before five. Margot went to her condo to call Norine about getting the funeral details settled, and Declan volunteered to pick up Taylor at Mieka's, leaving Zack and me with some welcome time alone.

After Zack made our drinks, we took them out to the terrace. There was enough breeze to ripple the leaves on the nearby ficus. We positioned ourselves so we faced the late-afternoon sun. Zack leaned back and inhaled deeply. "We have to build more time for this into our day," he said.

"Agreed," I said. "But I guess for a while, you're going to be spending a lot of time on Peyben business."

"Looks that way," Zack said.

"What's going to happen there?" I said.

"Nobody knows for sure. But I can make some educated guesses. I think Margot will ask Blake to take over as CEO until a new CEO is chosen. That's not what the board had in mind but a lot happened today that they didn't have in mind."

"Like what?"

"Like the fact that Margot was sufficiently in command to recognize what they were up to. The gentlemen of the board underestimated her. Margot's a helluva lawyer, but of course those bozos never took the time to check out her track record. They were condescending and smug, and they thought they could snow her with statistics and business jargon. She let them roll for a while and then she restated what they'd said – except she hosed the bullshit off the orotund phrases. That's when the board members knew she was on to them and started scrambling to take control of the situation."

"That must have been entertaining," I said.

Zack brightened at the memory. "It was a sweet moment, and Margot seized it. While the board was figuring out how to regroup, Margot gathered up her papers and told the board they were done for the day. She said the purpose of the meeting had been to take one another's measure and they'd done that. She also said that anyone who wasn't happy with the direction the company was taking should resign immediately. Then she gave them her barracuda smile and said, "Same time, same place, tomorrow?""

"I wish I could have been there."

"I do, too. Margot really was magnificent."

"How did Declan do?"

"He played it smart, too – shook hands, made eye contact, took it all in, and never left Margot's side."

"Declan's really coming into his own with this, isn't he?"

"Yes, he's the one who suggested that he and Margot and Blake and I meet tomorrow before we face the Peyben board again."

"Leland would be proud."

"Yeah." Zack's voice was hoarse with emotion. He

cleared his throat. "I should probably call Norine and Debbie. Catch up on the latest."

"I'll go in and make the salad," I said. I picked up our glasses and leaned over and kissed Zack's forehead. "This was nice," I said.

"Nothing like a time-out," Zack said. And then he hit speed-dial.

Zack's conversations were lengthy. When he finally came inside, he wheeled over to the salad bowl and picked out a cherry tomato."

"Anything new?" I said.

"Nothing at the office that can't wait. But Debbie did say there's a rumour going around North Central that a member of Red Rage was paid to kill Leland. It's all she has, so she's hauling in the bad boys one by one, but she's not optimistic. Gang members have a tendency to protect one another. Besides, the shooter has probably vamoosed by now – he could be anywhere." Zack turned his chair towards the hall. "Now I'm going to get out of this coat and tie."

All at once, the image of Louise Hunter, shaky and miserable, flashed through my mind.

"Hang on a minute," I said. "Zack, the night of the All-College, Louise told me it would be easier for her if Leland was dead – that way she wouldn't have to imagine his life with Margot. At the time, I just thought it was alcoholic self-pity, but now . . ."

Zack winced. "We're going to have to tell Debbie this."

"There's more," I said. "When Margot and I talked just after she found out that Leland had died, she told me that he'd had death threats – one from Louise, the night before the wedding."

Zack picked up his BlackBerry. "You can't sit on information like this, Joanne." He hit speed-dial and handed the phone to me.

I could tell Debbie Haczkewicz was taking notes as I told her about my conversation with Louise, and about Louise's threats to Leland. When I was through, she said, "I appreciate this, Joanne. I know you've been through a lot lately."

"Others are going through worse," I said.

I handed Zack back his BlackBerry. He'd been watching my face closely. "You do realize you didn't have an option," he said. "You had to tell Debbie."

"I know, but I feel as if I betrayed Louise. That night at Luther, the other parents were congratulating Margot on her marriage and admiring her ring. Everything Louise wanted was slipping away. She was desperate, and desperate people sometimes say terrible things."

"And sometimes they *do* terrible things, Joanne. You told the truth. Leland deserves that. If Louise had no connection with Leland's death, she'll have the unpleasant experience of being questioned by the police, but after they check out her story, she'll be fine."

"And if she did hire someone to kill Leland?"

"Then she's in big trouble, and she deserves to be. The Latin motto on my law degree is clear on that point. *Fiat justitia.* Let justice be done."

There was a knock on our door, and I shrank. "When do we tell Margot and Declan?"

Zack squeezed my hand. "In an ideal world, we could wait till morning."

"This isn't an ideal world," I said. "But we can at least wait until after dessert."

It turned out to be a good evening. As Zack poured the wine and we gathered at the dinner table to share Ed's savoury lamb biryani, there was a feeling of family. To one degree or another, we were all mourning something we had lost and would never recover, and that loss united us. The mood of the evening wasn't dark. Most of the conversation was easy and aimless. Only once did the grief break through. When Steve handed around his camera with the seeming endless series of pictures he'd taken of Hunter that day, Zack ribbed him gently about being a proud papa. Margot said, "Leland would have been worse," then she dissolved in tears. Steve was sitting next to her, and when he put his arm around her, Margot buried her face in his chest. "That's good, Margie," he whispered. "Let it out."

After we'd had dessert, Zack's gaze travelled around the table. "We've been putting this off, but it's time for an update. Debbie Haczkewicz says word on the street is that someone with serious money hired a member of Red Rage to kill Leland."

Declan broke the silence. "Why would anyone do that?" he said, and his voice cracked.

Zack's eyes sought mine. "Too soon to know," Zack said. "Declan, it's too soon to know if the rumour is even true. Debbie's checking it out, and she's talking to everyone who might have had a motive. Declan, I'm afraid that includes your mother."

Taylor moved closer to Declan and threaded her arm through his. He shot her a grateful look and breathed deeply. "Yeah. I can see why," he said, and his acceptance of the unthinkable tore at my heart.

Margot's face was a mask. "Anything else?"

"Nothing definite," Zack said. "But it's early times."

"I'm glad you waited till we were through eating to spring this on us," Margot said dryly.

"Timing is everything," Zack said. Suddenly, his composure broke. "Jesus, Margot, I wish this wasn't happening."

"Me, too," she said.

Steve stood up. "I'm going to exercise my authority as brother-in-law and take Margot home. She's had enough for one day." He turned to Declan. "I think you have, too."

As we said our goodbyes at the door, Taylor hugged Declan for a long time, and when he turned to go, she went straight upstairs to her room with a quiet "Goodnight."

I'd just started emptying the dishwasher when I heard Zack's cell ring in the living room. It was a long conversation. By the time he joined me in the kitchen, I'd finished setting the table for breakfast. Without asking, Zack poured us each some cognac. I watched his face as he handed one of snifters to me.

"Bad news?" I asked.

"The worst," Zack said. "That was Debbie. Sage Mackenzie just left police headquarters. The cops are on their way to talk to Louise."

"Sage has evidence that Louise was involved in Leland's murder?"

"Nothing concrete, but enough circumstantial evidence to raise questions. Sage still has friends on the force, so she's been following the Hunter case. Today she found out that the cops were investigating the possibility that someone in Red Rage had been paid to kill Leland, and apparently that triggered a memory.

"On Canada Day, Louise passed out after dinner and when Sage was getting her ready for bed, she saw a stack of cash in Louise's lingerie drawer. Louise has a thing about credit cards. I remember cautioning her about keeping large amount of cash in the house, but she never listened. Anyway, after Louise was asleep, Sage counted the money. There was $15,000 in the drawer."

"Wow."

"Wow, indeed," Zack said. "$15,000 is a substantial stash for incidentals, but Sage didn't say anything because as far as she was concerned there was no reason to. It was Louise's money, and she could do what she wanted with it.

"But today when Sage heard about the possibility that Leland's death was a paid hit by Red Rage, she was concerned enough to check out the lingerie drawer. The money was gone. When Sage asked Louise about it, Louise was defensive and hostile."

"So Sage went to the police."

"Not immediately. She apparently has real affection for Louise, so she struggled with her decision. Finally, Sage decided to be guided by her conscience. As a lawyer, she's an officer of the court. She has an ethical duty to tell the truth."

"So it's only a matter of time before they arrest Louise?"

"Sage thinks so. She's already called Sandra Mikalonis to represent Louise."

"This is so terrible," I said. "Are you going to tell Margot tonight?"

"No," Zack said. "Let her get some sleep. This is going to crush Declan, but maybe if I have a night to think about it, I'll come up with a way to cushion the blow."

"You're taking on too much," I said. "I love you, Zack. Last Christmas I was afraid I was going to lose you. I don't want that to happen again."

Zack swirled his cognac. "Neither do I, but what's that old saying about how we don't know how strong we are until being strong is the only option? We do what we have to do."

CHAPTER

19

The next morning as Zack dressed for the meeting with the Peyben board, he was sanguine. He and Sandra Mikalonis had talked earlier. The police had cautioned Louise to remain in the city, but they hadn't arrested her, so Zack had been able to present Margot and Declan with a best-case scenario. Margot was a shrewd enough lawyer to know that every best-case scenario has a flip side, but she hadn't pushed it.

When Zack left to pick up Margot and Declan, I walked across the hall with him so I could wish them luck. Zack felt they were on solid ground with the board. The initial meeting had been a feeling-out process. Now that everyone knew where they stood, Zack was optimistic that the board would support Margot and they could all get on with the business of running the company.

In less than an hour, Zack, Margot, and Declan were back in our condo and they were clearly gobsmacked.

"That was quick," I said.

Declan ran his hand through his dreads. "I'm still not quite sure what happened."

Zack shrugged. "Your stepmother showed that she has the makings of a first-rate poker player."

"Is anyone going to fill me in?" I said.

"Sure," Zack said. "The story is short and sweet. We walked into the boardroom at Falconer Shreve. The members of the Peyben board were sitting around the table looking as if they owned the place. Their chair stood up and announced that he was prepared to take on the role of CEO of Peyben and if Margot didn't agree to his appointment, the board would resign en masse. Margot didn't blink."

I turned to her. "So what did you do?"

"I said, 'Resignations accepted all around,' and then I said, 'Peyben thanks you for your service. Now get out.'"

"And they did?"

"Oh yeah," Zack said. "They got out, and when they left, smoke was coming out of their ears."

I laughed. "So you'll be looking for new board members."

"Blake's already drawing up a list of prospects," Margot said. "I actually feel pretty good about this."

"So do I," Declan said. "Those guys creeped me out."

Later that day, I drove to a shop that specialized in custom-printing T-shirts. I ordered three: one each for Zack, Margot, and Declan. On the front of each shirt were the words *Being Strong is the Only Option.*

Margot and Declan wore their shirts till the day of Leland's funeral.

Knowing that Leland's funeral would be emotionally gruelling, Zack, Taylor, and I planned a morning that would keep our family near Margot if she needed us but would give us a chance to recharge. The three of us had a long swim, then Taylor went to work in her studio, and Zack and I took tea and an armload of our condo's never-ending supply of magazines up to the roof garden, kicked back, and waited for sunshine and peace to work their magic.

As a rule, Zack did not handle leisure well. After five minutes exclaiming over the joy of doing nothing, he always found something to do. That morning, as he flipped through *Sports Illustrated*, reading aloud items he was certain would be of interest to me, I found myself taking a hard look at my dream of getting Zack to retire early. He had just finished giving me a précis of the high school careers of the some of the most promising new U.S. college quarterbacks when he took out his BlackBerry and began returning calls. I did not discourage him.

For an hour Zack contentedly thumbed responses and chatted away while I read *New Yorker* articles on how the dog became our master and how Thomas Hardy's reputation as God's undertaker still made him the most relevant of early twentieth-century authors.

By the time Zack had finished his calls, and I'd ordered the e-book of *Jude the Obscure*, we were hot and hungry. As we stepped out of the elevator, my phone rang, and Zack mouthed that he was going to check on Margot and Declan.

It was Norine. She must have been swamped with details about the funeral, but as always, she sounded in command. "Everything appears to be under control. Of course, appearance isn't reality."

I laughed. "Actually, with you, it generally is. Anyway, let me know if you need a hand."

"I will. But that isn't why I called. Joanne, I've been delving into the history of that strange file of clippings about your late husband's life. Patrick Hawley, the young man who found it, says there's a companion file. I told him to courier it directly to you from the Calgary office."

"Did Patrick say what was in the file?"

"No, and I didn't ask. But given everything that's happened, I think you should take it to the police."

"Given everything that's happened," I said, "I think you're right."

At Margot's request, we dressed for the funeral as we would for a summer gathering. As we turned onto the university campus, I knew that in suggesting comfortable clothing in light fabrics and pastels, Margot had chosen wisely. Those coming together to honour Leland would be dressed to remember, not mourn.

In midsummer, a university campus can be Arcadia. The lawns are lush, the trees are in full leaf, the flowerbeds are brilliant, and the tanned, leggy students, their lives bursting into bloom in the summer heat, are more handsome then they will ever be again. Sublime. But on that hot July day, we were on campus for the funeral of a good man, and the beauty of our surroundings bruised my heart.

Zack and Taylor and I were early for the service. The partners at Falconer Shreve had decided to accompany Margot and Declan as they walked up the aisle to take their seats. A young woman from the funeral home asked us to sign the guestbook, and after we had signed, she directed us to the room where Margot, Declan, and the partners would assemble. I wanted to be alone for a while, so I told Zack and Taylor to go ahead without me and I'd meet them in the chapel.

The Luther College chapel was a space designed to welcome students. The windows looked out onto the campus, the maple pews were arranged in semicircles that faced a simple altar, and bright pillows, large enough for students to sit on, were stacked in the room's corners. I found a place in the second row with space beside me for Zack's wheelchair, said a prayer for Leland and his family, and then repeated the mantra which had sustained me since Zack and I had looked at the rubble that had once been our home: "This too shall pass."

In the small hours I wondered whether the words were more comforting than true, but I clung to them, and finally, it seemed that the worst was almost over. The next day we were going to Lawyers' Bay, and we would be there until September. At the beginning I had believed that once we were at the lake, our lives would resume their old, comfortable rhythm, but too much had happened. The lake would be the same, but we had been changed. We had all paid in hard coin for what we had learned since the bombing of our house, but we'd made it through, and I was grateful.

There had been unfathomable losses, but there had also been gains. Blake Falconer was assembling a Peyben board that would accept the fact that the Village Project's priority was to give the men and women of North Central the background, training, and experience necessary for a decent life. Riel was proving to be an effective ally for Margot, and Zack had become one of his staunchest supporters. Even Declan, grieving the loss of his father, had begun to take quiet pride in the role he was playing in Margot's life. We had been wounded, but we would survive.

Louise, though, was a question mark. She had gone into seclusion, refusing to see anyone, including her son. Sage was with her 24/7, and she gave us regular and increasingly distressing reports of Louise's disintegration. There was one bright spot. Louise was not planning to attend the funeral.

When Norine notified Leland's out-of-province/out-of-country business associates about the funeral plans, she told them that Margot's preference was for a funeral that was small and private. In the past week, these associates had deluged Margot with towering flower arrangements and extravagant food baskets, but as the chapel began to fill, it was apparent that they had taken Norine at her word.

There weren't many faces in the chapel that I didn't recognize. Laurie and Steve and their five children sat with Margot and Laurie's tall blond brothers and their families. The women with whom Margot had celebrated her upcoming marriage on that idyllic evening beneath Linda Fritz's cottonwood tree were all there. Henry Chan, who was Margot's doctor, as well as ours, and his wife, Gina Brown, were sitting near the back. Many of Margot's Wadena friends whom I recognized from the wedding had come to offer condolences. As Margot had requested, no one had chosen the traditional colours of mourning.

"How's Declan doing?" I asked as I sat down next to Taylor.

"Not great," she said. "But okay."

Ed and Barry came in soon after, and when they spotted us, they came over.

"Is there room for us?" Ed asked.

"Always," I said. "And see if you can save places for Mieka and her family. They seem to be running late."

Barry smiled. "I imagine a fashionista like Lena takes a while to pull her look together."

"She does indeed," I said.

When Mieka and the girls arrived, Riel wasn't with them. I leaned close to Mieka and whispered, "Where's Riel?"

"He's doing something during the ceremony," she said. "He just wanted to check out the timing with Margot."

"I'm glad he's here." I looked down the pew at the girls and Barry and Ed and my eyes welled. "I'm glad you're all here."

Riel joined us just as the ceremony started. A pianist and a soprano, whom the bulletin identified as students at the conservatory, performed Leonard Bernstein's "A Simple Song" and then Declan, Margot, and her law partners moved up the aisle in silence and took their places. Margot was wearing a draped jersey dress the colour of sea spray and her blonde hair fell smoothly to her shoulders. Her face was drawn, but she was composed. She was carrying the carved box that held Leland's ashes, and when she placed the box on the altar, her hand lingered on it for a long moment.

There is something comforting about a funeral service that follows a ritual. A ceremony acknowledging the brokenness that comes in the wake of death is a reminder that others have faced the abyss and endured. Leland's service adhered to the traditional Protestant pattern of comforting words from the Gospels and psalms and prayers interspersed with music.

When Declan and Margot expressed their personal loss, their pain was searing, and I was grateful that we had the safety net of ritual. Declan played and sang Eric Clapton's "Tears in Heaven" – a tough choice, and he almost made it until his voice broke in the last chorus. Beside me, Taylor tensed and leaned forward, willing Declan to continue. He did, and he finished strongly.

Margot and Declan had worked together on the eulogy. It was highly personal, warm, funny, and revealing. It was also effective. In evoking the man they had known in a way that few of us had, Margot and Declan underscored the magnitude of our loss.

Riel's appearance addressed another loss. When Margot had finished the eulogy, Riel presented her with the multicoloured woven scarf that is emblematic of the Métis culture – disparate elements coming together to form an integrated whole. His words were simple: "This scarf honours your husband's work for the Métis people and the commitment he made to our future."

The young pianist played the opening notes of William Blake's "Jerusalem," and we rose to sing the final hymn. Zack's voice, strong, rich, and full-timbred, made the challenge of Blake's lyrics come alive. As he sang the final verse, I understood why Margot had chosen a slightly revised version of "Jerusalem" as the coda to her husband's funeral.

Bring me my bow of burning gold
Bring me my arrows of desire.
Bring me my spear! O clouds, unfold!
Bring me my chariot of fire!
I will not cease from mental fight
Nor shall my sword sleep in my hand
Till we have built Jerusalem
In this green and pleasant land.

In a display of ecumenism, Campion, the Catholic College, and Luther College were architecturally joined. Campion had a larger public space and better sandwiches, so the funeral reception was being held there. As Zack and I took the five-minute walk between Luther and Campion, he said, "Remind me. What's the purpose of these things anyway?"

"In theory, the reception after the funeral helps us reconnect with ordinary life," I said.

Zack snorted. "Then they should serve something stronger than tea."

Steve and Lori now had five children and Margot's brothers each had four, so including Madeleine and Lena, there were twenty-seven boys and girls under the age of twelve at the reception. Reconnecting with life was a necessity, not an option. The combination of fancy sandwiches, other kids, and plenty of space was heady. Life was all around us, and it was hard not to get involved.

Hunter, in her tiny dress with the appliquéd apple blossoms, was a great hit. Barry and Ed carried her around the room as if she were spun gold – as, of course, she was. Everyone was drained, but exhaustion in the company of others was still more palatable than being alone. So we pushed on – laughing quietly, exchanging reminiscences, commenting on the beauty of the service and the day.

When we left, I embraced Margot. "Why don't we go for a swim tomorrow morning?"

"Six o'clock?" she said. "I'm not training for the Iron Man."

"I'll meet you by the elevator," I said.

Taylor had decided to come home with Declan, so Zack and I were alone. "Wouldn't take many days like that to make a dozen," Zack said.

"You're right about that," I said. "I'm going to get out of this dress and into something comfortable."

Zack took off his jacket and loosened his tie. "What would you say to a nice tall gin and tonic?"

"I'd say, 'Where have you been all my life?'"

The sun was slanting in the sky, but the air was cooling and it was pleasant just to stretch out on the chaise longue. I sipped my gin and tonic. "I don't think I've ever been this tired."

"Neither have I," Zack said. "Let's turn in early."

I closed my eyes. "What time is it now?"

"Five-thirty," Zack said.

"Too early. We're adults. We have to stay up till at least six. But I hope Margot can get some sleep tonight," I said. "She was magnificent today. The moment when Riel handed her the scarf was electric and then that last hymn. Margot made sure that Leland's message came through loud and clear."

"We're building the new Jerusalem," Zack said. "So don't get in our way."

The next morning, the water Margot and I swam in still held the coolness of night, and we both emerged from the pool invigorated.

Margot towelled off and slipped into her robe. "Well, that was bracing," she said. "Now I just have to figure out what to do with the rest of my life."

"Why don't you try the 'one day at a time' model for a while," I said.

She shrugged. "That's probably not the worst idea you ever had. Planning hasn't exactly worked for me lately."

"You could take the morning off," I said. "Go up to the roof garden and read *What to Expect When You're Expecting*."

"I've read it," Margot said.

I smiled. "You are such a keener," I said.

"Always the girl with her hand up because she knew the answers," Margot said. "Don't worry. I'll find something to do. Actually, I have a meeting with Riel this morning about the Racette-Hunter Facility."

"Is that what it's going to be called?"

"It was Declan's idea – honour the two men who . . ." She bit her lip. "Well, you know."

"It's a strong name," I said. "Something people will actually use." We started back towards our building. "I'm going to be around most of the day so shout if you want company."

"I will." Margot hesitated. "Jo, I hope you know how much it helps just knowing you and Zack are there. And Declan couldn't make it through this without Taylor, I know."

"You'd do it for us," I said. I slipped my arm around her waist. "Do you realize that in a few weeks, getting my arm around your waist is going to be a stretch."

"I can hardly wait," she said. When her tears came, I was prepared. "Hormones," I said, and we both laughed.

When I went in to change, Zack followed me into our room. "I have to go into the office for a couple of hours," he said. "I've let things slide, and I have to get everything back on track before there's a real problem." He wheeled over. "If I leave now, I can be back by lunch."

I drove Taylor to Willy Hodgson and arrived home just as the courier truck pulled up in front of our building. There were two envelopes for me – both expected.

The smaller one contained a DVD-R Jill sent me of potentially usable footage of Leland and Riel; the larger one was from Patrick Hawley at the Calgary office. I took both upstairs, dropped the DVD-R into my laptop, and watched for a few minutes. It was all recent material: the presentation of the Métis scarf at the funeral, the press conference on the site of the shared multipurpose facility, and the ugly encounter between Riel and Leland outside the Conexus Centre. The footage would be useful when we started thinking about the shape the program might take, but right now it was painful to watch images of Leland, alive and full of plans.

I opened the large envelope from Calgary. Inside was a paper file, much like the file that Angus had brought me: an old folder stuffed with newspaper clippings and secured by elastic bands. I slid off the elastics. The clippings were all related to a particularly grisly murder from more than thirty years ago. A man had murdered his wife and her lover. A newborn and a ten-year-old child were in the room, but the man, whose name was Bryce Mackenzie, apparently couldn't bring himself to finish the job and he turned himself in to the authorities. There were many grainy photos of the three principals in the case. When I read the name *Bryce Mackenzie*, I got a shiver. But Mackenzie is a common enough name in this country settled by Scots. He was a good-looking man with a history of mental illness that was apparent in the pain in his eyes and the agony of his face. His wife, Merrill, had a broad forehead, a direct gaze, and an appealingly crooked smile. Her lover was an

Aboriginal man. When I saw that his name was Tom Delorme, my pulse quickened.

I read and reread the account of the murders and of the trial and the tragic denouement. When I was finished, I was shaken. The children who had been present in the room during the murders were Riel and Sage. According to all who knew her, their mother, a community social worker, was close to being a saint. Shortly before their marriage, Bryce Mackenzie had been diagnosed with what was then known as manic depression. Merrill endured her husband's mood swings: the days and months when he was manically active, promiscuous, and filled with delusions of grandeur, followed inevitably by the days and months of despair, fatigue, and suicidal depression. For ten years, Merrill never faltered in her devotion to her husband and later her daughter, and then she met Tom Delorme. When she gave birth to Riel, a child who was visibly Aboriginal, Bryce went berserk. He threatened Merrill, their daughter, and the baby, and when she took the children and fled, Bryce followed her.

At his trial, Bryce's lawyer fought to get him put in a prison with a hospital where he might receive treatment, but the Crown prosecutor was adamant, stating that a person who took the life of another human being must pay the full penalty, and Bryce Mackenzie had taken two lives and left two children effectively orphaned. The jury, who at first had been inclined to go easy on Bryce because they understood why a disturbed man might kill a wife who'd been unfaithful with a native, were won over by the Crown prosecutor's high-mindedness.

The jury found Bryce Mackenzie guilty of first degree murder in the deaths of Merrill Mackenzie and Tom Delorme. For each of the crimes, Bryce Mackenzie was sentenced to life with no possibility of parole for twenty-five years. The sentences would be served concurrently. Mackenzie was sent to the penitentiary in Prince Albert, where he was thrown in with the general prison population.

Three weeks into his sentence, Bryce Mackenzie hanged himself. By then, the Crown prosecutor had resigned and was running for office in an affluent constituency with a large number of voters who self-identified as supporters of law and order. The candidate needed their votes, and by reminding them of his lofty speeches about insuring that the punishment fit the crime, the former Crown prosecutor brought his voters to the polls. He won handily, and at the age of twenty-eight Ian Kilbourn became Attorney General of the Province of Saskatchewan, and we were on our way.

I closed the folder, slid the elastics back into place, and stared at the file. As Leland had said on our first evening together, "There are always casualties."

The contents of the second folder had rocked me. I was still trying to see where all the pieces fit when the phone rang. It was Jill Oziowy.

As always, Jill leapt right in. "We have a problem, Jo. I think I have a solution, but you may not be willing to go for it."

"Try me."

"Okay, hold on to your hat. NationTV's Regina station has it on good authority that Sage Mackenzie is within hours of being arrested for killing Leland Hunter."

My heart was a stone in my chest. "This doesn't make any sense," I said. "Are you sure?"

"Very sure."

"Is Riel involved?"

"No," Jill said. "But unless we manage this information, Riel's guilt or innocence will be a moot point."

"Because Sage is Riel's sister and people will believe he must have played some role in what happened."

"Right," Jill said. "But I think there's a way to salvage this. We have to let the public know that they were estranged, and we have to act fast." She took a breath. "I want you to talk to Riel about getting Sage Mackenzie to turn herself in. He can go to the police station with her, but it has be clear that Riel, the new face of North Central, is on the side of law and order."

"And so we come full circle," I said.

Jill was irritated. "I haven't a clue what you're talking about, but I do know that time is not on our side. You've got to talk to Riel."

"Jill, this is crazy. I can't ask Riel to get his sister to turn herself in."

"Why not? Sage is going to be arrested anyway. And from what I hear Leland Hunter's murder may not be the only charge against her. If she turns herself in, she can maintain at least a semblance of control." Jill paused. "There is so much on the line here, Jo."

"I know," I said. "The Racette-Hunter Centre has the potential to change the lives of the people in North Central."

"That's why this program we're working on matters so much," Jill said. "But you know as well as I do that if Riel is no longer seen as a credible representative, all bets are off."

My mind was reeling. "All right," I said finally. "I'll talk to him."

I called Margot and told her that I needed to see Riel. Then I brought both files of clippings into the kitchen and put them on the butcher-block table. Before I had time to think through what I would say, Riel was at the door. He looked worried. "Is everything okay with Mieka and the girls?"

"They're fine," I said. "But there's something we need to talk about. Let's sit down." Riel and I pulled up stools and I slid the file of his family's tragic history across the table to him. He looked through it slowly, then closed it.

"I don't understand," he said. "Who put all this stuff together?"

"Your half-sister," I said.

"Sage? But this happened thirty years ago. Why would she give it to you."

"Sage didn't give it to me, Riel. She misplaced it." I handed him the file with the clippings about Ian and our family. "Someone found it, put two and two together, and gave both files to me."

Riel skimmed through the second file. "So you're wondering about your late husband's connection to my family?"

"Yes."

"I didn't know about it myself until last Christmas, after Mieka and I became involved," he said. "When Sage found out I was seeing Mieka, she was furious. She told me about the history between our two families and said any relationship between us and the Kilbourns was impossible."

"But you didn't agree."

"No. I told my sister I wasn't having a relationship with the Kilbourns, I was having a relationship with Mieka, and what happened thirty years ago didn't have anything to do with us. Sage didn't see it that way. We haven't spoken since. Sage's choice, not mine." He rubbed his eyes. "I had no idea that she was this obsessed with the past."

"You're not responsible for what your sister does," I said. "And that's why I wanted to talk to you."

Riel's complexion was the colour of burnished copper, but as I told him that his sister was about to be arrested for the murder of Leland Hunter, the colour leached from his skin. By the time I'd finished explaining that to ensure his credibility as the voice of North Central and guarantee the future of the Racette-Hunter Centre, he had to show publicly that he and Sage were not allies, Riel looked ill and jaundiced. When I proposed that he urge Sage to turn herself in, he winced, but he didn't argue.

When I was through, Riel leaned towards me. "I'm having trouble believing this," he said. "I know Sage hated your family and she was furious about my relationship with Mieka, but she's always believed in the law. She was a cop. She's a lawyer. She's not a killer." Riel's eyes searched my face, seeking a sign that the charges against Sage were a terrible mistake. He found nothing to comfort him, and his shoulders slumped in defeat.

"Riel, it may be too late to save your sister, but it's not too late to save North Central."

Riel nodded. "My Grandmother Mackenzie raised Sage and me. We lived in a little bungalow on a corner lot on Osler Street. My grandmother came to that house as a bride. In her day, everyone in the district had a job, everyone had a garden, and everyone knew everybody else. She watched as the neighbourhood changed. At the end, she couldn't even sit on our front porch after supper. Our house was robbed, my grandmother was mugged, my sister was regularly harassed, and I was beaten more times than I can count. North Central went from being a good place to start a life to being the neighbourhood of last resort.

"My grandmother used to sit and watch the street through the front window. Whenever she witnessed some fresh horror, she would say, 'Somebody has to break the cycle.'" Riel's eyes were miserable. "I guess I'm it," he said.

After Riel left, I sat down and tried to bring coherence to my swirling thoughts. Sage had set Louise up. That much was certain. She'd planted the first seed with her phone call to Leland the night we went to Magoo's. Louise's disintegrating mental state made Sage's story that Louise hired a thug to intimidate an enemy plausible. And knowing I'd remember Louise's first intrusion, it must have been Sage who stole into our condo and rearranged the Fafard sculptures. Suddenly, it had seemed that Louise was capable of anything. We were prepared to believe Sage's story about seeing a large amount of cash in Louise's negligee drawer and to accept the possibility that Louise had hired someone to kill Leland. But it was Sage who did the killing.

That was the part that didn't make sense to me. There was no reason for Sage to risk everything to bring about Leland Hunter's death. I opened the file that contained the records of Sage and Riel's childhood and began leafing through the pages. When I came to the picture of a female officer taking ten-year-old Sage from Tom Delorme's house the night of the murders, I stopped. Sage's face was contorted with fury.

The night of her party, Linda Fritz said that Sage's anger management problem was so severe that she'd had difficulty carrying out her duties as a police officer. Linda's explanation for Sage's anger was simple and sensible: growing up in North Central, Sage had simply seen too much. And that was true. Sage *had* seen too much, and experienced too much, but her anger had taken root earlier, on the night she saw her father murder her mother and her mother's lover.

According to the newspaper accounts, Sage had picked up her baby brother and run outside crying for help. Even then, North Central was not a neighbourhood where a child's cries for help were answered. The newspaper quoted an outraged social worker as saying that Sage must have stood on the sidewalk crying for at least thirty minutes before a neighbour called the police.

At ten, Sage had been old enough to read the newspaper accounts of her father's trial. She clipped out and saved every picture and article. She wanted to make certain that she would never forget the tragedy of her parents' lives and of their deaths. But it seemed Sage also wanted to make sure that she would never forget who was responsible for those twin tragedies.

I turned back to the picture of Ian and me on the election

night when we did the impossible and won it all. I stared at our young faces. We had all the answers. We would make the world a better place. We would never forget that *Security for any one of us, lies in greater abundance for all of us.*

But we had forgotten, and Leland paid the price. His death had been an accident – collateral damage. I had been the one Sage targeted for death. Leland's concern for me had saved my life and taken his.

When I picked up the phone and dialled Inspector Debbie Haczkewicz's number, my heart was pounding, but my hand was steady.

CHAPTER

20

Sage's confession to the murder of Arden Raeburn was a punishing blow to Debbie Haczkewicz. For more than twenty-five years, Debbie had been a dedicated member of the Regina Police Force, and Arden Raeburn had been a good cop. Arden's death at the hands of a woman who had once been a colleague shook Debbie to the core. She was a professional who was secure in her judgments, but the fact that she had not been able to spot a rogue cop in her own midst was a burden she would carry with her. The morning she came to Halifax Street to fill us in on Sage's actions, it was clear Debbie's confidence had been eroded.

The rain had been steady since the early hours and showed no signs of letting up. After I'd taken Debbie's raincoat, Zack led us into the living room. On sunny days, the space was washed with light, but that morning the only breaks in the gloom were small islands of light from the table lamps.

When Debbie turned down my offer of coffee, I motioned to the reading chairs. Too tense to relax, she balanced on the edge of the chair closest to her. "It's difficult to know where to begin," she said. "But there are two salient facts: Sage loves her brother, and she hates you and your family, Joanne. Everything Sage did – and I'm still trying to get my head around what she did – was motivated by either love or hate.

"We had no trouble getting her to confess. She was eager to set the record straight. She arranged for the bombing of your house. She murdered Arden Raeburn, and after the member of Red Rage she'd hired to kill Joanne backed out, Sage took on the task herself."

For a moment, I felt light-headed. Zack reached over, took my hand, and then turned back to Debbie. "And Sage killed Arden because Arden suspected that Sage had lifted the damaging material about Riel," he said.

"It's more complex than that," Debbie said. "Riel's file was just the beginning, but it gave Sage an idea. She approached Red Rage and offered to remove incriminating evidence from the files of their members in return for future favours. She was selective, and careful, so her activities weren't detected."

"Then Cronus came to police headquarters and started asking questions," Zack said.

"And Arden had the rotten luck to be the officer Cronus approached," Debbie said. "Arden and Sage were friendly and when Arden mentioned her concern about the missing material, Sage offered to help her track it down. Sage said she didn't want material damaging to her brother to fall into the wrong hands."

"And Arden bought that?" Zack said.

"Sage was a colleague and a friend. When they found nothing, Sage convinced Arden the search was a waste of time, so she abandoned it." For a beat, Debbie seemed to lose her train of thought.

"But that wasn't the end of the story," Zack said.

"No. As a lawyer, Sage was clearly on her way up in the police force, but she and Arden continued to get together every so often for a drink or dinner. Everything was fine. And then one day, Arden was interviewing a member of Red Rage who'd been arrested for stealing an Oldsmobile. According to Sage, the boy proposed a deal. If he was treated with leniency, he'd name a cop who'd been known to lift incriminating material from the files of gang members. Apparently, Arden was skeptical, but cops are funny about loose ends, so she played along. When the boy identified Sage Mackenzie as the bad cop, Arden didn't believe him. After all, Sage had turned her back on a law career to come back to police work."

"But Arden must have been at least suspicious," I said. "Cronus's charge that someone had removed damning evidence against Riel had never been resolved, and Sage was Riel's sister. That must have raised some red flags."

"It did," Debbie said. "And Arden was thorough. She called Sage and told her about the accusations. Sage dismissed them as mudslinging by a gang member settling an old score. Arden seemed to accept the explanation, but Sage says she couldn't afford to take a chance."

"So she killed Arden," Zack said. He inched his chair closer to Debbie. "Did Sage know about the rough sex?"

"She knew," Debbie said, and her voice was thick with anger. "And she knew that the date with Cronus was always on a Saturday night. Arden was just going off duty when Sage called to ask if she could drop by Arden's apartment for a drink after Cronus left. Apparently, Arden was often depressed after her dates with Cronus, and Sage had come by several times to cheer her up."

Debbie walked to the window and stood with her back to us, staring at the rainy city. "This whole thing makes me sick," she said finally.

"I know the feeling," I said. "Why don't we give it a rest? You can send another officer to talk to us later."

Debbie turned to face me. She was grey with exhaustion. "This is my case," she said. "I'll do the interview."

"Okay," I said. "But at least let me make us coffee."

When I came back with the coffee, Zack was telling Debbie about the delivery man's convenient arrival the night Sage attempted to seduce him.

Debbie heard him out. "Sounds like the delivery man was planning a photo shoot," she said. Her eyes moved from Zack to me. "Blackmail?"

I set the coffee tray on the table between the reading chairs. "I don't think so," I said. "I think Sage planned to make sure I saw those pictures. She really does hate me, Deb."

Debbie took a mug of coffee from the tray. "You and your family are an obsession with her. She hated Ian Kilbourn because he'd prosecuted Bryce Mackenzie to the full extent of the law – showing no mercy for her father's mental illness. When your late husband died, Sage's obsession moved to you, Joanne. She blames you for everything that's gone wrong in her life: her rages, her inability to sustain a relationship, her estrangement from her brother, her chronic insomnia."

"I don't even know her," I said.

"But she knows you," Debbie said. "More accurately, she knows a lot about you. For years, she watched you from a distance, but since Christmas you've been, to quote Sage, 'in her face.' When she started at Falconer Shreve in January, she discovered that you were married to Zack. And that was just about the time that Riel told her about his relationship with Mieka. After that, as far as Sage was concerned, everything went from bad to worse."

"Is that why she blew up our house?" I said.

Debbie shrugged. "Sage was bent on revenge, and according to her, the explosion that killed Danny Racette provided a model. Her informants in Red Rage told Sage that Danny Racette's death showed the community that the penalties for people who co-operated with Peyben would be quick and deadly. She called in her markers from Red Rage, and they set up the explosion in your garage—"

"But we were at the lake, so she didn't kill us," Zack finished.

"We had to change the way we lived our lives," I said. "Why wasn't that enough?"

"Because Sage felt her world was under attack. Leland Hunter had co-opted Riel. Even worse, Riel had found a place in your family."

"So Sage hired someone to kill me."

"His name is Jimmy Raven, and when he backed out, Sage's house of cards came tumbling down. There were rumours that Raven had been involved in Leland Hunter's murder. We called him in for questioning, and when he realized that Sage wouldn't be doing any more favours for him and his pals, he fingered her. After that, it was just a question of putting together enough evidence to arrest her. Joanne, Raven made it clear you had been the intended target all along. And Sage underscored the point in her statement by repeating three times that the bullet that killed Leland had been intended for you."

"She wanted to make sure I'd always carry that knowledge with me," I said. "And I will."

Riel called at mid-morning and asked if he could come over on his lunch hour. When I opened the door to him, I was shocked. It seemed he'd aged fifteen years in the last two days. His skin still had the grey tinge I'd noticed when I showed him Sage's file and his eyes were dull and deeply shadowed.

When I stood aside to let him come in, Riel hesitated. "I didn't know if you'd see me," he said. "Mieka wanted to come, but she's been through enough. I thought we should talk about this alone."

Zack came up behind me. "Come in and sit down, Riel," he said. "The past couple of weeks have been tough for all of us."

Riel didn't move. "It's not going to get any better," he said. "Sage is my sister. I hate what she did, but I love her, and I'm not going to abandon her."

"You can appreciate why that decision might be difficult for Joanne and me," Zack said.

Riel nodded. "I can, but I thought you should know."

"How does Mieka feel about this?" I said.

"She's miserable," he said. "Mieka loves you, Joanne, but she also loves me. She doesn't want to lose either of us."

"She doesn't have to," Zack said, and he wheeled towards the living room. When Riel didn't follow, Zack turned his chair to face him. "An old law professor of mine used to quote Isaiah. 'Come now, let us reason together.' I think the time has come for reasoning."

Our talk didn't resolve anything, but as we reasoned together, Zack and I saw the depth of Riel's commitment to Mieka and the girls, and Riel saw that we were still prepared to accept him into our lives. As he walked towards the door, Riel's step seemed lighter and, for the first time in a long time, I felt the stirrings of hope.

August that year was the most beautiful month at the lake that anyone could remember. Day after day of high clear skies, warm sun, and calm waters. Kevin Hynd was taking advantage of his position as managing partner of the Calgary office to spend weekends in the mountains with his new girlfriend. The Hynd cottage was vacant, and so Margot and Declan moved in. The arrangement was serendipitous. Margot needed to be private but not alone, and having a cottage for Declan and herself with all of us close by was ideal.

The Winners' Circle, which a few short weeks ago had seemed a sad anachronism, suddenly had new life. None of us could banish Margot's grief, but each of us could find a way to ease her load. Jacob Wainberg was a merry little boy and Delia and Noah Wainberg developed a sixth sense about when Margot and Declan seemed to need a quick visit and an infusion of joy. Zack and Blake Falconer were able to handle some of the stress Margot was experiencing in finding herself suddenly in charge of a multinational corporation. Blake was knowledgeable about industrial real estate, and years as a trial lawyer had honed Zack's ability to judge character and made him fearless on the attack. Both Blake and Zack were useful allies. Taylor, Gracie, and Isobel supplied camaraderie for lighter moments. They had regular chick-flick movie nights and Margot became a regular.

I never had a sister, but during those hot August days, Margot and I became as close as sisters. We talked about everything – especially about Leland. I was with Margot when her baby moved for the first time. We both wept.

Imperceptibly but irrevocably the shape of Zack's life and mine changed. As the days of August grew shorter, it became clear that Blake and Zack would have to make a decision about their futures. Blake was still finding his way as CEO of Peyben, but he was sure-footed and he liked the work. Zack, who never did anything by halves, had committed himself to bringing the Racette-Hunter complex to completion within a year. It was a daunting task, but Zack was determined.

On the Friday before the Labour Day weekend, Blake Falconer and his daughter, Gracie, invited the families at Lawyers' Bay for dinner to confirm what we already knew: Blake was taking a year's leave of absence from Falconer Shreve.

The evening was bittersweet. Blake was clearly excited about this new direction in his career, but his partners seemed to sense that, ultimately, the leave of absence would become permanent.

Zack was uncharacteristically quiet during dinner, and when he suggested that we go down to the lake before we went home, I knew he wanted to talk. It was an achingly beautiful night. The sky was bright with stars in their ancient patterns, and the lake was like glass. I stood behind Zack with my hands on his shoulders. "It doesn't get any better than this," I said.

"Nope," he said. "This is a perfect stone-skipping night."

I bent down, picked up a handful of stones from the beach, and handed Zack a flat one. "Go for it," I said.

He grinned, aimed, and threw the stone. It bounced twice before it sunk.

"Not bad," I said.

"I'm out of practice," he grumbled.

I picked up another stone. In the next few minutes Zack worked his way up to four skips, then he threw one that sank without a trace. "Should have quit while I was ahead," he said.

"One of life's great lessons," I said.

Zack looked up at me. "I've been thinking about following Blake's lead."

"I figured that was what was on your mind at dinner," I said.

"So what do you think?"

"It's a big step," I said.

"It has an upside," Zack said. "Margot wants to work from home. Two of the condos on the floor beneath ours are vacant. Blake approached the owners of the other two and they've agreed to sell. As soon as they move out, a crew will come in to turn that floor into offices for Peyben. I'll be working regular hours. As long as we're living on Halifax Street, I'll be able to nip upstairs to have lunch with you or take an afternoon off so we can do whatever people who take off afternoons do. And here's the real kicker. We can have Willie and Pantera in the condo. I wrung that concession from Margot."

"I don't imagine it took much wringing," I said. "Margot's a dog lover. What about the other condo owners?"

"There aren't that many, but the dogs will be here on a trial basis. We'll have to make sure they're good citizens. We'll hire a dog walker."

"I'm the dog walker," I said.

"Okay, we'll hire you. Anyway, the upside of the deal is not to be sneezed at."

"You're right," I said. "So what's the downside?"

"I won't be practising law for a year."

"That's a lot to give up," I said.

He lowered his eyes.

"But not as much as Leland gave up," I said. "You can say the words, Zack. They're never far from my mind."

Zack took my hand in his. "Jo, we're never going to be able to make this right, but we can make it work."

"I know we can," I said.

"So what are you going to do this fall?" Zack said.

"Press on with April's Place."

Zack raised an eyebrow. "Is that the new name for the play centre?"

"Yes," I said. "The name is my idea, so be enthusiastic. Anyway, we now own the lots on either side of the old synagogue, so once Peyben gets the necessary permits, we'll be able to start construction. And Jill wants me to get moving on the mediation program with Margot and Riel while the interest is still high."

"Will there be time for canoodling in your busy schedule?"

"I'll pencil you in," I said. "And, Zack, we're going to have to make a decision about the house."

"I looked over the final report from the engineers," Zack said. "It seemed promising. According to them, the basement is structurally sound. If we want to rebuild, we can."

"The O'Neills say that if we start construction immediately, we can move back by Christmas," I said.

"Is that what you want?"

I shook my head. "No, and I've given it a lot of thought. The happiest time of my life was spent in that house, but whoever said, 'You can't retrace happy footsteps' was right. This summer has changed us all. Taylor's excited about the art she's making, and she's really looking forward to working with the Kids at Risk program. She and I have talked about moving back to the old house, but she wants to stay on Halifax Street."

"That surprises me," Zack said.

"It surprised me, too," I said. "But Taylor says she feels as if we belong on Halifax Street now. I feel as if we belong here, too – mostly because I want us to be close to Margot and Declan, but also because everything we're involved in is in the neighbourhood."

Zack looked out at the lake. "Remember that first night we had dinner with Leland and Margot and he took us up to the roof garden?"

I smiled at the memory. "All we could see was mud and construction hoardings, but when Leland talked about re-creating the kind of community that existed in the Warehouse District in the early 1900s I understood his dream."

"I understood it, too," Zack said. "Jo, I want to make Leland's dream a reality."

"Then we're in," I said.

"You're sure about this," Zack said.

"I'm sure. I want our family to be a part of the changes The Village will make in this city, and I want you and Taylor and me to be there the day that security fence around our building is ripped down."

"Leland and I talked about that," Zack said. "We decided we should celebrate with the kind of block party neighbours are supposed to have."

"Bushwakker's wild boar-burgers for everybody," I said.

Zack beamed. "And dancing to the Beach Boys all night," he said. When Zack spoke again, his voice was serious. "This isn't going to be easy, Jo. By the time our neighbourhood is safe enough for that fence to come down, you and I might not be around."

I shrugged. "At least we won't have wasted our time here."

Zack held out his arms, and we shared the kind of kiss a man and a woman in love should share on a summer night.

"That was nice," Zack said. "But it's been a long day – time to piss on the fire and call in the dogs, Ms. Shreve."

I bent, picked up another skipping stone, and handed it to Zack. "How about one for the road," I said.

Zack grinned and took aim. This time the stone skipped five times before it sank beneath the surface of the water. "How about that?" he said. "A personal best."

"That's all any of us can do," I said. "Let's go to the house."

ACKNOWLEDGEMENTS

Thanks to:

Rick Mitchell, retired Staff Sergeant in Charge of Major Crimes Section, Regina Police Service, for reading the manuscript and for giving me insight into the world of urban police officers and the lives of the people of North Central.

Lara Hinchberger, my editor, and her associate Kendra Ward, for rigorous but always thought-provoking and productive editing; Heather Sangster, for her keen eye; Terri Nimmo, for the dynamite cover, and Ashley Dunn, for her consummate professionalism and endless warmth.

Dr. Ingrid Kurtz, a fine surgeon whose knowledge about breast cancer is exceeded only by her empathy for the women who find themselves facing a daunting diagnosis; Dr. Najma Kazmi, who sees and treats the whole patient; and Dr. Linda Nilson and her colleagues at the Alan Blair Cancer Centre for their unfailing courtesy and kindness. A special thank you to Barb Nicholson and Ivy Jensen, who know the value of a warm smile.

Hildy Bowen for her help in more ways than I can count; Madeleine and Lena Bowen-Diaz for advice on Taylor's wardrobe; and as always Ted, who, after forty-three years, continues to rock my world.